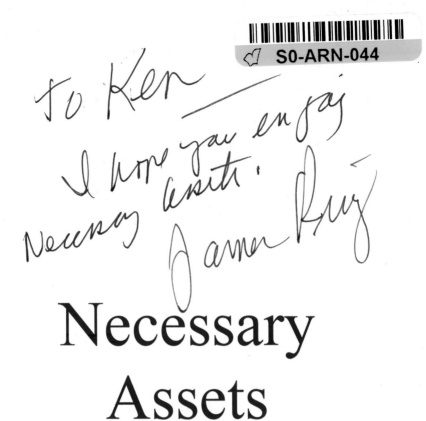

To Ken —
I hope you enjoy
Necessary assets.
James Ring

Necessary Assets

James Ring

Omni Publishing Co.

2013

Published by
Omni Publishing Co
www.omni-pub.com

Library of Congress cataloguing-in-publication data
Ring, James A.
Necessary Assets
ISBN 978-1-4909-9746-9
Printed in the United States of America
July 2013

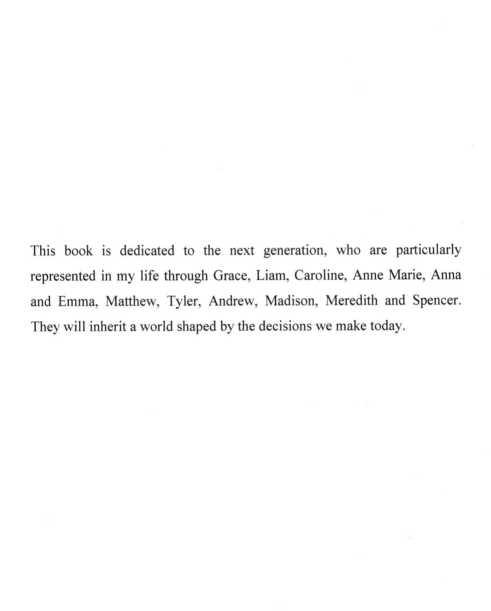

This book is dedicated to the next generation, who are particularly represented in my life through Grace, Liam, Caroline, Anne Marie, Anna and Emma, Matthew, Tyler, Andrew, Madison, Meredith and Spencer. They will inherit a world shaped by the decisions we make today.

Acknowledgement

The author would to acknowledge and thank my two primary readers. Award winning and now retired Boston TV reporter Ron Gollobin knows the art of writing, is a great teacher, and shared his talents generously. Ken O'Brien of the Profile Group enjoys an uncanny ability to find any plot inconsistencies and what he calls those "nits and nats," to which I was often blind. Both were with me for the long haul and are true friends.

How would a reader unfamiliar with this genre react to my story? I went to two forever friends who share the uncommon gift of truth telling to everyone in the nicest way possible. Jim and Marie McCrohons' reaction encouraged me to go forward in the process.

Retired agent colleague Arthur Ryall is an experienced genre reader. His advice and support were most welcome.

Thanks to my dear friend Muhammad Ali-Salaam of the Islamic Society and Cultural Center of Boston. Muhammad has been recognized by the FBI and law enforcement in New England for his efforts to explain Islam to non-Muslim law enforcement and help establish lines of communication which now serve as a national model. Muhammad did the same for me. He helped me get to the ending I wanted.

Thanks to Mark Medeiros of Slocum Studio for my website and business card design, some great photos, and an edited video.

Henry Quinlan of Omni Publications has a long history in the business and agreed to act for me as both agent and publisher. He assembled a team that allowed this book to move into the marketplace of judgment. Because of his experience, Henry was able to offer me informed choices as we progressed through the editing and publication process. Leonard Massiglia designed the cover and Theresa Driscoll performed the editing. Thanks to Henry and his team.

Merita Hopkins, my bride, made a wise choice a few years back. She was not going to be an editor, advisor, or technical consultant to my efforts. She had the ability to fulfill these roles owing to her experience as an FBI agent, lawyer and trial court judge. However, she realized before I did how hard it is to critique someone you love. Every time I got a reader e-mail that started with "I have just a few comments," Merita was there to point out what wonderful friends I had. When I asked aloud: "Why am I doing this? Why all the effort? Who cares?" Merita was there with a gentle word and a nudge forward. Not a push mind you, just a nudge. I am thankful to God every day for her presence in my life.

Well, here we are. Please enjoy Necessary Assets.

Author's Note

The word "asset" is commonly used to describe property or money available to pay a debt. It is also a widely used term in intelligence work. In this context, an asset can be hardware, software, electronic or human. If human, the product is often referred to as human intelligence, or "HUMINT." Synonyms for a human asset are spy, mole, spook and undercover agent.

Historically and presently, assets in all forms are an absolute necessity in detecting and preventing terrorist attacks. Connecting the dots is not easy and, as demonstrated in recent history, is not always done well or on a timely basis. A reliable human asset, who can tell you how, when and where a threat or attack will materialize, is beyond measurable value.

Prologue

Said Ali al-Wahishi got out of the battered, dusty pickup truck just before sunrise in front of the abandoned one-room schoolhouse in the village of Gerdi, just north of Peshawar on the A01 highway. The cool, sweet mountain air was a pleasant relief to the oil-laden pickup truck exhaust he had been breathing through rusted floorboards for the past several hours.

Wahishi's body still vibrated from the impact of rutted roads driven at night, with no headlights for the last three miles, in a vehicle whose abused suspension system was long ago suspect. Waiting for him in the schoolhouse was Haydar Abu al-Adel, al-Qaeda's number two in command. They were to meet alone. The day's first light enabled him to see his way into the schoolhouse without a flashlight, which might be seen by US electronic eyes. This was Wahishi's second summons to a meeting with Adel in three months.

"As Salaam Alaikum," Wahishi said to Adel as Adel arose from his sitting position on the floor.

"Alaikum Salaam," replied Adel. They embraced and kissed three times. There was no personal warmth in the expressed tone of voice or body language of either party. They both sat facing each other on wool mats placed over the damp concrete floor. Adel pulled a new-looking red thermos from a much-used, tobacco-colored, goatskin shoulder bag. He next brought out two porcelain cups wrapped in a dirty white cloth. He poured some welcome hot tea. They exchanged limited pleasantries in the still air, their breath forming white clouds in the coolness of the dim light of early morning. Wahishi remained reserved waiting for the senior al-Qaeda leader to tell him what this meeting was about.

Adel was a short, thin and wiry man in his mid-sixties. His hair and beard were grey and noticeably unclean, matching his well-stained robes. Body odor wafted from his presence. Wahishi knew Adel's physical appearance was intentional. No one ever gave him a second look or seemed inclined to be close to him. This persona enabled Adel to move about and conduct al-Qaeda business more effectively, free from prying eyes.

Wahishi by comparison was handsome, in his late-thirties, of medium height and athletic build. His hair and beard were still black, well-trimmed, and his robes were neat and clean. It was his eyes that made Wahishi memorable. Wahishi looked directly into your eyes as if he could read your innermost thoughts. His presence was always disconcerting to someone wanting to keep his innermost thoughts secret from Wahishi.

"When we last met," Adel began, "I told you how highly you are regarded in al-Qaeda. With more experience, maturity, and patience, we think you are capable of great things. In our last meeting, I told you of our concern about your criticism of our leadership and our strategy to simply outwait America's presence in Afghanistan and Pakistan. Ours is a long-term plan, proven trustworthy in the past. Yet since telling you of the discomfort we have for your criticism, you persist. Why?"

Wahishi slowly swirled the tea in the ancient, long-ago chipped, white porcelain cup. He took a sip, looked down into the cup, and then looked up.

"I told you before," Wahishi began slowly but deliberately. "Some of it is personal and some of it's not. I watched my brother vaporized by an American drone-fired missile. One moment he was smiling, saying goodbye to me and waving as he drove away. The next, without warning, he was dead with nothing left for us to bury. A second sooner and I would have been vaporized, too."

Adel looked solemn. "Many times we have expressed our sorrow over your loss, and our thanks for your good luck."

Wahishi continued to look fiercely into Adel's eyes. "Their drones, electronic warfare superiority, and anti al-Qaeda financial incentives to other Muslim countries all make this a war of attrition we are losing."

Adel started to interrupt, but Wahishi shook him off and continued.

"We cannot even communicate with each other except by messenger. We have failed to follow 9/11 with any significant attack. Instead we are on the run, hiding. Where have we instilled fear since 9/11? We are becoming irrelevant. We send out useless videos pretending to inspire our colleagues and instill fear in our enemies. We are just making fools of ourselves. Neither is effective. Instead, those videos highlight our weaknesses. You in the leadership refuse to listen. Perhaps it is time you heard."

Adel interrupted Wahishi with a quick wave of his hand. "You have no idea what we plan for the future and I cannot tell you now. You are a soldier and you need to learn a soldier's discipline, and to obey orders when given."

Wahishi countered with his own interruption. "There are many like me who are sick of scurrying about, hiding like rats, avoiding the daylight. Can't you see our inaction means America is winning and we are losing? Do you think your shoe and underwear bombers will bring America to its knees? We need to do more, now!"

Haydar Abu al-Adel sat back on his heels and took a sip of tea from his own porcelain cup and thought about what the young Arab in front of him had to say. It was true enough, but hardly respectful. He did not want to alienate this intelligent man with many followers. He was too valuable. He, Adel, must bring him into the tent and give him a difficult but important assignment, where he would be busy with little time to criticize. His sarcastic words about the current leadership were being repeated by others, more and more.

Adel sat forward again. "It is obvious you think our experienced leadership is inadequate. We too hear the murmurs of mockery, but they are from those who do not know of our plans. We see the fall-off in contributions from our supporters. You have not helped in this regard. Adel now smiled and said, "We have an important role for you to play now, but it requires patience and discipline. We are placing you in charge of all al-Qaeda operations in Yemen. We have been slowly moving our critical operations from the Northwest Tribal Area to there. Yemen is our future and there you will be in charge."

Wahishi was stunned. He came expecting confrontation and a dressing down for his outspoken views. Instead of a tongue lashing, he was getting a promotion. His first reaction was suspicion. Wahishi went on full alert but remained quiet as Adel resumed speaking with his measured voice and quiet demeanor.

"We have a good relationship with the Yemeni government. They pretend to be cooperative with the United States. Yemen will get access to US intelligence and will be plugged into their drone bases. The US military will be restricted by Yemen from acting unilaterally while on Yemeni soil. We will know what they are doing at all times. We need you to organize, unify and train our forces already in Yemen. The Americans already have a hint about our shift. We need to be ready for them when they realize the full extent of this relocation."

Wahishi looked Adel in the eye and slowly nodded his head. He said nothing. Adel continued by handing him a folded, food-stained white envelope taken from inside his robe. "Here are your contacts. I included some travel documents we made up for your new identity." Adel reached into his goatskin shoulder bag and pulled out a dirty, brown cloth pouch with a tie of string leather at the top. "Here is cash to get you started. Your financial contact in Yemen is experienced and awaiting you. We think the future for you is unlimited. But we must see evidence of your maturity and the required discipline to lead."

Again, Adel sat back on his heels and looked into his teacup.

Wahishi knew the meeting was at an end. Both men stood and embraced. There was still no personal warmth, no trust, evidenced between them in this exchange.

Each left thinking the meeting had been successful. The older leader believed he had pulled the too-impatient, too-ambitious, younger man back into the tent and put him into a position where any management weakness might be exposed. At least he would be too busy in Yemen to be a bother. He might even prove to be a good leader. They needed a leader.

Wahishi left knowing his criticism had found its mark. He did not share with his superior his own plan occupying his thoughts for some months. If no one else knew what he was thinking, no one could betray him. Wahishi was now in a position to lead. He could now create action, decisive action, which they would later sing about around camp fires in all of Arabia. He would bring respect back to al-Qaeda and to jihad.

Chapter 1

The Port of Naples, Italy

The four young men waited for over an hour for the loading and departure of the night boat from Naples to Palermo, Sicily. They had paid for two cabins, were assigned cabin numbers, but were not allowed to board until called. The steward made it quite clear that, for a gratuity, he would personally escort the four men to their cabins before the general boarding. They declined and remained in the public waiting area with a vast array of people, very few of whom seemed able to afford the steward's requested gratuity for early boarding.

One young man stood, stretched, and asked if anyone needed to use the men's room. The others declined. He sauntered off in the direction of the ticket counter and a sign for the men's room. Upon entering the men's room, the young man checked to see that none of his colleagues had followed him. He entered a stall, but left the door open to observe the entrance. He took a cell phone from his jacket pocket and placed a call to his Mafia family boss in Palermo, Zio Vincenzo.

"I'm in the Naples ferry terminal. We're taking the night boat and should be in Palermo at 7:00 am. Nothing has changed. They've told me no more. They aren't discussing anything new about the shipment, at least not in my presence. I think their leader, the one who does the talking to set up the shipment, may be having conversations with his associates when I am not present. They stop talking when I approach."

"Have they asked for any more information about cost or the proposed date for the shipment to leave Palermo?"

"No. Nothing."

"What else have they done in Naples? Who have they seen?"

"The one we call The Engineer has been off on his own a few times. I've been with the other two most of the time and I haven't seen or heard anything. I haven't been able to get away to speak with our people here in Naples. I don't know if they were following the one who went off on his own. I did see an *amico nostro* from Naples going on board the ship a few moments ago. I'm sure he accommodated the steward so he could carry out your request."

"I understand," said Zio Vincenzo. "I will be in the coffee shop after the boat docks. Bring them there and I will have others ready to take over. Perhaps it is better for you to leave them for a while."

The call ended. The young man washed his hands and strolled back to the waiting area where the three men were still sitting. As he approached them, he wondered what they had talked about when he was gone.

He'd been sent by Zio Vincenzo to find out more about the shipment and what these people were up to, but so far had failed to do so. The trio was friendly enough but they said little of substance to him about plans beyond the shipment.

He would make it a point to be absent from the cabins when on board so they would have a chance to talk among themselves in private. The microphones that Zio Vincenzo had the Naples people plant in their cabins should tell them something about the trio's immediate plans.

The North End, Boston

Retired FBI special agent Mark Patrick made a stop at the greengrocer's store on North Street to pick up some fresh figs, baby arugula, herbs, and fava beans for the dinner he planned to cook that night for himself and his wife, Liz Brennick.

On warm summer evenings years ago, Patrick used to sit on the stoop with some of the older neighborhood women and the talk would always turn to food and cooking. He eventually figured out that some of the older women in the neighborhood would pass on to him a recipe that did not include one or two key ingredients.

When Patrick finally caught on to this ploy, the women all laughed. "You thought we would give it to you all at one time, just like that!" Then there was a bit of raucous laughter among them at Patrick's expense. They openly admitted they never gave all the recipe ingredients to their own daughters-in-law. That way they could be assured their son would show up for Sunday dinner to eat "the way mama cooks it." Patrick was well-liked and had turned into an excellent cook, owing to his many North End instructors. Despite working for the FBI and the generational gaps, these women were his friends and he theirs.

Patrick's appearance prevented him from ever considering FBI undercover work. No matter how he dressed, no matter how practiced his mannerisms, Patrick always looked like a "fed" to the criminal element. Patrick was now closer to sixty than he would like to admit, but still had the same look.

The grey in his short hair was not total. There was still some surviving pepper mixed with the salt. Always clean shaven and always dressed neatly, more often than not in casual clothes, Patrick walked with the authority of someone who could still take care of himself. To say he was of medium height and full bodied would be an expression of kindness. He resembled a blocking back, not a wide receiver. As an FBI agent, he was trained as a SWAT team leader. He still looked the part no matter how much he preferred not to.

Patrick entered the Café Strada on Hanover Street and sat at a small table in front of a window opened to the street. The first warmth of the early summer drifted in. There are many cafés in the Italian North End, and he liked them all. Patrick exchanged a few nods with some other men in the café who quickly resumed their conversations. Patrick thought of the Sicilian proverb "never speak when you can whisper, never whisper when you can nod, never nod when you can wink, never wink when you can grunt...." For no reason he seemed to have picked up their way of communicating over the years. Patrick ordered an espresso and started to read his paper.

"Mark, you have a minute?"

Patrick looked up. It was Billy Evangelista. Evangelista and Patrick were more accustomed to seeing each other in a courtroom since Evangelista was a leading defense attorney for La Cosa Nostra (LCN) and Mafia members from New York to Boston.

"I always have time for one of the great criminal defense lawyers of our time," said Patrick with a smile. "I was just ready to have an espresso, will you join me?"

Once another coffee was ordered, Patrick and Evangelista exchanged some general conversation about the neighborhood, Evangelista's clients, other lawyers and FBI agents they both knew.

Evangelista sipped his espresso. "I see Liz from time to time in the courthouse or at Bar functions. She seems to enjoy being a lawyer again. She says she does not miss being an FBI agent or a prosecutor."

"That's true," said Patrick. "She enjoyed the FBI but being a prosecutor gave her a chance to get back to practicing law. She has been successful as a defense attorney in the few criminal cases she has taken since going into private practice."

Evangelista looked up and out the café window to the street. This had been a Mafia-run neighborhood within the recent past. He smiled. "Who would have ever thought this was possible years ago? Two FBI agents from the Organized Crime Squad come to live in the North End, get married, spend years putting my clients in jail, leave federal service, and then continue to live here. And now we are having coffee together."

Patrick laughed. "If it were fiction, it would be too far-fetched. What's up with you my friend?"

Evangelista smiled. Despite the fierce courtroom battles over the years, there existed a mutual respect for the jobs each had done.

Evangelista came to the point. "I was asked to contact you and say exactly the following. Someone you know needs to have a conversation with you. I have no idea what the conversation is about. I have been asked to represent to you personally that this is a legitimate request. They felt it best if you heard it from me first so you would not think you were being set up. I am assured this is not the case and the need for the conversation is legit. The person will contact you directly. You know the person."

"If it is legit, tell me who wants to meet with me."

Evangelista shifted in his seat nervously. "I would rather not be any more involved."

Patrick pushed away from their table. "I am long past the cloak and dagger scene. I just don't feel like having somebody set all the terms for a meet they want with me. It goes against my grain. Tell whoever it is to take two aspirins and call me in a couple of years when I really won't give a rat's ass. I don't work for the Bureau anymore."

"Okay. Okay, Mark. I am just a messenger. It's Mario Bocca who wants to see you."

Patrick was somewhat stunned. He figured it was a made guy but Bocca was different. Bocca was made into the Mafia in Sicily, came to this country, and was re-made into the New England family. Bocca was a capo in the New England family but reportedly now retired.

Patrick devised and led the now legendary FBI operation, the first-ever electronic bugging and tape recording of a Mafia induction ceremony. It was the Holy Grail. The FBI trotted out that induction tape at every Mafia trial in the country and overseas every time a Mafioso claimed, "What Mafia? There isn't any Mafia! It's a fantasy made up by the FBI to increase their budget."

Those tapes made the New England family the subject of a few embarrassing jokes inside criminal circles. Was Bocca looking to even the score? Patrick, after all, had been the architect of the induction eavesdropping.

"I see," said Patrick. He didn't know what else to say. It was clear Evangelista had done his job so business was over. Patrick knew Evangelista was smart enough to know this history and would have asked about any possible revenge targeting Patrick. Interesting, he thought.

"Tell Mario anytime," said Patrick. He was not going to ask Evangelista any questions.

As they walked out of the café, shook hands, and parted, the men inside the café observed what transpired, digested that data, and resumed their conversation. Something had happened. It was none of their business.

Patrick left the Café Strada, walked to the cheese shop, and told Felipe he was making the Bolognese sauce tonight. Felipe reached to a hook above his head and cut down a soppressata. "For the sausage," Felipe asked, "You want the sweet, right?"

"You have it, Felipe."

Patrick could not resist a few stuffed peppers. He also got a small container of garlic-stuffed olives for his martini. Liz preferred a lemon peel. It had taken a few hours to get his errands done, going from shop to shop, talking with people, saying hello, but that is the way of life in the North End. What the hell? He was mostly retired and could take his time. He needed to mull over this Bocca thing.

Sana'a, Yemen

Said Ali al-Wahishi was comfortable walking the narrow maze of walled pedestrian-paths near the Sug al-Milh, the historic salt market, in the ancient, beautiful and mountainous Yemen capital city of Sana'a. Yemen was now an important "ally" of the United States in their war on terror which, Wahishi truly believed, was a US war against the Muslim faith.

Strangers viewed these high-walled labyrinths, with clean pathways, as a system making escape almost impossible for an unwanted visitor put into a state of panic. Wahishi viewed these paths, as did the city dwellers, as a source of protection against those from outside seeking to conquer. It also offered protection from anyone, friend or foe, trying to learn your business. He often changed direction and pace to determine if anyone was following him. After fifteen minutes of this exercise, Wahishi knew he was clean. Satisfied that he was alone, Wahishi proceeded to a café which he kept under observation for another fifteen minutes. He watched his appointment arrive, look around and then be seated at an inside table, as previously directed. Wahishi observed nothing amiss so he entered the café.

"As Salaam Alaikum," said Wahishi to the person rising to offer him the Muslim greeting.

"Alaikum Salaam," responded Mustaf ben Afad. They exchanged the kiss of peace.

Afad bore a general appearance similar to Wahishi. He was also in his later thirties, more solidly built, and with a full, dark, well-trimmed beard and hair to match. They were dressed in modest but obviously high quality jilbabs. They both fit in with the well-to-do locals coming to the Sug al-Milh for male society and conversation in an interesting and active setting. The needed shopping could be done by the women.

These men did not know each other well, but each had earned a reputation within al-Qaeda that called for mutual respect. Wahishi also now had rank.

Afad did not have a formal leadership title in al-Qaeda. He started out overseeing the personal fortunes of many senior al-Qaeda leaders. Later, Afad helped structure al-Qaeda finances worldwide. He was unknown outside of al-Qaeda and was able to freely move much of their money as needed. He utilized multiple venues from world capitals to little known financial havens, all without discovery by enemy intelligence agencies that were desperately seeking al-Qaeda funds.

Since his meeting with al-Adel at the Gerdi schoolhouse and his assignment to Yemen almost a year ago, Said Ali al-Wahishi succeeded in unifying the al-Qaeda related groups in Yemen. They were now one well-disciplined body referred to by Western intelligence as al-Qaeda in the Arabian Peninsula or AQAP.

While directing this reorganization, Wahishi developed contacts with al-Qaeda affiliate groups in Northern and Western Europe, Africa and the Near East. He observed these groups also lacked leadership and a common vision of how to conduct jihad. Wahishi offered them both and it was not long before they considered him their al-Qaeda leader. In less than a year, Wahishi became the recognized leader, not only of Yemen, but all al-Qaeda.

With that recognition, money came to Wahishi from both private resources and governments favorably disposed toward Wahishi's view of jihad. They supported the return of fundamentalist Islamic Society guided by the sacred Islamic Sharia law. The former al-Qaeda leader acknowledged this reality after losing the needed funds to Wahishi. Thus, the leadership change was bloodless, just the way Wahishi had envisioned it a year ago.

Owing to his non-existent profile with intelligence agencies, Afad was sometimes asked by leadership to manage a sensitive project outside the al-Qaeda chain of command. Today's meeting concerned a project that Afad initially oversaw at the request of the former al-Qaeda leader. Subsequently Afad was directed to continue this role by Wahishi. To Afad's knowledge, he was the only one in al-Qaeda who personally spoke to Wahishi about

The Engineer's project. Afad never knew how Wahishi first learned of The Engineer's mission now in progress.

"I have done what you asked," said Afad. "I met with The Engineer. He acknowledges your leadership. His mission is ready to launch its final stage. He asks that he be allowed to continue outside the chain of command. Absolute secrecy is imperative to him and his teams. He has just about everything needed in place. I must make one final delivery of money and travel documents to him. The Engineer will then be out of contact until after the attacks have taken place."

"You gave The Engineer my assurances that I understood why this mission was set up outside the command structure and that he had my blessing to continue the same way?" asked Wahishi.

"Yes. I'll continue to be the only one with whom he communicates.

"Good. We are all set. Allah willing, in a short time the US will be under such a great demand to protect their citizens at home, they will not have the money or the resources to continue their current war against us. We will soon be freer to move around the world. Our newly reorganized groups are ready to once again make our jihad credible."

Said Ali al-Wahishi did not tell Afad his personal reason for agreeing to The Engineer's request for complete mission secrecy. Wahishi's needed plausible deniability. Whether The Engineer's mission succeeded or failed, the United States would respond with ferocity. There would be an immediate demand within the United States for retaliation with vengeance. Wahishi wanted that first US effort directed at the former leader and not him. He staked out the former leader like a goat as bait for a lion. He would be a continuing diversion for the US military effort and the person who would take the blame for being the first terrorist to use a nuclear dirty bomb.

Wahishi's new leadership role would remain a secret until this mission was completed and the United States had time to respond. He would be the "new" al-Qaeda. The only people that could say Wahishi knew of The Engineer's mission were Afad and The Engineer.

Chapter 2

Palermo, Sicily

It was 7:00 am in the port of Palermo. The night boat from Naples just docked and passengers were coming ashore. It was early for the tourist season. Some passengers towed roll-along suitcases as they walked the long, concrete, passenger pier from the ferry to the street. The younger people carried backpacks and knapsacks. They all looked as if the night's sleep on the ferry had not gone well. Vincenzo Torino's attention was focused on a group of four young men. Nothing seemed unusual about any of them. They were in their late twenties or early thirties and appeared familiar with their surroundings. Their dungarees, t-shirts and sneakers made them look like anyone else their age coming off the night ferry, probably to visit relatives or to find work. Palermo was doing much better financially than Naples. Their banks had far more money to loan for construction projects. Money from *la druga* had to go somewhere.

Vincenzo followed the men to a coffee shop about two blocks from the ferry entrance. The men settled in for some coffee, pastry and another round of cigarettes. Vincenzo walked into the coffee shop, talked briefly with the barman behind the counter, ordered a coffee, and went to the men's room. One of the young men at the table noted to his friends that he had the call of nature and would be right back.

To the locals, Zio Vincenzo looked like the traditional, old style Mafia. In his mid-seventies, he was short and stocky, with thick arms and hands like a lifelong stone mason. No matter what the weather, he always wore black shoes, black pants, and a white long-sleeve shirt open at the throat.

The young man and Vincenzo had a brief conversation in the men's room. Vincenzo passed the young man a cell phone, and the man pulled out a small envelope and gave it to Vincenzo. During the transaction, the young man told Zio Vincenzo that The Engineer was the one in the blue t-shirt.

Vincenzo exited the men's room, sat down at a table, and was served a coffee accompanied by a newspaper. Other men stopped by the table to respectfully wish Vincenzo a good morning. The coffee shop was one of his investments and the young man with whom he spoke was a member of his "family," an *amico nostro*.

While pursuing his morning routine in the coffee shop, Zio Vincenzo had an opportunity to observe The Engineer. He noted The Engineer was a little older and shorter than the others. He looked to be about five-and-a-half feet tall, and had an overall slim build with a less than trim midsection. He did not look like a person whose body was used to a regimen of exercise. This observation seemed to be confirmed by his sallow complexion. The Engineer had dark hair and a matching beard that was short and scruffy looking.

The four young men, three of whom were oblivious to the accord being paid to Zio Vincenzo by the other patrons, or by Zio Vincenzo's interest in The Engineer, finished their breakfast and walked out.

Vincenzo finished his coffee, walked into a back office, pulled out yet another cell phone and called his cousin and fellow family boss, Aldo Torino, in New York. Zio Vincenzo shared the same views as his cousin as to what they must do to stop some very bad business, which would adversely impact the lives and fortunes of many.

Vincenzo updated Aldo Torino on what transpired this morning. "They have arrived in Palermo. I have someone with them and some others keeping a loose eye on them. They wire-transferred $30,000 from a bank in Milan to the shipping company to set up an account. That money came to Milan via a London bank. Our banking connections in London are looking to find where that money originated, but so far no luck. If they find anything, we'll let you know. Within the next couple of days, this group wants to ship a container of "machine parts" to New York City. While they readily admit the container will be something other than machine parts, they are holding their plans very close. They are clear the container must not be opened and are adamant that we guarantee our shipping methods will not subject the container to any physical inspection upon reaching New York. The $30,000 is a down payment of the $75,000 we are charging them. The rest is to be paid in cash prior to sailing. To pay us that amount in cash, you know whatever they are shipping is bad."

"What would the shipping cost be for a legitimate container?"

Zio Vincenzo smiled and said, "About $3,000."

"How did you come up with the $75,000 figure?" countered Aldo.

"We thought the more we charged them the more they would believe we were the right people to use. We didn't want them going elsewhere where we couldn't find out what they were up to." Vincenzo chuckled, paused for a moment, and added: "We told them how expensive it was to bribe US Customs. You figure if this were a load of *la druga,* the cost would be cheap for the potential profits. In the end, the more we charged, the more they believed."

Aldo responded, "I'm glad you are on my side. What is your sense of things now?"

"My man reports these are serious people putting on an act of nonchalance. One of them may be an engineer of some sort. There have been no more questions about customs inspections in New York. They are assuming there will be none. Have you heard anything more from our mountain friends?"

Vincenzo was referring to information that was developed from an old Sicilian poppy supply connection in Afghanistan. The people in Afghanistan had done business for years with yet another Palermo family that was still in the drug business. This line of work was not for Vincenzo or Aldo. However, this family in Sicily told Vincenzo and Aldo about their friends in Afghanistan known as the poppy people. The poppy people were asked by others to share or find a resource who could smuggle goods for them directly into to the United States. The poppy people also learned those seeking the smuggling connections were al-Qaeda from Afghanistan, now operating just across the border in Pakistan. Not wanting to see anything bad happen to their Sicilian friends, with whom they still did business, the poppy people checked further. They worried that al-Qaeda would use them to get what they needed and cause a problem with their long established Sicilian friends. The Sicilian drug family, after talking to one of Vincenzo's people in Palermo, asked the poppy people to find out more. They did.

Vincenzo heard the poppy people kidnapped someone in the al-Qaeda group. Reportedly, that person told what he knew before he died. The poppy people reported al-Qaeda was putting together a post 9/11 operation that required this container to be smuggled into the United States. The poppy people thought the container would contain armaments, explosives and possibly radioactive material or a suitcase-size nuclear bomb. If either of the latter two was present, they would have the makings of a dirty bomb or an independent nuclear device. This was not considered good for anybody's business. The poppy people were asked by the Sicilians why they believed nuclear material or a small device might be involved. This effort to drill down to the supporting facts just did not pan out. The poppy people just insisted that whatever was going to happen would involve nuclear material of some sort.

The poppy people assured the al-Qaeda operatives they had just the right Sicilian Mafia connections and their container could follow their poppy/heroin route. al-Qaeda would get their container into New York uninspected. al-Qaeda seemed satisfied the Sicilian Mafia was capable of doing what was needed, and would do anything for the right price.

"Did the disappearance of the person the mountain people spoke of cause any alarm among his colleagues?" asked Aldo.

"I am told these people made inquiries, learned nothing, and now assume their person was grabbed by a hostile intelligence agency. The group in question believes their person had no knowledge or information that could jeopardize their plans even assuming he was made to talk," said Vincenzo.

"Wrong to assume," thought Aldo.

"How sure are you of this?" asked Aldo.

"This is our best information at present. I am sending you an envelope, with a courier on tomorrow's flight, containing current photos and copies of passports being used by these three. The passport copies are courtesy of our friends in Naples. Also included is a memory stick containing recordings of conversations from the cabins shared by the three men on the ferry last night. They speak in Arabic among themselves. I will have one of my people who speaks Arabic listen to it. If there is anything of immediate value, I will call you back. My soldier with them says it is unusual how little they talk about business. He also noted they do not seem all that interested in Muslim prayer rituals nor do they appear to be religious."

"Do you think these three know the whole story?" asked Aldo.

"One appears to know more than the others. The other two seem to be more along for the ride. The apparent leader of the three we call The Engineer. He has told our people he was educated as an engineer. His two associates have also referred to him as The Engineer. We have followed them and call him by that name. Our people have the sense The Engineer is the one behind all of this, but they need more time."

"How will they get their container to Palermo?" asked Aldo.

"They haven't said, only that it will be here at an agreed-upon time before the ship leaves. Give us more time to see what we can learn now that they are here. We are using some friends with technical expertise so we will attempt to find out with whom they are speaking and what they are saying, even among themselves."

"I understand," said Aldo. "Please let me know as soon as you learn anything else."

Chapter 3

Franklin Wharf, Boston

At 6:30 pm, Liz Brennick arrived home to their Franklin Wharf condo from her Boston law office. Patrick had the Bolognese sauce simmering. Some fava beans were shelled and on a plate along with pecorino romano cheese. Patrick wanted this accompanied by a martini not yet made. The baby arugula was to be served with a little olive oil, and the figs would be dessert.

"What kind of pasta would you like tonight?" he called to Liz who was changing into her khakis and a t-shirt.

"How about farfalle? That holds the sauce well," responded Liz entering the hallway.

"As my love commands," replied Patrick politely looking to collect his first kiss of the evening from the weary lawyer.

Patrick thought Liz the most beautiful and elegant woman he had ever met. After many years of marriage, he still held that same opinion. Her tall, slender build, the still beautiful dark hair and flawless skin, allowed her elegant look to continue unfettered. Ten years younger than Patrick, Liz maintained her obvious excellent physical appearance through diet and regular exercise. She made every effort over the years to install these two regimens into Patrick's lifestyle. She met with limited success. Liz never looked like the "fed" she was at one point in her career. However, she continued to look like someone who could take care of herself.

A few years back, Patrick and Liz left the 525 square-foot apartment they originally shared. It was in a modest, four-story walkup brick building located in the North End. After ten years, this apartment was just too small. Patrick and Liz bought their current two-bedroom condo on the waterfront. The condo building originally had been a warehouse on the docks. Their unit had tall ceilings, a fireplace, two bedrooms, and a deck looking out on Boston Harbor.

Franklin Wharf was a renovation project they enjoyed doing together with the help of a contractor. It took them living through the dirt and dust for weeks on two separate occasions, but eventually the work was done. When the weather became just passable, they sat out on the deck to enjoy a martini and often dinner. They wondered what the neighbors thought seeing the two of them sitting with jackets on having dinner on the deck. Patrick and Liz learned in Paris that people sat in the outdoor cafés all the time, regardless of the weather. If the weather turned cold, you just put a jacket on or sat a little closer to each other. Patrick favored the latter solution.

Immigrants living in the North End at the beginning of the twentieth century raised large families in one- and two-room apartments. There was only room enough at home to eat and sleep. The streets served as the family living room. Social clubs were centered on devotion to a particular saint whose statue was sometimes carried from the local village church in Italy. It was in these clubs where the men spent their non-working time. While the communal bath houses for families were now gone, the social clubs were still active and an important part of the community. The weekend feasts were still held on the streets by the clubs in the North End each summer to honor their saint. The feasts continued to be well-attended and an attraction to many non-Italians.

"Are we having a martini tonight?" Liz asked.

"My weekend has officially started," said Patrick. "Unless you are working tomorrow, your weekend has also started. If so, you are entitled to a martini. I left the shaker on the counter for you to do the honors."

Who made the martini in the family was solely based on merit. Liz made the better martini, always shaken, not stirred, with a few ice crystals floating on the top. They drank a martini on weekends but not on "school nights."

"Let's have our martini on the deck," said Liz.

"I'll get the fava beans and cheese and see you there."

"My trial scheduled for Monday was rescheduled to Wednesday," said Liz.

"Why don't we get up early and grab a coffee for the drive to Southport. I would like to see about some late afternoon fishing." Patrick loved to saltwater fly fish.

"That sounds good to me. I don't have to come back until Monday morning," said Liz.

After retiring from the FBI, Patrick worked for a national consulting company doing mostly corporate due diligence. The work was interesting and often international. Patrick was amazed at the growth of information available through the internet and eventually through various commercial databases. He could do needed research from a laptop, refine the questions that had to be answered, and then hire former colleagues at home or abroad to do any necessary legwork.

Patrick, wanting a less structured environment, next started his own corporate consulting practice and sublet an office from a friend who ran a marketing business at King's Wharf. He still walked to work when he chose to go into the office. He did not work Fridays. That was his family errand day, which gave him and Liz more free time on the weekends.

Patrick in the past liked to travel for pleasure, but not so much for business. Now, he liked to travel less, at least by air. The barriers erected in the name of "security" after 9/11 did not seem to increase public safety as much as they seemed to give employment to ill-tempered people bent on abusing the discretion given them in a time of need. It seemed to Patrick that a lot of personal ugliness was being buried under the label of national security. On that score, the terrorists had already achieved their goal of disrupting the daily lives of a large segment of American business and society.

"Since you didn't answer me, I shall take that as our plan," said Liz. "What are you thinking about, I seemed to have lost your interest or at least your attention," she said with a smile.

"It is not good for a wife to know her husband so well. That is in the Bible," said Patrick turning his head aside so Liz would not see his smile. He next looked back to note Liz's reaction to his humorous provocation.

Liz turned her head slightly toward Patrick, raised her nose, looked down at him and finally responded: "So are some other passages that are similarly revolting. Shall we start down the list?"

"Only if we can go immediately to Saint Paul where he instructs wives to be subservient to their husbands," said Patrick with a huge grin.

"I used to detest Saint Paul until I studied him and realized that he was being greatly misinterpreted by willfully ignorant men seeking to feather their own nests at their wives' expense. I shall not bite on that one. Care to try again?"

They both laughed out loud. It was something they did a lot. Liz wished Patrick would smile more often. She worried at times he was too serious. Patrick and Liz were really good friends. They were also in love. Patrick often said God was good to him when he was able to marry his best friend.

Liz followed her original inquiry saying, "So don't try and dodge me with your lame effort to engage in biblical history. What were you thinking about?"

Patrick relayed to Liz the details of his conversation earlier in the day with Bill Evangelista.

When he finished, they both sat quietly nibbling fava beans, pecorino cheese, sipping their martinis, and watching the harbor boat traffic. They were as comfortable being quiet together as they were talking.

After this welcome period of joint reflection, Liz looked up to Patrick. He smiled knowing her lawyer mind was ready to proffer a question.

"Why you, why now?" asked Liz.

"I truly have no idea. As Sherlock Holmes said to his friend, 'Insufficient data my dear Watson. We must await more information.' In addition I was also thinking about you and me, where we have been over the years, and how we are both happy people. We are very lucky living where we do, having church, friends, and families who still reasonably like us."

18

They both resumed their quiet reflection.

The early summer warmth of the day did not last into evening. The chilly harbor breeze took over. They ate on the deck wearing jackets. While they were eating the fresh figs, accompanied by a glass of *vin santo*, the phone rang. Patrick got up, walked back inside, and answered the phone in the kitchen. A few moments later he came back to the deck.

"Are you available to give me a few moments of your time Monday morning at eleven?" Patrick asked Liz.

"Sure. As I said, my trial was postponed. I don't have any appointments."

"That was Mario Bocca. He wanted a time and place. I told him 11:00 am in the Boston Aquarium lobby. He said it would only take a minute, so I figured it wasn't worth more of an effort other than to make it very public, in an area where there are a lot of visitors."

"Still no idea what it is about?"

"No. He didn't seem very happy to have to speak with me."

"Okay. I'll back you up. I think it warranted."

Both Patrick and Liz obtained Massachusetts permits to carry concealed weapons after he retired and she became a prosecutor. Patrick had often been asked if he still carried a gun. He always found a way not to answer the question directly. He had not carried a gun since he retired, but he did not want people to know that. No real reason, it was just the way he was. If anyone had any ideas, they would have to consider the fact that he might be armed. He thought it a good idea for them to exercise this license privilege on Monday.

Chapter 4

East Boston

Billy Evangelista, after speaking with Mark Patrick, met the next morning with Mario Bocca at a diner in Day Square in East Boston.

"I told Patrick exactly what you told me to say to him," said Evangelista. "I tried not to tell him it was you who would be calling him, but he insisted on knowing."

"It makes no difference," said Bocca. "I called him and we are meeting Monday morning. It won't take me thirty seconds to deliver the message and, believe me, I don't want to be in the bastard's company any longer than that. I can't believe that people from over there asked me to speak with him."

Evangelista realized that Bocca was saying more than he should but he did not want to interrupt Bocca or even make an effort to caution him about this conversation. He had seen Bocca angry before and did not wish to see it again. He kept quiet and merely nodded as Bocca rattled on, working himself into frenzy.

"I told them what this bastard did to our family, about the FBI recording our induction ceremony. But they said it did not matter. Can you imagine that? My people from Sicily don't respect me. They have no say over here. They are giving me orders when I am not even in their family anymore. I am in the New England family and they can't give me orders. Suppose someone saw me meeting with Patrick and got the wrong idea. They specifically said I was to tell no one of my conversation. They don't even know I talked to you to get to Patrick."

When Bocca finally slowed, and paused for a breath, Evangelista said, "Perhaps you just need to do what they asked and then forget about it. If someone sees you with Patrick and starts asking questions, you can tell them to talk to me. Otherwise, this smells like something to stay out of."

Bocca had not vented enough. He did not catch the drift of Evangelista's words. "We took a close look at him years ago, and I am sorry now that we never took him out."

Evangelista was not going to be part of any such conversation. "Whoever made the decision not to do something that stupid should be thanked. Attacks like that are just what caused everything to fall apart over there."

"Yea, but they had the tapes of us swearing the new soldiers into the family. They took those tapes to Italy and Sicily and played them at trials over there. They even have been played in movies. It makes us look real stupid here, and everyone is still pissed at us and won't do any business with us."

Evangelista merely nodded. He wanted to end this conversation before it went any further.

"I'll meet with Patrick because they asked me to. I will say what they told me to say. Then I hope the bastard gets run over," said Bocca.

Evangelista confirmed that Bocca would meet with Patrick, say exactly what he was asked to say, and do nothing more. They finished their coffee and left.

Chapter 5

Southport, Massachusetts

Before moving to Franklin Wharf, Liz and Patrick purchased some land in the town of Southport, Massachusetts, located seventy miles south of Boston on Buzzards Bay. This land was in the middle of the woods. There they built a post and beam house with an open floor plan that some likened to a "tree house." They worked with the builder, doing a lot of the interior work themselves. This was especially helpful when their limited construction loan proceeds ran out.

Southport enabled Patrick and Liz to get out of their small city apartment on weekends and holidays. There they had a little more room to enjoy the company of their families and friends. Southport was also a place where they made new friends and attended the local Episcopal Church. In reality they had two lives. One was in the city they loved, and the other in the beautiful countryside of Buzzard's Bay, adjoining working farms and great salt water estuaries.

Upon arriving in Southport, Patrick and Liz stopped for their mail at Brant's General Store. There were very few general stores still authorized by the US Postal Service to handle mail. The post office tried to dismiss Brant's from their service in the name of efficiency, but soon they calculated, rightly so, that the opposition battle would be joined by the locals and the somewhat influential weekenders who came to Southport. The post office measured the cost, real and political, muttered, and went away leaving Brant's as a post office, as it had been for a couple of hundred years.

Their house was located four hundred feet from the road. Going up the long gravel driveway Liz said, "Look, the lady slippers are out."

The lady slipper is the somewhat unknown pink state flower of Massachusetts. Patrick and Liz had adopted the custom of inviting the neighbors to stop by to view them, as they had one of the few spots in town where they grew in abundance. Liz would make sure she had a supply of tea and cookies for those who came to view the flowers and wanted to sit and chat for a few minutes

Patrick called his fishing pal John Peabody. "Anything doing this week?" asked Patrick.

"I had three charters this week and we hit stripers in the river and outside. I don't think the blues are here yet," said Peabody.

"You interested in going down to the beach around six to fish the inlet into Bourne's Pond?"

"I guess it would be a holiday for a fishing charter captain to go fishing if he stayed on shore. Is that your logic?" asked Peabody.

Peabody ran two fishing charter boats. He used an eighteen-foot flat bottom boat for the rivers, and a twenty-three-foot center console for outside in Buzzard's Bay or over to the Elizabeth Islands. John Peabody was a recognized authority on salt water fly fishing and knew the local waters well. He and his wife Joan were some of the first friends Patrick and Liz made in Southport years ago.

"Tell Joan we'll be back around eight o'clock. She is invited here for dinner. Since I'm going fishing with you, dinner probably won't be fish."

"You don't spend enough time on the water to be a good fisherman, but I'll go with you anyway in hope of improving your skills," chuckled Peabody.

"I'll pick you up at five forty-five. Bring the dog. I may need some worthwhile company," responded Patrick.

Peabody and Patrick got back to the house about 8:15 pm. To the surprise of Joan and Liz, they caught a keeper. More correctly stated, John landed the striper on a fly while Patrick and the dog watched. The fish was filleted and was awaiting the grill. The martinis were poured and another pleasant dinner was at hand.

Sunday morning, Patrick and Liz went to the eight o'clock service at St. Mark's Episcopal Church in the village. The service was over by nine fifteen. The pastor seemed to feel the need to recap the sermon's main points after she spied a few congregants nodding off during her sermon. They stayed for coffee and a little conversation with their fellow parishioners before heading down to the local village eatery called the Bluefish. They, unlike more pretentious places in the area, served breakfast all day long. .

"Don't you think you should talk with someone in the FBI about Bocca before you meet with him, just to catch up with what's going on?" asked Liz.

"I think that if the FBI knew what was going on they would have told me that Bocca was going to call me for a meeting. No, I would rather see what he has to say first. Who knows? It could even be personal although, from the tone of his voice, I didn't think he was all that excited to meet me."

"Enough of this serious stuff. We are now properly churched. What would you like to do today?" smiled Liz.

"Perhaps we can take a walk on the beach and later consider a romantic interlude. The Red Sox are playing tonight. We can cook out and listen to the game on the deck."

"A fine plan", said Liz. "You continue to bring added value to this marriage."

Chapter 6

Boston

Patrick and Liz pulled into the parking lot at Franklin Wharf Monday at 10:45 am. Both carried their revolvers. Considered old equipment by today's 10 millimeter semi-automatic standards, they were still efficient for their purposes. They exited the parking lot, turned left, and walked along Commercial Street onto Atlantic Avenue. It took ten minutes to reach the Aquarium. Just before arriving, Liz went ahead of Patrick to enter the lobby first and have a look around. She did not think Bocca would remember her. She was right. Liz walked right by him as Bocca's attention was focused on Patrick, who was now some thirty feet behind her. She saw nothing to alarm her in the crowded lobby.

"Good morning Mr. Patrick," said Bocca, not extending his hand.

"Good morning to you Mr. Bocca. How can I help you?"

Bocca's face contorted into a sneer at hearing this innocent suggestion. "As you know, I am retired," said Bocca. "From everything," he added in a low mumbling growl.

Patrick just nodded.

"I have received a very specific request from friends outside this country. They asked me to contact you. I am to tell you that things are different today than when you were in the FBI, yet the need to communicate sometimes remains the same where there are matters of important mutual interest. Your FBI knew Lucky Luciano during World War II. They got him out of jail to have peace on the New York docks during the war."

"If you want someone out of jail, you are talking to the wrong person," said Patrick.

"Listen, please," said Bocca. "I am saying only what I was specifically told to say. There is a problem that needs to be addressed. My former associates need to talk to someone and they have asked me to speak with you to see if you would agree to a meeting to hear out this problem.

They also request that you not involve the FBI until you hear them out. You don't need them for protection. You know that. They won't deal directly with the government and you are someone not with the government but yet known to my associates. If you agree, give me a time and place. If you do not show up, they will know you changed your mind."

Patrick looked into Bocca's eyes. He could tell that Bocca was doing something that went against his grain, but he was doing exactly as he had been instructed. Patrick quickly considered the downside, thought a minute, and then said: "What is the time frame?"

"None. They are ready anytime."

"Tomorrow at 1:00 pm in the café at the Boston Public Library in Copley Square."

"At that time someone will approach you. They will tell you that I'm not available. I have gone on a fishing trip to Sardinia. I have no idea who this person will be. I have no idea what the nature of the problem is or why they have chosen you. I am also to tell you that the person who will talk to you has full authority to speak and act on behalf of my former associates. That is important for you to understand from the start. They have chosen me to deliver this limited message. That is all I know. I cannot answer any questions you might have. It's how they wanted it. I asked Evangelista to speak with you first. I was afraid you might not come if I called you out of the blue. I will give them the time and place. Goodbye, Mr. Patrick. I hope I never have to talk to you again."

Bocca walked off.

Definitely old school thought Patrick, who enjoyed a respectful relationship with a number of made guys. To someone like Bocca, conversation with a cop should never take place unless you were paying one off.

Patrick waited a few minutes, saw nothing out of the ordinary, and walked down Atlantic Avenue to King's Wharf. He went inside the lobby where he waited for Liz. When Liz arrived, they found a bench outside where Patrick could securely relate to Liz his conversation with Bocca.

"Your thoughts?" asked Liz after hearing the story.

"There is still no real information. Someone wants to have a conversation with me. They don't know me personally so they went through Bocca to set it up. It would appear that it has something to do with the Sicilian Mafia rather than the American LCN. I get the reference to Luciano."

"What happened with him?"

"The government let him out of jail and deported him to Italy, never to return. In return, Luciano guaranteed labor peace with all the unions on the docks during the course of the war. There would be no delays in getting needed war materials to the American fighting forces."

"It worked?"

"Yes, and the Sicilian Mafia later worked with American military intelligence providing information assisting the Allied invasion of Sicily. After Sicily came under Allied control, US forces allowed local Mafia bosses to participate in re-establishing local government and reconstruction. In 1928, Mussolini put the Mafia out of business in Sicily. The US put them back in business after driving the Germans out of Italy. Il Duce had been captured and dispatched. The Sicilian Mafia won with a little US help."

"So it seems the Mafia needs to speak with the US government, they refuse to talk directly, and they want to use you as a go-between."

"Ah my love, you always capture the essence without verbosity," smiled Patrick.

"Now would you be asking for my help at lunchtime tomorrow or have you found someone else more reliable and trustworthy," said Liz, with a twinkle in her eye.

"I have found no one to match your ability and, more importantly, your hourly billing rate."

"Is it cheap you are calling me?" queried Liz with a feigned look of anger.

"I am not entering that trap. Tomorrow I shall buy you lunch as a reward for your assisting me in my civic duty," said Patrick.

They both laughed.

"Seriously," said Liz, "You don't see any problem with this meeting and their request that you not tell the government about it ahead of time?"

"No, there could be some things that need to be discussed before getting a government bureaucracy jacked up. There is a little 'feeling out' going on here and I don't find that unusual. Bocca made it quite clear and, it is true, if they wanted to harm me they could do so. Bocca does not know what this is about."

"Puccini is on the bill at Covent Garden tonight. Shall we go?" inquired Liz.

Chapter 7

Patrick took the MBTA Green Line to Copley Square. He walked across the street and entered the front door of the Boston Public Library. The BPL, as it was commonly known, is regarded as the finest public library in the country. An architectural gem, well-appointed with murals and artworks tracing the history of the Commonwealth, the BPL serves as a foundation for cultural and educational excellence in the city. The BPL is one of the most used and loved buildings in Boston. Patrick felt he was entering a very special place every time he visited.

A couple of years ago, a café was established on the north side of the first floor just off the garden courtyard. A more formal dining area was adjacent. Patrick walked into the café.

Liz was already seated at a table where she could view both areas. Patrick sat down and waited. In a few seconds, someone was standing in front of him. He did not even notice where she came from. She just appeared.

"Good afternoon, Mr. Patrick. My name is Maria. May I sit down?"

At the same time, Patrick instinctively stood.

Patrick was not expecting this. He shook hands with Maria. Her handshake was firm, her smile was electric. She was beautiful. Maria was dressed in a beige suit, a white silk blouse, accompanied by minimal but what appeared to be very expensive jewelry. He guessed Armani for the suit. She was tall, shapely, with black hair, dark eyes, and exuded a look of quality and intelligence. He would guess her age to be about thirty-five.

After both were seated, Maria said, "Mr. Bocca is in Sardinia on a fishing trip. I am here to have a conversation with you on a matter of importance to this country."

Patrick's first reaction to Maria was to go on full alert, put on his best stone face, and reveal no observable reaction. Maria had to know she was not what Patrick expected. She would want to measure his response to her. Patrick instinctively wanted to deny her that. Maria said the right words to authenticate her contact with Bocca. He would stay on guard and see where this conversation was going.

Patrick just nodded.

"First, let me say it is necessary for you to understand I am here as a principal with full authority to speak and to make necessary decisions. I believe that Mr. Bocca made that clear. However, he has no idea who would speak with you nor is he aware now, or will he ever be, of our subject matter."

Patrick nodded again with his stone-faced expression unchanged. He needed more information. He was having an internal debate about how to proceed.

After a pause, Patrick said, "I understand what you have said so far. You asked for this meeting. I am here."

It was Maria's turn to nod. Patrick decided to ask Maria a few direct questions to see how she handled them.

"Are you telling me that you are made?" asked Patrick, with his eyes locked on Maria.

Maria momentarily broke eye contact with Patrick, lowered her head, looked at her watch, then looked back to Patrick and answered: "If you insist on asking an arcane question, the answer is yes." She didn't break eye contact while answering. Maria knew Patrick was taking her measure and it didn't seem to bother her.

Patrick considered that Maria could just be a well-coached actress and perhaps Bocca, or more likely one of his smarter colleagues, might be trying to embarrass Patrick by having him carry a baseless story back to the FBI. Not likely, he thought, but Patrick was ready to notch this conversation up a bit.

"Since when have women been made?" was Patrick's next question.

Maria seemed a little more disturbed by this question. She adjusted her watch and said in a low voice, "Since this thing of ours decided to come out of the dark ages, reform itself into the modern world, and take advantage of all its potential resources. Italian women have always had a role. Some families decided to formally admit to the reality of what has always been. Things are different today. Bocca is retired and I am here ready to do business, if we can proceed?"

Patrick was impressed. He talked to enough made guys, and listened to enough wires over the years, to experience the understated influence of women in the Mafia. Their influence was in fact significant. The Sicilian Mafia was a far more matriarchal-controlled society than many recognized. Patrick thought Maria spoke like the real thing.

"You've done the 'right work,' to use an LCN expression?" asked Patrick.

Maria offered her best stone face while holding direct eye contact with Patrick. She did not alter her expression in the least and responded immediately, saying: "I understand your question Mr. Patrick. Things have changed. This thing of ours imposed that requirement in the old days when perhaps 'hits,' as you infer, may have been more necessary. In the end it meant very little. Having participated in the ultimate act of violence was not an accurate gauge of future behavior. Those who had it in them to be informers did so regardless of their participation in a murder. Besides, the authorities are willing to forgive almost anything these days of those who would testify for them."

"Let us be clear. You want me to accept you are a made-member of the Sicilian Mafia, have a position of authority, and you want me to pass some information to the FBI?"

"In a word, yes. I know you find me and what I have to say surprising. I don't intend to deliver a lecture on the current management structure of our thing. For an organization to survive, it has to adapt. You think of crime. We are almost totally legitimate. We are part of the world economy. We are not going away. Organizational control has been ceded to more innovative members who have a new business model, which is not yet published or well known."

Patrick's level of intrigue increased. While keeping an open mind, his gut reaction was that she was for real. This was going to be an interesting conversation.

"What do you want to talk about?" asked Patrick.

"Before we continue, perhaps you could nod to Ms. Brennick. She has a concerned look on her face and probably would like to know everything is okay."

Score one for Maria, thought Patrick. She knew about Liz and how Patrick would have back-up. Patrick turned, looked at Liz, smiled, shrugged, and focused back on Maria.

Maria began, "Muslim terrorists intend to use a Sicilian transportation company, part of our operation, to smuggle arms, explosives, and possibly some radioactive material into the US. Even worse, they may even have a small nuclear device. The shipment will originate for us in Palermo. Our contacts are being paid to deliver the container uninspected from there to New York City. Our contacts have a certain reputation, shall we say, for the successful delivery of difficult shipments."

"Does that spell smuggler?" asked Patrick, generating a slight smile by Maria in response.

Maria continued, "Understand what is harmful to this country and its economy is also harmful to our personal, familial and economic interests. This is about preserving civilization as we know it. Our interests are in seeing that these people do not succeed. We can do this by indirectly sharing our knowledge with your government."

Patrick digested this information, nodded, and asked, "And what is it you want from me?"

"We don't want to share our organization, personnel, or have any form of direct contact with your government. We want nothing from them. Nothing," said Maria.

"I understood about the government," said Patrick. What do you expect from me?"

"If you agree, I will pass information onto you. You can pass it on to the FBI. Do what you think is necessary to stop this insanity. However, we do not wish the public to know we are the source of any information. We do not want my identity known, not that you know it now, or will in the future. If someone tries to identify me, or initiate their own independent contact, we will disappear."

"Can I say this information is coming from your organization?" asked Patrick.

"To those who must know, the answer is yes," responded Maria.

"That my contact is a woman who is made?"

Maria smiled, almost to herself, before responding, "I did not think you a sexist, Mr. Patrick. Was your wife a female FBI agent or an FBI agent?"

Patrick smiled sheepishly. "I see your point. Gender isn't the issue. The information is."

"Yes."

"Obviously, Liz has observed you," countered Patrick.

"We assumed you would have very discreet backup for a first meeting. Who better than another former FBI agent and your spouse, Liz Brennick? We trust in her discretion as well," said Maria completing her analysis.

Patrick pressed on, "How imminent is the threat? How good is your information?"

Maria paused for a second and then responded, "We think the event planned will be sooner rather than later. It is difficult to get a clear picture. These terrorists limit their information sharing to those who have a role. Few know the whole plan. Most have just a piece of the puzzle at best. If captured, they cannot give up the whole plan. However, we do have contacts in several countries picking up information so we are getting a little more of the picture, but not enough to be specific yet."

"How good is the information?" queried Patrick, realizing he was apparently going forward with Maria's request. "I am going to get a lot of people excited when I relay this information. Their first question will be 'how good is your source? What is the source's history of furnishing reliable and accurate information in the past?' We just met. We have no past. How would you suggest I answer these questions?" asked Patrick.

Maria was thoughtful. It was clear she was making a decision about how to answer Patrick's question. Then she spoke in the same low voice: "In January of this year, *The New York Times* reported a story about the arrest of a Russian civilian named Oleg in Tbilisi, Georgia. He was arrested trying to smuggle into Georgia one hundred grams of enriched uranium. Oleg claimed to have four to six pounds of this uranium available for sale, enough to make a small nuclear bomb. The article went on to say that the authorities were alerted to details of Oleg's attempted sale by Georgian government spies in South Ossetia."

Maria continued, "Check with the Georgian authorities and you will find the story about spies in South Ossetia was false. You will learn that these authorities were alerted to Oleg, and his effort to sell this uranium, via a detailed and untraceable email. The email contained all the necessary information for them to identify Oleg and make the arrest. They tried to trace the email and failed. There were no spies. That was a cover story for the media."

"Your organization gave this information to the Georgian authorities resulting in Oleg's arrest?" queried Patrick.

"Yes."

"May I use this event to establish your bona fides with those with whom I will speak?" inquired Patrick.

"Yes. Look, I know you will be asked questions you cannot answer. However, for this to work, you will soon need to believe I am who I say and my information is credible. We are talking about a substantial threat to this country by some extremely serious and capable terrorists."

"You know that once I contact the FBI, a story like this will get their full, immediate, and aggressive attention," said Patrick.

Maria replied, "We know that. Our contacts are not being given enough specifics at this point other than the container is to be delivered to the docks of New York City. We have drawn some conclusions on our own. On February eighth, an article in *The New York Times* discussed how New York City was going to be a test site for equipment designed to detect the presence of a dirty bomb or nuclear device entering the city. One of their leaders, whom we call 'The Engineer,' has made specific reference to this article and asked a lot of questions about whether we would able to avoid this type of sophisticated technical search if it were in place. He was assured such equipment would not be a problem, but the issue was moot because the equipment does not exist and is not in place."

"So you think New York is the destination port?"

"Yes. This is consistent with all we know and is what they've told us. We also think this news article put them on alert as to what type of cargo inspections in New York could threaten their plans. They seemed a little more willing to talk because they needed to be assured we could provide ways around any inspection threat. The problem for them is getting the container into the country. Once in the country, they can move the material about as necessary."

"Do you know the identity of the specific Muslim terrorist group behind this?" asked Patrick.

"No, we are working on that. We believe they are definitely under the al-Qaeda umbrella, but which faction we don't yet know. The people who referred the terrorists to our network are in the poppy smuggling business in Afghanistan. It was these people who were asked by the terrorists about using their poppy smuggling routes and contacts. We call them our mountain friends. They feel the same way we do about nuclear terrorists. They are trying to find out more. We are following a money trail in hopes of answering these questions."

"What is it you expect I am going to do now?" asked Patrick.

"Tell the FBI what I have told you. They can check with the rest of their intelligence colleagues, which I am sure they will do. They can see if the ever present 'chatter' they monitor has anything to offer. We will tell you what we know as we learn it. I repeat, we will not work directly with the FBI, the CIA or any other government group. We will not introduce any of their agents into our process. If we find someone trying to end run what we are doing, we will cease contact, for good," said Maria.

"You've made that very clear. Anything else?" asked Patrick.

"My colleagues do not need unnecessary conflict with these terrorists. Don't forget, to them we are also infidels."

"What about emergency contact?" asked Patrick.

"I know how to contact you," Maria said.

Patrick interrupted Maria as she began her next sentence. "I love your watch."

Maria looked at her watch and then back to Patrick. She smiled. Patrick had earlier noted something was out of place with her jewelry. Her watch did not match her look. A moment ago she moved her arm, and Patrick saw the very thin antennae wire running up her arm inside her sleeve. Her "watch" was an electronic device designed to alert the wearer to the presence of a transmitting device or body recorder. Patrick had seen them before on important, high ranking members.

Maria nodded toward the watch. "It enabled me to be more frank with you. Had you been wearing a transmitter or recorder, this conversation would not have even started. To continue, if you need to speak with me, put the chairs on your balcony on the left or west side instead of the right side where they are now. I must go now. I will be in contact shortly."

With that, Maria got up and walked out. Patrick saw no one leave either before or after her. It appeared she was alone. How long had they been watching his balcony?

Chapter 8

Patrick and Liz sat on a park bench between Trinity Church and the Boston Public Library. There was no chance anyone was overhearing this conversation. It took Patrick a little while to recount his conversation with Maria. Liz asked few questions, and then only to clarify exactly what Maria said. When he finished, they both sat for a few minutes taking a brain rest.

"What do you think?" asked Liz.

"I think she is real. She is direct. There is a very real, potential problem. My guess would be this is not the first dirty bomb or suitcase size nuclear device threat that has come to the government's attention. So far, such an attack has never occurred. However, I have a feeling I do not like. For the Sicilian Mafia to expose themselves as they have done just now means they are concerned. If the Sicilian Mafia is concerned, I am definitely concerned. I think I need to set up a meeting with the FBI."

"Who will you talk to?"

"A couple of months ago I was contacted by an agent named Robert Delgado. He is assigned to start up what basically would be an intelligence network among former agents now employed in the outside world. They want to make sure that the FBI office is in contact with all potential sources of information. Delgado explained this program to the former agents. I emailed him with a question, and we later talked. Rather than making a big deal out of this at the moment, I think I will go through him to set up a meeting with the international terrorism people."

"What about the Director?" asked Liz.

"He has more than enough on his plate. He spends all his time testifying before seventeen different congressional committees about what the FBI does or does not do. I don't see how he ever gets anything done. Going through channels is, I think, the right step at the moment."

Liz and Patrick both knew FBI Director Carter Simms since he was an assistant US attorney in Boston over 20 years ago. They happened to meet him a few months ago in Boston while attending a talk that Simms was giving. After the program, Patrick and Liz shared a few moments of conversation with Director Simms, who followed up by sending them a photograph taken of the three of them after the event. In a note to them, Simms observed all three were sharing a good laugh when the photo was taken.

"What are you going to tell them about Maria?" she asked.

"I have been thinking about that. At this point, I will just draw a bright line and say nothing about the physical attributes of the person I met with or where we met. I don't want them going behind my back pulling footage from every video camera inside and outside the BPL, trying to identify everyone in the building at the time when I was meeting with Maria. I will strongly suggest they not divert their attention trying to figure out the source's identity. It will not advance their effort. I will tell them I do not know who the person is, where to find the person, or how to make contact. I see no need to tell them about my speaking with Evangelista and Bocca; it just adds more people with no potential profit. Maria and her friends would pull the plug if they thought the government was trying to identify them."

"When?" asked Liz.

"Now," said Patrick.

Patrick had Delgado's number in his cell phone so he punched up the number and got Delgado's voice mail. Patrick left a message saying he had come across some information that may be important for the FBI to hear and asked Delgado to give him a call back at his earliest convenience.

"Now my love, since you were not provided breakfast at home, may I invite you for a late lunch? I am famished."

"That would be fine. I can work at home afterwards."

Patrick asked, "How long will your trial take?"

"About two weeks. I don't think the other side wants to settle but we will meet with the judge one final time before the jury is seated."

"Why don't we pay a visit to Giovanni, have a plate of pasta, a salad, and if you really push, a glass of red wine."

"Deal," said Liz. "Such a beautiful afternoon, why don't we walk back to the North End?"

They walked arm in arm over to Newbury Street and headed toward the Public Garden, checking the shops and chatting along the way. They passed through the Boston Common, over City Hall Plaza and crossed to Hanover Street and into the North End.

Giovanni was glad to see them.

"Where have you been? I have not seen you for so long," said Giovanni giving both Liz and Patrick the obligatory and welcome kiss on both cheeks. He stood between them both, put an arm around each shoulder, and marched them over to the bar to say hello to his wife, Carmella. After another series of greetings, Giovanni marched them to a table and asked what they wanted to eat. It was a simple question. He would not bother getting a menu.

"Just a plate of pasta with some marinara sauce, insalata mista, and a couple of glasses of your fine Sicilian red wine," said Liz.

Patrick nodded his assent.

"You two don't eat enough. I will take care of this." Giovanni walked away muttering to himself. He instructed a waiter in Italian to bring a bottle of mineral water to the table, two wine glasses and some small plates for an antipasto that Giovanni was going to surprise them with.

Patrick regretted that as a child he had not spoken more with his great grandmother in her native Italian. His great uncles were also a source of the language for him but, by the time he was in the FBI and working the LCN, he primarily taught himself. The books and tapes he used helped somewhat, but the real lessons came when he asked friends in the North End to speak with him only in Italian, forcing him to learn how to survive using the Italian language. Later, after two fairly long, personal trips to Italy, his fluency increased. Liz had actually learned Italian just by being with him.

Giovanni returned with a plate of grilled vegetables drizzled with green Sicilian extra virgin olive oil, a dish of black cured and spicy green olives, and bread to soak in more Sicilian olive oil seasoned with rosemary and sea salt.

"Eat this while I fix your pasta," said Giovanni, walking off singing to himself now that he had properly set the table for his guests.

They demolished the vegetables, ate the bread and olives, and pronounced themselves hungrier than they thought.

"Maybe just being here with Giovanni makes us hungry," said Liz.

"Not too late to order more," smiled Patrick.

"If I know Giovanni," Liz said, "he is not finished. Let's wait until the pasta comes and see what else he has planned for us."

Twenty minutes later Giovanni came back with two plates of linguini with marinara sauce. He also happened to have a plate of fried eggplant accompanied by a few fried squash flowers.

"The first of the season," Giovanni said with pride, referring to the squash flowers. "My cousin just brought them in. He got some squash in the ground early and the frost did not get it. Enjoy!"

Now Giovanni walked away singing loudly in Italian for all to hear. He was as much an entertainer as a chef but, whatever he did, it came from his heart.

They left a good tip for the waiter, who never got to serve them. On the way, out goodbye kisses with both Giovanni and Carmella were affectionately given and received. Coffee was declined, as they would stop by the Café Strada on the way home.

Walking down Hanover Street, Patrick's cell phone went off. He stopped, stood to the side, and answered.

"Mr. Patrick, this is Agent Delgado returning your call."

"Call me Mark, please. I have some information that I have been requested to pass on to the FBI. I thought it might be what your program is designed to pick up. I would like to see you in person as soon as possible. It might save some time if you could have one of your folks from international terrorism available."

"Hold on," said Delgado, "Let me see who is around in the morning?"

"Would first thing, say eight-fifteen, be okay?" asked Delgado.

"That is fine," said Patrick. "See you at One Center Plaza then. Good afternoon."

In front of the Café Strada, the men were smoking their cigarettes out on the sidewalk. The mayor was a terror against smoking and the city had banned all smoking from anyplace that served anything to eat, drink, or had the smell of food or drink. Well, it was pretty inclusive anyway. In response, the men just stepped outside the café to comply with the law and to avoid any possibility of confrontation with the smoking police, who could be lurking nearby. Besides, it was a nice time of day to be outside with the late afternoon turning toward evening.

After coffee, they walked the five blocks back to the condo. Liz went to her desk and started going over her trial material. Patrick wanted to do some computer research.

He found the two *New York Times* articles mentioned by Maria, carefully read each one, and then printed out copies. Patrick regularly read articles about what Homeland Security and other agencies were doing to protect the United States post 9/11. He also followed the public testimony of various government officials before congressional committees, which, while carefully scripted, was still informative. From time to time Patrick needed to know these things to advise his own clients. Patrick was not a big fan of Homeland Security. He thought the creation of the large Department of Homeland Security was solely a political reaction to 9/11. It did not in itself solve a lot of the known intelligence gathering problems. It just created a more weighty bureaucracy with too many chiefs and not enough workers in the field. As the printer was whirling away, Patrick was ruminating about how government intelligence gathering had changed over the last thirty years to the point where it now almost exclusively relied upon some form of electronic or technical interception of the opposition's communications.

Immediately prior to 9/11, the CIA had no experienced case officers in the needed regions abroad. They were downsized when US Intelligence policy wonks decided to rely primarily on their technical and electronic eavesdropping capability. The use of live informants was discouraged, as they were often bad people themselves who would sometimes cause the responsible agency, and the administration, embarrassment, bad press, and reveal some poor judgment. The favored electronic plan worked for a while, but when the terrorists learned through experience about US electronic intelligence gathering, the terrorists stopped using technology to communicate. People delivering messages by mule were not likely to be electronically intercepted. American intelligence had not counted on the enemy going backwards in time to defeat the tools of their modern intelligence collection. Now, post 9/11, it would take any agent sent to one of these important countries years to get established and become productive. The learning curve for field work could not be ignored. The CIA reportedly was one of the few government agencies after 9/11 to hire back some of the old hands that had been retired off. This helped fill the gap, but the real damage to intelligence gathering had already been done.

Under administration pressure, inflamed by the political left, the CIA was forced to issue its own guidelines for how agents were to record the identity and operate all terrorist informants. The result has been that most

CIA agents are reluctant to operate live sources. Needed human intelligence often has to be begged from close allies who are always reluctant to endanger their own sources. Singular data reaching the wrong hands can often lead to the informant's identity and death. Why share human intelligence so difficult to obtain with a country refusing to share any operational risk?

The FBI was being hounded over its use and handling of criminal informants. Restrictive guidelines were put in place to correct all the real and perceived problems of agents operating criminal informants. The overall tenor of these changes was to make sure real bad people could not be used as informants. Real good people, who could now qualify to be informants, of course did not know anything about crime much less terrorism. Thus the FBI had no worthwhile informant program. How could you have an active member of al-Qaeda as an informant? He was doing evil and illegal things by the very nature of his being in al-Qaeda. If you did not have him as an informant, what hope did you have of ever finding out what al-Qaeda was planning? The agents responded to these bureaucratic moves by just not having informants.

It was different administrations and their intelligence gathering philosophies over the years that led to this present state of electronic intelligence domination. Using the budget process, administrations enforced their will that electronic intelligence gathering would be primarily relied upon to protect the country's national security. Dealing with bad people as informants or spies was a nasty business that sometimes reached the press. Electronic intelligence gathering generally did neither. Congress more favorably funded those programs that relied upon this strategy. Many thought they had found an alternative to dealing with people or countries that did not meet our nation's democratic, human rights, or legal standards of civil behavior. Not everyone agreed with this decision. The administration strategists were warned in a Department of Defense report as early as 1994 against this almost total shift away from human intelligence to electronic intelligence gathering. The administration believed itself smarter than their career intelligence officers who, after all they thought, were just defending their rice bowl.

When Patrick again read the now printed article about the nuclear detection equipment to be installed, apparently only in the Staten Island port terminal, he was not impressed. His first reaction was why tell the enemy what you have and what you don't have. Didn't they realize that telling the American people what they intended to do in the future to protect them was actually telling terrorists what is not being done now? How would this make any thinking person feel more secure?

Patrick hoped that this type of article might just be disinformation designed to fool al-Qaeda. His instinct told him otherwise.

Patrick also knew only a very small percentage of overseas cargo containers were ever inspected upon entry into the United States. Some proposed security plans called for cargo to be inspected by US agents in foreign ports and then sealed before shipment to the United States. Patrick could see the value of keeping any potential danger physically away from our shores. However, he did not believe such a plan could be effectively pursued, even by the best of people, on foreign shores. There we were just not the home team.

Patrick also knew the deadlines for inspection of commercial freight aboard passenger planes had come and gone, without substantial compliance. There were only spotty inspections of cargo planes. Yet the TSA would bust the chops of the elderly couple, make them stand in long lines, unpack their toothpaste, take off their shoes, and submit to body pat downs that every day were becoming more invasive, degrading, and lacking in common sense. TSA was willing to piss off passengers, which caused airline travel to shrink. The same TSA did not want to offend the politically powerful airlines and their lobbies by demanding action that would increase their operating costs, which were difficult to pass on to their declining passenger base. They never got around to fully inspecting what was sent commercially in the belly of the beast.

While passengers stood in more lines, airlines noted they were laying people off. They had no money for costly inspections. Some claimed the technology was non-existent or just not up to needed operational standards. Many of the congressionally-legislated requirements still lacked implementation.

In reality, the threat possibilities against the United States were so numerous that government could not address them all. But this would never be said out loud by anyone wishing to remain in government service. Patrick thought the government should be more realistic, perhaps more forthright, when discussing terrorist threats with citizens. Citizens already had figured out a lot of this on their own. Certainly the enemy had. After all, Oleg did not seem to have a problem getting four- to six-pounds of enriched uranium.

Patrick next turned his research to dirty bombs. In government parlance, they were termed a Radiological Dispersal Device. Perhaps the words dirty bombs were just too graphic? The theory was that most of the death and destruction would come from the conventional explosive used to blast the radioactive particles into the air. Long-term sickness and death from exposure over time was less certain. However, there was no effective technology to decontaminate an affected area. The material had to be physically removed from all surfaces in the contaminated area and transported to some recognized, safe, containment storage facility. The material would not lose its radioactivity for many lifetimes. Patrick thought this would certainly enliven the NIMBY groups. Can you imagine, thought Patrick, lower Manhattan being covered in radioactive dust? Do you think anyone would ever live, work, or visit there again? Perhaps having areas like that would do more harm to the psyche and economy of the country than outright destruction.

Patrick finally shut off the computer. He learned more than he wanted to know, at least for tonight. A nuclear device that could generate a 15-kiloton explosion, with all of its fallout problems, would fit into the back of a van. Hell, thought Patrick, put the bomb in a van and ship the van into the United States. How many vans does the United States import in a year? How many of them are ever searched?

Patrick decided to go to bed. Liz was still working. As he said his prayers that night, Patrick thought about the Muslim terrorist praying to the same God as he, but asking for blessings on his effort to destroy infidels. The Muslims, Christians and Jews all claimed to be the descendants and children of Abraham. All traced their religious beginnings to this founder of monotheism. Patrick was praying to the same God that he might be an instrument to prevent this madness. Patrick wondered what God thought? He knew that Abraham was pissed!

Chapter 9

Manhattan, New York

After leaving Patrick at the BPL on Tuesday afternoon, Maria Torino took a cab to Logan Airport and the shuttle to New York's La Guardia Airport. Upon arriving, she went to the lower level where the limousine was waiting.

"Good afternoon, Ms. Torino," said the driver.

"Good afternoon, John. How is your day?"

"Traffic is not bad. It is spring, sunny, and everyone in New York seems to be happy. I am sure it will change but right now the city is in a good mood. Your father would like you to join him in his office if you have time."

"Fine, let's go to the office and after that I can let you know about the rest of the day."

Maria always liked the drive into the city from the airport. Today it gave her a chance to collect her thoughts to report to her father what she thought about her meeting with Patrick.

Maria was married after graduate school to a medical doctor who had no idea as to the extent of her family's business interests. She met him when she was in an MBA program at NYU. He was just starting a surgical residency in the city. Her husband, George, got along well with her family, which included both her parents, two brothers and a sister. After Maria got her MBA she went to work in her father's international business conglomerate. By most standards it was a small business, with about $500 million a year in revenues. Today, the business was much larger. It operated under various names and a group of domestic and foreign companies that were all privately held but related. It would take anyone a long time to figure out who owned what. It was a matter in which no one seemed to have any present interest. It was the way she and her father wanted it.

When George had a significant career opportunity offered to him in Los Angeles, it was time to move from New York. She tried the West Coast life for a while, but it just did not work. She came back to New York and her father's business. While she and George remained friendly, their careers took them apart and they divorced. She, in a way, was glad she had no children. There were grandchildren enough through her sister and two brothers, and she thoroughly enjoyed her nieces and nephews. Even more, she enjoyed working with her father in all aspects of his business. She felt what she was doing was exciting, and she liked that. Maria had a number of male admirers in the city and she never lacked for an interesting dinner partner. She, like her father, respected a modest lifestyle but enjoyed a life with style, nonetheless.

Their company headquarters was located in a small, mid-town office building that her father purchased years ago. Tenants helped support the building at first but over the years, as his companies grew, tenants were no longer necessary. The family businesses now occupied the whole building. John Turco drove for her and her father and was treated as part of their immediate family. He was also an *amico nostro*.

Maria took the elevator to the fourteenth floor and went to her father's office.

"How did it go?" asked Aldo Torino. He gave his daughter a kiss on both cheeks.

They sat on two high wingback leather chairs in front of his desk. She reported to her father in a succinct and factual manner. Anyone listening would think she was reporting on her first contact with a potential business acquisition.

When she finished, Aldo asked, "Do you think we are dealing with the right person? Will this work?"

"My first impression is that Patrick is what was described to us. He had his wife covering the meeting as we thought. I came away with no significant negatives and thus have no reason to tell you that we cannot go forward as we have discussed."

Aldo nodded absorbing what Maria said.

"Is there news from Zio Vincenzo?" Maria asked.

"No. There is nothing more we can do until we hear more from him. I have continued to think this over and believe what we are doing is right for our families and for the good of our thing. But, I know there will be pushback if word of this gets out."

"How bad?" asked Maria.

"There is a whole element that has no idea of what some of us have created right under their noses. They will be very angry at first, fearing they have somehow lost opportunities to make money and then fearful about what else they may not know. Greed still rules. Others are not ready to hear about the formal role granted women in some families. They still think you should be in the kitchen kneading the pasta."

"Shall I get out one of Mom's aprons?"

"As long as it has a pocket for a small computer," he said with humor.

Both realized their present course of action could have negative ramifications, but they had crossed that bridge and had no intention of turning back. With the support of Zio Vincenzo in Sicily and other similar thinking family leaders, Maria and her father believed they had the necessary backing for any immediate needs.

"I think we need to get John involved. If there is any plan that calls for these terrorists to come to New York, we may have to act directly if it turns out we cannot rely upon the authorities. We should at least be ready for this contingency. If we keep John up to date, he can begin lining up the necessary resources. Will you handle this?"

"I will speak with him immediately," said Maria.

Maria excused herself to go to her office. They tentatively agreed to have dinner that night.

Aldo Torino sat in his office reflecting on how and why these changes had come about. His father took him as a very young boy, along with the rest of the family, out of Sicily just before the war. Mussolini had earlier declared war on the Sicilian Mafia. Il Duce feared their political power and treated the Mafia like any of his other political problems. He made them disappear.

Aldo's father brought the family to New York. Aldo's first cousin, Vincenzo Torino, remained behind in Palermo as his father was a less well-known Mafia person and not on Il Duce's elimination list. Giovanni Badalamenti was their early childhood friend in Palermo. Giovanni's father was on Il Duce's elimination list so he and his family moved to Buenos Aires. Eventually each of her uncles' sons followed their father's family tradition and became members of their fathers' Sicilian Mafia families. It was her two uncles and father that spearheaded the reform of the Sicilian Mafia families to insure their survival. Some of the Sicilian Mafia families, less open to change, were not even aware of what was happening.

These three men, along with other similar thinking allies, slowly and quietly disconnected from the old traditions. They reformed how and with whom they did business. It was they who recognized the value of women and established their full role in *la famiglia*. It was Aldo, Vincenzo and Giovanni who convinced their colleagues that they needed to furnish this information to the government now for their common good. This was certainly bad business, which made it everyone's business. It needed to be stopped.

Later that day, Aldo stopped by Maria's office to see if she was still available for dinner at Illario's. He also mentioned that he had spoken further with Zio Vincenzo and they could discuss it on the way over.

"I spoke with John," said Maria. "I explained to him we may need some resources. He is putting together a group that will be at our disposal until we resolve this matter."

"Ask him to include anyone we have who has the needed technical expertise," said Aldo.

"Already done," said Maria. "The equipment is being gathered and will be on standby."

"I will come by around 6:30."

"See you then."

Chapter 10

Boston

Patrick woke early, which was unlike him. He loved the early morning hours but generally was unwilling to exercise the necessary effort to get out of bed. Consequently, he did not enjoy many sunrises. On the other hand, Patrick was somewhat of a night owl. He often stayed up late. Liz was normally a morning person but was sometimes corrupted by Patrick's bad habits.

By the time he sat on the outside deck, with his first coffee of the morning, the sun was well up and the harbor was alive with both commercial and pleasure boat traffic. The din of the morning city traffic was rising. The air was cool from the breeze off the water but the early June sun was starting to build in strength.

Liz appeared shortly on the deck with her coffee. "I was thinking," she said, "that you need to come up with a name for Maria so you won't make a gender mistake when talking with the FBI. If you agree ahead of time that you are not making any representations as to the gender of the person and will use a code name, they will not feel as if you are fooling with them if you use the word "she" in error at some point. Give them a code name at the start and you are all on the same page."

"That seems to be a solution to the problem I was just thinking about. Got a suggested name?"

"You want me to do all the work?" she smiled.

"Hurry and drink your coffee," said Patrick, "Because until you do, you are a rotten human."

It was generally Liz who fixed the morning coffee on weekends when they were home. Otherwise it was a stop at a nearby café. However, when they went camping, it was a great luxury for Liz to stay in her sleeping bag inside the tent while Patrick got up with the sun and fixed the coffee. For some reason he loved to get up when camping. Of course, sleeping on a tent floor with only a pad under the sleeping bag does not lend itself to lolling around in the morning. Liz loved the thought of Patrick being up first, hearing him bang around the campsite, getting the pot ready and the camp stove going. She knew shortly she would smell the first aromas of the black gold mixed with the fresh morning air. To Liz, it remained one of her special memories.

As Patrick was finishing his pleasant recollection of early mornings while camping, Liz said, "Vespa."

"The motor scooter?" he asked.

"Yes, but the word means a wasp or a hornet. It does remind me of the sound the old motor scooters used to make in Italy. Simple enough to remember. It almost sounds feminine."

"Simple is best. Okay. Problem solved. Want to go for breakfast?"

"No. I need to do a little more reading before I go to court. Give me a call on my cell after you get through. Maybe we can meet for lunch?"

Patrick walked the two blocks down Commercial Street to Sal's. Sal served the best breakfast in the North End. Patrick could not adhere to the Italian tradition where breakfast was just a piece of bread and some espresso, laced with sugar, which held until the large noontime meal. Patrick needed breakfast. Sal was only open for breakfast and lunch, and closed at 2:00 pm. All walks of life ate at Sal's, but most were from the neighborhood. Sometimes people from the hotels wandered through after asking the concierge where to get some "real food" for breakfast. Sal had a knack for remembering what everyone ate the last time in and how they took their coffee.

"Good morning, Sal."

"Morning, Mark. Coffee with milk?"

"Please."

"Two over easy, bacon well, dry Italian toast, okay this morning?"

"Sounds good to me? Where is your mom? Give her the day off?"

"Yea. Want any juice?"

"No, not today," said Patrick as he walked over to look at the headlines on the papers in the news rack."

"Anything I need to know about the world this morning?" asked Patrick as he looked over the headlines.

"Not that I can see. The Sox won last night. Pitching is still good. I'm still a believer."

Sal was what you would call a real sports fan. During football season, he was known to let his mother and sister run the café while he traveled to another city to catch the Patriot's Sunday away game. Pictures of his favorite Celtics and Bruins players were on the walls where they had hung undisturbed for years. No need to change what you liked.

Sal's place only held about twenty people and it filled quickly. Patrick grabbed a local North End weekly newspaper and read it with his breakfast. This paper made you realize you were a member of a community that cared to report on the small things of community life. It was alive, breathing, and caring of its community members.

It was a fifteen-minute walk from Sal's to One Center Plaza on Cambridge Street, which housed the Boston FBI Office. He arrived at 8:20 am. He was intentionally five minutes late. Patrick went into the reception area on the sixth floor. There were two desks behind a large floor-to-ceiling Plexiglas that looked like it was designed to stop a small tank. Before you reached what passed for the counter, there was a metal detector to pass through, or you could walk around it. He was not sure what it meant. He walked through it with everything in his pockets and no alarm sounded.

Patrick gave his name to the lady behind the Plexiglas and asked for agent Delgado. She offered him a seat while she located Delgado.

As he sat in the waiting room, Patrick thought how the reception areas of FBI offices had evolved over the last twenty-five years. At one time there was no glass, no barrier, generally two desks for receptionists, and a picture of J. Edgar Hoover on the wall behind the receptionist along with a picture of the sitting president (more of Hoover's equal in the eyes of some), or the Attorney General (always considered a lesser figure then Hoover). The receptionist had a panic button that could immediately summon armed agents. Patrick could only recall it being used once, and that was for a mentally disturbed person. Now, the security of the attending personnel required that there be a barrier between them and the public. Patrick thought this was a metaphor for some of the FBI's problems today.

There were many things that had changed over time, but not by their own design. Circumstances seemed to take the FBI away from their much needed direct contact with all segments of the public. This eroded their opportunities to garner public support for their ongoing programs. Without substantial public support, their job was far more difficult.

A side door opened and a tall, young man about thirty, with dark hair cut short, a muscular build, and a huge smile extended his hand as he approached Patrick.

"Mark, nice to finally meet you. Please come in. I have a conference room for us. May I get you a coffee?" They shook hands. Delgado had the FBI handshake, firm but not overpowering. They taught it in new agents training.

Patrick smiled silently to himself. He could remember when FBI agents were not allowed to bring coffee into the office! He started to comment to Delgado about this old restriction but decided Delgado would not be interested or impressed by anyone who actually was willing to work under such conditions. As he walked through the door of the conference room, he tried to recall why that was so and when it had changed. He could not remember.

The only difference between this conference room and any other FBI conference room Patrick had ever been in was the carpeting and window treatments. They were not in a government building run by GSA, and thus the minimum civilian standards provided by the landlord were far superior to any in a government building. Patrick observed that one could go from the reception area to this conference room without passing into FBI working space. Another security measure he presumed.

"Mark, please sit down. How can I help you?" asked Delgado.

Patrick explained that he was being used to relay information from the Sicilian Mafia to the FBI. How the meet was setup or who observed it was not important for this conversation. He did not mention Liz. He was sticking to basics to get the information where it needed to go. Patrick described in full detail his conversation with Maria, leaving out anything to do with her gender. He did represent that the person admitted to being made in the Mafia, and that Patrick believed that to be true. Delgado was taking no notes so Patrick knew he would be telling this story again to someone who would be taking notes. He knew the conversation was not being recorded as they had not asked his permission to do so. It did not take long.

Delgado absorbed everything Patrick had said without interruption.

"I wanted to hear what you had to say first. I made arrangements for us to be joined by agent Susan Crowley who is assigned to foreign terrorism matters. Would you mind if I asked her to join us?"

"Not at all," said Patrick.

Delgado made a call and asked the person on the other end to join them in the conference room. Within seconds, the door opened and they were joined by a woman in her mid-forties, short with an athletic build, obviously a runner. She had blond hair with a touch of grey, blue eyes, and a firm, FBI-approved handshake. She appeared to be a serious woman with a pleasant disposition. After they were introduced she sat across from Patrick and alongside Delgado.

"Mark had some interesting information brought to him, which he believes is being furnished to him by the Sicilian Mafia," said Delgado.

Crowley showed no reaction.

"Mark, I know you told me everything, but could I ask you to repeat what you told me to Susan since it will be her responsibility to carry this matter forwar

Patrick proceeded to relate to Crowley exactly what he had just told Delgado. This time she was taking notes. When Patrick finished she asked a few questions to clarify her note entries. She was also a very precise person.

Crowley next asked, "You call this person Vespa. Why don't you want to tell us who the person is?"

"I told you I do not know the person's name, or where the person can be located. I do know that if this person feels that the FBI is trying to identify Vespa, they will walk away. That is what the person said and I believe it."

"And you feel that if you tell us any more about what Vespa looks like or where this meeting took place, we might make some effort to identify that person?"

"Exactly," said Patrick.

"What is wrong with that?" asked Crowley.

"It was the only thing they asked not be done. It does not seem unreasonable under the circumstances. So if you make this effort, make some noise, stir the pot, what is the advantage? If they should find out and stop the conversation, what is gained? I just don't see the present need or any upside to doing that. You have plenty of other things to do. You can evaluate where this information fits into current intelligence. See if the information about Oleg pans out."

Crowley did not agree or disagree. Delgado said nothing.

"Mark, would you mind waiting a few minutes while I speak with my supervisor? Before you leave, I want to make sure that we have a good plan of communication and we each know what to expect from the other in the immediate future."

Patrick nodded his assent. Delgado offered coffee again, and Patrick accepted this time. Both were gone from the room. Patrick sat there trying to imagine himself in the position of Crowley and Delgado and what management was going to say when they heard this story. The coffee took long enough so he figured that Delgado stopped to have a word with Crowley and with whomever she was speaking. Best to take some time and get this off on the right foot, thought Patrick.

Delgado returned with the coffee. He asked Patrick who he currently knew in the Boston office. Patrick acknowledged that he knew some but not many of the current agents. He did know many of the support staff still serving in the office. In fact, Patrick had just renewed many of these friendships when he recently spoke at a retirement party for a long-term support employee who had been very helpful in Patrick's Organized Crime program. Patrick was always very conscious of the fact that the support staff was essential in every case and their efforts needed to be recognized.

Some years back, when the FBI Director came to Boston with the Attorney General for the press conference about the recording of the LCN induction ceremony, Patrick requested the Director meet privately with the support staff who had worked very hard on the case. The Director agreed. He also knew the value of what these people contributed. Everyone was happy.

Crowley came back to the conference room. "I have spoken with my supervisor, George Fisher. He, in turn, has spoken with the Assistant Special Agent in Charge for terrorism matters, that being Phil Kirby. Fisher also has spoken with Jerry Craig, who presently is supervisor of the LCN OC Squad. We would like to have some more time to talk among ourselves. We will need to talk with FBIHQ, see what may be going on in their world that we don't know about. Then we can get back to you for another meeting if that is convenient. However, ASAC Kirby has just told me that he wants to speak with you now. Would you mind?"

Patrick noted not only what she said, but how she said it. The last part seemed to be tinged with a little frustration.

"I know this is not what you expected to start your day with. On the other hand, it would be worse if there were anything to this and the FBI did not learn about it or did not handle it well. So let's do what is necessary to get this off on the right foot," said Patrick.

"I will be right back," said Crowley, as she again left the room.

Patrick and Delgado enjoyed a few minutes of conversation about which former agents now in the private sector were presently in a position to assist the FBI in various types of investigations. They both were in agreement that FBI intelligence gathering needed to be put back on track to succeed in their mission.

Crowley came back into the room followed by a man in his late thirties or early forties. He was shorter then Delgado, heavier, and looked like he spent a lot of time at his desk. He had light brown hair, was balding, and had a little flab around the neck. What stood out, and what Patrick noticed most, was the look of someone who was not good at handling pressure. Patrick did not like to make snap judgments, but he often made snap observations.

Crowley introduced Phil Kirby to Patrick. Kirby sat down without offering to shake hands. He appeared to have forgotten this business and social custom.

"Why do you think the Mafia has chosen you, of all people, to receive this information?" asked Kirby.

Patrick thought for a moment, and then said: "I don't know, but when they tell me I will be more than glad to tell you."

"You must have some idea," Kirby said in almost the same poor, unimpressive, theatrical tone that a lesser qualified criminal defense attorney uses to cross examine an agent testifying in court. It is the same tone where one seeks to insinuate to the jury, "You really don't think this guy is telling the truth, do you?"

"I do not see where any speculation on my part adds anything to what is known. You know what they said to me. Draw whatever conclusions you like. I prefer to wait and see."

"I understand you lived in the North End while all the mob cases were going on, even after the induction ceremony. You must be pretty cozy with those guys to know they wouldn't bother you?"

Patrick observed that Kirby was sailing his own boat for whatever reason. His questions were a matter out of Crowley's or Delgado's control. Kirby was acting as if his cross examination of Patrick would result in more information than Crowley or Delgado had obtained.

Patrick did not respond to Kirby, which seemed to piss him off. This is just what Patrick intended his silence to do.

"Why do you refuse to tell us all you know about this person you say is Vespa? What are you hiding? How do we know you were even contacted?"

"Are you suggesting that I have just violated title 18, section 1001 of the United States Code and furnished false information to a federal officer?" asked Patrick with a look of stone on his face.

Kirby did not respond, but his face did get more flushed. Patrick just sat there. He would not be the next to speak. Since Kirby came in carrying his own ball, neither Delgado nor Crowley was going to let him play with theirs.

Finally, Kirby said, "I just need to know how to answer all the questions Washington will ask me."

"Do you think Washington will ask you if I am making this up?"

"Well, it is a possibility."

"Do you believe that I am making any of this up?" demanded Patrick.

Kirby knew that Patrick was going to make him back down or accuse Patrick of a crime, neither of which Kirby was willing to do at this moment.

"I don't know one way or another," said Kirby

Patrick turned to Delgado and Crowley and asked, "Is there anything else the FBI would like to ask me today?" Each looked to Kirby who said nothing. Obviously he got the import of that question.

"We have all your contact data on file," said Crowley. Let me just recheck the cell phone number."

It was a good thing she did because they had an old cell phone number.

Both Crowley and Delgado provided Patrick with all the necessary contact data for any time of day or night. Crowley said she wanted more time to think this over, talk with her supervisor, and get back to Patrick to set up another meeting. Patrick said he would immediately let them know if he heard from Vespa during the interim. Patrick left Kirby and Crowley in the conference room and walked out with Delgado.

In the hallway, Patrick ran into Rose Phillips, secretary to the Special Agent in Charge. Rose had been in the Boston office before Patrick was even assigned there. Talk about someone who had seen it all, it was Rose. She was one of the most dedicated humans to ever work for her country and the FBI. Their affection and respect for each other did not go unnoticed by Delgado. Rose asked Patrick if he had met the new SAC yet. He said no. She offered to set up the meeting anytime Patrick wanted. Rose also sent her love to Liz when they parted.

Delgado took the elevator down to the street level with Patrick. It was obvious he wanted to say something, but did not know how or what to say.

"Don't worry about it," said Patrick. "There were jerks in the FBI when I was an agent, there are now and there will always be. After all, agents are selected from the human race. The best thing we can say is that there are far fewer than in most places. I can take care of myself with them."

They shook hands and parted on the street.

Chapter 11

Boston

Whenever he felt his knowledge insufficient on a given subject, Patrick would do research. He loved learning. Patrick always believed that to be a good investigator, you had to be a curious person about life in general and be constantly willing to put some effort into improving your overall state of knowledge. The internet made so much information immediately available to the public. It was like having the world's greatest library at your fingertips all the time.

What he had been following for a few years was the FBI's response to demands for their reorganization post 9/11. Many in Congress felt you could not have a bureaucracy that operated under constitutional guidelines and be the same agency tasked with catching foreign and domestic terrorists who wanted to commit mass murder in the United States. A discussed alternative was to create a whole new agency to investigate terrorism and leave the FBI with its more historical, criminal-based role.

Various study groups would cite the example of MI-5 in Great Britain. They conducted terrorism investigations but when the case matured to an arrest and prosecution matter, they turned the case over to the police and crown prosecutors. In the City of London, that meant Scotland Yard.

The creation of Homeland Security seemed to obscure this question of what the FBI should be. During this period the FBI did make changes to better focus on terrorism. Of course, some thought the changes did not go far enough while others thought the FBI went too far, and were trampling constitutional rights. Equal criticism from both spectrums probably meant they were right in the middle where they needed to be. They needed to be effective at what they did, and always constitutional in their execution. Politicians could, and sometimes did of course, hold two opinions on the subject at the same time depending on which audience they were addressing.

Patrick walked to his small office at King's Wharf. He turned on his computer, went through his emails, checked the national and local news, and made a few client calls. His mind wasn't on his work. He called Liz but she was not around. He did not bother calling her cell. He didn't want to bother her. He had in mind going to Southport early but it was only Wednesday. He needed to check out Liz's schedule for the rest of the week.

Patrick spent a couple of hours reviewing the content of various reorganization proposals for the FBI, which a variety of interests wanted Congress to consider. In the end, it all made little sense so he decided to stop for a late lunch.

Patrick left his office and walked over to Felipe's. He ordered a sandwich to take home. It was prosciutto with provolone cheese, lettuce, tomato and onion mounted on a fresh baked roll drizzled with a little olive oil. "A gift from the gods," thought Patrick as he walked home. Sitting out on the deck overlooking Boston Harbor, he ate his sandwich and thought about what he knew about the FBI's current structure and what tactics they might employ to resolve the current problem. Patrick had no desire or intention to be any more than a messenger in whatever followed. He felt as if he had done his time in public service. He retired before he was worn out and was quite willing to leave today's problems to others who were more qualified, up to date, smarter, and, if the truth be known, younger. However, the vision of ASAC Phil Kirby did not exactly fill him with confidence.

Patrick decided to do a few chores around the condo. He still held out hope he and Liz might go to Southport a day early. He and Liz shared the house workload. Since Patrick now had more time than Liz, he cleaned, did errands, went to the cleaners and did the food shopping. The only thing he was not allowed to do was the laundry. Liz had been taught by her mother all the proper techniques for washing and folding clothes. Patrick's mother had somehow missed passing these valuable instructions on to Patrick or, if she had done so, he failed to learn them. In any event, after remedial lessons by Liz had failed to improve Patrick's performance, she gave up and issued an edict that Patrick was not allowed to do laundry.

Patrick walked two blocks to the cleaners on Battery Street.

"Good afternoon, Mark," said Hien, the eldest daughter of the Vietnamese family who ran the laundry. "How many shirts today?"

"Three for me and just one for Liz."

Patrick used to throw their shirts in together until Hien pointed out they charged more for a lady's shirt than a man's. He always thought this was a sexist and illegal pricing system, but this was how it was done.

"How did your exams go?"

"I got four As and one B," smiled Hien, very proud of her accomplishment.

"Congratulations on a great semester. You worked really hard so I hope you will enjoy some time off from school. Now you only have a full-time job."

Hein's mother was sitting in the corner doing clothing repairs. She had a big smile on her face. She was very proud her daughter was going to a local community college, was an excellent student, and still worked six days a week in the family laundry business.

Patrick liked and admired this family. He gave them what business he could. However, he still did business with an Italian laundry he used for years before Hien and her family opened five years ago. So his suits and coats went to the Italian cleaners and his shirts, sweaters and miscellaneous garments went to the new Vietnamese cleaners. What a great country, thought Patrick.

Not wanting to go back to the condo, not wanting to go to work, and not wanting to do much, Patrick went to the Café Strada for an espresso.

"Hey Mark, how are you doing?"

Patrick turned and saw Renaldo, one of the two brothers who ran the local pharmacy on Hanover Street.

"Fine Renaldo, how is business?"

"Good. Can I join you? Do you have time?" asked Renaldo.

"Sure, sit down," said Patrick motioning to the waiter for another espresso.

Patrick knew their business was good. While one of the super pharmacy chains had opened a competing store in the North End, all of the locals continued to go to Renaldo's. It took no time to figure out their overall prices were no higher and Renaldo and his brother put a lot of effort into helping their customers. More than once, Liz went to their pharmacy to get a prescription filled only to realize she left her wallet home. No problem. Either Renaldo or his brother would insist you pay the next time. Their trust inspired great customer loyalty. Both brothers always had time for a kind word for someone in need. A little encouragement and a smile were part of their medicinal treatment. It worked. Patrick dreaded the day when they might retire.

After the first sip of the potent, black liquid laced with sugar, Renaldo got down to business.

"What do you think of those new trash receptacles on Hanover Street? They compact the trash so they don't have to be emptied so often."

"Great," said Patrick. "I notice that the streets are a little cleaner. With so many tourists, the barrels were always overflowing. This seems to have solved the problem for a while."

"Mayor Corso came down himself to check them out and see what the merchants thought of them," said Renaldo. "We told him it was great, but if he could only get the meter maids under control and stop giving out so many parking tickets, things would be better for business."

Patrick laughed to himself. He knew Mayor John Corso well and always admired his enthusiasm and his energy in serving the neighborhoods. But no matter how much he ever did, no matter how many improvements, it was still not enough. Corso understood human nature very well and never let the "glass half empty" people bother him. He just went at it every day and for the many years he had been mayor, the city kept improving.

Next was the subject of the Red Sox. "You think they have it this year?" asked Renaldo.

Answering this question could be dangerous. Some Red Sox fans took serious umbrage to any negative comments about their team. Others seemed to have an ongoing love hate relationship with the Sox. To offer a neutral response that did not make you sound like an idiot could be difficult. You could have the "if" conversation where a caveat is put on every observation, leaving a back exit for the speaker should the comment not be well received. Patrick just answered the question.

"I like the team. I think they have talent, heart and a great coach. The rest is in the hands of the baseball gods."

"A wise answer," said a smiling Renaldo. The Italian language had many subtle nuances, which many native speakers had learned to translate well when speaking in English. Renaldo was one of those who conversed well whether speaking in Italian or English. He enjoyed the art of conversation and Patrick enjoyed the time they spent together regardless of the topic being discussed. There were some who believed that among Italians, he who was the loudest won the argument. This was in fact uncommon. Patrick often heard some of the most elegantly put phrases come from the most unsuspecting lips.

Patrick finally reached Liz. "Any chance of us going to Southport tonight?"

"Sorry, I have to be around tomorrow, at least in the morning, but we can shoot for getting out mid-afternoon."

"Deal," said Patrick. They agreed to have a late dinner at home, which Patrick would cook. The cupboard was bare so he had to make a few stops.

Patrick went to the greengrocer's on North Street.

"What are we cooking tonight?" asked Arturo, the store owner. Arturo had taken over the store from a man who appeared to be in his eighties when he retired. Every day except Sunday, every month of the year, the store was open from 7:00 am to 6:00 pm. He never spent a day out sick. Patrick admired the old man's work ethic. Arturo worked the same way. Patrick never knew the old man's name even though he had shopped with him for a few years. Patrick didn't know why this was so. It was just the way it was.

"I just want a few things for tonight. Have any chanterelle mushrooms?"

"No, but I have some nice cremini."

"Okay, I'll take half a pound. I have this very simple recipe for some homemade pasta with a light mushroom sauce that seems really easy to fix."

"How so," asked Arturo?

Patrick explained.

'Well, I finally got a recipe from you," smiled Arturo. "It is a pretty basic mushroom sauce, but you explained it well. Good luck and let me know how the cremini work in the recipe."

Patrick got what he needed for the night and left for home. Later, when Patrick was ready to put the mushrooms into the iron skillet, the phone rang.

It was Susan Crowley. Patrick glanced at the clock on the stove; it was 7:45 pm.

"Can we get together first thing in the morning? George Fisher and I have talked to headquarters and they have asked us to get back to you immediately."

"What time, and do I presume your office again?"

"If you don't mind," said Crowley, "It would be helpful to us. Would seven thirty be too early?"

It was for Patrick. He didn't want to start the meeting on an empty stomach and intended a stop at Sal's for a little breakfast on the way over. He also didn't want to jump each time they asked. Crowley agreed to his counter suggestion of eight fifteen.

Having set the meeting, he went back to the mushrooms. The pungent, earthy aroma created when they hit the pan told him the cremini mushrooms would do just fine. Patrick was enjoying a glass of pinot noir while cooking. It's a great country, he thought, and that was as hard as he planned on thinking for the rest of the night.

Chapter 12

When he walked into the FBI office at 8:15 am, Susan Crowley was waiting in the reception room. She escorted him back to the same conference room. Crowley introduced him to her supervisor, George Fisher. Fisher was in his late forties, balding, slim, another agent with a stern looking face and the body of a runner. Fisher in turn introduced Patrick to agent Vincent Baker, a man in his late thirties, who looked more like an academic than an FBI agent. Dressed in tan slacks, a blue button-down, no tie, and a brown tweed sport coat, he looked relaxed. Baker was six-feet tall, built like an outside receiver, large hands, dark curly hair, and a big, warm, friendly smile.

Baker explained he was assigned to the FBI headquarters desk that covered all foreign and domestic investigations of al-Qaeda.

"What you told these folks yesterday certainly got my attention," said Baker, "and that of my al-Qaeda colleagues at headquarters. With your permission I would like to ask you to repeat what you told Susan yesterday. I would also like to record this as well as future conversations with you. That way we can share your information more quickly with others on the case by converting it into an electronic format. Is that okay with you?"

Baker handed Patrick a written consent form requesting the needed permission. Patrick reviewed the form, signed it, checking off the block acknowledging the consent would remain in effect until Patrick revoked his permission. Patrick proceeded to provide the same information he had done twice yesterday. He knew growing pains would exist until the investigation got organized and underway, which he did not expect would take long.

Baker took no notes, but paid full attention to every word said and intently studied Patrick as he related the story. Patrick knew Baker's primary mission was to do a personal evaluation of Patrick, his credibility, and assess whether and how the FBI could go forward with or without Patrick.

When Patrick finished, Baker asked, "You won't identify Vespa at this time, is that correct?"

"I don't know the identity of Vespa, which I thought I made clear."

"Let me put it another way. You won't tell us what you do know about Vespa, where you met, or anything that might help us identify Vespa?"

"That is correct," said Patrick. "Vespa made clear if it is the FBI's intent to expend their efforts in trying to investigate Vespa, determine identity, and trace Vespa back to others, then Vespa would cease all contact. I believe Vespa. It is consistent with how I think the Sicilian Mafia would handle something like this. While I understand your desire to be in full control, and while I would like to introduce you to Vespa and be done with any involvement in this, it is not how the cards were dealt."

"Vespa will not help us introduce an undercover person into this situation?"

Patrick was beginning to feel abused. "That is what Vespa told me. I have told you what I know, what I think I can do, and what I will not do. Live with it for now. Is there anything else you want to talk about before I leave?"

"Will you take a polygraph about what you have told us today?"

"In my twenty-five years as an FBI agent I was never asked to take a polygraph about anything. Why should I start now? If you have some information that causes you to doubt my credibility, then we can discuss that. Otherwise I am not interested, as a civilian, in keeping your polygraph examiner employed. Besides, I always have believed that polygraph results are as valid as the examiner is qualified, and that not all examiners are competent in their analysis. There is a reason why polygraph examinations cannot be admitted as evidence in court."

"I did not mean to upset you."

"I am not upset. I think that you just wanted to see how I would react to a baseless and somewhat accusatory question. I want to leave no doubt in your mind. When the Psychological Profile Unit at Quantico reviews the tape of this conversation this afternoon, you can tell them for me that I am only slightly pissed. They can incorporate that thought into their findings to you."

"We may have to reactivate your security clearance in order to speak with you about certain classified matters. That means we have to update your background. Can you update your personal post-retirement information with us so we can do that?"

Patrick smiled. "My first impression of you was that you were not an ungracious person.

Seems I was wrong. You seem more interested in bureaucratic bullshit than you are in setting up a system of communication that works. I do not give a rat's ass what your secrets are. I do not want to learn anything from you, about your work or what you think. I am in a position to tell you what this group says. You can do with it what you like. As long as these terrorists do not intend to blow up Boston, I do not feel compelled to do any more. If that ever changes, we will have to have another conversation on this point."

"Anything else?" asked Baker.

"I will give you what I get. I handled LCN member informants for years. I know how not to give information away even when asking questions. However, you and I both know that if I do not have certain information, I cannot give it away either intentionally or inadvertently. I am retired and intend to stay that way."

"We want your cooperation," said Susan Crowley. "We don't need to have a male ego contest going on here."

"Don't worry," said Patrick. "Baker is just playing with me to see what I am made of and I am trying to tell him. I am not sure he is listening or has the capacity to understand. You will excuse my prejudice against people like you from FBIHQ, Mr. Baker. My experience with those from Washington, who drifted out to the field from time to time to be more than desk jockeys, was never good. They rarely had anything to contribute and seemed more interested in improving their potential for career advancement."

"Well, things are quite a bit different today," said Baker. "You probably are not aware of some major restructuring that has gone on at FBIHQ and how we manage cases."

"I did read in *The Washington Post* two weeks ago about the FBI change over to the 'desk officer' system utilized by MI-5 in Great Britain. I believe the article went on to say FBIHQ is interested in learning the most it can about a terrorist group even if that means letting it stay in play longer until the details of the group's operations are known. This, of course, needs to be done without increasing any threat to the public. I was also interested to see that the FBIHQ policy wonks were copying ideas from the FBI National Organized Crime Strategy. That plan was devised and used against the LCN years ago. You now want to borrow from that plan to incorporate into a present-day terrorist investigative strategy. The organized crime strategy worked because dedicated people participated in its drafting and committed themselves to making it work. As you may know, I participated in the design and implementation of that strategy. My point is that copying any strategy won't work without a broad base agent commitment. You cannot achieve success by administrative fiat. You need the right people committed to a valid, workable concept."

Baker smiled. Patrick knew Baker was playing him but did not know why.

"That wasn't secret information, was it?" asked Patrick.

Fisher looked like he had not a clue as to what was going on. Crowley looked pissed that time was being wasted.

"Shall I pass your thoughts onto Director Simms?" asked Baker.

"Don't bother. He's heard my thoughts before," said Patrick.

Patrick stood, "I will call Agent Crowley if Vespa contacts me again. You can do as you wish. Will someone escort me out?"

Crowley looked at Baker who said nothing. She rose and walked out to the reception room with Patrick.

"I don't know what to say," said Crowley. "I don't know what just went on in there." She meant it.

"You people work it out amongst yourselves. I do not have a dog in this race. More importantly, I don't want one. I am not interested in being a junior G-man. Been there, done that, not interested. As I grow older, my threshold for bullshit goes down so I don't waste a lot of time nor do I appreciate it when other people waste mine. If we don't speak again, it was nice to meet you."

Patrick walked to the elevator, said hello to someone he knew getting off, and went down to Cambridge street. Patrick's first thought was to blame himself for not being more understanding, or for being too brusque. On reflection, he realized that Baker was jacking him up on purpose. He walked through City Hall Plaza, across the newly opened Rose Kennedy Greenway and down Hanover Street. Patrick turned into the Café Strada, grabbed a copy of the community newspaper, and sat at a window table. When his espresso came he added some sugar, which he did not always do. It gave the coffee an extra jolt.

Coffee and newspaper finished, Patrick rose and walked to Fleet Street, down to Commercial, along the waterfront and over to King's Wharf. The sun was warm and compensated for the chilly air coming off the water. The water would not get warm until well into July. Christopher Columbus Park had been ripped up and substantially rebuilt. Recently re-opened, it was a jewel in the neighborhood. The playground was occupied by mothers with young toddlers. The laughter of children could be an uncommon sound for some city streets. With Boston's outstanding parks, it was a familiar sound. It was also a sign to Patrick that the city parks would continue to add to residents' quality of life for a long time to come. Here was another generation that would have memories of playing as a child in a park directly on the Boston waterfront.

As he approached his office, Patrick saw Vincent Baker and Susan Crowley leaning against a brick wall separating King's Wharf from its dock area. They were looking at what had to be a 120-foot private yacht tied up next to a harbor cruise ship.

"If you are interested in buying, I am not selling," said Patrick.

Both Crowley and Baker laughed.

"Can we use your office to finish our conversation?" asked Baker.

"Sure, come on in. I think we can fit three people."

After they were seated as comfortably as they could be in Patrick's small office, Baker was the first to speak.

"ASAC Phil Kirby told headquarters he thought we should subpoena you to a federal grand jury and make you tell everything you know about Vespa. He also thought you were 'cozy' with the LCN in Boston and perhaps should be looked at with some suspicion since you choose to live in the Italian community. Kirby thought there had to be more to the story as to why the Sicilians chose you to be a messenger."

Patrick said nothing.

"I came up myself to take a first-hand look. Kirby is a known idiot. But, he still he has a position so I couldn't totally ignore his view. I am satisfied that we can handle this together, if you are willing?"

"So what happens with the apparently unhappy Kirby?"

"For the time being, he is not in the day-to-day picture. The desk officer concept you referred to is in effect. I can direct the field as to how the inquiry is to be conducted, including personnel management, so the investigation can be efficiently conducted and coordinated on a national and international level. After our meeting this morning, I just directed Kirby out of this investigation for the time being. I will be responsible as the desk officer for al-Qaeda. I propose that your contact with the FBI be through me and Susan."

Crowley gave Patrick some more contact info.

Baker provided Patrick a phone number. "This is a direct line to me at all times." said Baker. "If for any reason I do not answer, you can tell the person who does to find either Crowley or me, which they will do immediately. If time is really critical, you can give the person answering the information you wish to pass on. The number is for a twenty-four hour call center for my group, and when you give your name, they will know who you are and why you are calling. No other explanation is necessary."

Crowley said, "Would you mind if we gave you another cell phone to use? We arranged for it to be your same number. It will encrypt your telephone conversations with us. Your other calls will work the same as they do now. You will notice no difference either way.

"Okay," said Patrick. "When?"

Crowley took a phone from her pocket, opened it, dialed in some numbers, hit send, heard a beep and said: "You are all set. This encrypted phone is now set for your cell number. Try it out if you like."

Patrick balked. "How do I know you are not handing me a phone just to make it easier for you to listen in?"

"Are you familiar with the DCS Network?" asked Baker.

"Digital Collection System, used by the FBI to hook up to service providers' mediation cells so they can monitor cell phones, digital telephone transmissions and instant messaging, among other things, without leaving their office. I think it is all part of the national build out of the digital phone system. I did not steal your secrets. I saw this information on a computer geek network discussion. I am only retired, not dead," said Patrick with a smile.

"Right," said Crowley, suppressing her smile so as not to offend Baker. "No more lease lines and having to make a physical connection to the subject's landline phone. Now, when we get the court order, we serve the provider and they route the phone conversations from a mediation switch site directly to one of our monitoring centers."

"The point is," said Baker, "we would not have to give you one of our instruments if we wanted to see who you called or wanted to listen in. We would get a court order and monitor any phone of yours that we knew about. Right now we want to make sure that our enemies, or some of our supposed friends, are not listening to our conversations. Many foreign governments today have good electronic ears even here in the US. We just don't want anybody listening when we talk."

Crowley took the encrypted phone, hooked up a wire from it to Patrick's phone, and downloaded all of Patrick's personal phone data and contacts into the new phone.

"For your convenience you can use either phone, but we prefer you use encryption when you talk to us."

Patrick nodded slowly.

"The information about Oleg in Georgia was accurate," said Baker. "Georgian state authorities received an email that they were unable to trace. It outlined Oleg's overall plan to sell the material, his schedule of meetings, their locations, his vehicle information, a copy of his driver's license with photo, everything they needed. They took it seriously. While they never knew the source, they wanted to protect the email information and at the same time sow some potential dissension among the terrorist group. Hence they created the phony story about a spy in the midst of the Georgian operation."

"So you believe Vespa has good information?"

"They proved to be accurate about Georgia. We will evaluate here as we go along. At present, there is certainly prima facie evidence to make us take Vespa very seriously. We will be anxious to have you hear from them again," said Baker.

"By the way," said Crowley, "Is the GPS active on your personal cell phone?"

"Yes," said Patrick. "In case I ever went missing, Liz would be able to track me through the phone."

"Well, it is also active on the encryption phone, but we will not be tracking you. We would only do so in an emergency."

"Okay," said Patrick. "Also assume that I will brief Liz on what I am doing. If you have any problem with that, say so now."

"We don't," said Baker. "Before I leave today, Susan and I will brief the SAC in Boston. Crowley and George Fisher will be reporting directly to him but only for a short time. The SAC is heading to Iraq on special assignment with Evidence Recovery Teams. When he goes, Crowley and Fisher will report directly to me, not Kirby."

"I will let you know as soon as I hear anything," said Patrick. The meeting ended. Patrick felt a lot better than he did earlier in the morning.

Chapter 13

Manhattan, New York City

Maria and her father left the office and walked to a nearby restaurant. Illario's was a small, elegant, and expensive restaurant that catered to a very select audience. They were patrons who could afford to eat well and who wanted their personal surroundings to match the quality of the food and drink. Linens, fine china, an exceptional wine list, attended to by an attentive and competent staff, added value to their dining experience. For that value, these patrons were willing to pay.

"Good evening Mr. Torino, Ms. Torino," said Dominic, the maître d' and brother of the owner. "I have a table available and Francisco will be with you tonight."

There was always a table available for Mr. Torino

Francisco appeared immediately, providing his own welcome and explaining the evening's specials. He invited them to order whatever they wished, noting the chef could certainly accommodate any off-menu desires. They worked late and had no desire to cook at home. Since Maria's mother had passed away a few years back, they came here often. Once a month, Illario's would send a bill to Aldo Tornio's office. He would never review it. He gave it to his assistant and told him to add 25 percent and pay it immediately. He also left a generous cash gratuity for the waiter after each meal. Aldo Torino appreciated the hard work and effort by people who cared about whatever they did.

Dinner was simple. They ordered egg drop soup, linguine with a tomato basil sauce, lightly grilled tuna, and insalata mista dressed with a dark green, nut flavored, virgin olive oil. For dessert, a plate of fresh fruit and a selection of cheeses were sufficient. He also had ordered a 1999 Brunello that complimented the meal well but remained unfinished, owing to its youth.

They spoke of many things but nothing to do with the conglomerate. They left that in the office. Family, friends, politics, sports were topics that often came up. Business or mercantile theory could be discussed but not with direct reference to the conglomerate.

Somewhat breaking with tradition, Aldo said, "I would like you to make sure that you keep in mind what resources we may need in the event you are not successful with your trip north."

"You think our efforts may not work?"

"I don't know. I just don't want to wait, do nothing, and then find out they are incapable of addressing the situation. I do not think the problem should ever reach New York. I will stress this when I talk to Vincenzo. There is a lot of water between there and here, and perhaps somewhere in the middle would be a convenient place for the problem to end."

"What if this group already has people here in New York ready to act? What about them? Couldn't they just be resupplied by others we may never know about? We were just lucky this time that the matter came to your and Zio Vincenzo's attention and you were able to insert yourselves."

Aldo laughed softly while looking at Maria.

"During the war, Vincenzo left the pre-seminary school as a teenager to join his father fighting the Germans. He actually ran one of the best anti-

63

German intelligence networks in all of Sicily and Italy. What is this, some sixty-five years later he is going back into running another network; this time against terrorists? We must all be crazy."

"Well, he has one success already," smiled Maria, appreciating her father's point of view. "The business in Georgia was handled well and hopefully we can do the same here."

"We just have to feel our way through this one," said Aldo. "There is no manual to consult. I do not greatly trust the people you have met with. They have their own agenda and their own image to maintain. Their world is not our world."

"Yes, but 'the enemy of my enemy is my friend.' Perhaps we just start on that basis and see where it goes."

"Just keep in mind that if it is necessary for us to act unilaterally, I want to have the necessary resources available and in place. We may not have enough time to act unless we prepare now," said Aldo.

"What is that Latin phrase you used to quote? *Para bellum, sevis pacem.* If you want peace, prepare for war?"

Aldo smiled. "Why can't you quote something pleasant that I've said?"

"Oh, I do, all the time," smiled Maria.

"I intend to do whatever needs to be done to make sure that product, or whatever it is, never enters this city. If some less well-intentioned friends of ours should seriously entertain working with these people just to make money, I will no longer honor them as friends and will treat them as enemies. There is the old rule: 'whatever is bad for business is everyone's business.' If we were seen to be doing business with these people, the world would descend upon us with a fury never before seen. No, I can act this way for the good of all our friends. I will act as necessary and explain later."

"I understand. I'll continue to use John to line up what is needed."

"Yes, when people hear from John they know for whom he speaks. Your name should not be out there at all. No *amico nostro* from this country should be used. The friends of ours here are riddled with informants. Use only our own people."

Maria nodded.

Chapter 14

Southport, Massachusetts

Early Friday morning, Patrick and Liz were in their nine-year-old Volvo sedan headed to Southport. Each had a cup of coffee, the sun roof was open, and the sun was sponsoring another fine New England early summer day, which by far was not the norm. Sometimes the month of June was hard to distinguish from the month of March. Not this year. Today was to be enjoyed.

Since her trial had cancelled, Liz was joining Patrick on a day off. They had planned on doing a little yard work around the house to neaten up from the remaining ravages of winter. The young man who cut their grass had already made some effort to clean the flower beds so the perennials could get an early start. Patrick and Liz had done a major cleanup in May, but still more was needed. After this, the gardens would mostly take care of themselves for the rest of the summer. A little fresh mulch now and the benefit of planting perennials would take over.

"After our chores are done, what do you have in mind for fun today?" inquired Patrick.

"They just opened another hiking trail on the preserve behind Brant's and I thought we might give that a try."

"You expect me to do laborious labor in the yard and then go on a hike?" said Patrick with a feigned look of fear on his face."

"Are you too old to handle that?" inquired Liz.

"Ah! When sweetness fails you resort to a challenge that I shall accept gladly."

"Speaking of coercion, have you heard anything more?"

Liz was up to date on whatever Patrick knew.

"No, it was only Tuesday, and today is Friday, so I didn't expect anything this soon. These things never seem to develop fast but, when they really get started, it can be a roller coaster," replied Patrick.

Liz resumed, "I think Vespa will be efficient with her contacts. I don't think there will be much chit chat between the two of you."

"I agree," said Patrick.

Into their working clothes and out in the yard, they spent the next two hours as planned. After working in the garden, they fixed some tuna fish sandwiches and sat at the dining room table looking out into the woods and enjoying nature. Patrick's cell phone rang.

"Hi Mark, it's Vincent Baker. I just wanted to test this phone, make sure the encryption worked and that the signal was strong enough in Southport."

"It is now. A couple of months ago, my carrier put up a new cell tower and now we have great reception at the house, on the river and even in the village. So that shouldn't be a problem. Anything new with you?" asked Patrick.

"Nothing. The drums are silent. We are hearing nothing of value in all the chatter we can find," said Baker.

"I will let you know the moment I hear anything," said Patrick.

"Thanks Mark."

They drove down to Brant's General Store and turned west for a mile to the dirt parking area for a new hiking trail. Patrick carried an old walking stick, which was his tradition. The stick was made thirty years ago by a hiking friend. It stood about five-feet tall and had a painted duck's head mounted on the top. It had seen a lot of miles and was a few inches shorter then when first made. Patrick never seemed to get around to putting a metal piece on the bottom to prevent the wood from wearing down.

Liz had longer legs and walked at a faster pace. She wanted exercise. Patrick liked to stroll. Somehow they still managed a great hike to end a very nice day outdoors.

Chapter 15

Patrick and Liz attended church services at St. Marks and, as usual, walked over to the Bluefish for some bacon and eggs. They split an order of pancakes. They would be active all day and would not eat again until dinner. The Bluefish was starting to fill up. It appeared more sailboats were being launched each day. The weekenders had decreed that the sailing season was on. Of course, the local sailors had their boats in the water since April and enjoyed a great spring season. The weekenders seemed to require warmer sailing weather.

After finishing breakfast, Liz and Patrick walked two doors up to Muldoon's Variety Store. Muldoon's carried whatever you needed and was a year-round local market used by all the village residents. During the summer, the boat people increased the business enough to make it worthwhile year-round. In the rear of Muldoon's was the best meat market in the area. It was presided over by owner Herbert Muldoon, who believed in passing along the town gossip along with the latest local news while he cut your meat selection. His showcase space was limited and sales were sometimes infrequent during the winter months. Thus, like the butchers in the North End, you told Herbert what you wanted. He then entered the meat locker, came out with a large piece of meat, from which he cut the requested piece to the exact size desired. Buying a piece of meat from Muldoon was a social event not to be hurried. You learned town politics with a dose of Muldoon humor. Muldoon was a good man who always had the best interest of the town and its residents at heart. Patrick and Liz shopped there whenever possible to make sure that his business remained open and a vital influence on the local community.

"Good morning, Herb," said Liz.

"Why did you bring him?" inquired Muldoon.

"He followed me from church to breakfast to here. What is a poor girl to do?"

"Call the police," said Muldoon. "Here take my phone."

Patrick laughed. It was customary for Muldoon and Liz to gang up on him to provide a little merriment for themselves.

Patrick spoke: "I realize that you are only open until noon on Sundays, and since it is now ten thirty, I wonder if there is enough time for me to obtain a couple of rump steaks that I might grill this afternoon?"

Muldoon smiled, walked into the meat locker and came out with the large slab of meat, laid it on his table, took out his cutting knife and, ignoring Patrick, said, "how thick would you like them Liz?"

Liz directed his knife to the desired spot and said, "Two, cut just that size, please."

As Muldoon was performing his cutting and weighing, he did happen to offer a few comments about the new trash regulations just passed by the board of selectman and how they might impact Patrick and Liz.

"Anything else in the paper I need to know about?" asked Liz.

Muldoon thought for a moment and said, "No."

Muldoon's wife was at the cash register at the street end of the store. Patrick put the meat on the counter and took out his wallet to pay. "Again, I wish to offer you my condolences on being married to the man. May your children inherit looks and brains only from you."

Having completed all three of their Sunday morning routines, Patrick and Liz left the village feeling accomplished. Liz drove home so Patrick could relax and enjoy the ride around the harbor and through the seaside community where people had been summering for generations. Just as she pulled to the end of their driveway, Patrick's cell phone went off.

"Good morning Mark, this is Maria. I need to give you something. Could you meet me in the Providence area around 6:00 pm.

"Liz and I are driving back to Boston tonight so yes, we could swing over to Providence and then head up to Boston. Where?" asked Patrick.

"Greene Airport, at the shuttle ticket counter, say 6:00 pm."

"Okay. I will see you then."

Patrick went into the kitchen and drizzled a little olive oil on the rump steaks, and sprinkled some fresh-chopped garlic and freshly ground salt and pepper. He shook some dried, mixed herbs that he combined himself on the meat. It was one of his little secrets. He then covered the steaks with plastic wrap and put them in the refrigerator to marinate.

"Why don't we grill the steaks about four o'clock. After dinner and clean up, we head over to Providence, meet Vespa, and drive back to Boston."

"Sounds like a plan to me," said Liz.

"The Red Sox are on at one o'clock – why don't we listen to the game out on the deck? Maybe while we listen, we can fill our deck pots with the herbs we bought last week," Patrick suggested.

The rest of the afternoon was spent on the deck. The Sox won, which made the day even better. The steaks were grilled medium rare and served with a salad of arugula, lettuce, cherry tomatoes, sliced yellow peppers, and dressed with olive oil and balsamic vinegar.

After they finished dinner and cleaned up, they left. Driving some scenic, back-country roads, it still took only forty-five minutes to reach T.F. Greene Airport in Warwick. Traffic wasn't heavy. Patrick pulled into the short-term parking lot. He and Liz held hands as they walked across the street and went up one level to the shuttle ticket counter. Liz waited outside while Patrick walked inside the terminal. Vespa was waiting. Patrick looked up at the arrival board and noted the last two flights to arrive at Greene were from Philadelphia and Baltimore. Vespa followed Patrick's eyes and smiled. Patrick had no idea the conglomerate had a fractional ownership in a Lear Jet and that Vespa had arrived at Greene through the general aviation terminal, and not through a commercial carrier. For her, it was like taking a cab across town in Manhattan.

They shook hands. Vespa was dressed in a brown pants suit with a white blouse. Again, both looked like Armani to him. Very stylish noted Patrick. Interesting woman, he thought.

"We have been reliably informed that the three people who want to ship the container to the US are in fact known as al-Qaeda. This information was furnished to our Sicilian associates by their contacts in the Afghanistan/Pakistan area that we call the poppy people. So if you are trying to identify these three men, Afghanistan or Pakistan may be a place where they are known."

Vespa handed him a sealed eight-by-twelve inch manila envelope. "Inside are copies of three passports that these people used when staying at a hotel in Naples. Besides the passport photos, there are some other photos taken while they were in Naples. Their cabins on the night boat to Palermo were bugged by us. Here is a memory stick containing conversations recorded of the three men speaking in Arabic. We understand the FBI has the ability to identify people through known voice exemplars, so they may be of help in identifying who these people are."

Patrick smiled. He wondered if Vespa would also suggest running the photos through a terrorist photo recognition database. He had the sense he was talking to someone experienced in terrorist investigations rather than a member of the Sicilian Mafia.

Maria continued, "They have arrived in Palermo and are there now."

"Why are they in Palermo?" Patrick asked while taking the envelope from Vespa.

"The man in the black jacket in the photos we call The Engineer. He has indicated engineering is his area of education or experience. He seems to be the leader and the other two seem to be along to serve him. They have an ocean shipping container that they want delivered to New York City and are paying handsomely to insure that it undergoes no inspection of any kind from Palermo through arrival in New York City. Once we give them a shipping date, they will have the container somehow delivered to a Palermo dock that is under our control. We cannot hold them off much longer, so we will give them a shipping date of this Wednesday."

"How do you know for sure they are al-Qaeda?"

"As I said earlier, these three men eventually were put in contact with people in Afghanistan, the poppy people, known to our Sicilian associates. They were obviously looking to use what they thought were drug smuggling routes to get some material into the US. It is the poppy people who are telling us these people are al-Qaeda, are planning a post 9/11 event in the US, and believe this event will involve the use of radioactive material."

"How could they find that out but not know the whole plan?"

"We are telling you exactly what we know." said Vespa. "I am told the poppy people in Afghanistan kidnapped someone affiliated with this group. They forced this person to tell what he knew about these three people, who they were, and what they were up to. They believe this man told them what little he did know, which is exactly what I have told you."

"The FBI will want to have this person interviewed."

"I don't believe interviewing a dead person is a viable option," said Vespa without showing any form of emotion. "al-Qaeda knows this person has gone missing but believes he was grabbed, and is being held, by a hostile intelligence service. They assume he talked but believe this man knew nothing about their plans. In fact, while he only knew a little, he knew far more than his own people realized."

Patrick was now anticipating the FBI. "You know they are going to want to know exactly where these people are, start following them, and not have amateurs in control of an investigation that is this important," said Patrick.

"Understand our problem," said Vespa. "We got matters this far because we want to see these people stopped. Friends in Afghanistan felt the same way. However, none of us wants to be informers to any government. The more people know about this, the more chance there is our involvement will be disclosed by someone in government who may see a chance to kill two birds with one stone, so to speak. Get rid of some al-Qaeda members and some Mafia people at the same time? Neither you nor the FBI can control this possibility. If al-Qaeda finds out what we are doing, it would not be pretty for us and there is no hope that we could ever do this again in the future. This may be the second time we are able to stop a nuclear or dirty bomb attack. It does not seem that they are going to stop trying. It is in your interest that we are not disclosed, not only for our present safety, but also for the future."

Patrick was silent for a minute trying to think what else he should be asking.

"What do you plan on doing now?" said Patrick, realizing what a weak question he asked.

"Give them Wednesday as the day their boat leaves. See if they show up with the container or see if they back out and are just testing us. If the container shows up, the boat will sail. It will be a slow boat with a few mechanical problems so the crossing time will be a little longer than normal. We will have one of our own on the boat with a satellite phone so we can be in constant contact. After that we look for some suggestions from you, but keep in mind our own interests for survival that I have explained to you."

Patrick's head was swimming. He knew he should probably be asking other things but he could not formulate any more significant questions. He did ask, "You assume the target is New York City?"

"We don't know for sure. We only heard there was a post 9/11 operation in the US, mentioned along with the words radioactive material. We are being asked to smuggle a container into New York City. These people are known in Afghanistan as al-Qaeda. Those are the facts and we have no more."

"What are they doing now, today, in Palermo?"

"They have a hotel room. It is bugged by us. So far the bug has told us nothing. They are not talking about this when alone. We have a man with them, arranging the shipping, as it were. The moment we hear anything new, it will be reported and I will contact you."

At this point neither one could think of anything more to say.

Patrick looked directly at Vespa. "I want to thank you personally for what you are doing. I know it was not an easy decision and probably not an entirely popular decision in your group to do this. Can I ask that you call me tomorrow evening just so I can hear from you even if there is nothing to report? I may need to communicate something from the FBI to you."

"I will call you tomorrow evening at seven. It was an easy decision for us to make. We are Americans. It could have been unpopular because we have no love for informers. So far for us, a potential internal conflict has not occurred. I don't want to see that change. While I do not want Liz to be part of our conversations, tell her she does not have to wait outside. Good evening."

Vespa walked over to the escalator, took it down to the baggage level and out of Patrick's sight.

Patrick walked outside, met Liz, and they both walked to the car. Liz offered to drive so Patrick could use his cell phone. Patrick filled Liz in on his conversation with Vespa.

After Patrick finished, Liz said, "My first reaction was 'oh no!' Then I thought this could be worse. This could be happening and no one knows about it. That would be a real problem. This one is at least manageable. Something bad may be preventable."

Patrick called Baker and left a message saying he would call Crowley. Patrick called Crowley and after a brief overview of his conversation with Vespa, she asked if they could meet first thing in the morning. Patrick suggested it might be worthwhile for her friend from DC to also be there. The meeting was set up for eight o'clock Monday morning.

Chapter 16

Boston

Patrick spent a few more hours that evening on the internet researching data on dirty bombs. The subject was well documented. It was the subject of some films both commercial and documentary. Everyone seemed of the opinion a dirty bomb was going to happen. It was only a question of when, where, and how bad it would be. If the terrorist wanted to create fear, the dirty bomb seemed to Patrick to be an efficient and effective way to achieve that goal. One expert referred to it as a "weapon of mass disruption," apparently to denigrate its potential harmful effects. Of course, thought Patrick, if you wanted to compare it to a nuclear device, it would seem minor. However, a terrorist with access to a dirty bomb could effectively destroy an entire city through fear alone. Would anyone want to visit or do business in New York City after there was any amount of radioactive dispersion?

Cleanup technology for radioactive contamination, Patrick learned, was described as being unsophisticated with the words "muck and truck" being used. This meant any contaminated surface would have to be physically cleaned and all the resultant materials and debris, including the now contaminated cleaning agents, would have to be considered contaminated nuclear materials and disposed of accordingly. Who was going to wash off all the tall city buildings? How would the material be collected? What about the material in the storm drain system? Could the nooks and crannies of a dense city environment ever realistically be cleaned up with this primitive technology?

What about the disposal part? Even if you could collect all of the radioactive material, where would you truck the materials? Patrick did not recall any state offering to be a radioactive waste dump site. The not in my back yard acrimony would start. By the time the argument ever got resolved, Patrick humorously observed to himself, the radioactive material would render itself safe through time alone. Of course this would be countless lifetimes later.

If a dirty bomb were ever detonated in the United States, congressional hearings would go on for years as blame would have to be assigned. This process would further sap the resources of the intelligence and law enforcement communities. The blame game would keep the ugliness in the news constantly. It would not be a healthy process for the people, an economy or a government, thought Patrick. It would be the constant negative news drone. The media's expert analysts and pundits, providing all their prognostications and projections, would paralyze the country with fear.

The conventional explosives used in a dirty bomb would result in some immediate deaths. Added to the mix would be the fear of long-term health issues, which would depend on the type of radioisotope utilized in the bomb. Mounted to that whole process would be the negative psychological impact not only on the city, but the country as a whole.

al-Qaeda had stated its goal was to destroy the US economy. How would investors react to such news? A dirty bomb could be the ultimate fear weapon of the terrorists to coerce governments, whole societies, into accepting their ideological objectives. Patrick was depressed. This was real. Someone, he thought, has already been doing some good work to so far prevent this type of atrocity.

"Are you finished on the computer yet?" inquired Liz.

Patrick explained what he had been doing. "It has been right in front of us even before 9/11. It has been written about, studied, PBS has done a special, and yet the subject has not really been on our minds. Are we immune to even thinking about this threat?"

"We've been told so much about so many horrible ways terrorists can attack our society, I guess it's hard to think about one more than the other until the actual event confronts you."

"Do you realize," asked Patrick, "that the United States has a shortage of laboratories to test the thousands of people who might be exposed to radiation if a dirty bomb is detonated in a major city? They only have current technology to test for six of the thirteen radiological isotopes that would probably be used. Further, it is estimated that with current resources, if only 100,000 people were subject to some type of possible exposure, it would require about 350,000 individual tests to be performed on just these 100,000 exposed persons. These tests, with presently available facilities, would take two years to complete. Come in and be tested and we will tell you in two years how soon you or your child might die. I found this information in a just-released congressional report."

"If that is the case and a device went off, I would fear the psychological damage more than the actual physical damage. Hiroshima and Nagasaki each caused 40,000 immediate deaths and up to 100,000 each over the years. The psychological damage is still with us," said Liz.

"I don't know that we as a country are prepared for this possibility." noted Patrick.

"Perhaps that is the answer," said Liz. "We can't prepare for every evil that someone may want to inflict on us. It is impossible. The news you mentioned gets published, people read it, and go on about their business leaving the problem for 'others,' whomever they may be. Perhaps we are to the point where our human psyche can take no more?"

Patrick remained depressed. Deep down he did not want to be burdened with these thoughts. Then, he had to admit, given a choice he would leave it to "others" to worry about. Fate did not seem willing to allow him this option.

Patrick did not sleep well that night.

Chapter 17

Patrick called ahead to Sue Crowley to ask if she or Baker wanted him to pick them up a coffee. They did.

Crowley came to the reception area and escorted Patrick back to the same conference room where Baker was waiting for them. Patrick thought of all the years he spent in this FBI division. Now all he knew of the Boston FBI office was the reception room, the hallway, and this conference room. Yes, he thought, he was definitely an outsider.

"Vespa called me yesterday for a meeting. We met last night."

Patrick then recounted exactly what Vespa said. Both Crowley and Baker were stone-faced. At one point Patrick thought he noted some fear in their eyes. Finally Patrick produced the envelope that Vespa had given him last night.

"The envelope is sealed," noted Crowley.

"I wanted to let you see it as I got it. I have learned over the years, not too well mind you, to make some effort to control my curiosity where matters are not under my control."

Neither Crowley nor Baker smiled at Patrick's effort at humor.

Baker took the envelope and opened it in a manner to protect the envelope from further fingerprint damage, without being too obvious in so doing. Patrick noticed. This furthered his suspicion that Baker and Crowley still maintained an interest in identifying Vespa. That is why Patrick didn't make an effort to protect the outside of the envelope.

"We need to get our people and others active in Sicily right away," said Baker with urgency. "We can't leave the Mafia to respond to this for us."

"You must have been listening to my conversation with Vespa last night. I said exactly the same thing. I remind you of Vespa's response. They cannot have it out there that they are cooperating with any government. al-Qaeda will target them and a battle between the two would ensue. Some in government may be inclined to believe this may be a good idea, but the Mafia wouldn't agree. This is the second time they have been in a position to prevent a terrorist act. If their cooperation ever becomes known, there will never be a third time. They would have no future value."

"You want me to tell the Director and the inter-agency intelligence group that we have amateurs out there doing our work, and we are sitting by doing nothing about it? Are you going soft?" Baker asked.

"I don't work for the Director anymore. When you are ready, set up a call with Carter Simms. I'll explain it to him myself. I also remind you that I haven't heard you come up with any better proposal or solution."

"Tell us who Vespa is, everything you know. I'm sure when we get to him we can reason with him."

"What do you mean by reason?" asked Patrick.

"Convince him to do it our way. Give us everything and get out of the way."

"What would you say that I haven't already said to convince Vespa?"

"What we would do to him if he does not cooperate!" replied Baker.

"I don't know why you think your puny threats would work. Vespa says if you do this, if you try to identify Vespa and force direct contact, they will walk away. You cannot find Vespa without my setting Vespa up, and I do not see anything so critical that warrants me doing that. Seems they are making all the right moves so far. By the way, would you kidnap, torture, and murder an al-Qaeda soldier to make the person talk? Sounds to me like someone in Afghanistan did."

Neither one responded.

Patrick mentioned the research he did last night, making the observation that it seemed to him this country was totally unprepared for a dirty bomb going off in any American city. Crowley looked at Baker but neither said anything.

"As I said before, I'm not interested in finding out your secrets. I am doing just what I agreed to do. When you have any suggestions or answers, or a message to go back to Vespa, let me know." Patrick stood up.

"Give us some time to study this information – the passport data and photos – and we will get back to you. Are you available at noon?" asked Crowley.

"My office," said Patrick. "I don't feel the warm and fuzzies here. I'm beginning not to like this place. Will you escort me out, or can I walk out by myself?"

Crowley was required to escort him to the reception area. They had no further conversation.

Patrick walked through City Hall Plaza to Hanover Street and down to Café Strada. He drank a double espresso while he read the newspaper. It took his mind off of things for awhile and gave him a chance to regain his balance. He was getting pissed and he didn't want to be in that state. The Red Sox were doing well, the pitching was holding up, and the hitting was dynamite. The season was looking good.

He stopped by the greengrocer's to see Arturo and pick up some oyster mushrooms, homemade pasta and some hot peppers. "You are quiet today," said Arturo. "What's up?"

"It's just Monday and I realize how much I still hate Mondays."

He dropped off the groceries at the condo and walked down to the waterfront to his office. Liz had gone to her office so he had no one with whom he could talk. He thought about the morning's events. In the end, he realized it was not up to him. He would have to just let it play out.

At 11:00 am his cell phone went off. He thought it would be Liz and he was ready to answer with some witty greeting, but refrained.

"Mark, this is Carter Simms calling. How are you doing? It has been a while. You are on the encrypted phone so we can talk."

"Well Carter, I'm surprised to hear from you but, upon reflection, I also guess I'm not. What can I do for you?"

"Agent Crowley and Vince Baker have just brought Bob Wilkins, the Assistant Director for Counterterrorism, and me up to date. I would like to get your view on where things stand if you don't mind."

"Not at all," said Patrick and he proceeded to review the morning's contact with Crowley and Baker.

"What are your thoughts?" asked Simms when he was done.

"Actually Carter, I was hoping to hear something from your side of the house other than wanting me to identify Vespa so they can confront this person and force them to do it their way. This has already been discussed with Vespa, as I have explained. It will not work as far as I can tell and it's just wasting time. But I'm not hearing anything concrete from your people to help move forward."

"Can you work with Crowley and Baker?" asked Simms.

"Yes," said Patrick without hesitation. "But they both seem to have a lot of pressure on them. They don't know me. They are operating like radios that only receive and do not transmit. They have their protective guards up. I've told them I'm out of the business, don't want their secrets and am not a threat to them – but the current level of trust in our conversation is not helpful."

"Such a petty thing as an updated security clearance, believe it or not, has created some of this problem," said Simms. "I have resolved that issue myself, personally re-activating your top secret security clearance. That takes away legal barriers for information exchange. I must tell you, though, there are people down here at FBIHQ and at DOJ who favor putting pressure on you to get control of Vespa."

Patrick could feel himself getting cranked up again. He knew exactly what they would do to make him more pliable to their point of view. He would be served a subpoena to a federal grand jury. When he appeared, he would be served with an immunity order that would take away his right to not answer their questions. If he refused to answer their questions in front of the grand jury, after being immunized, he would have to appear before a federal judge who could put him in jail until he changed his mind.

"Do what you think you have to do." said Patrick. "If you wish to move legally against me, I will give you the name of my attorney and you can have Justice contact him directly. When it is all over, you will still be where you are now and I will be in federal court with a motion to quash, seeking a public hearing and defending a contempt citation. By the time you get through pissing around, the whole affair will be public and probably moot one way or another."

"Ah, Mark, you make me a prophet. I told them that would be your response."

Patrick said nothing.

"Mark, people down here are very nervous. They are even more so when they are not in control and will have to answer questions when something goes wrong."

"How do you think I feel?" said Patrick. "I don't have any sense that the FBI considers me any more than an obstruction. If something goes wrong, then the obstruction, namely me, will be dragged out as the reason for failure. I think in Washington today, more so than ever, success has many fathers but failure very few."

"How can we resolve this?"

"Why is it that I'm supposed to come up with the answer? You guys are the ones with the authority to investigate. You are the experts. You have all the worldwide intelligence. Why don't you guys come up with some possible scenarios? We can kick them around until we find something that is workable and that everyone is comfortable with."

"I have to meet today with the Director of National Intelligence, the Homeland Security Director, and some key people in Congress on intelligence, to get them all up to speed. That is all I do these days – make sure all the bases are touched. In fact, it is what I am ordered to do. I was trying to get a feeling from you as to how we can get this going down the right path."

"I am not setting Vespa up. I know that would cause the information flow to cease. Their moves have been pretty good so far, except for that thing in Afghanistan and that was not their doing. Whether or not the bugs they are using are legal in Italy I don't know, and frankly don't care. These people will not help a formal prosecution. If the boat sails, I know we will get its identity. You can keep an eye on it all the way over, and the US has the resources available to address any in-flight meetings, if you get my drift. Why not let it play out a while longer and see where we are. Meanwhile, you have a lot more to work on with the latest photos and passport data provided by Vespa. See what facts this inquiry turns up and then further plans can be made based on this the new information obtained. It is basic investigations 101, unless such procedures have gone out of style."

"I don't disagree but today people want to define everyone's role," said Simms. "Who is in the loop? Who is not? Who has a piece of the investigation? Who is in charge, either inside or outside of the US? Right now we don't exactly have clear jurisdiction."

"You have had years to design protocols, form groups and develop plans. If you don't have it done by now, what makes you think you can do it at all?"

"Retirement has not changed you at all."

"Well then, you take what you have, go with it, and solve it by committee. If I hear from Vespa again, I will call it in. As long as Boston is not under threat, you can do what you want. That way whatever comes down is not on my conscience. I had hoped the FBI had not changed so much as to be ineffective."

"I can assure you that isn't the case, Mark. We still have the best people and the best minds. There are just more bases to touch and people to be accountable to."

"I'm glad you are there to do the job and I'm here and don't have to anymore. It's not of my liking."

"Believe me, I understand how you feel. It will work out. You are dealing with the right people and I am listening to them. You know me and what I stand for. I also am willing to walk away from this job if that is what it takes to get someone's attention. I still have my place in the White Mountains. I still dream of retiring there soon in peace and quiet. Hang in there and we will talk soon."

Chapter 18

At noontime, Vincent Baker showed up at Patrick's office bearing an extra cup of coffee. They got right to business.

"The three Italian passports are phony. The supporting documentation is completely fictional. They did not use an existing identity to build on. Nothing checks out so the passports have told us little except that they were not done by amateurs. The Italians are checking to see if the passports can be linked to any other known passport forgeries. Maybe a connection can be found there, but it will take time. The photos have been run through our international terrorist facial recognition program. We got a hit on The Engineer but we still don't know exactly who he is."

"How is that?" asked Patrick.

"Identities are easy to change, faces are not," said Baker. "This fellow has been photographed once by German authorities in Bonn coming out of a suspected al-Qaeda safe house. That was three years ago. Last year he was photographed meeting with a fundamentalist cleric in London. This cleric is suspected of being a communications point or message center for al-Qaeda in Europe. al-Qaeda continues to stay away from any communications system that can be electronically intercepted. The last hit we got, however, is a little different."

Baker showed Patrick a photo that appeared to be taken in an Arab market place. It was of two men talking, one of whom Patrick recognized as The Engineer.

"This photo was taken in Karbala, Pakistan, about six months ago by Pakistan intelligence. We believe the man with The Engineer was in charge of trying to set up a roadside bombing program in Afghanistan, similar to what was done in Iraq. He is an Afghan but not al-Qaeda, so far as they know. Possibly Taliban. Pakistani intelligence believes The Engineer was sent to Pakistan by al-Qaeda to serve as an instructor or technical adviser on how to make and deploy roadside bombs."

Patrick studied the photograph. "Pakistan intelligence never identified him? Never found out where he came from or where he went after?"

"It became somewhat of a moot point after the Pakistan authorities raided what they thought was a safe house. It turned out to be a bomb factory. They discovered this when during the raid a firefight ensued and the place blew up, killing everyone inside. They found only small bits of human remains. They swept them into a pile and buried them before anyone could save DNA samples. The police there just didn't care about DNA evidence. "

"But our man was not there?"

"They thought he was, but now we see apparently not. We have FBI agents over there now. They are requesting the entire Pakistan investigative file on this group in an effort to identify anyone associated with him. We'll try to identify The Engineer from that end. Whatever information they come up with will immediately go into our database here."

"So what do you think now?" asked Patrick

"You have at least one al-Qaeda type with a very good but phony Italian passport, with ties to al-Qaeda in Bonn and London, and a direct tie to a Pakistani bomb factory. He has two people with him who are probably Arabic but carrying phony Italian passports of the same quality. All in all, we have a serious problem, especially when you add into that mix what Vespa has told you."

"What is next? Let me rephrase the question. What do you want me to do?"

"Find out from Vespa if it would cause them any problem if they told us what hotel they are in, and whether it would be a problem if we took over the surveillance. We think it is critical not to lose contact with any of these three individuals in Palermo since they are the only live bodies we can connect to the current threat. We would make no effort to involve any of the Italian civilians these people are meeting in Palermo. We just cannot afford to let these people out of our sight."

"That sounds reasonable. I'll call you when I have an answer."

"Somehow we have to find out for sure what is in their container. Is there any radioactive material? If so, we don't see how we can take the chance and let it land in the US. That is the debate going on at FBIHQ right now in conjunction with CIA and Homeland Security. How far can we let it go in order to develop the full conspiracy, but not be the cause of harm landing on our doorstep when it could have been stopped?"

"These are tough issues," said Patrick. "I know the FBI doesn't want to be premature in making arrests but needs to be in a position to allow a conspiracy to operate just long enough to make sure you have it all."

"Yeah – it's great in theory but it's hard to practice. How do you know when you have let a dangerous situation go on too long? How do you balance risk to the public with the need for more information? How do you know when you are, or are not, in control? We will be testing all of these thoughts as we go forward with this case," said Baker.

"I wouldn't doubt that Vespa may soon have more recordings of the three, and perhaps a better sense of what they are doing. If so, I'll get it to you immediately. It may help you get started in Palermo."

"Great. Just call the 24/7 operations center. I'll get it right away."

"Hungry?" asked Patrick.

"Starving," said Baker. "I took an early flight this morning and couldn't handle a bag of peanuts for my breakfast."

"Let me take you to Sal's for lunch. I don't think you have anything like it in DC. Besides all the sandwiches in the world, his mother makes homemade pasta dishes. He also serves breakfast whenever he is open, so you still have that option."

"Pasta with Italian sausages and a little red gravy sounds like a great breakfast to me right now," said Baker.

Chapter 19

Boston FBI Assistant Special Agent in Charge Phil Kirby was sitting in the office of Assistant United States Attorney Harvey Bottom. Bottom was the prosecutor designated by the US Attorney in Boston to represent him in providing legal assistance the Boston Joint Terrorism Task Force, known by its acronym of JTTF.

Each FBI field division set up and led a JTTF within the geographic area their office covered. Other members of a JTTF usually included other federal investigative agencies, government agencies that had a needed technical or scientific expertise, and state and local law enforcement. The underlying concept of a JTTF was that everyone who could contribute in a terrorist investigation would participate. All federal, state and local assets were drawn together under one roof to maximize resources and information sharing.

Bottom and Kirby had been talking by phone daily since Patrick first contacted the FBI.

Bottom knew whatever Kirby knew about Vespa. Bottom had advised Kirby on how he thought Kirby could get control of Patrick and the source called Vespa. Kirby wanted to please Bottom, and Bottom wanted control of the investigation through Kirby and the FBI. It would make Bottom's career and he would take Kirby along on his coat tails. However, the initial effort did not work. Since then, Bottom had been instigating among his friends and fellow thinkers at DOJ, trying to force the FBI to go along with putting a squeeze on Patrick. So far this effort had not worked.

Bottom was in the middle of a rant. "There is no reason why this old fart shouldn't set up Vespa for us. Vespa is Mafia for christsakes. What is he, a friggin' apologist for these assholes? I can't believe they don't just yank his pension and put him in line."

"Patrick is well respected at headquarters and among the agents," replied Bottom. "He is very convincing when he says Vespa will bolt if anyone tries to identify him or set him up. He even told the Director this. The Director was possibly open to taking a stronger stand with Patrick, but after talking to Patrick, the Director wants to wait."

"The problem," said Bottom, "is the longer Patrick controls Vespa, the less likely you will wind up in charge of the investigation. They already implemented the new desk officer system at FBIHQ, which puts Baker in charge over you to coordinate an international terrorist investigation. If we could get control of Patrick and Vespa, we would control the information flow and have a shot at making FBIHQ put you in charge over Baker. I hear Patrick told Baker you acted like a real asshole when you met."

"I pushed Patrick exactly the way you suggested," responded Kirby. "Now you tell me that was wrong?"

"No, no" said Bottom. "It was worth the try. Now we'll have to apply some real pressure. It won't take long and I think Mr. Patrick will be more than willing to let us direct the activities of Vespa and get himself out of the picture altogether."

"How do you plan on doing this after Patrick's conversation with the Director?"

"There are colleagues of mine in Washington who believe the Director and his FBI are not the best people to be handling this case. The overall investigation should be put into the hands of someone more favorable to the thought process of the DOJ and the whole national security team the administration has in place. These people know that I'm reliable and they wouldn't mind seeing me direct this inquiry using the Boston

JTTF. I know how to be a team player and make sure no one looks bad. Those that play will look good. It's all about positioning, and I am going to position Patrick right back to his little retirement."

"Are these people at DOJ?"

Bottom smiled. "Not only DOJ, but also in the office of the Director of National Intelligence and at Homeland Security. There are those in the intelligence community who think the FBI Director should not attend or even be part of the morning intelligence briefings given to the President. Their role in terrorism investigations needs to be diminished. No offense to you."

"What happens if Patrick won't go along?"

"He won't have a choice. He will be answering to the legal system. He won't have his good reputation intact when I get through with him. We will attack not only his reputation but also his pocketbook. The first wrong move he makes, I'll have his pension yanked. It's expensive to fight the government, especially when you have to use your own money," said Bottom.

"How are you going to do this?" asked Kirby.

"Never mind for now. You just make sure I know everything the FBI knows, and I want to know it before FBIHQ. Don't let me down on this. When Patrick starts whining to FBIHQ, I want to know exactly what he is saying and to whom he's complaining. You got that?"

Kirby nodded.

"Make sure I get copies of whatever he gives Crowley or Baker, and I want it before it goes to FBIHQ. I want to make sure the people who agree with me are in our information loop before the material even goes to FBIHQ."

As Bottom walked Kirby from his office, he suggested to Kirby that he continue spreading the thought among the active and retired Boston FBI agents that something was not right with Patrick, and he may need to be looked at.

Chapter 20

After lunch, Patrick decided he needed to go for a walk, get some exercise, work out some demons, relieve tension, and get back in balance. His system was revolting against stress and a nice walk was called for.

Patrick had eaten a light lunch. He wasn't hungry. Baker, on the other hand, demolished a plate of eggs, home fries and Italian toast, with two sweet Italian sausages covered in red gravy.

Patrick stopped by the condo and changed into his walking shoes. He briefly stopped by to say hello to Peter, the parking booth attendant, and then headed north up Commercial Street toward the Charlestown Bridge. He crossed the bridge and walked over to the Charlestown Navy Yard, past Old Ironsides, and into the area that had been converted into condos. The Navy Yard was now its own residential community. While the Constitution was still berthed there, the US Navy had little presence beyond the Commandant's House and a few buildings. Civilians now occupied most of the Navy Yard. It was a beautiful place to live, with a view looking back across the harbor onto the waterfront and the tall buildings of downtown Boston. Besides walking the streets, you could walk down all the old piers. Some had condos built on them while others still served their function as dry docks for ship repairs.

As he reached the end of Charlestown marked by the Mystic River, he looked across to Chelsea. This was another town being revitalized by those who wanted to live in or near Boston and no longer wanted a long commute from suburbia. Called home by immigrants representing many foreign countries, and having come out of bankruptcy just a few years earlier, Chelsea was developing a spirit and vibrancy once again. The evidence that this community was revitalizing itself was its rising real estate prices. The down-side was these prices now threatened to drive out the economically marginal souls of the community. Perhaps they could learn co-existence this time?

On his return route, Patrick walked into the North End and up the hill on Salem Street to the Old North Church. As he was going through the walkways of Old North, he stopped to look at the garden. It was a garden done in the eighteenth century and now maintained by the parishioners. Every plant was labeled, neat in rows, and the June sun was starting to produce a good response with the early flowers. He and Liz were married at just about this same time of year at Old North. They stood overlooking this garden after the ceremony, listening to the bell changers create their magnificent music. It was always a special place to them. He looked up across the prado and recalled how he and Liz, along with the entire wedding party led by a violinist, walked through the park going to a friend's restaurant on Hanover Street for the reception. Some young girls – nieces and friends of the family – held up the train to Liz's wedding gown during the entire walk to avoid soiling from the sidewalk. Some older Italian ladies observed the entourage from their apartment windows and waved white hankies to express congratulations to the bride. Motorists blew their horns and pedestrians clapped. The whole party stopped by the firehouse on Hanover Street to say hello to the firemen sitting on the sidewalk. It was just a wonderful community moment.

"Mark, I have found you daydreaming?" said Tom Hughes, the Vicar of the Old North Church.

"I plead guilty, Your Honor," said Patrick.

"Hope they were good thoughts," said Hughes.

"I was admiring the garden. We were married this time of year. We stood here, by the garden, with all the guests just so we could listen to the bell changers before heading off to the reception." Patrick explained to the vicar the details he had just recalled and ended by saying, "I remember it all with great fondness."

"What a wonderful thing to be able to plead guilty to," said Hughes.

Patrick and Hughes then continued a discussion from a previous conversation about the mission of St. Paul to the gentiles and what the relevance of his letters are to the modern day reader. The discussion lasted about fifteen minutes but occupied Patrick's mind for several hours that afternoon.

At exactly 7:00 pm, Patrick's home phone rang. It was Vespa. She spoke without identifying herself.

"Can you meet me in the park at the end of King's Wharf?"

"I can be there in ten minutes."

"Okay," said Vespa, and she hung up.

Patrick put on a sport coat and walked down Commercial Street to the park at the end of King's Wharf. In the days of colonial Boston, King's Wharf was the leading commercial dock. King's Wharf was well situated near the old counting and commercial houses as well as the former seat of the king's provincial government.

Vespa was seated on a granite slab looking out over the small sailboats on their moorings at the end of the wharf.

"The three were in the Hotel Villa Palermo on Via Messina Marine yesterday afternoon, Palermo time. They were supposed to have dinner with the shipping contact at 8:00 pm. They did not show up at the restaurant so he went back to the hotel. He was able to check the room and they were gone, as were their bags. They were not being watched full time as it was too difficult without being detected. A number of ferries departed

Palermo during that period of time so they could have gone back to Naples, or anywhere. We just don't know."

Patrick knew it was impossible to maintain tabs on anyone who was constantly looking over their shoulder. You had to play it loose and risk losing them if you didn't want to get made and spook the quarry. There was a particular form of bureaucratic doublespeak that went along with this proposition. Headquarters would order that the field surveillance must not lose the target, and the agents must not be "made" by the target. These orders do not work when the target is looking for you. However, if the surveillance was successful, headquarters could take credit. If things went badly, and the agents were made, headquarters had warned them and they failed to heed the appropriate warning. No matter what, the score would be headquarters one, agents zero.

"What are your people doing or expecting next?" asked Patrick.

"Nothing. We have $30,000 of their money. Our people feel they will hear from them soon enough. Who knows, something may have put them on alert. They could just be playing us to see how we respond to their absence, or checking to see if there is any heat."

"Nothing in their conversation to indicate a problem?" asked Patrick.

Vespa pulled out a memory stick. "On this stick are digital recordings of their brief hotel room conversations. I am told there are no meaningful or helpful conversations. Everything seems normal."

Patrick accepted the memory stick and put it in his jacket pocket.

"Here are the full details of the hotel they used, room numbers, names used, and the restaurants and coffee shops they hung around the last couple of days. The name of the shipping office is not included as we don't want attention there at this time."

"I'll give this to the FBI." said Patrick.

"I would also suggest you dump your cell phone and get another not connected to you. I will not meet with you again unless absolutely necessary. I think you will draw some negative attention from the government. They will not be happy with this news and will want you to discuss your source of information. They may even follow you to find out who you are meeting. So for the time being, we have no more meets."

Patrick replied, "I'll get another cell with a new number in the morning. Here is a payphone number at Quincy market. Call me on this number at noontime tomorrow and I will give you a new cell number that will also have text messaging. Here is an out-of-the-way email address that I have. I have not used it except to send test emails so the ISP won't shut it down. It would take anyone a little while to find it."

"Depending on the circumstances you may not be able to recognize my voice when I call. I have voice altering equipment to use if I feel it is needed. In any event you will know it is me from the conversation, which will always refer back to the end of our last conversation," said Vespa.

Patrick nodded. He thought it strange that he was making plans to communicate with the Sicilian Mafia so his government would not be able to monitor him doing so. He felt awkward doing this, but knew it was necessary in the short term. Some people were going to be pissed, maybe justifiably so.

"Someone looks at the chairs on your balcony several times a day so we still have that for a backup."

Patrick nodded again. "I will talk with you at noon. If for any reason that fails, call that same number at 3:00 pm."

"Okay, Mark. Have a good evening." Vespa started to walk off.

"One more thing," said Patrick. "It has been bothering me about the man in Afghanistan who can't be interviewed. I don't know exactly how to say this, and I am not being judgmental, so I will just say it. I don't want your people doing harm to anyone to get information to give to our government. It was not how I did business and, in the end, I believe it does more harm than good. We either stand for something or we don't. It's just that simple."

Vespa's face went red, her body tensed and her eyes drilled right into Patrick. "I did not say we did it, nor did I ever indicate that we approved of what may have been done. It was done by people beyond our control. I do note what you say." She turned and walked off. She was upset. It was not hard to tell. Patrick thought that perhaps he could have expressed himself differently, could have sounded a little less goody-two-shoes – but that was the way it came out. It had to be said and he could not take it back now.

When Patrick got home, Liz was finishing the file she had to review for a client meeting in the morning. Patrick explained what Vespa said.

"Things don't always go smoothly. I'm sure there will be more of this, but try not to be a jerk. What's next?" asked Liz.

"We've agreed to my using a new cell phone for our contacts." Patrick took the FBI cell phone from his pocket, turned it off, removed the batteries, and placed it in his desk drawer. He took his personal cell phone and turned off the GPS feature. He would turn on the GPS feature on the new cell phone when he got it tomorrow. Somehow, he thought the tenor of his conversations with the government might change. "I'll get a perfectly cheap cell phone with a prepaid card in the morning using cash."

"When will you tell them what Vespa said?" inquired Liz.

"I'll call Crowley in the morning and offer to meet her at my office. I don't feel like going to their office anymore. I don't really get warm feelings when there, so why bother?"

"I will be in court after my 9:00 am meeting. I'll get out at one. If you want to buy lunch for a damsel in luncheon distress, I'm available."

"How is it you can eat like a horse and never put on any weight? I look at a bagel with cream cheese and put on five pounds."

"Stop whining and promise me lunch."

Chapter 21

Patrick was out early the next morning. Using cash he bought a cheap, basic cell phone with a prepaid card for five hundred minutes. He didn't have to produce ID since it was prepaid, but he had to give a name and address for registration of the new phone number. He used his name but the clerk misspelled it. The clerk also accidentally reversed his street numbers. Oh well, errors do happen. He still carried his original cell phone so anyone calling that number could reach him, just not on the FBI encrypted model.

Patrick made it to his office by nine thirty. He called Susan Crowley at the FBI office and set up a meeting for twelve thirty in his office. That way he would already have talked to Vespa, and then could meet Crowley and give her the memory stick along with the most current data on The Engineer and his friends in Sicily. Patrick took some time to sit and just think about what his options were, depending on what changes occurred. He worried that he could have done more to get the Sicilians talking directly to the FBI. However, he realized again, the option was not his and he could not change what he did not control.

Patrick knew the most recent developments with Vespa were not good. He was still in the middle and the FBI did not have "control" of the source of information. Patrick knew from his conversation with Carter Simms there was a view at headquarters suggesting Patrick should be "ordered" to set up Vespa. Simms rejected this idea because he knew Patrick well enough, but it still meant the thinking existed and was probably shared by some in DOJ. They might risk blowing the source to get control. If they were not experienced, they would never see their failure would lead to total Mafia silence. If they could not convince Simms, they might try to end run him. What would they try next? Patrick thought he knew. If they did, he would need some legal help. He thought it best to line up that help right now.

It was 10:45 am. Patrick called William Welby, his lawyer.

Welby was in. His office was located in Boston Place, directly across the street from Patrick's office. Wharf. Patrick needed a half hour of Welby's time. He was told to come right over. Welby and Patrick went back over twenty-five years. Welby had been an Assistant United States Attorney when they first met. He was one of the most respected attorneys in Boston, handled both civil and criminal matters, enjoyed a great record of service within the Bar, and feared no one.

It took Patrick only fifteen minutes to provide Welby a summary of the last week. Patrick and Welby discussed what Patrick thought might happen next, and Patrick asked what Welby could do to help. They jointly made a plan. Their discussion was completed in thirty minutes.

After his conversation with Welby, Patrick went to Quincy Market. At noon he was standing by the pay phone. Vespa called on time. There were no changes to report. Patrick gave Vespa his new cell phone number. Vespa would be more circumspect about her calls to Patrick. Without saying, they both assumed there would be more effort to find out from Patrick how to identify his source of information. Patrick felt some coldness in Vespa's voice. He thought Vespa was still angry. She was. She was infuriated Patrick could even presume torture and murder were her cup of tea. She wondered if she and her father were wrong to have gotten involved with Patrick. Should they have handled this on their own? One Palermo traffic accident could take care of all three terrorists. The ensuing police investigation, including accident reconstruction reports, would not be an issue.

Vespa was in the car with her driver John Turco. He was well respected by the Palermo families. Turco had never been introduced to or mingled with any of the American LCN. He was completely unknown to them. On the other hand, John made it a point to know by sight the key LCN leaders in New York. John believed in the proverb "keep your friends close, and your enemies closer."

"I want to talk with my father. I am going to ask him to have you leave tonight to visit with Zio Vincenzo. We need to make sure there is no communication error. If these fellows show up again, perhaps you might get a look at them so you know what they look like in person. We need to pick up the thread again because the link back to Afghanistan is broken at present." John merely nodded his head.

Vespa went up to her father's office and invited him for a coffee. They both knew this meant they needed to have a walk and talk. The authorities had not yet mastered electronic surveillance to intercept conversations of targeted people walking on Manhattan streets. Too much background noise existed for any directional microphone to be effective.

While the human ear could, to some extent, tune out noise or sounds not relevant to the immediate conversation, a microphone could not.

Once outside, Maria outlined why she thought they should send John to Palermo to meet with Zio Vincenzo. Aldo Torino agreed. However, he added, "You are upset. You should not let Patrick upset you. We are risking our lives so something evil may not happen. Patrick is merely carrying messages with no personal risk to him."

"I know. It is just that he does not see the difference between now and the past. Why should he assume anything bad about me?"

"Why do you care what he thinks?"

"Patrick has put labels of violence on me because I am Italian. I carry on your tradition, which Patrick knows well, but I resent his labeling me."

"It comes with the territory *cara mia*. You have now vented. Let it go. Send John. Tell him to keep it low key. I do not want anyone here to know he is over there seeing Vincenzo. It will just raise questions and perhaps link us to what is going on."

She smiled, gave her father a kiss on both cheeks, and went off to find John to send him to Palermo.

At 12:30 Crowley arrived at Patrick's office. Patrick gave her the memory stick and explained what happened in Sicily. Her first questions were: Could the Sicilians locate The Engineer and his friends? Did they expect further contact, or was this it? Patrick explained any answer to these questions would be a guess not based on fact. It was their feeling that The Engineer was not finished with the Sicilians and while they could not explain what was going on, they would do nothing and just wait. Patrick said anyone making overt inquiry and stirring up dust in Sicily right now would probably learn nothing new and would only create problems.

Besides when did any overt inquiry ever turn up any information of value in Palermo? It was not how things were done there.

Crowley was a professional. She said she would get the data immediately to Baker in Washington and they would be back in touch as required by the circumstances.

It was shortly after 1:00 pm. Patrick called Liz's office. She was finished her morning project and was hungry. Liz did not suggest it would be nice for Patrick to take her to lunch, she told him so.

They both sat under the large rotunda at Faneuil Hall reserved for the patrons of the many food stalls. Both had a roast turkey sandwich carved right from the bird itself. Not bad. They had little conversation. Both preferred to watch the growing hordes of tourists as they explored this diverse food market looking for the best thing to eat. With all the food choices available, representing the cuisines of many countries, it was hard to decide. If you liked to people watch, this place was one of the best.

After their sandwich, Patrick walked Liz backed to her office. He wanted to bring her up to date on his contact with Bill Welby and what thoughts caused him to seek Welby's advice. They discussed his visit to Welby's office and Patrick's need to know Welby would be his legal advisor.

"Why didn't you discuss your legal concerns with me before you talked to Bill?"

"Look," said Patrick, "Bill can be dispassionate, you cannot, at least when it comes to your favorite husband."

"Well I agree with your approach to the problem. If it becomes necessary, Bill is the best lawyer for it."

"I think it will become necessary," said Patrick.

Chapter 22

Tunis, Tunisia-The North Coast of Africa

The Engineer sat with his laptop in a Tunis coffee shop that provided free internet access. He was in the middle of a daily ritual. The Engineer was online reviewing the print and electronic media available for three American cities. He had been doing this for almost two years. He knew as much about what was going on in these cities, and probably more, than most local residents. He made it his job to know about and be part of each of these cities, to be as knowledgeable as the most dedicated citizen, even though he had never physically been to any of the three. One of the cities was Washington DC.

The Engineer concentrated his efforts there on congressional hearings and criticism citing purported failures of the current administration to address protecting the public from potential terrorism in the United States. The Engineer was a one person intelligence agency on this subject. It was really so easy to do with the internet combined with the openness of American society. When he zeroed in on a topic of importance, he would often locate and read the testimony of various government leaders as they were often required to testify before innumerable congressional committees claiming oversight of their activities. He could easily see what the FBI, CIA, or more recently the Director of National Intelligence, were telling Congress about their ongoing efforts. Congress used these hearings to assure the 'American public they were on the job and that American citizens could feel safe from terrorists' threats.

"Salaam Alaikum," said the newcomer. The startled Engineer looked up, smiled, then stood and greeted the newcomer enthusiastically with the kiss of peace.

"Alaikum Salaam," said The Engineer to the man who just appeared at his table. They both sat. Both ordered the strong Arabic coffee as The Engineer managed to discretely close his computer screen without offending his guest at the table.

The Engineer came from Riyadh, Saudi Arabia, and learned his fanatical brand of Islam in the local madras that the Saudi government said did not exist, and, if they did, would never teach their young charges a radical brand of Islam.

The Engineer first met his newly seated guest, Mustaf ben Afad, in Afghanistan where they both fought with al-Qaeda against the Americans. Both had been sent at earlier but different times to a training camp in the tribal area of Pakistan as new military recruits.

Mustaf ben Afad's family was from Iraq. He was a devout Muslim. Before being recruited to al-Qaeda, Afad worked in his father's bank. While Afad was an adequate soldier, it was soon discovered his real talents lay in money management. He left soldiering and began handling the personal financial affairs for many senior al-Qaeda leaders. Afad was present today because he was asked by the former al-Qaeda leader to serve as the personal link between him and The Engineer regarding his proposed project.

After the coffee was served, Mustaf lowered his head and said in a quiet voice: "At 3:00 pm Friday, please appear at the shop of the rug merchant listed at this address. You will give the greeting to the proprietor and then say you are there to pick up a small rug your wife left to repair a burn hole. You will write this series of numbers on a paper and show it to the proprietor. The proprietor will take out a rug, wrap it in paper, and give it to you."

The Engineer waited for the next sentence because it meant he had the final approval.

"You will not open the parcel until you are in a safe place. Inside you will find 150,000 in euros. There will also be British, Italian and Saudi passports that will guarantee you safe entry into any country."

This answer meant that the current al-Qaeda leader, Said Ali al-Wahishi, had now given his personal blessing to The Engineer's plan.

"May Allah be praised," murmured The Engineer instinctively.

"Allah Akbar," responded Mustaf.

They finished their coffee in silence. Mustaf got up and left without saying a word. What do you say to a martyr?

The Engineer left the coffee shop and slowly walked the streets of Tunis toward his hotel room. During the walk he thought about how only he, Afad and Wahishi were the only active al-Qaeda members who knew the full details of the plot The Engineer was about to unfold. Wahishi wanted to make sure the project was feasible and would be a worthy addition to his overall plan to destabilize the United States economically and politically. Today's meeting confirmed Wahishi was satisfied.

As he walked, The Engineer thought about how his plan moved into its first action stage, under the former al-Qaeda leader, when The Engineer was put in contact with two newly trained cell leaders who were resident US citizens. He met them separately in London through Mustaf ben Afad, who set up the meetings. The cell leaders had seen him at their training camp but were never introduced to The Engineer and knew nothing of his business until this first meeting. Afad didn't participate in the details of either meeting. The Engineer provided each cell leader only limited information about the overall mission, but it was enough to assign each leader specific intelligence gathering objectives. They were not told, nor did they ask, what the ultimate object of their efforts was to be.

It was intentional that these two cells were trained independently of each other. However, for secrecy, logistics and efficiency, al-Qaeda needed to train them at the same place, at the same time. They did not want any team member, if captured, to be able to give up any of the other team members. The Engineer arranged the London meetings so each leader did not know the other was participating in the same plot.

The Engineer had the option of combining the two different cells into one action group to use against his targets. However, that was a decision he did not need to make now. It remained a possibility but he was not going to discuss his whole plan with either of them now.

The Engineer's next step after these and some other London meetings was to arrange getting weapons, himself, and some key material into the United States. Only then would he again meet with the cell leaders and review what they accomplished in their intelligence gathering missions. He would next assess the manpower and equipment he had in place, how viable his plans were, and whether or not there should be one combined or two separate actions against the infidels. After this review, he would decide the eventual targets. There were many variables that could still impact this decision.

The Engineer's thought process was interrupted when he arrived at his hotel. Present in the lobby were his two associates. They had helped him with logistics over the last couple of weeks, but they had no idea as to his overall mission. He would need them to do a few more errands. Then they would be dismissed to return to Afghanistan as The Engineer disappeared.

Chapter 23

The North End, Boston

At nine thirty Wednesday morning the door buzzer rang at Patrick's condo. He was still at home. "Yes?" Patrick responded to the buzzer.

"This is Special Agent Fred Rickman of the IRS Criminal Bureau. I need to speak with you. May I come up?"

"Sure," said Patrick as he rang the buzzer that opened the entrance door downstairs. Patrick heard the elevator arrive at the fifth floor so he opened the condo door and stepped into the hallway. Exiting the elevator was a man about thirty-five years old, short, with a receding brown hairline, and overweight by about forty pounds. He was puffing and seemed to need to catch his breath even though he had just taken the elevator. Patrick stood in the doorway as the man approached and displayed his credentials. Patrick examined them closely and noted from the photograph that the man's weight gain was in recent years.

"How may I help you?" asked Patrick.

Rickman reached into a pocket, pulled out a piece of paper and handed it to Patrick. As Patrick started reading, Rickman said, "I have been asked to personally serve this subpoena by Assistant United States Attorney (AUSA) Harvey Bottom who is assigned by the US Attorney to the Boston Joint Terrorism Task Force, to which I am assigned."

Patrick listened as he continued to read the subpoena that called for him to appear before a federal grand jury in Boston on Thursday, the next day, at 10:00 am.

Then Patrick looked up at Rickman, smiled, and said, "Is there anything else?"

Rickman looked somewhat lost at Patrick's response and said, "Perhaps I could come in for a minute and we could talk?"

"Why? Is there something else you need to tell me that doesn't appear on this subpoena?" asked Patrick.

"Well," smiled Rickman, "Perhaps this subpoena could disappear if you agreed to cooperate with me and AUSA Bottom."

"In what way?" asked Patrick.

"We know about your conversations with Vespa and the FBI. You are retired and should not be doing this. We want you to turn Vespa over to us. The FBI will still be able to participate."

"Perhaps you could tell me your qualifications for investigating terrorism, Mr. Rickman?"

"I worked criminal tax cases for fifteen years before being assigned to the JTTF a year ago."

"I see," said Patrick. "I was just wondering how they trained an IRS agent to work terrorism, but apparently chasing tax evaders is a good enough training ground."

Patrick was achieving his goal. He could see Rickman getting flushed and irritated.

"Let me tell you something. The IRS is going to make your life miserable unless you smarten up and cooperate with me and AUSA Bottom. Your smart ass FBI friends are history. There are all kinds of federal agents willing to work with the assistant US attorneys, and we are just as good as the FBI in their best day."

"Anything else?" asked Patrick with his most patronizing smile.

"The FBI may not let us know all that is going on, but we know enough from Washington and we have the means to put you between a rock and a hard place. You will do business with us, or wish you did, when we get through with you and your taxes."

"Are there any other threats you wish to make before you leave?"

"What do you want me to tell Bottom?" demanded Rickman as if laying out a trump card.

"Well, since I have said nothing so far, I would suggest you inform Mr. Bottom of exactly what you threatened to do to me, using the power of the federal grand jury as a lever."

"Tomorrow, 10:00 am, and if you are not there, we'll get a warrant and arrest you."

"Good day Mr. Rickman," said Patrick, as he gently closed the door.

As he walked away, Rickman had a nagging feeling that this had not gone the way he or Bottom wanted. Patrick was a smart ass. Rickman had the feeling that Patrick was using him somehow, but he could not put his finger on what exactly was bothering him.

Patrick went to the phone, called Bill Welby, and explained to Welby what had just transpired. They agreed that an affidavit would be filed in federal court by Welby supporting a motion to delay the appearance required by the subpoena. They had both anticipated this move when they talked previously and knew what they needed to do.

Patrick went to work. He did have some matters that were timely and he did not want to keep the clients waiting.

About 11:30 am, Patrick got an email copy of a motion, filed by Welby on his behalf with the emergency federal judge, requesting a two week continuance on the appearance date for the subpoena. Additionally, the motion contained an affidavit from Patrick reciting the statements made by Agent Rickman during the service of the subpoena. Rickman's statements appeared unprofessional and achieved the effect desired by Patrick to indicate the AUSA was using the federal grand jury and the powers· of the IRS improperly. The court was also advised that further filings would likely be forthcoming in the form of a motion to quash the subpoena itself. By return electronic notice a few hours later, Welby was advised that federal judge Morris West had scheduled a hearing for 9:30 am the next day, one-half hour before Patrick's scheduled appearance.

Chapter 24

Patrick walked over to Sal's for a light lunch, as he planned on cooking dinner.

"Hi Mark," said Sal. "I haven't seen you for a couple of days. Started another diet?"

"I have no need of a diet," claimed Patrick with a smile. "I'm at my perfect fighting weight. How about a panini and a small side salad?"

"Done," said Sal. "By the way, that guy who attacks women is at it again up near the firehouse on Hanover Street. Been quiet for months, now it starts up again. Seems like the same guy, but instead of 2:00 am it was 7:00 am. The woman was walking down Charter Street to work."

"Was she hurt?"

"No, he got a grab; she screamed, then broke away and ran. The victim gives the same description as the prior victims. Cops think maybe the guy was in jail for six months and that is why the attacks stopped for a while."

Patrick knew the description was of a tall, Caucasian male, dark complexion, in his mid-twenties who normally wore jeans and a hooded sweatshirt. He also knew in prior months some of the neighborhood men were going out for very late coffees and walking the neighborhood looking for this guy. Patrick thought that practice might be resumed with this fresh attack. Everyone walked in the North End day or night without fear. No one was going to let this jerk spoil that. Patrick's bet was if the next woman could see the attack coming, and managed to get off an early scream, this guy would be history given the closeness of the neighborhood.

As Patrick ate, he and Sal discussed the Sox pitching lineup for the next couple of days. Sal got busy so Patrick left after eating to make room for more customers in the small restaurant. Patrick walked up Fleet Street to Hanover, right near the firehouse. Patrick did not see anyone around fitting the attacker's description but he thought he would look anyway. Renaldo was out in front of the pharmacy.

"You hear about the guy this morning?" asked Renaldo.

"I did" said Patrick, "just now, from Sal." Renaldo nodded. Enough said. Renaldo stood there looking up Charter Street as if he expected the suspect to appear.

Patrick turned left and went down to Parmenter Street into Arturo's.

"You hear about the guy on Charter Street. Back again?" asked Arturo.

Patrick agreed he had heard about it. Arturo gave his view of what should happen to this individual when apprehended.

"I don't think the court would approve of your sentence," said Patrick.

"They won't have to," said Arturo, not smiling.

Patrick thought he should change the subject.

Patrick reached into the refrigerated case and took out a box of fresh pasta. "How about some arugula, romaine lettuce, and a pound of your best tomatoes, even though they are not ripe?"

"You aren't complaining about my tomatoes, are you?" asked Arturo.

"Not directly, but I'll mix them with some canned tomatoes to give them some flavor."

"All you people are the same," said Arturo. "You buy an Italian cookbook, think you know how to cook Italian, and then have the nerve to be picky about your produce. A good cook can make delicious gravy without complaining about the tomatoes."

"You have gotten the last word in, for now," said Patrick as he walked out the door.

Patrick went into the Café Strada for an espresso. There was a newspaper on the table so he sat and read for a while. Nothing in the news, thought Patrick. He read the local North End paper for the listed activities in the community. He didn't plan on attending anything at present but liked to see what was going on. The park support groups were active with cleanups and fundraising, and the mayor's advisory group was meeting over some zoning variance requests. The café had the front windows open so Patrick watched the pedestrians going by, noting how everyone seemed joyful at being able to shed their winter coats. Only someone who had passed a long New England winter could really appreciate that feeling.

Patrick stopped at the cheese store. Felipe started to speak, but Patrick said, "I heard about the woman on Charter Street." Felipe just nodded. Patrick asked him if he had any of his homemade fresh cheese, which was a white, medium solid cheese. Felipe made it when he made the mozzarella. The cheeses tasted differently and had different textures but were alike in the process, which is why Felipe made them at the same time. Felipe went in back, came out with a four-inch round tub containing a fresh cheese. He wrapped it in his white paper and Patrick was now on his way back to Franklin Wharf.

Patrick turned off Commercial Street into the parking lot of Franklin Wharf. Peter, the daytime parking lot attendant and a good friend of Patrick's, waved Patrick down. Patrick stopped to listen to Peter's summary of today's news. He had great knowledge of the local neighborhood.

"You hear about the woman on Charter Street this morning?"

"I did," said Patrick.

Patrick had often seen Peter during the day in the attendant's booth reading his Bible. Peter set a very high standard when it came to helping others. Peter was an example of good will and straight talk, and the residents at Franklin Wharf, as well as everyone in the neighborhood, thought well of Peter. Patrick listened to him with attention.

"Can't you get your friends in the police department to do something? You and Liz know the mayor. His wife, she is from here. He doesn't want this stuff going on in our neighborhood."

Peter did not live in the North End. It made no difference to Peter. This was still his neighborhood, and he was looking after his neighbors.

"I'll check and get back to you Peter. The police put a lot of effort into this before and it stopped. They will get it started again."

"I just don't want to see anybody hurt because nobody said anything."

"Okay, Peter. I will check and talk with you tomorrow."

Liz could never understand why it took Patrick so long to do a few simple errands and walk home. His walk, as always, was filled with conversation and friends.

At home, Patrick fixed a marinara sauce with fresh basil and a blend of ground parmesan and pecorino cheeses for the topping. He served it with a salad of romaine lettuce mixed with arugula, olive oil and balsamic vinegar. It was simple yet so delicious. Liz picked up a bottle of Australian Malbec on the way home. After dinner they went out on the deck for coffee and some fruit. They watched the glow from the setting sun light the steeple of the Old North Church and spill onto the sails of the boats finishing their evening on Boston Harbor. Patrick brought Liz up to date about the hearing scheduled for the next morning in federal court. He also made sure she knew about the attack on Charter Street. This reminded Liz that she needed to talk with Mayor John Corso's wife, Gina, so she left the deck and went to the phone. A few minutes later she was back.

"Gina was not home but the mayor was. She will call me back. I mentioned to him about Charter Street and the mayor said he has had about thirty calls today asking what he is doing about the problem. They are on it big time."

Patrick then made a call to a friend who was a detective in Area A. He was in. They were on it. Patrick would be able to give Peter a good report in the morning.

Palermo

By Wednesday evening in Palermo, John Turco had already met with Zio Vincenzo. They enjoyed a modest supper of fresh goat cheese, ripe olives, pasta with aioli sauce, and some fresh fruit. Zio Vincenzo brought John up to date. They agreed that what they needed to do was already in place. However, John did ask about the family's resources at the Palermo Airport. They were considerable since the *aeroporto* was an important part of their business. John suggested a photo of The Engineer might be circulated to their key people at the *aeroporto* with a request to notify Zio Vincenzo immediately if this person was observed. Vincenzo agreed. It would be done.

Chapter 25

Boston

Bill Welby called Patrick at eight thirty to make sure he was all set for the hearing and had no further questions. Welby never left anything to chance.

On the way out, Patrick stopped at the attendant's booth to tell Peter of Liz's conversation with the mayor last night, and of his own conversation with the Area A detective. Peter seemed satisfied, for now.

Patrick walked down Commercial Street to Atlantic Avenue, the same route as to his office. He then turned left and walked over the old turn bridge, now strictly a pedestrian passage, to the new federal courthouse. The courthouse was now ten years old but it was still called the new courthouse. It seems courthouses do not come along that often, so fifty years from now they would probably still be calling it the new federal courthouse.

There was a great cafeteria on the first floor looking out through four stories of glass, back across the harbor, to the downtown area of the city. It had one of the best views of any building in the city, as it sat directly on the harbor's edge. It was the entrance to what people called the Seaport District. Patrick got a coffee and a bagel, nodded to a few people he saw, and sat down at a table to have breakfast and wait for the hearing to start.

"Hello Mark, how are you? What are you doing here?" asked Claudia Bell, a local reporter.

Patrick got up and gave Bell a kiss on the cheek. For years they had been friends, respected each other, but had enjoyed some rather harsh professional disagreements in the past. After all, it was Boston.

"In the order in which you asked, I am just fine, I'm having breakfast, and enjoying the view."

Bell smiled, clearly noting that Patrick had not answered her question. She also took it as an indication that, if further inquiry were made, Patrick would again not answer her question thus abrogating her need to make any further inquiry of him. She would enjoy the conversation and then find out her own way. She loved playing the game of finding out what Patrick didn't want her to know when he was in the FBI. Maybe there was a reason they could play again?

Bell brought Patrick up to date on her family news, as did Patrick. They talked about former comrades in the media, the FBI, as well as mutual friends. They looked around the cafeteria, seeing various people they had known over the years. A few even stopped by to say hello to them and accuse Patrick of leaking government secrets to Bell. This was not the first time he had been accused of leaking. He and Bell knew the truth.

After Bell left, Patrick proceeded to the fourth floor courtroom of Judge Morris West. Judge West was still engaged in another hearing that had started at 9:00 am. Patrick saw Welby sitting in the back of the courtroom and went over and sat next to him. In the front of the courtroom, Patrick saw AUSA Harvey Bottom seated with IRS Agent Fred Rickman. A few other were seated with them, and they were all talking together. Patrick surmised these were more members of Bottom's personal posse of federal agents, just waiting to see Patrick get his ass kicked.

At 9:30 am the other hearing ended and the clerk called the matter of the federal grand jury in the matter of John Doe. Welby went inside the enclosure to the defendant's table and sat down as AUSA Bottom assumed the government table. Judge West appeared to be reviewing some filings.

"Mr. Bottom, I have a request from Mr. Welby for a two-week continuance for his client to appear before the FGJ scheduled for today. Do you object to this continuance, Mr. Bottom?"

"Yes, I do, Your Honor. While the time frame may be tight, I note the witness is here in the courtroom and there is no reason why the witness cannot comply. It is the government's opinion that this witness is using a delaying tactic to avoid cooperating with the US government as required by that subpoena." Bottom appeared to be quite content that he was able to point out that Patrick was there, as if his trap had worked and Patrick would be sent down forthwith into Bottom's hands to be questioned under oath. Listening to Bottom, Patrick could feel his stubborn streak coming to life.

Patrick observed Bell walk into the courtroom just as Bottom made his last statement. Rickman motioned to Bottom and nodded toward Bell. Judge West could see it all. He was no fool. He knew who Patrick was, and looked down to read some more. Patrick suspected Judge West was now reading the affidavit by Patrick on his conversation with Rickman. When he looked up, Judge West started to look a little pissed.

"Mr. Welby, you are appearing on this witness's behalf?"

"I am, Your Honor."

"What is your position, Mr. Welby?"

Patrick felt like he did not have a name, and with Bell in the courtroom that was just fine.

"My client is cooperating with the US government, Your Honor, just not to Mr. Bottom's liking. This subpoena was served yesterday morning. There is no matter of expediency alleged by the government to require this witness to provide immediate testimony. I have had no conversation with Mr. Bottom as to whether or not my client is a subject or target of any investigation by Mr. Bottom. Certainly, the affidavit provided by my client as to the conversation with Mr. Rickman at the time the subpoena was served would give any counsel pause as to the government's intention toward my client and perhaps, even further, whether Mr. Bottom and Mr. Rickman are off on a personal vendetta."

Bottom jumped up, "Your Honor, I..."

"Hold on Mr. Bottom," said Judge West, "Why not give me a chance to speak. What do you say as to the representations made by this affidavit submitted by Mr. Patrick as part of this pleading?"

Patrick could see Bell's pen come out. The mysterious, potential witness was just given a name.

"Your Honor, I have not had a chance to speak with Mr. Rickman in detail about the service of this subpoena, but I do know Mr. Patrick was less than professional with Agent Rickman when he was served." Bottom was pleased he was able to take another shot at the uncooperative Patrick.

"Mr. Bottom," said Judge West, "are you telling this court you had enough conversation with Agent Rickman to know some of the details of the service of this subpoena wherein you allege Mr. Patrick was not professional, but you cannot inform this court as to whether Mr. Rickman threatened to use the powers of the IRS and this federal grand jury to 'make his life miserable' unless Mr. Patrick cooperated with Agent Rickman and you?"

"Well, Your Honor, I have not gone through with Agent Rickman word by word what was said."

"Is Agent Rickman in the courtroom presently?"

"Yes, Your Honor."

"Mr. Bottom, you will call Agent Rickman to the stand now. I am not wasting any more time."

Rickman took the stand, was sworn in by the clerk and sat down in the witness stand.

Bottom started to ask Rickman a question but Judge West cut him off.

"Will the clerk hand the affidavit of former FBI Agent Mark Patrick to Agent Rickman?"

The clerk did so.

"Agent Rickman, have you had an opportunity to read this affidavit?"

"Yes, Your Honor"

"When and where?"

"Yesterday afternoon"

"Second part of the question, please. Where?"

"In Mr. Bottom's office, Your Honor."

"Are the representations made by Mr. Patrick in this affidavit an accurate representation of comments made by you when you served the subpoena yesterday?"

"Well, Your Honor, Mr. Patrick was…"

"Agent Rickman, a simple yes or no is in order."

"Yes, Your Honor."

"You said these words to Mr. Patrick, as he recites in his affidavit?"

Rickman thought for a moment. He was tempted to deny making the statements to Patrick. He did not want to get in trouble with the IRS for threatening someone. On the other hand, suppose Patrick recorded their conversation? He hadn't thought of that until now. He realized if he lied now, and Patrick had a recording, he could be in more trouble. After doing this quick analysis Rickman responded to the judge's question, "Yes, Your Honor."

"You may step down Agent Rickman."

Rickman left the witness stand and went over and sat behind Bottom without looking up or making eye contact with anyone. Now he realized why Patrick had goaded him.

Bell kept writing.

"Mr. Bottom, Mr. Welby appears to have a valid concern, based on the testimony of Agent Rickman, of exposing his client to you without full preparation and legal analysis with his client. You know that, absent some exigent circumstances, one day is not enough time to do so. You are experienced enough to know that. I hope you are not wasting this court's time. I think you need to speak with Agent Rickman on the proper way to serve a subpoena. Having said that, Mr. Bottom, I realize you are entitled, within some limitations, to call your witnesses and carry out your investigative responsibilities on behalf of the executive branch of government."

Bottom was up again, "Your Honor."

"Not now, Mr. Bottom. You need to speak with Mr. Welby and try and work this out. This could have been done before this hearing. I am postponing the appearance of Mr. Patrick until one week from today, when the grand jury sits next. If a motion to quash this subpoena is filed prior to that hearing, I will hear it at nine thirty that morning and rule from the bench. Court is adjourned."

Judge West left the bench. Welby packed his bag and walked over to Patrick. As they exited the courtroom, Bottom came out and went over to Welby.

"Look Bill, we got off to a bad start. Rickman got a little pissed off after Patrick yanked his chain. Why don't we go down to my office and talk so we can get this thing going forward. You know he'll have to answer my questions sooner or later."

"Mr. Bottom, I have not been able to converse with my client at any length. I am busy until early next week. Would you care to submit your questions to me ahead of time in writing so I can review them? That could possibly allay my fears that you and the IRS are trying to make some type of tax case against my client. I also need to review whether I should be talking with you or the DOJ Inspector General regarding possible criminal conduct by Rickman in threats made to my client."

"Come on Bill, Rickman was busting his balls. We want to know who Vespa is and we want access to him."

"Why don't you call me Tuesday afternoon of next week and perhaps by then I can give you some idea of the position of my client. And also, Mr. Bottom, you know as an experienced prosecutor I can give my client advice, but the ultimate decision is the client's. Have a nice day."

Patrick and Welby took the elevator to the main floor and walked over to the glass wall in front of the cafeteria. They exchanged their observations about the hearing. As they were parting, Patrick said, "look at that."

Coming off the elevator was Bottom, followed by Claudia Bell. Bottom was talking and Bell was writing. Patrick knew Bell, as a reporter, would write what Bottom was saying regardless of whether she believed it or not. In an hour or two, Patrick's old cell phone would go off and it would be Bell formally asking for comment based on what was said in court and what Bottom slipped to her "in confidence" after court. For those comments, Bottom would be quoted as a source familiar with the investigation of Patrick. Patrick could feel his blood start to boil but he knew this was coming and had prepared himself. Still he was pissed and getting more so. This is what bothered Patrick a great deal about what any reporter does. Patrick and Bell had seriously argued this subject for a number of years, with no one giving up or gaining any ground. When the article came out, it would be all about what Bottom had to say alongside of Patrick's "no comment." It would make him look stupid, or worse. But, he had been there before.

The newspaper could drag this out for a few days getting comments from "knowledgeable sources" to speculate on what it would take for the government to make a tax case against Patrick. There would be opinions expressed about why a former FBI agent would refuse to testify as requested. This of course would lead to columnists questioning why Patrick should be paid his government pension while refusing to testify.

As Patrick walked back to the condo on this fine morning, he did smile when he thought about the possibility of just calling a press conference and telling the whole world what he knew. Maybe it would be a way to stop whatever the terrorists were planning. But he knew, in the end, it would not. It just made him feel a little bit better to imagine what he could say at such a fantasy news conference.

Chapter 26

Patrick was no sooner in his office when Vince Baker called him from FBI Headquarters.

"Why didn't you call us yesterday when Bottom made his move on you?"

"What good would that do? Some of your associates in Washington already tried to convince Director Simms to strong arm me to set up Vespa. I figured their next step was to link up with the DOJ attorneys and try using a subpoena to get me to come running to you. I went to my lawyer instead, and we are prepared. There will be no negotiations. They have sandbagged you as well as me, unless you were in on it. If you were not part of the plan, then it is clear they don't care what you and Simms think and they are going to do what they want. Telling you about the subpoena would not have stopped them. It would have just served as their opening gambit."

"The Director is talking to the DNI, the CIA and the AG."

Patrick laughed. "I've been off the dance floor for a while, but you and I both know the Director should not be talking. He should be cutting someone's balls off and daring them to do it again."

"What are you going to do now?"

"If I hear from Vespa, I'll notify you or Crowley as I have agreed to do. Otherwise I'm going to find my fly-fishing rod and do something that is both useful and fun."

"What I mean is, what are you going to do about the subpoena for next week?'

"Leave it in the hands of my competent attorney, who knows exactly what I will do and what I will not do, and then so employ his legal talents."

"What am I to tell the Director when he calls me in about fifteen minutes?"

"Exactly what I said about what he ought to be doing."

"Will you be serious?"

"Believe me, I am. I have spent my whole life fighting bullies. Now I find in my retirement, the bullies will not leave me alone. What's more, they purport to be on the same side. I will not work with assholes. I do not have to play your games. I am out. You people seem to either be willing to put up with or are incapable of stopping this negative, disruptive behavior. In either case it does not elevate my opinion of the JTTF structure in Washington or the ability of our intelligence community to get its act together."

"So what are you going to do?"

"Frankly my dear, it is none of your damn business. Bottom tried the squeeze play. Apparently he didn't think you, the Director, or the FBI are much of a problem or he would not have done it. Score one for the bureaucratic assholes."

"I will call you back after I talk to the Director. I will also talk with our general counsel."

"Don't bother calling me. I've told you what I will do if I hear from Vespa. If I feel lonely, I'll just call a press conference and bring the media up to date about everything I know, which still may be more than you know. Then the Bottoms of the world can explain to the public the logic of what they are doing."

"Mark, don't be a jerk. You know you won't do that."

"You ask Carter Simms if he thinks I will do exactly what I say I'll do," said Patrick before he carefully placed the phone in its cradle.

Patrick didn't feel better, but he felt somewhat relieved. He feared that it was going to take a grotesque tragedy to stop them from moving the same chairs around on the deck of the sinking ship, calling the new arrangement a success. Did anyone in their right mind think the

Department of Homeland Security was effective and efficient? Mergers and marriages of mediocre organizations merely led to larger organizations still suffering from mediocrity. All the changes in the country's intelligence and anti-terrorism capabilities were all too often just moving the same deck chairs around. The purpose, of course, was to convince the American public that Congress was on its game and looking out for the voters. Somehow, thought Patrick, the voters were not that dumb. They understood the ongoing charade and did not feel any safer.

People like Bottom, and those behind him, were just bureaucratic survivors. Their biggest mission was to see that they had a spot at the podium if things went well. If things did not go well, no blame would fall to them because they were not out front making the decisions and being held accountable. They never got their shoes dirty. They were never in the trenches dealing with the mud.

Patrick needed to walk. He left the office and walked downtown to the city hall area, up over Beacon Hill, and down to the Boston Common. After thirty minutes he felt like a coffee so he headed toward the North End and the Café Strada. He noticed at least two members of the surveillance team while on the Boston Common. He identified one more as he walked down Hanover Street. Patrick knew now that Bottom was really pissed and was using his posse to follow him and find out with whom Patrick was meeting. Patrick did one of his better versions of playing Denny the dunce, oblivious to all, so the surveillance team would not realize he had made them.

"Hey Mark, join me for a coffee," said Giovanni.

"Shouldn't you be in the restaurant with Carmella?"

"She is mad at me right now so I thought I would come up here for a few minutes and let 'absence make the heart grow fonder,' if you know what I mean," said Giovanni.

After they got their coffees, Patrick sat at a table with its window fully opened to the street. He and Giovanni enjoyed some pleasant conversation on a variety of topics. About a half hour later, Giovanni stood, looked out, stopped and said in a low voice, "Mark, if you don't mind me asking, are you in any kind of trouble?"

"Why do you ask?"

"When you walked by my restaurant, I was looking out the window. I thought two men were following you. So I came up for a coffee and to see you. I saw the men talking together after you came in. Since we have been here, I have seen them change positions on the street but they appear to be watching this place. They look at each other and they look at us. Can I help you?"

"Tomorrow you will read in the paper I was in federal court today because someone in the government believes I should be talking to them instead of my former colleagues in the FBI. They are not getting their way. I was threatened by the IRS if I did not cooperate to their satisfaction. They want me to immediately testify before a federal grand jury but that has been delayed. I think they want to know everyone I am in contact with so they can figure out from whom I got some information about some bad people. I have provided that information to the FBI, but not directly to Department of Justice attorneys. Their noses are out of joint. That is as much as I can tell you now. I don't want my friends involved."

"I wasn't prying. I only wanted to know if I could help. You didn't have to tell me all that," said Giovanni.

"Yes I did because you will read a lesser version tomorrow. I don't want you to know less than the paper," smiled Patrick.

As Giovanni was leaving the table, he leaned over to Patrick and said *sotto voce,* "I am going back to my restaurant. Please stay here. Have another coffee on me. Stay for at least ten minutes. Just do what I ask. Okay?"

Patrick never saw Giovanni like this before. He had a strange smile on his face. "Okay. I will," said Patrick.

Giovanni walked in the direction of his restaurant. About five minutes later Patrick heard a loud commotion on the street. He stood and leaned out the café window looking up toward Prince Street, and saw that two Boston police officers had one of the surveillance guys up against a wall and was patting him down. The man was yelling at the cops, which did not seem to improve their disposition especially after one of the cops pulled a gun from the waistband of the dungaree clad man. A crowd was gathering.

Another man arrived on the scene and started talking loudly to the two cops. Patrick saw it was the second member of the surveillance team. He was showing a black credential case to the cops. The cops gave the gun back to the first man, but it was quite clear from the shouting and hand waving that relations were still not cordial. Eventually the scene broke up and the crowd dispersed.

Patrick left the café and walked up Hanover Street heading to the condo. Renaldo from the pharmacy was out front. "They thought they had the guy attacking the women up on Hanover Street a few minutes ago," said Renaldo. "This guy fit the description and someone called the cops to check the guy out. The guy was giving the cops a real hard time claiming he was a federal agent of some sort. Turns out the guy worked for the IRS. Another IRS guy was with him. What would they be doing hanging around dressed like that – to catch tax cheats?"

Patrick smiled. In fact, he laughed. Now he knew what Giovanni had done.

As Patrick walked down the alley to North Street, he thought how it was the simple things that sometimes brought one so much joy. When he got to the condo the phone was ringing. It was John Peabody.

"Why don't you get out of Dodge so we go fishing tomorrow? If Liz has to take the bus down, Joan will pick her up at the bus stop. We can have dinner here."

"Good plan. Count me in. I'll wait until Liz gets home, and then drive down tonight so we can get an early start. Besides, I don't want to be in Boston tomorrow."

"That doesn't sound good. I thought you were finished with all that stuff and could lead your own life?"

"So did I," said Patrick. "We can talk tomorrow."

"When Patrick finished, his cell phone rang. It was Claudia Bell. "Mark I have some questions to ask about your court appearance today. Are you willing to answer them?"

"I have no comment," said Patrick.

"How about a comment off the record?"

"It won't do any good Claudia. Now is not the time."

"Bottom gave me his views suggesting you are refusing to cooperate with a government investigation, suggesting the word obstruction may be used formally in the future. Are you in tax trouble? Are you a subject or target of an investigation?"

"What do you think?"

"It doesn't matter what I think or even what I know. I have to report what is happening, and this is happening and I have to report it."

"Even if you don't have it right and you are being used by Bottom so he can get what he wants?"

"Bottom is with the JTTF. He does not do taxes. So why is he trying to hustle me to write something bad about you?" asked Bell.

"I think we need to leave this where it started, no comment."

"But if you say that and I write that, it makes it look like Bottom has something going against you and you are hiding."

"I'm a big boy. I've been here before. No comment, my friend, but thank you for calling. You will do what you think you have to do, but, in reality, you know you can choose not to do something you think is wrong. We have been there before. I saw Bottom feeding you after court. I was awaiting your call. Have a great rest of the day."

Nothing left for Patrick to do but to fix dinner. One look in the refrigerator told him that it would be meatless, and would involve two portabella mushrooms that he saw lurking about. He thought for a few minutes and then it hit him. He would make a mushroom risotto with chicken broth and serve a side salad of romaine lettuce with the last of the arugula added in. He checked the cabinet and confirmed he had a full box of risotto rice. He was in business. He would be a hero with Liz tonight. This was one of her favorite dishes.

When Liz hit the door, Patrick had a chilled white wine ready. No martinis until the weekend, which officially would start tomorrow night. Patrick caught Liz up on the news of the day. He could see that Liz was really upset and ready to engage, until she heard about what Giovanni had done. The story made her laugh heartily. She was angry at Bell for not having enough restraint to wait to get the story right rather than being the first to break the news. She realized this was heresy to any reporter, but said it anyway.

"I just don't want to see junk written about you because of some internal government pissing contest. Why is it that inadequate people always seem to drain from the positive and effective people, and no one does anything about it."

"Some would say that is an accurate description of government, my dear."

"How clever," said Liz.

"Both you and I have been through this before. Those who want to believe the bad will do so, regardless of what you say. Your family, friends, and those you care about know who you and I are. They know the good and the not so good about us. God knows it all. So what do we care after that?" said Mark.

"For now!" said Liz without any smile.

"Let me bring a smile to your face when I describe our menu for tonight!"

It did.

After dinner, Patrick called John Peabody. They changed their plan and decided to fish the incoming tide on Friday afternoon. Joan would pick Liz up from the bus stop at 7:00 pm and they would all have dinner at the Peabodys' when everybody got back.

Chapter 27

Tunis, North African Coast

At 3:00 pm Friday, The Engineer left his hotel room and began wondering through the Medina. This ancient city center best reflected the political, economic, and cultural roots of Tunis and its Mediterranean trading heritage. The alleys and intricate passageways of the Medina hosted its noisy, vibrant market stalls and its trading system for textiles, carpets and olive oil. It could be confusing to a stranger. The number of market visitors was augmented in recent times by the increase in foreign tourism. The money spent at the stalls by tourists for souvenirs supported the families of the small craft shops. While the tourists were not bold enough to eat at the market food stands, they bought their trinkets and took photographs of market activity they were unable to see at home, no matter where they were from.

Tunis had a population of one million or so. The city had been occupied, since its founding in the second millennium BCE, by every political and military power that had enjoyed success in the Mediterranean area. It started to fully succeed as a city in the seventh century after adjacent Carthage was destroyed. The Medina was built to be the new city center of a Tunis now under the control of Arab Muslims.

The Engineer frequented Tunis over the years as it was a city, and Tunisia a country, where not too many questions were asked. He was familiar with the winding alleys, the passageways, and the organization of the various merchants stalls based on their product offered for sale. Tunis also had a radical political flavor. The Arab league had been headquartered in Tunis from 1979 to 1990. The Palestinian Liberation Organization was headquartered in Tunis from the 1970s until 2003. Tunis also had a large Italian population and the Tunis Carthage International Airport offered sufficient connections to the rest of the world.

The Medina was an easy place to determine if you were being followed. These same conditions also made it easy to lose a surveillance, if desired. You entered a coffee shop by the front entrance facing the market, but that did not mean you had to leave the same way. After making sure he was not being followed, The Engineer enjoyed his coffee and quietly exited into a side passageway that took him to a rug shop to which he had been directed by Mustaf ben Afad.

As he entered he observed a short, very thin man with a neatly trimmed dark beard, standing behind a large wooden counter in the middle of the shop. He had very intense brown eyes that did not soften when smiled at by the potential customer who entered.

"Salaam Alaikum," said The Engineer.

"Alaikum Salaam," replied the shopkeeper.

"My wife left a small rug with you hoping you could repair a burn hole. It is a wedding gift from her favorite uncle."

The shop owner smiled and pushed a small piece of paper and a pencil in front of The Engineer. "Would you write your address here for me, sir, so I can search my records?"

The Engineer wrote the series of numbers that had been given him by Afad and slid the paper back to the shopkeeper, who then looked at the numbers. The shopkeeper then walked to the rear of the shop and disappeared behind a large rug hung from the ceiling. He emerged a few moments later with a small rug neatly bound with brown cord. He placed the rug on the counter and wrapped it with brown paper.

"Tell your wife the hole has been completely repaired and no damage can be seen. I have wrapped it for you so nothing can spill on the rug as you carry it through the Medina."

The rug merchant completed the transaction by charging The Engineer a modest amount for the "repair."

When he finished, the shop owner said: "Thank you for your business. Allah Akbar."

"Allah Akbar," replied The Engineer as he picked up the package, nodded to the man, and walked back out into the throbbing wave of people in the market area.

The Engineer went directly back to his hotel room, removed the outer wrapper, cut the cord binding the rug, and inside found 150,000 in euros as well as British, Italian and Saudi passports, each bearing his picture and the prerequisite information. Also included was some additional documentation, a driver's license, identity card, and a few tax receipts for purchases in the respective countries. These he aligned with the appropriate passport to carry in his wallet to serve as backup documentation for the passport being used. It was all here, as Afad said it would be. He took out 20,000 euros for his immediate needs. He hid the passports.

The Engineer was to meet his two associates at a food stall in the market at 2:00 pm. He put the remaining euros inside a large, brown envelope that he took with him as he left his room. The remaining 130,000 euros would get to the United States another way. When he got to the food stall, his two associates were waiting. They drifted into a corner to talk.

"You will go back to Palermo this afternoon and tell our friends they will be shipping the container. I want to know if they can receive the container on Sunday and how soon thereafter the container can be shipped. What is the expected arrival date in New York? Also see what they have available for cell phones so I can dump the ones I have. I want to be able to make international calls. Maybe they have prepaid cards? I will meet you Sunday in front of the Hotel Palermo at 2:00 pm. I will call you if things change or if I am late. Otherwise just wait for me there."

The pair acknowledged his instructions and left. They would shortly be on a flight to Palermo. He would not be far behind if things went well.

The Engineer left the area and walked around the outside edge of the Medina to insure once again he was not being followed. After moving in and out of alleyways and around stalls for fifteen minutes or so, he ducked into the shop of an olive oil trader who was also a Hawaladar. While roughly described by some as a money changer, under the ancient banking system known as Hawala, this person was more than just a money changer. He was a person with whom you could entrust large sums of money that would be returned to you or another as you directed at a foreign or domestic location chosen by you. Tribal custom and history all dictated the Hawaladar would act on your behalf with honor and efficiency. He had no controlling political philosophy. Hawala was a system of transferring money across political borders without the payment of taxes, bribes, or adhering to any particular monetary regulations.

In its early days, Hawala enabled traders to be active to the far ends of the Silk and Spice Roads without fear of robbery. The money would be put into this system to be claimed by the trader, or his designee, at a destination point. The Hawala system itself had a complex set of couriers, promissory notes, and debt transfers to third parties for collection, the methods and details of which The Engineer did not need to know. The Engineer just knew Hawala worked. For a small percentage of the funds, Hawala enabled a sophisticated trading system to develop long before technology caught up to the trader's need for currency security. The Engineer just needed to know the money, minus a small percentage, would be where he wanted it when he needed it. It always was.

The Engineer and the Hawaladar, named Dihab, had done business before. In fact, he had previously given Dihab money that he planned to pick up after arriving in New York. To this money, he was now adding the 130,000 euros in the envelope just delivered to him by the Hawaladar at the rug shop. For security reasons, The Engineer did not want to use the same Hawaladar that Afad used to transfer funds along the entire route. Instead he used Dihab, and The Engineer would reclaim this money upon arrival in New York. Out of caution, The Engineer would transmit the pickup code numbers to Afad. If The Engineer was captured or killed before he claimed the money, Afad could see that it was retrieved and used by another jihadist.

When back in Palermo, The Engineer needed to give the two associates money to get back to Afghanistan. They were not part of the overall project. Their role with him ended in Palermo when the container was in place and ready to ship to New York. If they were captured and talked, they could never lead anyone to him after he arrived in New York.

After his arrangement with Dihab was completed, The Engineer went back to his room, packed his small shoulder bag and laptop, and took a cab to the Tunis Carthage International Airport where he was scheduled on a flight to Palermo at 8:00 pm.

Palermo

The Engineer made his scheduled arrival late Friday night at the Palermo Airport, located in Punta Raisa about thirty kilometers outside the city proper. The Aeroporto Falcone-Borsellino was named after two anti-Mafia judges who were viciously assassinated by the Mafia in 1992. Their deaths marked the beginning of the end for the Sicilian Mafia bosses who foolishly ordered their murders and also began a series of bombings and murders designed to intimidate the Italian government. It was the most expensive mistake the Sicilian Mafia ever made. These murders galvanized not only the government but also the public in an unprecedented and joint opposition challenging the very existence of the Mafia. The Mafia had come out from under their normal cover in the deeper shadows of society to openly challenge the government. The Mafia dared the government to challenge their power over both the civilian populace and the government itself. What the Mafia had failed to anticipate was the public had reached the point where coexistence with the Mafia could no longer be tolerated. The public anger was the fuel behind a no longer tepid Italian government response to the constant public recklessness being exhibited by the Mafia. It was the public outrage that insured the Mafia would never again be as powerful.

The Engineer did not intend to go into the city to join his two associates, nor stay at the same hotel. Instead he went to a hotel that was just outside the airport but part of the airport modernization project that was recently completed. Millions of dollars had been spent on airport and nearby business development areas, and now it was hoped legitimate business profits could be reaped. He needed to get some sleep, as he had to be back at the airport early Saturday morning.

Chapter 28

Boston

Patrick was up early Friday morning. When first awake, he started thinking about the events of yesterday and rather than let it bother him again, he got up, dressed, and went out. When he came back with a cup of coffee for the drive to Southport, Peter was in the attendant's booth. As Patrick started to walk to his car, Peter asked, "Are you all right?"

"What prompts the question my friend?"

Peter held up the morning paper, front page, city section, above the fold, to an article captioned "Former FBI Agent Seeks to Delay Grand Jury Appearance." The byline was, of course, by Claudia Bell. The article went on to recite what she had observed in court yesterday, noting Fred Rickman's unusual testimony to include the admission of making threats to Patrick. Then came the predictable "source close to the inquiry" adding a few comments about "the need for a former FBI agent to respect a subpoena, cooperate with the government paying his pension, and how such a person was not above the law."

Bell did point out that Patrick was not known to work terrorism when in the FBI and thus the activity by the JTTF did not readily make sense on its face. She also noted that IRS agents were working the matter, and if it was terrorism, it was strange that FBI agents were not involved. Her inquiry at the Boston office of the FBI and at FBIHQ received "no comment." Bell ended the article by saying there was some rumor that Bottom had tried to force Patrick's cooperation for some unknown matter, and Patrick had called Bottom's bluff. More would be known next Thursday when Patrick was scheduled to appear before the federal grand jury, whose proceedings were not public.

"Are you in any trouble, Mark?"

"No," said Patrick. "Thank you for asking. I know it comes from your heart."

Peter had a strange look in his eye. "Then I guess that IRS agent dressed up in street clothes on Hanover Street yesterday afternoon has nothing to do with this article?"

"Peter, you are too suspicious," laughed Patrick. "You will have to talk to Giovanni about that one."

"If you need any help, if there is anything I can do, let me know. Whether you want it or not, I am adding you to our church prayer list."

"That help I will gratefully accept."

"And the white, four-door sedan parked halfway between here and the coffee shop contains a guy that followed you on foot when you walked out to get coffee. He hopped back in the car when you stopped to talk to me."

"I wasn't paying attention. I must be getting old," said Patrick. "They will come with me shortly when I leave. We'll see how good they are. Tell Liz when she comes out, just so she knows they've been around."

"Will do. Anything else?"

"If anyone asks you, tell them I said I was leaving the country. For your personal information only, I am going fishing in Southport. You have the number there."

Peter just smiled. "You're okay. I can tell."

"I told you that. Now let me get going."

Patrick drove north toward the Charlestown Bridge, and then left on North Washington Street. The white car was with him and made the same lights as Patrick. From here Patrick could go downtown, to his office on the Surface Artery, or go onto the Expressway to the airport. Each choice had several more turn options within the next half mile. He drifted left to make it look like he was going to the airport but went right at the fork to take the expressway south. One quarter mile later he got off at Purchase Street, but instead of turning right to his office, he went left into The Seaport District. Three blocks later he was on another ramp that would put him back on the expressway going south. Being this close to Logan Airport flight traffic, Patrick doubted the surveillance team had aerial assistance. He didn't see any above him. Bottom and his people wanted to see what he was doing. What a waste! He was on the expressway going south when he got off one exit, stopped at a light, then got on a ramp going right back onto the expressway. There was no one with him now. He sipped his coffee as he enjoyed the sixty-seven mile ride to Southport.

At 3:00 pm Patrick drove up to John Peabody's house in his Southport car. It was a fourteen-year-old Volvo station wagon with low miles and in good shape. Most of what he needed in terms of equipment, which was not much, was in the back of this car and remained there throughout the summer. Need a clam rake? Look in the wagon. Need an anchor? Look in the wagon. He loved driving this car because it owed him nothing. The water was still cold so he brought along his waders. They were in the back of the wagon for the season.

On the way down to the beach from where they parked John asked, "You okay?"

Patrick just looked at him trying to figure out what to say.

"Joan and I saw the paper this morning."

Patrick told John everything he had told Giovanni, Peter, and a little more about the IRS following him. Patrick assured John he was doing the right thing, which he could not discuss with his friends, and that he appreciated his and Joan's concern.

"We never want to know your business. We just want to know if you are okay, and if there is anything we can do?"

"Just be who you are, and when this is over maybe I can explain more."

Enough said. John would tell Joan and there would be no more conversation on the subject unless Patrick brought it up. It made Patrick think about the nature of friendships and how lucky he was.

The luck did not hold for the fishing. John was using a 10-weight graphite rod with a shooting head and fast sinking fly line on the reel. A green colored wet fly was securely tied on the tippet. He caught four small striped bass, but no keepers. The blues were not in yet.

Patrick was using an 8- to 9-weight rod with a sinking line tied with a brown wet fly to imitate the small bait fish. He had tried several different flies, but no fish for him. They moved up and down the cut for about one quarter mile from where it started at Buzzards Bay. When they got back near the car, Patrick figured he might as well practice casting with his new 5-weight rod. There seemed to be only small stripers in the cut, and Patrick thought it would be more sporting to try and catch one on the lightest rod possible.

On his third cast he had a fish on. It was striping line fast. He cranked down on the drag, which seemed to make no difference. He looked up and John was laughing at him. Fifteen minutes later Patrick still did not have the fish in. He didn't want this to go on any longer because if the fish got too tired, it might not recover when released. He started reeling the fish in without regard for the leader breaking.

"It is about time you put the wood to that fish," said John somewhat instructively.

Patrick was not as good as John, and he knew he had not been direct enough early on with the fish. When he got the fish almost in, his leader snapped. Off went the fish with his fly. "Maybe this 5-weight won't work for stripers. I should save it for fresh water."

"It will work," said John, "You just need to improve your technique. Want some help?"

"Sure," said Patrick. John did this for a living and Patrick was glad to accept any instruction from John. Twenty minutes later Patrick understood why he lost the fish and what he might do differently the next time.

Joan noted the absence of fresh-caught fish for dinner when she arrived with Liz. It made no difference. Knowing Patrick's usual fishing results, Liz and Joan stopped at the fish market and bought a couple of tuna steaks to grille. Patrick was in a world he liked.

John and Patrick made plans to go to the state park the next afternoon at low tide to dig some cherrystone clams. Patrick loved them raw, and also used them to make a fresh clam sauce to put over linguini. When Patrick got back to the house he was just plain exhausted. He had no doubt he would sleep well tonight.

Chapter 29

Palermo, Sicily

The anti-terrorism division of the Italian national police had been briefed by the FBI legal attaché from Rome as well as the CIA station chief. Photos of The Engineer and his two associates, and their history at the Hotel Villa Palermo, had been provided. A discreet surveillance was set up in the hotel and the surrounding area. Additional general surveillance was set up in the port area in an effort to locate these individuals. Their photographs were entered into the facial recognition system for all of Italy's airports and train stations that had been so equipped to date. After the train bombings in Madrid, the pace of the train station installations had picked up but it was far from complete.

Earlier, at the Aeroporto Falcone-Borsellino, both the facial recognition system and the passport computer system failed to alert the authorities to the return of the two associates on a flight from Tunis that Friday afternoon. The system had been hastily installed and not all the personnel had been properly trained on the system's usage. What controlled today's failure was a software malfunction. Passports were being reviewed manually.

A surveillance team assigned to the Hotel Palermo, on the off chance that the men returned, saw the two associates arrive by cab and go into the hotel. A second surveillance team on standby joined in immediately, and they in turn were soon joined by two more teams. They had a total of twenty surveillance team members in the area. Their instructions were clear. Under no circumstances were they to allow the two associates out of their sight.

The two registered at the Hotel Palermo using the same phony Italian passports from the previous visit. At least they were consistent. But now a passport crime had been committed on Italian soil, and witnessed. The associates could be arrested at any time. After registering, the associates immediately went to their room where they remained for several hours. No outside calls were made and no one knew what they were doing. Later in the afternoon, the two associates returned to the hotel lobby, found a couple of newspapers, and sat in the lobby reading. Later they walked around the area near the hotel checking the posted restaurant menus. Soon they chose a restaurant and went inside. By the time the soup course arrived, their room had been bugged, the telephone tapped and a visual surveillance system was in place. The police occupied the rooms on either side of them.

All of this did not escape the notice of the hotel staff. While the police were unaware of the Mafia's interest in these men, Zio Vincenzo was aware of their interest. A quiet word from Don Vincenzo let everyone know that this was not a police matter that concerned them or any of their friends. They were to ignore what they saw or heard, except to report everything they saw or heard to Don Vincenzo. People took that request seriously. There were more eyes and ears tuned into this pair than they ever could have imagined.

After dinner, the two associates strolled to the dock area. They appeared to just amble after their dinner. They talked but did not seem serious, nor did they seem to be concerned for the world around them. In short, they were not suspicious looking at all. After walking about for forty-five minutes, they wound up back at a coffee shop near the hotel. They had coffee and watched the soccer game on television. One of the associates went to a payphone, inserted a coin, and had a one-minute call. The surveillance team member inside the coffee shop was unable to overhear any conversation. The phone was not tapped, but it would be soon. When the associate sat down, he did not immediately converse with the other but instead resumed watching the soccer game.

When the game ended, the two associates walked across the street, entered the Hotel Palermo, and went to their room. That had very little conversation in the room. Soon the room was quiet, except for the distinct sounds of the two people in deep sleep.

The cab driver who delivered the two associates from the aeroporto to the Hotel Palermo was now in police custody. He was being held incommunicado until the Italian authorities could determine if he was a member of an al-Qaeda cell. All indications were he was just a cab driver doing his job, but they wanted to make sure. If they were wrong, he could alert the two associates. So they decided to hold him until court on Monday, noting there were serious deficiencies regarding required safety conditions of his cab.

The cab driver was led to believe he had been seen with some drug suspects and was asked to recount his entire day. The authorities did not want to highlight their specific interest in the two associates and their pickup at the aeroporto. The cab driver enumerated all his fares for the day to include the two associates. He had picked them up at the airport lower level cab stand. They gave him the name of the Hotel Palermo. He drove them directly there. He could recall no conversation during the drive. The two associates paid him in cash and, it being late in the day, he decided to quit after this fare. They did not ask him to come back or request his cell phone number for a future pickup.

With this information, it did not take the police long to track the associates to the flight arriving from Tunis. All videos from the airport were made available, and the two were successfully traced from the time they got off the plane until they got into the cab. The associates' passports were subject only to a physical inspection, and because of the software malfunction were not run against any of the critical data banks to alert the authorities. The plane's manifest was obtained and inquiry was now being conducted in Tunis to identify all flight passengers. There was no indication that The Engineer had been with them on the flight. All airport video for that day, and the day before, was being reviewed at both the Tunis and the Palermo airports by individuals given a picture of The Engineer and asked to review hours of video to see if he passed through either airport. The work was mind numbing, but this was the only choice. The facial recognition system was not responding to an inquiry of his photograph.

Chapter 30

Saturday morning at precisely 6:00 am, The Engineer's alarm clock sounded what could have been a late call to morning prayer. It was not such a call for him. He got off the bed, stretched, looked outside into the early morning light, and then proceeded to the bathroom where he splashed some cold water on his face. He brushed his teeth, dressed, and left the room. He went to the lobby where he looked at a flight board for the airport. He walked outside in time to catch a shuttle bus to the airport terminal. Once inside he walked around until he found a stand selling coffee. With his black coffee in hand The Engineer proceeded to the second floor, where he could watch the arrival of a small, twin-engine turbo prop cargo plane arriving from Tbilisi, Georgia. Few knew Tbilisi to be the sister city of Palermo and even fewer people ever thought how this status was being exploited by criminal groups in both countries.

When the plane's props stopped turning, a cargo handler's cart appeared next to the rear hatch. The airport employee stood on his empty cart, unlatched the cargo door, and began to unload boxes onto his cart. After the boxes were unloaded he reached inside and detached two red fire extinguishers, one from each side of the hatch. Each appeared to be the same size, about thirty inches high. These were placed on the cart and the employee drove off. The Engineer sat for a few minutes, finished his coffee, and took the shuttle bus back to the hotel where he got his bag and checked out. The Engineer stood in front of the hotel. Ten minutes later an older black Fiat pulled up. The Engineer got in. The Fiat was being driven by the airport employee whom The Engineer watched unload the plane's cargo. The Engineer did not notice the doorman's intense interest as he got into the Fiat.

The Italians quickly passed the word to the CIA and the FBI that the two associates had returned to the Hotel Palermo. They were under physical and electronic surveillance but there was no indication as to what they were doing. They had not met with anyone. Now the question was what Washington wanted done in the event the two associates caught on to the surveillance and tried to elude the followers. It was decision time, and the people on the ground needed some direction.

FBI Director Carter Simms was notified and he called an immediate meeting with AD Bob Wilkins, al-Qaeda desk officer Vincent Baker, and by secure phone from Boston SAs Susan Crowley and Supervisor George Fisher. Their first objective was clear. They needed to identify these people. They didn't know who these people were, much less what they were up to. The intelligence to date, while sketchy, was serious enough that no one believed they could lose contact with these two again. They needed to identify them and The Engineer who, it was noted, was still missing. There was agreement among them. If it looked like the two associates made the surveillance and were going to take off, they should be taken into custody.

Carter Simms called the CIA Director to share the group's conclusions. The CIA Director and his team agreed with this course of action. The joint operations room was activated. Vince Baker would oversee the operation for the FBI, for the time being, as it was still considered an al-Qaeda terrorist activity. The FBI legal attaché in Rome, along with the CIA station chief, would communicate their thoughts to the Italian authorities who were in charge of what would or would not be done. Information from the Palermo surveillance, both physical and electronic, was being fed real time into the FBI joint operations center. Everything was in place to proceed. It was luck that put them back on the trail. The question was, whose side would luck favor next?

The two associates were up early Saturday morning, had coffee and a pastry, and walked down to the dock area where they spoke with a man in front of a trailer being used as a temporary office for a shipping company. They went inside and came back out in less than ten minutes. Photos of all the parties were obtained and a request was already in process to bug the trailer. The Italian police had not been told that the Americans had a source of information on what was going on inside the shipping company. This information was being closely held by the Americans until things could be sorted out. The Italian police had respect for such nuances of information management. They would not be disturbed in the least when they found out they had not been told the whole story.

The two associates strolled back to the city center. They seemed to be in no hurry and appeared to be window shopping. They drank another coffee, read the newspaper, and spoke to no one else. Around noon they wandered into a drugstore. The nearest surveillance agent did not go in behind them, but waited for orders. He was told to go in to see what they were doing and he passed them coming out. Neither had anything in his hands, so either they bought nothing or had their purchase in a pocket. No inquiry was made.

Keeping twenty surveillance people in a congested area unnoticed by the two associates was not easy, but it was done effectively. It did not go unnoticed, however, by some of the keen eyes in the neighborhoods. Zio Vincenzo could get a pretty good idea of what was going on just by listening to the information coming in to him from his people in the neighborhood.

"How will he get the container delivered to the dock? Where is it now?" said one associate to the other.

"I don't know. He only asked us to find out about the shipping schedule. They can handle any container he sends, and, if it is delivered Sunday, they will be there to receive it. They will have the container on a boat to New York early in the week, probably Tuesday."

"Did you see that drawer-full of cell phones in the shipping office? Those guys must buy every cell phone stolen from tourists in Palermo. He just gave us three phones for nothing. We were ready to pay."

"No. These phones are not stolen. If a phone is stolen, the owner just cancels the number and the phone is shut off. They get these phones through their contacts that work for phone vendors. Once the phone is listed under phony data, it is good until the bill does not get paid, which will take at least forty-five days. You can chose to keep it going by paying, as long as it looks like the payment is coming from the phony ID behind it. Some of the others are used with SIM cards that use prepaid amounts of time. There is no billing so they are good as long as your card has time. Not only did he give us three phones, he made sure they were all fresh. The larger phone is the one listed under the phony ID and is a satellite phone. It can be used on a boat crossing the ocean."

"Let's tell The Engineer the guy charged us 100 euros for each phone because they are fresh and non-traceable. Then we'll have 300 euros to split."

"Okay."

The associates were still oblivious to the surveillance about them as they returned to the hotel. They watched another soccer game in their room. The electronic surveillance learned little until one associate asked the other what time their meeting was tomorrow. "He wants us in front of the hotel at 2:00 pm."

The Italian authorities now had the shipping company under physical and electronic surveillance. Those affiliated with the shipping company assumed they would be subject to physical and electronic surveillance when the authorities focused on the activities of the associates. In this case, they were not concerned because Don Vincenzo told them not to be.

While the associates were enjoying a soccer match on TV, The Engineer was in the apartment of the airport cargo handler on the outskirts of Palermo. He was on his computer checking the news for his three US cities. He was amused to read the testimony of the mayor of New York City, who just testified before a congressional committee. It seemed all the promises made by the federal government to have a nuclear material detection system program up and running in key US American cities, especially in New York City, had gone underfunded and was not yet close to being in existence. The New York City police commissioner further lamented that the federal government failed to issue sufficient regulations to protect US nuclear waste, which could be used for a dirty bomb. "Securing the Cities" was the name of the underfunded program and, as yet, also non-existent program. The Engineer laughed to himself. Perhaps the Americans would give him some credit. His efforts would definitely result in the money being appropriated in the near future. The Engineer had worried that the Americans might have a nuclear material detection program in operation and functional. In the past he might have thought such a news article, as he was now reading, was false information put out to entrap the unwary in an operation such as his. Now he was convinced the news reports from the political process were in fact feeding him valuable operational intelligence.

When he finished on the computer, The Engineer used his cell phone to call a second shipping company on the mainland. He did not want all his supplies shipped to the United States through one company. For security reasons, it was better to split the armament shipments. That way if something went wrong, he would be fully operational if one container got through. One was going through the Italian Mafia and the other through a mainland shipping company owned by the Camorra in Naples. The shipment of "machine parts" was just being delivered into the hands of the latter shipping company and would be leaving Naples shortly. Only The Engineer knew of this second shipment. He did not inform his two associates. They had no need of this knowledge, as they were not involved. The Engineer was banking on the fact that this container would also get through a non-existent or weak port security operation. It would take a physical search of the container to find his supplies. He was willing to risk that a search would never happen. Even then he had yet another back-up plan.

Mustaf ben Afad arranged for The Engineer to make contact with a new al-Qaeda cell located in the United States. The sole function of this third cell was to acquire weapons, munitions, explosives, and various types of advanced and powerful small arms for al-Qaeda missions in the United States. They were even working on obtaining their own reconnaissance drones. Contributions to the al-Qaeda cause from certain oil rich countries, who wanted to export terror and maintain their own internal peaceful existence, helped bring their terrorist activity to a whole new level. It was true that 9/11 had been a shoestring operation financially, but that was years ago. Their financial world was now completely different.

The cargo handler was in the other room. He heard The Engineer speaking on the cell phone but paid no attention to the conversation. The Engineer said, "The container is being delivered to your pier by my carrier, as we speak. The paperwork is with the shipment and in order. I understand the container will be loaded aboard ship tomorrow, and will sail in two days. It will arrive in New York for pick up by my carrier within seven days. I will call you to check to make sure there are no customs delays before I arrange to have my carrier pick up the container."

There were a few moments of silence, and then The Engineer said: "The money has been electronically deposited into your account for the container. Good, that is confirmed. I have my personal ticket and arrangements have been made for me to board any time before the ship sails Monday at 4:00 am. I will arrive in New York before the container. Yes, I understand. We are complete. Thank you and goodbye."

He then made a second call and arranged to have the other container delivered to the Palermo shipping company dock that was contacted by his two associates. "Yes, I want it delivered at noontime Sunday. The shipping company already has the documents for the container and expects your Sunday drop off." The Engineer had the rest of the needed money, in cash, required for the Palermo shipping company. He was not waiting for the associates to tell him he could deliver the container to the dock in Palermo. He knew they would have already made that arrangement.

The cargo handler was only half listening and not interested. He had no reason to be otherwise.

The Engineer researched what shipping companies had passenger accommodations available. Many he found did. It was another way to help pay the fuel costs as long as the passenger did not expect to be entertained. The food was not bad and the accommodations were clean. More importantly, nobody was trying to introduce themselves to tell you their life story. He made the necessary travel arrangements using his newly acquired, clean, Italian passport, which he used for the first time coming from Tunis. He planned on traveling on a different ship than either of the two containers. He would arrive in New York before the containers. The Engineer made this second set of shipping arrangements without anyone's help, or more importantly, knowledge. This portion of the plan was known only to him. He needed to get his fire extinguishers to New York. Those he could not readily replace.

Chapter 31

Southport

Both Patrick and Liz worked around the yard on Saturday. No big projects but it took all morning just to neaten things up a bit and complete a few small items on the never ending "to-do" list. By early afternoon, Patrick did not feel like clamming so he called John and cancelled. Around 4:00 pm, Patrick had a call from Bill Welby. "What do you want to do about the next week? Do you want to file a motion to suppress the subpoena and get that argument started to give you some time?"

"I think we need to do that and I've been thinking about what to say in the motion."

"Any answers?"

"The Department of Justice Informant Guidelines, I think, don't allow an FBI agent to operate an informant that is actively committing violent crime."

"Go ahead."

"What about filing an affidavit under seal stating they want me to identify an informant to the Justice Department, when the Justice Department themselves could not operate that person as an informant according to their current guidelines. We have told them the source is in the Mafia. Therefore they know the person speaking to me is a member of an ongoing, violent, criminal conspiracy."

"The government has alleged that much in their LCN indictments for years," replied Welby.

"My point exactly. I don't think an FBI agent, under existing guidelines, can operate someone as an informant within the US who is an admitted member of the LCN or al-Qaeda, or any other criminal/terrorist group for that matter. The government cannot authorize an informant to be a participant in a constant state of crime."

"So it would be your position that since they cannot operate this person as an informant, under the current guidelines, they cannot demand Vespa's identity from you," Welby concluded.

"Yes, and while the guidelines do not apply to foreign counterintelligence investigations, they cannot claim this inquiry is a foreign counterintelligence investigation because they have subpoenaed me to a US criminal grand jury. Also, al-Qaeda is operating as a criminal organization in the US so the guidelines have to apply in this case," explained Patrick.

"That is an interesting point," said Welby. "Tomorrow I'll get some research started to see what kind of argument we can fashion and put it in a draft motion to quash the subpoena. This may cause a hearing to be scheduled for next Thursday, depending on how Judge West sees it. If the judge orders you to testify, I'll ask for a stay to give us time to appeal to the First Circuit."

"The good part about this miserable public circus is we can frustrate these ego maniacs and perhaps cause some intelligent discussion about the effectiveness of the current guidelines. This is an issue they have to face sooner or later but, at present, there seems to be no one willing to expend any personal or political capital on the subject. They have their heads in the sand when it comes to informants in organized crime and terrorist groups. Maybe this can start a productive political and public discussion."

"I'm so glad you are retired Mark. I would have to increase the size of my firm just to defend you if you were still an active agent."

"Do yourself a favor. The Red Sox are on at four o'clock. Watch the game. Goodbye."

Liz got up, walked across the room and turned on the TV. "I should be so glad you are retired and free from constant stress as you enter your declining years. I'm putting the pre-game show on so you can gently work your mind into a state of leisure as you watch the Red Sox win."

"You are certainly a gracious and caring lady. What else will you be doing for me today?"

"Ignoring you. You know I could shoot a lot of holes in your theory about using the guidelines to quash the subpoena."

"I know. I'm doing it just to focus attention on that problem and create some legitimate appeal issues. That way, when I refuse to tell Bottom what I know, you won't have to see me in jail on a diet of thin gruel."

"You could use a few days on a diet of thin gruel!"

"You are so mean to me," he frowned.

"Stop whining," said Liz with a smile. "On the other hand you will jack up Bottom and company a bit, and somehow I think that pleases you. Perhaps they will start acting like adults and stop playing this silly game while there is a potentially serious problem that needs to be addressed. If there were more women involved you wouldn't be having this problem. Too much testosterone involved here."

"A wise and beautiful woman you are," said Patrick turning his head as if he had a serious thought to ponder.

"Flattery does not work on me when it is so patently obvious," quipped Liz.

Chapter 32

Palermo, Sicily

John Turco and Zio Vincenzo sat under the grape arbor enjoying a glass of red wine, some olives and cheese, before the extended family sat down for the midday meal. It was just after noontime. This outside dining room was host to many "family" conversations through the years. John Turco had participated in some as a young man before going to New York to work for Maria and her father. Zio Vincenzo was not a blood uncle, but certainly he was that close in Turco's heart.

"What do you think?" asked Turco.

"The police have them surrounded. Their rooms are bugged by the police. Our bugs are still in from their last visit. We made sure they got the same room as the last time because we left the bugs in and did not have to rewire the room. So in that respect we know what the police know, which is only that they are back."

"The dock?" asked John.

"Be patient. That is why they are back. Well, two of them anyway. They have contacted us. We told them what was needed. We are waiting for the container. Our man is still talking with them and has given them some cell phone equipment. The authorities are conducting surveillance of us and them so all is in order for the next move. The police will eventually come to us as a serious member of the business community and ask for our help. It will be freely given. It has all been worked out. We will do whatever they ask regarding the container. We will be glad to help and comply with all their requests, as any good citizen would. We will be part of the solution, not part of a problem."

"That should protect our interests publicly. What about the people from Afghanistan who sent them here?" asked John.

"They understand all. We share a common goal. There will no suspicion on any of us," replied Vincenzo.

"Have we heard anything from the aeroporto?" asked John.

"Nothing yet."

"Can I have your permission to walk by the Hotel Palermo tomorrow afternoon? I would like to get a look at the three of them. I would know what they look like in person, for the future."

"That is a good idea," said Vincenzo. "Please be discreet. The area is loaded with police and we don't want them to take any note of you, nor have you inadvertently appear in any photographs."

Turco nodded his understanding.

After a nod by Zio Vincenzo to his wife, the food started to appear on the table followed by family members young and old. There seemed to be no formal seating arrangement, other than Zio Vincenzo at one end of the table and his wife of many years at the other. John Turco was already seated to Zio Vincenzo's right, but when he got up to make room for someone else, Zio Vincenzo patted his hand and nodded for him to return to that seat. He was a guest of honor. Nothing else need be said. Having the children mixed in with the adults seemed to make the children more attentive to the conversation of the elders around them. In turn, the natural smiles of the excited children seem to infuse some of the elders with instant smiles of their own. There was a reason why this midday dining tradition remained strong even in the face of adverse cultural influences now present in Sicily.

Giorgio Tomasso, a young Palermo detective, normally worked swindles perpetrated on the elderly. Like most other detectives present today, he was pulled off his regular assignment and directed to review airport tapes looking for the man in the photograph provided to him. It was a photograph of The Engineer. It was late Saturday evening when Giorgio was reviewing, for the second time, a tape from a camera that covered the airport bus stop just outside a baggage area. It was not the stop closest to this baggage area but one about thirty meters removed that caught his attention. A man, who boarded a bus, for a moment seemed to avert his face away from an obvious camera. Giorgio called over his sergeant.

Further review of the tape showed the man on the bus, but he never looked back toward the loading area. "Get the tape from the baggage area," said the sergeant.

"I already looked at that," said Giorgio.

"This time don't look at the people picking up bags. This guy only had a carry-on. Instead, look at people walking in the background and see if you can find him and an image of his face."

Giorgio complied.

About an hour later Giorgio called over to the sergeant again.

"I did what you said. I saw the man in the background passing by the carousel and heading out the door. But again, he had his face down so I could not get a look. So I pulled the tape covering the escalator coming down into the baggage area, and there he is with a full facial image. I think it is him."

The sergeant thought so too.

They pulled one more tape that covered an intersection of two concourses just before the escalator, and they could see the man had entered the intersection from Concourse B. The sergeant went to get his superior while Giorgio began tracing the man back down Concourse B to determine his arrival gate. It was easy. The man had been on the evening flight from Tunis.

"Are you crazy?" asked the bus driver. "You show me a photograph and want to know if I recognize that person as a passenger on my bus last night?" Since they had the time and place of the pickup, the bus driver was easy to identify. Since it was about the same time of evening, he was also at work and available.

"Unless there is something really unusual, I never look at their faces."

The detectives reviewed his route with him just to make sure there were no unscheduled stops. Their job was to find someone who may have seen The Engineer get off the bus. Parking garage camera recordings were being pulled. Manpower was being shifted to follow all bus opportunities that might lead them to find where The Engineer went, once on the airport shuttle bus.

Having been assigned to conduct a general but discreet inquiry at the hotel just off the airport proper, but serviced by the airport bus, the police showed the photo of The Engineer taken from the escalator security camera. The photograph also showed the clothing that he was wearing when he got on the bus. The manager and assistant manager on duty did not recall seeing the person, but a check of the registration records from the time when the bus arrived Friday evening suggested a few possibilities that had to be checked out. None of the names matched the name from the Hotel Palermo. It would take some time for the police to do background on each of the guests who checked in at this time, plus everyone else staying at the hotel. They had more than one location around the airport that needed this type of inquiry, and manpower was running short.

According to the hotel managers, there was camera coverage of both the exterior and interior of the hotel lobby. They would immediately summon in the person responsible for the video system to download and make copies of that data for the police. The police decided not to show the photograph to the entire staff at this point. They had no indication The Engineer had come to this hotel. They did not want to cause any undue attention. They would wait to review more of the guest data and wait for the chance to review the entry and lobby tapes from last evening.

The doorman heard the police were looking to see if someone checked in last night. He did not connect this inquiry with the person he saw leaving this morning. The police doing the inquiry were too inexperienced to realize the doorman is quite often a more fertile area for information about the comings and goings in a hotel. The detectives also had not been fully briefed, so they did not realize how critical their effort was.

By the early hours of Sunday morning, the hotel manager reported to the police that the employee responsible for the video system still had not answered their call, but they had left a message for him on his cell phone. They would let the police know as soon as they were in contact with the man. Yes, they would ask him to come in right away so they could access and copy the video data. It was, however, early Sunday morning and, after all, the man was single. The police understood but needed him right away, single or not. Promises were again made to find him immediately.

Chapter 33

The Engineer was not up early. Morning prayer did not seem to be an immediate concern. The cargo handler was a little surprised. He had been told he was to help an important warrior of Islam. He assumed the warrior would begin the day with morning prayer to Allah. He did not.

The Engineer first stirred around 8:00 am, and got up immediately. He declined the cargo handler's offer of coffee and instead went directly out. His first errand was to drop off three bags at a self-check bag storage facility at the ferry terminal. One bag contained his limited clothing supply and travel items. The other two bags each held a thirty-inch long fire extinguisher, each packed in its own cardboard box, much as it had come from the factory. After storing these items, The Engineer took a leisurely stroll down to the dock area.

He did not go close to the shipping company. He just wanted to get the feel of what was going on, or not going on, in the area. He was establishing a baseline for the degree of weekend morning activity in the dock area. He saw no reason to stop the noon delivery of the container. He also saw no reason to alter his backup plan.

The Engineer leisurely walked back to the area of the hotel and selected another coffee shop. He sat inside where he could get an overall view of the front of the Palermo Hotel. He was not expecting to see the two associates. He had some time to kill and thought he would use it to get a feel for the area. The Engineer wanted to see if he could observe anything suspicious to indicate the associates may have attracted police attention after going back to the shipping company. They were not well trained, and he could never be sure what they might do wrong to bring attention to themselves.

There were three surveillance teams on duty. They had been told by those monitoring the microphones that the two associates were still asleep. The associates could not move without the microphones picking up their activity, so the attention to duty on the outside was somewhat in a stand-down mode. It would remain so until they were notified the associates were awake. It was this lax state that prevented The Engineer from detecting the surveillance presence in the area. It also was this lax state that allowed him to walk around the area without being noticed by any of the surveillance teams, of which each member carried his photograph.

At 11:30 am, The Engineer left the café and started back to the cargo handler's apartment to make his final arrangements.

About fifteen minutes later, the associates were up and went to the lobby to have some coffee and a pastry. They had nothing to do until 2:00 pm, when they were scheduled to meet The Engineer in front of the hotel. Before their feet hit the pavement in front of the hotel, the police were inside the associates' room doing a search. They found the cell phones. The police inspected all the cell phones, determined their makes, models, and phone numbers. They paid particular attention to the satellite phone and even used it to place a call to headquarters so the call could be electronically analyzed for any other available internal data. This call was then deleted from the phone's call log. There were no other items of interest in the room, so everything was replaced as found. As the items were put back, they were compared to a photograph taken before each item was moved they could be returned to the exact same spot.

At exactly noon on Sunday, as directed by The Engineer, a tractor trailer carrying an overseas cargo container arrived at the shipping company. It was directed to an empty dockage slip where the container was lifted from the truck by crane and placed on the ground. The cartage company was a prominent one in Palermo, and the driver, upon being asked indirectly, indicated he had just hauled the container out of their storage yard where it had been stored for more than two weeks. The driver knew nothing more about the container other than what appeared on the shipping manifest. The truck had completed its delivery and was out of the yard within fifteen minutes.

Chapter 34

The container delivery truck had no sooner exited the yard when news of the delivery was transmitted to the surveillance teams covering the two associates. The team onsite at the shipping company was asking the team monitoring conversation inside the shipping company for any information on potential movement of the container. There was none so far. It was not much longer before Vincent Baker was notified at the FBI command center. He called Susan Crowley. He wanted her to know in case more information reached Mark Patrick through Vespa. The arrival of the container caused everyone's blood to flow more quickly. This was the first measurable sign that the potential threat had meat on its bones. There was now a factual basis on which to evaluate Vespa's information.

At 1:00 pm, The Engineer decided it was time to leave the cargo handler's apartment. His host was lying across his bed taking a nap. The Engineer walked up to the bed, took a pillow, placed it over the .32 caliber automatic in his right hand, and fired one round in the back of the cargo handler's head. Death was instantaneous. The gun made no loud noise. No neighbors were alerted that a shot had been fired. The Engineer knew the link between him and the delivery of the fire extinguishers had to be broken.

The Engineer walked out of his host's apartment building and toward the Hotel Palermo. He was early for his meeting with the two associates, but intentionally so. The Engineer intended to observe the area again before meeting with them. By 1:25 pm, he was back in the coffee shop where he had been earlier in the morning. He sat at a different table, but one with a front view of the Hotel Palermo. It was not long before he noticed something that bothered him.

At first it was the movement of people that seemed out of sequence from what he had seen a few hours earlier. It was not suspicious movement, but just movement that did not fit. He kept watching and realized it was something he was sensing but could not directly see. He could not put a finger on it. Was it nerves? His training had taught him to respect what he felt, even if he could not identify the reason behind the feeling right away.

The Engineer did not know, nor had he ever seen, John Turco. So when Turco seated himself at an outdoor table at the coffee shop across from the hotel, The Engineer did not notice him nor pay any attention to him. Turco attracted no one's attention. Turco ordered coffee and began to read his newspaper. He did notice, out of the few people on the street, some seemed to be paying particular attention to the front of the hotel. It was still just an observation but one he would not ignore.

At 1:50 pm, the surveillance teams at the hotel were notified the associates were on the move and had a meeting in front of the hotel at 2:00 pm. It was like someone barked a command to attention. Everyone on the surveillance went to full alert. This is what The Engineer now observed, and what he knew to be different from earlier that morning. He began to put faces to movement that was paying too much attention to the front of the hotel. Faces that lifted up from a newspaper too often to look at the hotel entrance. A group of three women were in conversation standing nearby, one of them constantly watching the front of the hotel. What was a feeling a few moments ago was now a fact to The Engineer. The hotel was under surveillance.

At 1:55 pm, the associates were standing on the street in front of the hotel. They appeared to be just chatting. The Engineer could see watchers around his colleagues. He took out his cell phone.

The associates' cell phone went off.

"Pronto."

"I am running a few minutes late. Why don't we meet at the shipping company?"

"Okay."

The associate put his phone away. "He is running late and wants us to meet him at the shipping company."

The other associate just nodded.

The Engineer knew that his two associates, and most likely his container, were blown. He did not know how, and right now it did not matter. He sent the associates to the shipping company in order to have the surveillance teams vacate the immediate area. The Engineer needed to make his escape. This need now took precedence over all else.

The two associates started walking. They were oblivious to their new circle of acquired friends. The surveillance teams were moving slowly but seamlessly with them. They observed the cell phone call and assumed the associates were en route to their meeting. The Engineer could see the surveillance move with the associates. He got up and went out the back door of the café, which he had noted earlier in the morning for just this possibility. "Training pays off," he could recall his instructor saying. The Engineer hoped to be able to tell the instructor how right he was.

The Engineer dropped his cell phone in a trash can and slowly walked in the opposite direction.

Turco saw the two associates, observed the call, and saw them walk off on foot after the call was terminated. It was only then that he noted the surveillance teams. He was looking for them earlier but didn't see them until the associates started moving. Not wishing to have any further involvement, he got up from his table and walked away in the opposite direction, newspaper folded under his arm. He got a good look at the associates but it would make no difference. He would never see them again.

A block away, John Turco saw a man walking at a right angle to him about ten meters away. He could not be 100 percent sure, but he thought it was the person in the photograph called The Engineer. Then he saw the man turn and look back over his shoulder. He could see a look of concern on the man's face. It was unmistakable. Turco did not know what to do. The man started moving more quickly, and now seemed to be looking around himself even more. Turco decided to do nothing, not because he was afraid, but because it was made clear to him that he was only there to get a look and observe. He knew he could recognize The Engineer if he ever saw him again. He continued on in a different direction but one that took him back to Zio Vincenzo so he could report what he had observed.

Chapter 35

The two associates were seated in the office of the shipping company speaking with their contact.

"The container came in at noon. It's sitting on the pier. We expect to have it loaded by tomorrow afternoon and on its way by Tuesday evening. Do you have the rest of the money?"

"No. The money is carried by our friend. He should be here any moment. He was to meet us in front of the hotel but called and said he was a few minutes late and would see us here."

The electronic surveillance team immediately sent this information to the outside physical surveillance teams. If The Engineer showed up, the decision had been made to arrest all three. Now there had to be at least twenty-five pairs of eyes on the lookout for The Engineer.

The contact decided to see what the associates knew about the container. He also knew their conversation was an open line to the police.

"Do you want to inspect the container or check its security?"

"No," said one.

"Well, it's sealed, so if you want to look you need to break that seal. Otherwise our international shipping seal will be put on before we load it onto the ship."

"You can wait and ask him if he wants, to but it's of no matter to us."

"Want a coffee?"

"Okay."

The coffee was made as the associates watched a soccer game, which never seemed to end, on TV.

After coffee, the contact said, "I can't hang around here all day. I was only here to do you guys a favor. If he is not coming, I would like to close up."

The associates looked at each other quizzically.

"Why don't you call him?" asked the contact.

"He has our number, we don't have his."

"What happens if he gets hit by a bus?"

Neither one responded.

"How do you expect to ship this to New York? On credit?"

The associates said nothing and looked at each other.

"Here. This is my cell number. Call me sometime today to let me know what you want to do. Give me your cell number."

One of the associates complied.

"Do you have anyone to check with about getting the money?"

"We will have an answer for you after we find our friend. He must be delayed."

"Okay. I will talk to you later today."

Those on the electronic surveillance team thought the person in the shipping office was a big help. He seemed to ask the same questions they would like to have asked. This person did a pretty good job of finding out what the associates knew. It didn't appear they had much knowledge or were concealing anything.

The associates returned to the Hotel Palermo and resumed watching soccer. They were overheard conjecturing about what happened to The Engineer. They questioned why he did not follow through and meet them at the shipping office. They were not totally invested in the process and were quite willing to watch the game and wait. By evening the status had not changed. The associates went to dinner, took a leisurely stroll, went back to the hotel room and watched a movie. When they went to bed, they still had not heard from The Engineer. They did not seem as confident as earlier in the afternoon.

The Italian authorities were in constant communication with the FBI Operations Center. Everyone was willing to let the status quo remain in effect at least until morning to see if The Engineer materialized. Meanwhile, they would all have to consider what to do if he did not.

Some were in favor of taking the two birds in hand, along with the container, and starting an all-out public search for The Engineer. Assuming the container was full of arms and or explosives, they could bring substantial weapons charges against all of them even if they didn't know the entire plan. Better to be safe than sorry.

The other view was to continue the surveillance and wait until the other side took some sort of action. If they had control of the terrorists' supplies, what damage could they cause without them? If the surveillance of the two associates was made, they could always take them into custody. This was a more aggressive approach. Experienced agents knew something could always go wrong with the surveillance and the two associates could literally wander away. If that happened, heads would roll and blame would be assigned. Careers would fail.

The view from the Italian side was what one might expect from a government that changed its leaders every few years, or less. "Why should we take the responsibility? Let the Americans tell us what they want us to do. If it goes right, we are part of the success against terror. If things do not go well, it was the decision of the Americans that was ill-advised and the Italians were only assisting in an American-directed endeavor."

This was the thought process that prevailed among the Italian leadership. It was not the thought process of the troops on the ground, but then the leadership had not asked for their input. The leadership also suspected that the Americans were not telling them everything they knew and, at this point, they thought it best not to ask.

Back at the FBI Operations Center, Vincent Baker and Bob Wilkins had been on the phone with Director Carter Simms, who was also in contact with his counterpart at Homeland Security. Earlier, the CIA considered itself the primary operator in Italy. They now took the position they were only assisting in an FBI-directed investigation.

Everyone knew it was decision making time. The Engineer was still missing. They had a container of potentially dangerous material. They could not let the container transit any farther. The Homeland Security Director was "waiting to be advised" of the FBI's next step. The CIA Director was willing to assign "whatever resources the FBI needed."

"Everybody is protecting their butt. Some collegiality we have in the anti-terrorism and intelligence community. I am certainly glad our 9/11 experience has put us in a better position to act as a unified government in the fight against terrorism," quipped Baker. It was clear he was exasperated with the report from Carter Simms.

"They are just protecting themselves from an operation they think may be going bad," said Wilkins.

"It is what it is," said Simms. "We got things on hold for a few hours, so let's think this over and see what we can come up with. We need to give Palermo our input before morning and before the associates get up."

"The Italians can make sure the container isn't going anyplace. It will give us a little time to see if Patrick comes up with anything new," said Baker.

They all had some things to do, and a lot to think about.

Chapter 36

It was late Sunday morning before the hotel employee in charge of the video system responded to the messages on his cell phone. He had been to a party, met a girl, turned his phone off and had not gone home. He agreed to come in and download the lobby video camera and the one from the front of the hotel.

The captain in charge of the Italian detectives assigned to do the airport inquiry had not checked his cell phone or home phone messages after getting home late Saturday. He was tired and went to bed. The commander was not aware the detectives had identified The Engineer getting off the plane from Tunis, and getting on the airport shuttle bus. While the identification was not airtight, it looked like good information. Because the commander did not know, he could not pass this information on to the anti-terrorism division that had assigned him this investigation.

The commander was still at home late Sunday morning when the airport detectives telephoned him to advise the inquiries regarding the bus were negative. They still did not know where The Engineer exited the bus. They did think they would soon have the video from the hotel to determine if The Engineer had gotten off there. The commander asked what they were talking about. They explained the messages they had left the night before on his home and cell phones, and what had been done to identify The Engineer and determine his movements. The commander was now embarrassed at his lapse in checking his messages and decided he would not report this "possible Engineer sighting" until they had "firm" information. Giorgio and his sergeant thought the man had gone a little soft.

The associates were up earlier than usual Sunday morning. The listeners at the Hotel Palermo could tell they were now concerned that The Engineer had failed to show up yesterday and had not called. They were clearly beginning to think something was wrong and they needed to start thinking about what to do. There was nervousness in their voices that was not present before. The associates went down to the lobby for some coffee and rolls.

They looked around as if their answer might be in the lobby. It wasn't. In the elevator on the way back to the room, the associates made a decision to leave Palermo immediately. They had no further assignments at this point, and if anyone questioned them, they could say The Engineer had abandoned them.

The listeners heard noises, which they correctly interpreted as the associates packing their few belongings. They alerted the outside watch.

The on-site Italian police commander immediately requested instructions on what to do if the associates checked out of the hotel. The commander was advised they were in the process of getting information from the US authorities and would be back to him shortly.

It was too late.

By the time the associates hit the street, they were now on full alert. Their senses were activated to a higher level than existed over the last few days. They were worried. A worried animal is far more intuitive and cautious. There were no taxis at the stand, and rather than wait for one to be called they started to walk. Within a block they felt the movement around them that should not have been there this time of morning. They felt the surveillance. One panicked, dropped his bag, and started to run. The onsite commander gave the arrest order. Within moments the two associates were in custody, separated, and on their way to police headquarters. No one spoke to them. Hoods were placed over their heads. They were left to wonder about their future.

The onsite commander notified his superiors of the arrests and noted he had no choice once the associates started to run. His standing orders were not to lose them, and to take them into custody rather than lose them. The information was passed on to the FBI operations center. No one disagreed with their actions. They did what had to be done. The anti-terrorism division now had a container of what they thought were probably illegal weapons of some sort. They had two unknown males in custody who could face a lot of time in jail for the weapons alone, without even considering possession of phony passports. Lastly, they had a potential bomb maker and al-Qaeda operative who was missing. Had he been spooked or was he just temporarily out of contact? Why had he not shown up? Where should they search now?

It was agreed that they would continue the surveillance on the container and the shipping office in the event The Engineer showed up. Two Italian anti-terrorism agents were stationed inside the associates' hotel room in case The Engineer showed up. The outside surveillance of the Hotel Palermo would continue in place. The instructions to all participants were that if The Engineer was located, he should be taken into custody. Overt investigation would not begin until they had an opportunity to fully sort things out and get an idea of what the associates might have to say, if anything. The associates' arrests would not be publicly reported.

Chapter 37

Palermo

John Turco reported back to Zio Vincenzo. He had seen the man in the photo going the opposite way of the two associates. The man appeared to be concerned. John thought he might have made the Italian surveillance, as he had, when the two associates started toward the shipping office. Zio Vincenzo already had a report from the shipping office and was informed minutes after the associates were taken into custody. He put his own people in the shipping yard to make sure nothing untoward happened to the container. He was awaiting a report from his contacts in the police to see what the story was with the two associates. He had already given a full report to Aldo Torino in New York. It was decided that John Turco would remain with Zio Vincenzo a while longer to see how things worked out, as he was the only one on their team who could recognize The Engineer.

Washington, DC

The FBI Terrorist Operations Center got an oral report of the arrests. They were actually in the process of asking the Italians to arrest the associates if it looked like the surveillance was made. They had correctly concluded the associates would now be on full alert, given The Engineer's failure to appear. In such a case, the associates could have standing instructions from The Engineer as to what they were to do. A well prepared terrorist operation would have such alternative plans in place. Baker was actually happy the onsite commander acted with initiative. Baker told the commander this when he personally called to thank him.

Palermo

None of the agencies knew the results of the investigation at the Palermo airport. The data from the hotel cameras had been copied, picked up, and delivered back to Giorgio Tomasso and his sergeant on Sunday afternoon. They immediately began viewing the data. Now they clearly could see The Engineer, with his bag, getting off the bus at the hotel Friday evening and registering at the hotel. Since they had the exact time and the photo of the clerk checking him in, the details of the Engineer's room would soon be available. The new camera data from the front of the hotel clearly showed The Engineer being picked up early Saturday morning in front of the hotel. It was a vehicle driven by a man wearing an airport cargo handler's uniform. They were able to view the license plate on the vehicle as it pulled away from the front of the hotel. The Engineer had his bag and did not appear to be coming back. All hotel security tapes were being obtained from that moment until the present to determine if The Engineer had returned at any time.

The owner of the vehicle was confirmed to be a current cargo handler at the airport. Only at this point did the captain at the airport notify the anti-terrorism division of the earlier, and now fully confirmed, identification of The Engineer. The major in charge of the Italian anti-terrorism division was dumbfounded that the initial information had not been provided to them on Saturday. It was now Sunday evening, and they were learning for the first time details about the arrival of The Engineer back in Palermo, and about a car that had picked him up from the hotel Saturday morning. They had a new lead to locate The Engineer. Several teams of terrorism investigators were dispatched immediately to the airport to oversee the inquiry. The captain was relieved of his duty. Other officers were assigned to occupy positions at the hotel until it could be determined if The Engineer had returned.

The anti-terrorism division immediately contacted the CIA and the FBI operations center to provide this new information and to set up the next course of action. Most importantly, a team was dispatched to the apartment of the cargo handler once it was determined that he was on a day-off. Surveillance was set up outside the apartment while a phone tap was being arranged. A walk-through of the apartment building told them nothing. The building concierge was located. Yes, he knew the cargo handler. No, he had not seen him go out today. No, he did not recognize the photograph of The Engineer. The concierge was taken into protective custody until they could sort this out.

A telephone call was placed to the apartment. There was no answer. Adjacent apartments were quietly vacated. Listening devices were drilled through the walls. No sounds. Video feeds were inserted and no movement was observed. A SWAT team was ordered to make a quiet entry and secure the apartment. They did and found the cargo handler dead in his bed.

After insuring no one else was in the apartment, they quietly backed out while the surveillance continued. A search was ordered to see if the cargo handler's car was parked in the area. The body was not going anywhere and they wanted to talk this over before bringing public attention to the apartment. The cargo handler's body remained in his apartment Sunday night while others watched to see if The Engineer would show up.

Chapter 38

Southport

After attending the 9:00 am service at St. Mark's Episcopal Church, Patrick and Liz went to the Bluefish for breakfast. Surprisingly, it was not crowded.

"The usual?" asked the waitress, not even bothering to bring a menu. She did bring the most important items of the moment, two cups of coffee. Mark added some milk and Liz some cream. Liz nodded in the affirmative to the waitress, adding "please." Mark was thinking of changing his standard order of eggs-over-easy with bacon and dry sourdough toast to one of the fruit-based waffle dishes, just to see what the waitress would say. But she looked frazzled this morning, so he also just nodded and said "Thanks."

"What do you want to do today?" asked Liz .

"It's such a nice day with warm sunshine; I'd like to work around the yard. A few more garden areas need some cleaning out and I would like to start getting my pots ready for the tomato plants. What about you?"

"I don't feel like much. I'm tired today. I think a long, solitary walk would be nice if you don't mind."

"Why don't we hook up around game time and listen to it together on the patio. We can have a little lunch around mid-afternoon or start an early supper."

Around 3:00 pm, Patrick made an administrative decision to start supper. After supper, he thought, they could head back early to Boston. Liz had a trial starting Monday and could use a little prep time in Boston. Patrick looked at the two-dozen clams he bought after deciding not to go clamming. He would make the clam sauce. The clams were soaking in a pail of fresh water.

The meal took half an hour to fix, and it restored Patrick and Liz back to their prior state of good humor, which seemed to have been temporarily misplaced.

"What do you have tomorrow?" asked Liz.

"I need to talk with Welby about filing the motion to dismiss the subpoena. I have to pay a little attention to some of our creditors by paying bills. I also have some writing to do, and will make some tactical plan to stay on your good side."

Liz smiled and picked up the plates. If one cooked, the other cleaned up. When done, they drove back to Boston. The Red Sox won, so it was a good afternoon.

Boston

Monday morning Patrick called Bill Welby asking about the motion to dismiss the subpoena.

"I thought about it," said Welby. "I know how you get when you get annoyed. But Judge West will expect me to act like an adult, so I am going to call Bottom and talk with him before I file a motion for the world to read."

Patrick said nothing.

Welby continued. "I'll tell them my point is simple. You cannot subpoena what you already have access to. If FBI Washington has chosen to cut you out, talk with them. Don't subpoena us. If you continue, we'll ask for a hearing and subpoena those who have the information. We'll ask questions and make public the information my client has turned over to the FBI."

"What about Bottom feeding the media and hinting I've committed some crime?"

"I'll suggest to Mr. Bottom that he may want to point out to Ms. Bell that he may have been rash in his comments about you, and it was all a misunderstanding."

"What if he doesn't do that?"

"Let's take one step at a time and resolve the subpoena. I think DOJ Washington feels that Mr. Bottom is out of control and may wish to discuss that with him personally."

"You've talked with someone at Justice, haven't you?" Patrick was suspicious that Welby had worked this out to avoid an adverse public display between Justice and the FBI. Not good for the public image.

"Are you authorizing me as your lawyer to work this out, subject to your approval in the end, of course?"

Patrick thought Bill Welby had such a nice way about him when he wanted to tell Patrick to keep quiet, quit being a pain, and let him resolve it.

"As you see fit," said Patrick. He hung up not wanting to waste any more of Welby's time. He knew something had changed the discussion.

Patrick went for a light lunch at Sal's. It was difficult to do. He needed to lose a few pounds. He ordered a hamburger with lettuce, tomato and onion. Sal looked at him.

"You down in Southport last weekend?" asked Sal.

"Yea, we came back last night."

"On Saturday those guys that normally wear suits were in dungarees and spending a lot of time looking up your way. They were constantly in here for coffee. They must think I'm blind. Anyway, I heard they were related to the guy the police stopped the other day up on Hanover Street. I haven't seen them since then."

"Thanks Sal. I will explain later."

"No need," said Sal as he left to wait on someone else.

When Patrick left Sal's, he stopped by Franklin Wharf to see Peter. "I heard my friends were back this weekend?"

"They haven't been around since Saturday," said Peter without looking up from tickets he was sorting.

"Did you work Saturday?"

"Nope."

"Okay, I'll bite. How do you know they were around if you weren't working?"

"You don't have a need to know," said Peter.

Patrick let out a belly laugh. Peter looked up, smiled, and went back to his tickets. Patrick went upstairs. There was a message on the home phone to call Vince Baker as soon as possible.

Patrick removed the FBI-donated cell phone from his desk and called Baker. Baker would expect him to use the encrypted phone that he no longer carried.

Vince Baker summarized what had gone on in Palermo over the last couple of days. The two associates had returned to the hotel and set up the delivery of a container for noon Sunday, which did occur. They thought The Engineer was supposed to be there for a 2:00 pm meeting Sunday but he never showed. The associates did not appear concerned until Monday morning, at which point one of them made the surveillance and started to run. Both were taken into custody.

Baker told him the investigation at the airport had some delayed reporting. It was now clear The Engineer came back from Tunis Friday night, stayed over at the hotel, and was picked up Saturday morning by a guy who worked as a cargo handler at the airport. They traced the cargo handler to a residence on the outskirts of Palermo. They made a quiet entry Sunday night and found the cargo handler dead, with a small caliber bullet in the back of his head.

"What do the associates have to say for themselves?" asked Patrick.

"Nothing, but they haven't been challenged yet. They don't seem to realize the Italians know their passports are phony. The Italian anti-terrorism unit is waiting to get a clearer picture of what was going on before speaking with them. Each one is in solitary at present. They still have the apartment, hotel and shipping office staked out in case The Engineer returns."

"What's in the container?"

"They haven't opened it. They're waiting for court authority. They took a dog trained for explosives for a walk by the container. The dog reacted. In fact the dog went nuts."

"It looks like Vespa's information is right on."

"I wanted to give you this update in case you were contacted by your friends. There are some specific things we are doing, which I do not need to go into at present. If you hear anything please get in touch with the command center, ASAP."

"Okay."

"The Director dispatched two Evidence Recovery Teams (ERT) and a half-dozen agents to work with the Italian anti-terrorism police. I think they are there now. They will work with the Italians to gather and process physical evidence from the cargo handler's apartment. They will process the container at some point. We don't want to lose any potential forensic evidence and the Italians asked for the ERT assistance."

Patrick grunted.

"By the way, your attorney has talked with DOJ and that subpoena issue will be resolved shortly."

Patrick said nothing.

"One last thing," said Baker, "would you start carrying that phone we gave you? We can't use the encryption if you don't carry the phone."

That comment immediately alerted Patrick. Did they have their own surveillance on him? Was he paranoid? No, they could not resist the temptation. They were tracking the GPS on the phone they gave him. Even they wanted to know where he was. Tough luck for them. The encrypted phone would remain in his desk.

Later in the afternoon Patrick went up to the coffee shop for an espresso. His new cell phone rang and he went outside to answer it.

"Mark, I want to let you know what we heard from our end."

It was Vespa.

"So, what's happening?" asked Patrick.

Vespa began to relay information furnished by Zio Vincenzo and John Turco, who had returned from Palermo. Patrick learned a few things that he had not heard from Vince Baker.

"We wanted our own presence in Palermo," said Vespa. "The person we sent was one of our own. He observed the associates waiting for someone in front of the hotel about 2:00 pm. He saw one of the associates take a call on a cell phone and then the two of them walked toward the docks. Our person noted the surveillance moving with the two associates."

"I guess they had a lot of people there because they didn't want to lose them," said Patrick.

"Our person was well acquainted with the photograph of The Engineer that was circulated to the police. When he walked away in the opposite direction, he spotted The Engineer looking at the two associates and the surveillance that was moving with them. The Engineer appeared disturbed but in control as he walked quickly in the opposite direction."

"So your people think The Engineer spotted the surveillance when the associates started to move?"

"Yes, that is how our man saw it at the time."

Vespa continued. "You know about the cargo handler that was found dead in his apartment?"

"Yes."

Vespa continued, "The police will find out that he was a small time smuggler linked to a Camorra family in Naples. He was not a member, just an associate. The Camorra used him as a link with some of the Russian groups in the Balkans. One of our associates at the airport hotel knew the cargo handler. He used to buy small amounts of drugs and some knock-off handbags from him. This associate happened to be in front of the hotel Saturday morning and saw the cargo handler pull up in his car. The cargo handler had just gotten off work. Our person was just getting ready to say hello to the cargo handler when he saw a man with a bag come out of the hotel and get in the cargo handler's car. They drove off. He thought nothing of it until the police showed the picture of The Engineer later Sunday at the hotel. This man did not tell the police anything about what he saw. The police saw the whole thing on the hotel entrance video cameras anyway. The police traced the cargo handler once they got the license plate of his car from the video."

"So The Engineer knew the deceased and met him at the hotel Saturday morning."

"Yes, and the police traced The Engineer back to the Friday night flight from Tunis," said Vespa.

"You know as much as the police."

"Pretty much," said Vespa.

"There are explosives in the container. The bomb sniffing dog reacted before it even got close," said Patrick.

"What are your people doing now?" asked Vespa.

"Just listening to what comes in. They have the container, the two associates, and the cargo handler is dead. The associates are not jailed in the general population, so no one can talk with them. From what the person in the shipping office said, the associates appear to know little about the container. Can you let us know if you hear any more about the cargo handler?"

"We have a relationship with the people in Naples. We have made initial inquiries but cannot ask too much. When they find out he was murdered in Palermo, they will probably ask us to use our contacts to find out what happened. That will give us a chance to see what they will tell us about the cargo handler's recent activities."

"Can you let me know immediately if you find out anything about the deceased?"

"Yes. By the way, I understand you have made the papers and are suspected of being a tax cheat."

Patrick started to get angry but realized Vespa was teasing him. She did have a sense of humor. He laughed instead.

"Yes, but that's only a cover story I created to protect some Martians that landed in my back yard. After what I know now, I expect the subpoena will be re-thought and will not be an issue going forward."

"I will let you know if anything new is learned."

"Thank you." Patrick snapped the phone shut. He was concerned that the two associates had little to tell. The fact that the cargo handler was dead indicated he was in possession of information that The Engineer thought required a murder to protect. Concentrating on the cargo handler was critical. Patrick knew that Vince Baker concluded the same thing. That's why the ERT was sent over to work the crime scene. They would need all the help they could get.

Patrick went back inside and re-ordered his espresso. The old one was now cold.

Chapter 39

The Atlantic Ocean

The Engineer had been comfortably at sea almost two days. His attention to planning had paid off handsomely. His second shipment had been delivered to the port of Naples, where it was loaded onto a freighter. It would be delivered to New York City. The Sicilians were not the only ones who had a reputation for bringing disputed goods into the United States without inspection. He had been put in contact with elements of the Camorra of Naples by the baggage handler. This was the group for which the baggage handler dedicated his smuggling talents. For the right price, they would deliver anything and they were not as curious as the Sicilians. It cost a little more with the Camorra, but not enough to make a difference. He had the container delivered by truck to the Port of Naples, where no one questioned anything. The Camorra reigned supreme. At one point in the history of Naples, the city government paid the Camorra to collect their port taxes. The merger of organized crime and government always produced strange bedfellows. The freighter with the container would ship out tonight. The Engineer would be in New York when it arrived.

The Engineer thought his accommodations were quite comfortable. The food was very good. The crew was courteous and, most of all, non-inquisitive. He was an Italian citizen traveling on an Italian passport on an Italian freighter sailing from Naples to New York. His Italian was good, but a native speaker he was not. Under the present circumstances, he did not have to do more than grunt a few words and he was left alone.

The Engineer had picked up his bags from the Palermo ferry terminal-locker immediately after observing the surveillance of the two associates at the hotel. He had earlier purchased a ticket and made a berth reservation for that day's ferry from Palermo to Naples. His associates had no idea of his travel plans, and could inform no one when questioned. There was no problem in boarding the ferry earlier than other passengers. He did not want to be seen by any of the authorities in the waiting area. He presented the steward with a generous tip and the steward immediately understood that the available waiting facilities in the dockside terminal were not as comfortable as they should be for a man of The Engineer's generosity.

The Engineer did not ruminate over what happened in Palermo. There could be many explanations, but none of them could impact his future plans. He would waste no energy worrying over the past. He needed to review his plan and make any necessary adjustments. He had oversupplied himself with the necessary armaments in the event he lost any of his materials. While he would like to have it all, he could do well with just half. He also had the option of making a contact with another cell in the United States to pick up more supplies, if that became necessary. His present feeling was that the need did not justify the risk.

The Engineer lay on his bunk sorting things out in his mind. He recalled his first conversations with Mustaf ben Afad about his plan to attack America directly. They were in the tribal area of the mountains in Pakistan. The old leadership was still in place. The Engineer was making his point that he wanted al-Qaeda to adopt and support his plan, yet he did not want the plan known to the general leadership of al-Qaeda. He had his reasons, as he explained to Afad.

"Information about the 9/11 attacks did leak out. But the Americans and the Western intelligence were not clever or coordinated enough to put the information pieces together to foresee and prevent the attacks. I don't want to take such a chance again. I want to talk to you about a plan. If you don't like it, it stops here. If you do like it, we can make it happen and no one needs to know the entire picture except you, me, and our leader. I think you will see why if you wish to proceed."

"Go ahead," said Afad. He knew The Engineer was probably the best bomb maker al-Qaeda had. He had been active in Afghanistan and Pakistan on their behalf and was always effective at what he did. The Engineer had been sent several times to Europe to teach some splinter groups bomb making. The Engineer was used by many in al-Qaeda as a consultant for their creative bomb making ideas. Afad did not mind being asked to present The Engineer's plan to their al-Qaeda leader. Afad knew their leader was desperately seeking a way to show the membership he was still capable of conducting bold and effective jihad.

The Engineer continued, "The attacks on 9/11 were a great success, but they have not been followed up. The Americans have gone back to their normal lives. We need to do more now."

"We attack all over the world. Everyone knows al-Qaeda is still alive and well," responded Afad, knowing what he said was not true.

"We need to get out of this war of attrition and do something that will shock the world into fearing us anew," said Afad. "We did a great terrorist act on 9/11, but the fear of our terrorism has diminished with time. The buildings have been quickly cleared. They had their funerals and mourned.

151

They had their investigating commission. Then slowly everyone drifted back to normal. The economy of New York did not collapse. The 9/11 attack did not have the lasting effect of creating a fear of terror that was hoped for. I propose that this time our attack leaves results that cannot be quickly cleaned up. These results will be seen on the nightly news for years to come. I propose we destroy at least one or, preferably, two famous American cities. We will destroy what a city needs to function, but we will leave it standing as a monument to their inability to protect themselves from our attacks."

"Will this be a martyr's mission for you?" Afad asked.

"No, I can serve Allah more if I survive this mission. Others will be involved who may have to be martyrs, but not me." Both men smiled just a little.

"Tell me your idea."

The Engineer did.

After a few weeks of waiting for an answer, Afad finally got back to The Engineer. "You have been authorized to use two cells we have recruited. They are all US citizens who want to join our jihad. They will go on the Hajj and after that continue to our training camp. You will oversee their training from a distance. While the two teams will train together, they will not be allowed to have social interaction. They will be using false names even during training. You will determine the specifics of their training needed to implement your plan, and I will see to it. This is part of our long-term project to develop warriors from among US Islamic followers. It will be far easier for them to move about as citizens. It will be far more hurtful when it is realized that Islamic US citizens are part of our jihad. The political value of US citizens participating in these attacks will add greatly to the fear, confusion, hatred, and distrust the attacks will generate."

"The training period will take three months to complete. It will be six months before the teams are ready and in place," said The Engineer.

"Yes. Meanwhile you can utilize the information we have developed on the sale of nuclear materials to arrange your own purchases that cannot be linked to us. Western intelligence has offered huge rewards for any information about our efforts to obtain nuclear material of any kind. I don't want to expose what we have already accomplished by tying that work to this mission. We have been negotiating for some time to obtain an actual nuclear device. We hope for success in the near future. I will give you what information you need to make necessary contacts, and the money to supply yourself with the radioactive material needed."

The Engineer nodded his agreement. There would be parallel operations to purchase nuclear materials, carried out without the possibility of one exposing the other. This also insured his operation would be more secure.

Afad laid out the terms and manner in which he would provide The Engineer with money. The money would be available to The Engineer in increments as he accomplished various milestones agreed upon in advance.

Afad was good to his word. The two teams were brought to the training camps. They were in fact part of a larger effort of al-Qaeda to recruit American Muslims into the ranks of the Martyrdom Battalion. The money came as promised. Doors were opened to The Engineer without specific questions being asked. The last payment in Tunis, along with the new al-Qaeda leader's blessing, gave The Engineer all he needed to put the final plan into action.

The Engineer felt the comfortable vibration and steady drone of the ship's engines an aid to his deliberations. As he lay in his bunk, he had a soothing feeling as he mentally laid out his course of action after he landed in New York. He wanted to be as dramatic as possible with the resources he still had available. He always held out the possibility he would consolidate his operation. At present he believed that was not his best course of action.

Chapter 40

Washington, DC

While The Engineer was lying in his ship's bunk, Vince Baker returned a call from Patrick.

"Have any good news from the source?

"We have spoken, but not a lot is new. They seem to know what you know. There are a few minor differences."

"Such as?" queried Baker.

"One of their people was also watching the hotel, saw the associate take a cell phone call, and then walk toward the dock area. Their person next saw The Engineer observing the entire scene from a distance then turn and walk in the opposite direction. The person recognized The Engineer from the photo.

"Where did The Engineer go?"

"Unknown. The individual was there only to observe and did not follow him."

"Where did this person get the photo?" Baker's voice carried a snide tone in the delivery.

"He was probably the same person that provided the photograph to Vespa, who in turn gave it to me, which I gave to you, if you'll recall. We only have our photos courtesy of these people." Patrick was developing a tone of his own in response to Baker.

"When were you going to tell us about their having someone who saw The Engineer there?" Baker did not like what Patrick said and continued with his negative tone.

"I just did. If there was any delay it was because I was speaking to my lawyer, whose fee I am personally paying, about a court appearance I have scheduled for Thursday to answer a subpoena from the same government you are working for."

"It hasn't been cancelled?" said Baker in a somewhat incredulous voice.

"What did I just say?"

Baker said nothing in response.

Baker continued after a moment's pause: "I was also calling because they opened the container in Palermo. The contents were something else. We were quite surprised at the type of armaments and munitions found. It is more advanced material than normal for the average terrorist, if that makes any sense. It was all heavy-duty attack material, including laser guided anti-tank 66 mm rockets, heavy machine guns with armor piercing rounds, high explosive grenade launchers, plus other goodies one may want in order to take out a fortified position."

"What does all that mean?"

"We don't know, but I haven't finished. There was close to 2,500 pounds of C-4 and Symtex. The Symtex was old and probably from the Eastern Bloc arena, but in good shape. The C-4 may be what we gave the Northern Alliance when they became our allies. We're running the taggants so we'll have a general idea of where the plastic was manufactured and sold. We need to find out where it's been so we know more about The Engineer. In any event, it's all serious stuff."

"Anything else you think I should know?"

Baker hesitated and Patrick picked up on the hesitation.

"There is more that concerns us, but at present I am limited as to what I can say."

"I understand. I told you all along I am only a conduit and I don't need or want to know your secrets."

"Look, Mark, this is very serious. We have a concern that would make these armaments seem like a minor problem, if you get my drift."

Patrick was silent for a moment then said: "Is it intelligence you have picked up that is causing your concern, or does it relate to more things in the container that you don't want to discuss?"

"When your source provided some bona fides for us to check out, we learned about the arrest of an individual and the recovery of very dangerous material that came from the old Soviet Union. We're concerned that some of that material is in play with this case. That is based on physical evidence, not intel."

Patrick said nothing.

"I'm telling you this in the event your source comes up with more information regarding this material."

Patrick ran through some possibilities in his mind. He knew the two associates were not talking and appeared to know little. He asked, "What about the cargo handler? Figured out his role yet?"

"He's a small time smuggler for the Camorra out of Naples with some ties in Tbilisi. We are concerned about what was brought into Palermo on a flight from Tbilisi Saturday morning. He unloaded it before he picked up The Engineer from the airport hotel."

"And important enough to get him killed in the process?"

"That is exactly our concern. I'd like Susan Crowley to meet you for a conversation. We need you to pick up on any subtleties with your source that may be helpful in figuring this out."

"Direct questions to the source?" asked Patrick.

"Not at this time. We're still running down the cargo handler's background, bank accounts, cell records, relatives, travel, to get a picture of who he is and where he has been lately. We don't know if the Camorra had a hand in any of this? We ask you to have an open ear for the time being. Is that okay?"

"Not a problem. I'll wait to hear from Susan."

When he hung up, Baker felt badly that he had not told Patrick the details about radiation detected by the evidence collection team from the cargo handler's apartment, his locker at the airport, and the trunk of his car.

They also had the same radiation readings from the cargo door area of the airplane, which they located in Georgia. There was a trail of radiation cookies that told them the cargo handler had unloaded something that was giving off radiation. He had put it in his locker and in the trunk of his car, and later taken it into his apartment. From there the trail was cold. Now a reason existed as to why someone would murder the cargo handler.

The Italian police identified The Engineer as a visitor to the cargo handler's apartment. He was seen by neighbors Sunday morning, leaving with three bags. Patrick did not need to know all that. He needed to know enough to handle talking with the source, but no more. It was the need to know routine. The old World War II saying was "loose lips sink ships." A secret can be kept if only one person knows it. The Bureau did not believe that one agent should be discussing matters with another agent unless that person had a need to know. Following that thought, Baker decided that Patrick did not need to know all of the details, just the drift of their major concerns. That is what he got. Baker ignored the nagging feeling that he was treating Patrick shabbily.

Chapter 41

The Atlantic Ocean

The Engineer continued from his bunk to recall his private conversations with Afad, who asked him, "Why should we use a dirty bomb? Shouldn't we wait until we have something more powerful available?"

The Engineer immediately responded, "If you explode a nuclear device in a city, the city will disappear. Perhaps those that support you will feel that the world is not ready for such an act. They could turn on you fearing you might even do this to your friends with whom you have a disagreement. Perhaps it would make you too dangerous. A 'friend' may find it justifiable to act against you and curry favor with those seeking your elimination."

The Engineer knew this statement could anger Afad and get him in trouble, but he knew he had to address this issue directly or Afad would have no respect for him.

"Is it not true the West considers a dirty bomb to be a weapon of mass disruption, and not as serious as a nuclear weapon attack? Don't they denigrate the effects of a dirty bomb?" Afad asked.

"You have read the literature. Yes, these are dirty bombs. But the reality is they never have had to deal with one. They have just talked about it. They never have had to deal with its effects. I say let us put them to the test. They will fail. They have wasted their time and are not prepared."

"Please explain that further?" asked Afad.

The Engineer knew that Afad's questions were those of their leader, who was using Afad to test his competence to carry out this plan. The Engineer expected this and was quite willing to carry on this conversation with the leader, through Afad.

"There are continuous efforts in the American Congress to force the administration to protect its citizens from any form of radiological attack," said The Engineer. "Their discussions reflect the concerns of the American people, and their fear of nuclear terrorism. Congress is a great source of information on the state of preparedness for a dirty bomb. Members of Congress tell the world what the administration has not done to protect their constituents. They complain that their proposed cures languish because of a lack of interest by the administration. They have gone so far as to claim that Congress actually has passed laws that have been denied implementation, even after signed into law by the President."

The Engineer continued, "They do not have a national system to detect the movement of nuclear material. The administration responds by saying the laws passed are not funded by Congress, or that the laws cannot practically or physically be implemented. They never say they won't do it. They say it is just a matter of time, money, and equipment that works. In short, they have made none of this a realized priority. That is why my plan will cause all of this failed policy to be exposed. The result will be a demoralized public with little confidence in their political leadership and in their government to protect them."

"You think the disruption you plan will result in contentious national discussions about their lack of effective planning since 9/11?" asked Afad.

The Engineer responded quickly, "When you see absolute gridlock in one city as everyone tries to flee from reported radiation, every other city in the US will realize they also are trapped. Their evacuation routes will fail. They cannot manage normal commuting traffic, much less panicked efforts by a citizen population forced to flee a city. Can you imagine a better example of governmental impotency?"

"This will lead to assigning blame and political paralysis?" asked Afad.

"Yes. Absolutely," said The Engineer. "Instead of a city disappearing and all the cameras looking at a hole in the ground, my plan will cause more than physical destruction and deaths. The city will stand visible but unpopulated, and useless for many years. Can you imagine the financial loss that will be caused? Think of the insurance claims and lawsuits? What impact will this have on the economies of other US cities? Will people want to live in US cities? Where will they go?"

"I am still unclear about why you think cleanup is not a possible or viable option," said Afad.

"I have all the literature on the problems associated with cleaning up nuclear contamination in a city environment. I will submit it for your and our leader's review. I also will provide statements by various members of Congress on the subject. I also will provide comments of civilian experts who speak to the government's lack of adequate preparation and education of their first responders and the overall public. I can show you statements of comfort to the public that are known to be wrong."

"Give me some more detail on the cleanup of contamination," said Afad, probing more deeply.

"The technology to clean up a nuclear contaminated area is described as "muck and truck." There is no science to remove nuclear contamination. The only method is to physically remove the material from the site. You need to sandblast the buildings. You need to physically remove the contamination and debris from every crevice of every building. You need to tear up the streets and purge the drainage culverts."

Afad raised an eyebrow, which seemed to suggest The Engineer should continue.

"But for all this you need to have people who will be willing to work in such a contaminated environment. How can the workers be protected from the radiation they are cleaning up? Will they be sick from the clean-up work? Even if you had the will and the people to clean up, the contaminated material must be taken somewhere. Where will that be? Who will pay for all of this? In the end, I predict they will just abandon the geographic area. Do you think they could ever agree on where to dump all this nuclear waste? They can't agree on where to put a wind farm. No. They will argue and criticize each other forever. This will provide al-Qaeda an opportunity to speak out about the ineffectiveness of Western democracy to serve its people in time of crisis. The young people in the Middle East will see this and not be so enamored of Western democracy."

"You firmly believe the psychological damage caused by a dirty bomb can be as important as physical damage?" queried Afad.

"I think it is even more important," said The Engineer. "As a terrorist, I want to attack the psyche. People will see they are powerless against us. Fear will dominate their every word and action. Panic will be a frequent occurrence. How can they respond? Increase the rewards on our heads? It has not done them any good so far!"

After this meeting concluded, The Engineer sent Afad news articles and data he gathered from the internet, congressional public sources, and from media outlets on the state of preparedness of Homeland Security. These articles addressed programs and plans relative to the protection of the American public from acts of terrorism, and which plans have not yet been implemented. Some of these plans concerned the failure to inspect ships' cargo at American ports, and the failure to have nuclear material detection capability in ports of entry. All were relevant topics. The Americans had even failed their own deadline to inspect the cargo of airline passenger planes. They have scanned people and suitcases for years, but do not scan what goes into the cargo bay. The Engineer could not believe intelligent people could put so much effort into passengers and so little effort into any form of cargo screening.

While the United States locked down and hardened the methodology of the last attack, the creative terrorist was looking for a new method of attack. The Engineer thought Western security was vulnerable because they focused too much on the past and not enough on the possibilities of the future. This was the gap he sought to exploit.

Chapter 42

Washington, DC

Vince Baker was in a meeting with FBI Director Carter Simms, updating him on what the Evidence Recovery Team had developed so far in Sicily.

"The ERT examined the cargo handler's apartment, which the Italians had preserved very well. He was shot at close range while asleep. It was an assassination. The Engineer was identified coming into the apartment with the cargo handler Saturday morning, and going in and out until Sunday morning. Someone identified him leaving with three bags earlier Sunday morning, but then thought they saw him back after that. That was the last sighting of The Engineer. The really bad news is that they picked up signs of radiation from both a gamma and an alpha source in the apartment closet."

"It gets worse I hear," said Simms.

"The Carabinieri found the cargo handler's car parked on a neighborhood street. ERT examined it and found the same traces of alpha and gamma isotopes in the trunk. They immediately went to the cargo handler's locker at work. The radiation detector showed the same results. They checked all the cargo carriages but found nothing. They got the records for what he handled Saturday morning and identified a plane from Tbilisi that he unloaded."

Baker continued, "The Georgian authorities immediately found and examined the plane. They used devices similar to ours and got the same response from areas on each side of the cargo door. Meanwhile, the Carabinieri pulled the video from the cargo tarmac. The video shows the cargo handler driving in a cart up to the plane, unlocking the plane's port side rear cargo door, and removing four boxes that he put in the cart. He was observed removing two thirty-inch red fire extinguishers from brackets on each side of the cargo door and placing them on the cargo cart. Then the cargo handler drove the cart away to the terminal. The removal of the fire extinguishers does not fit. They were not cargo and not part of the aircraft's equipment."

"The airline?" said Simms quizzically.

"We don't have any evidence they are involved. The cargo handler was a small time smuggler for the Camorra in Naples. He did mostly smaller amounts of drugs and high-end counterfeit products brought in from Tbilisi. He was the kind of guy who could get you drugs, watches, handbags, and gold necklaces all without taxes."

"So now the Camorra is smuggling nuclear material?"

Baker shrugged. "We don't know one way or another. The authorities in Georgia have run into a dead end about how the fire extinguishers got on the plane. They were not part of the aircraft gear. The brackets are still on the plane, but no one knows who put them there. We can assume the fire extinguishers are the source of the radiation, given the pattern of where it appears. We, along with the Italians, are running down everyone who was in contact with the cargo handler. The Carabinieri took a shot with the two associates even though they are not talking. They threw the photo of the cargo handler in front of each one separately, and neither one reacted. More importantly, they did not seem to understand why this photo was being shown to them. Only a guess, but no one is betting either of them even knew the cargo handler."

Simms pressed on, "What about the container in Palermo?"

"No sign of nuclear contamination there. It is all heavy duty ordinance, like what's needed to assault a fixed position with heavy fortifications. Laser guided, armor piercing, anything you would not want pointed at you is there. Lastly, there is more than 2,500 pounds of C-4 and Symtex!"

"Where do the taggants tell us?"

"The C-4 is ours, apparently given to the Northern Alliance in Afghanistan when they agreed to help us fight the Taliban. Seems like they might have had a little left over, which they sold on the black market to generate some extra spending money. The Semtex appears to be sourced right out of the eastern bloc but the details are still being run down. There is so much Semtex for sale on the international arms market we will probably never know its history until we get someone talking. It is the amount that worries us. It can do some major damage."

"Somehow I think I have not yet heard the really bad news."

"You're right," Baker paused. "Put the C-4 or Semtex together with the radioactive material and you have a dirty bomb."

"How much material could they get into the two fire extinguishers?"

"Everyone is trying to guess that one. Depends on how much shielding they provided to protect anyone handling the extinguishers against gamma material emissions."

"How much?" repeated Simms.

"Enough to make a very substantial dirty bomb," said Baker.

"Remind me, don't we have their container of weapons and explosives in our possession?" said Simms with a degree of frustration.

"Yes", said Baker.

"I'm glad we at least have that," sighed Simms.

"Aren't we all?" responded Baker.

"What now?" asked Simms.

"Everything is going out to the intelligence community as we speak. Our close anti-terrorist allies are included. We have lots of legwork left to do before we can try to put the big picture together. We are going to start beating the bushes to find The Engineer. He is the bomb maker. We need him off the street."

"What about the associates?" asked Simms.

"Not talking. Nothing we can do about it right now," replied Baker.

"Is this case on the Director of National Intelligence's meeting agenda for this afternoon?"

"Yes," said Baker. "All the agencies have been briefed. Everyone is trying to identify The Engineer."

"Has Patrick heard any more?"

"No. I spoke with him earlier today and gave him a sanitized report."

"Why a 'sanitized' report? I gave him all the necessary clearances!"

"Some in our shop persuaded me that he might give too much away if he decided on his own to ask direct questions of his source. Sometimes the Camorra and the Sicilian Mafia don't get along."

"How does that make sense? The Mafia came to him in the first place? They want no one to know they are furnishing us information."

Baker shrugged.

"This is not making sense to me. Why cut him out at this point?"

"He has that subpoena bullshit that the AUSA in Boston dropped on him," said Baker weakly.

"Shall I call the US Attorney up there?"

"He has already disavowed what Bottom is doing, but won't order him to stop. He has not been briefed, to his displeasure, on the nature of Patrick's source info. If the truth be known, he is playing both ends against the middle."

"So we are leaving Patrick out there, hanging, alone?"

"His lawyer has talked to Justice, who was going to order Bottom to drop it. I don't know if that has actually happened."

"I suggest you pay this matter closer attention. What did Patrick say he would do? Hold a press conference to explain why he is being harassed?"

"Oh, he was just blowing some wind."

"You don't know him. I do. Believe what he says. If you can't resolve this with DOJ, set up a meeting for me with the AG. Don't let this slip from your attention again."

"Okay." Baker thought this would be a good time to leave, especially after Simms returned to the paperwork on his desk without further acknowledging Baker's presence. Simms was angry. As Baker thought about it, he really abandoned Patrick to Bottom's aberrant behavior. He had not sought a quick end to the interference and meddling by Bottom. His lack of action had to encourage Bottom to pursue Patrick. Baker felt he had enough aggravation on his plate. He didn't want more. But Baker now sensed he had been acting more like a bureaucrat than an FBI agent. He thought he might spend a few moments in meaningful self-examination.

Chapter 43

Boston

Patrick was sitting in Bill Welby's office. There was a scheduled appearance before Judge West tomorrow.

"I sensed a change in Bottom's tone yesterday morning. I thought he was going to drop the subpoena idea. By late afternoon he was off again, full of bravado and bluster. Something happened during the interim. I talked to some people in DOJ and it seems no one wants to take responsibility for Bottom's current venture. No one is telling him to stop. As a result, I filed the motion to quash the subpoena. Judge West will hear it at 9:30 am."

"What about witnesses?"

"I told the judge's clerk I planned to call witnesses but, since it was only yesterday that Bottom informed me that he was objecting to our motion to dismiss, I haven't had the proper time to notify the proposed witnesses and arrange for their subpoena service."

"So how far will it go tomorrow?"

"I don't know. The judge will hear my legal arguments. He does not have to allow witnesses. It's possible he could order you before the grand jury. On the other hand, he may smell a game here and not want to be part of it. He can continue the hearing to allow us to call witnesses."

"What names have you given them?"

"I only alluded to witnesses. I didn't have to name them in the filing. I just said we would update the court on witnesses at the hearing tomorrow."

"Do you still agree with the names we discussed before?"

"With your consent, I will name Susan Crowley, Vincent Baker, Bob Wilkins, and Director Carter Simms. I will also name the DOJ representative to the Joint Terrorism Task Force in Washington as well as the DOJ representative to the FBI twenty-four hour situation room, or whatever they call it. I have to get their names."

"Do you intend to identify the potential witnesses by name in open court?"

"No. I will offer the court and Bottom my list in writing. It will be less inflammatory. We'll push the issue if Bottom continues with his foolishness."

"If the media gets those names, they will know the matter is about terrorism. It may also mean there will be more curiosity about my comings and goings. The IRS will have to compete with the media for parking spots around my office and condo."

Welby said nothing.

"Okay. This time I'm not stopping for coffee. I'll just see you in the courtroom at nine thirty. We will make the decisions after we see what happens at the hearing," said Patrick.

"Have a good day, Mark. I have some interesting clients that require my attention."

Patrick smiled as he walked out of Welby's office.

When he got back to his office, Patrick had a message from Susan Crowley requesting a meet. He called her back. She would be at his office in ten minutes. She arrived with two coffees. Patrick knew she assumed he wouldn't come to her office. She must have been waiting nearby in order to get the coffee and be there in such a short period of time.

"Baker asked me to meet with you to insure no little points had been lost in the shuffle of information, and that you are up to date," said Crowley. She proceeded with her briefing to Patrick.

Crowley told Patrick about the radiation detected in Palermo at the cargo handler's apartment, his car trunk, his work locker, and finally around the plane's cargo door. Patrick realized that Baker had withheld this information. He wondered why. Patrick said nothing to Crowley. It was not her doing.

Crowley made it clear they were desperate for information about The Engineer. A lot more people in Washington were paying attention to this case. The recovery of the container of arms and explosives was bad enough. The existence of nuclear material, explosives, and The Engineer missing, had a lot of people justifiably nervous.

"So the fact that you have the container and the explosives has not allayed fears?" asked Patrick.

"There are two camps," said Crowley. "One is congratulating itself on preventing a terrorist act and the other is worried the container contents can easily be replaced, and the problem is far from over."

"Which camp is pushing Bottom to get me in front of a grand jury and force me to set Vespa up so they have direct contact?"

"According to Phil Kirby, I'm not allowed to discuss that. The issue is alive in both the FBI and DOJ. However, the people pushing the issue think you will cave in to the pressure."

"I understand," said Patrick. "Just tell me where Baker stands."

"Baker got into trouble with the Director for playing information games with you. He realizes now that you need our full support. Some earlier waffling on his part may actually have encouraged others to indirectly support Bottom in his current effort. I believe he is working to unravel the situation at present."

"And this is really why he wanted you to meet me. He wanted you to tell me this?"

"Yes. Baker wants me to tell you that he is disappointed in himself. He acted like a bureaucrat. He thought you might understand."

"Okay. I can live with that for now. Do you have any suggestions for me for tomorrow's hearing?"

"No. I'm afraid not."

"Thanks for the coffee. I will let you know if I hear anything."

Patrick went back to work but found his concentration lacking. As he started thinking about tomorrow's hearing he became infuriated. What wasted time and effort. Those causing these useless diversions would never be held accountable within their own agencies.

Patrick's mood grew darker. He was not able to concentrate on his work. A nice walk was the answer for what ailed him. He went out to the Harbor Walk and headed north and over the Charlestown Bridge into the Charlestown Navy Yard. He found a coffee shop and sat outside with his cup watching the harbor traffic. After twenty minutes or so, he reversed course back over the bridge, turned left on Commercial Street and headed back to Franklin Wharf. When he got to the parking lot, Peter came out of the booth.

"How is your day going?"

"I think I was feeling a little sorry for myself and was generating some internal anger. So I went for a walk and had a coffee."

"Did it help?"

"The walk, yes. The coffee, no."

Peter laughed. "Your friends have been around. Seems to me like they lost you."

"They probably did. I was on foot roaming around in the Navy Yard. They may not know what to do if they have to get out of their cars."

"You are in a bad mood. Go take a nap and when you wake up you can have a re-start for the rest of the day."

"Thanks for the advice."

Patrick went upstairs and took a short nap. When he awoke, he felt cleansed as if some of the dirty cloud hanging over him had dissipated. Patrick went into the kitchen, looked in the refrigerator, and didn't see a whole lot. He noted a bunch of celery and looked at the bookcase of cookbooks over the refrigerator. Fannie Farmer would know how to make celery soup. He found it on page sixty-four.

Chapter 44

Thursday morning Patrick left Franklin Wharf at about nine o'clock for the twenty-minute walk to the federal courthouse. He arrived at Judge West's courtroom just as the judge was coming onto the bench. The courtroom was more crowded than he expected. Harvey Bottom was seated at government's counsel table, and behind him was Fred Rickman along with Bottom's personal posse of IRS agents. They were probably some of the agents assigned to follow him around. He looked them over so he would know them again, just in case. They all seemed to turn and look at Patrick with some element of disgust. Patrick wondered if he ever looked at a defendant like that in court when he was an FBI agent. He thought if he had, he owed some apologies.

Claudia Bell was in a group of media people. He recognized one TV reporter who looked naked without his ever-attendant camera, which was not allowed in a federal courtroom. It also looked like some of the assistants from the US attorney's office had come to watch the show. He saw no one from the FBI. They knew how to avoid controversy. Bill Welby was standing at the defendant's table. Then it struck Patrick. This is what he was. He was a defendant in the courtroom today. As this thought hit him, he started to get really angry. Welby looked at him, seemed to understand what was going on in Patrick's head, and motioned for him to sit in the row just behind Welby. Patrick did so as court was called to order.

Judge West started: "I see we have not resolved this issue. Mr. Welby has filed a motion to quash the subpoena of Mark Patrick. The motion is opposed by the government. Is that where we are gentlemen?"

Both counsel agreed that this was the present standing of the case.

"Mr. Welby, it seems to me that the ball is in your court for the moment. Why don't I hear what you have to say? Then I'll see what Mr. Bottom thinks about it."

"Very well, Your Honor," began Welby. "It is my client's position that the court should quash the government's subpoena on several grounds. Mr. Patrick has come into possession of some information that concerns possible criminal acts. From the first moment he received this information, he communicated it forthwith and in a most timely manner to FBI agents here in Boston and in Washington, DC. It is our knowledge that this information has been shared by the FBI with other responsible law enforcement and intelligence agencies. In short, we believe that all responsible agencies have been appropriately notified. Apparently Mr. Bottom, and the US Attorney in Boston, have not been briefed to their satisfaction by the forces controlling this inquiry and have decided to utilize their subpoena power to force Mr. Patrick to tell them what he already has told the authorities. In short, Your Honor, Mr. Bottom, is using the federal grand jury process to circumvent the lack of shared information from Washington. There is no evidence at this point that Mr. Bottom has any jurisdiction to investigate any criminal matter resulting from the information known to date."

Bottom was up out of his chair, like a schoolboy, demanding the teacher's attention. "Your Honor, I would like to recite our jurisdiction in this matter."

"Mr. Bottom, would you mind waiting until Mr. Welby finishes outlining his argument?"

Bottom sat down.

Welby continued. "Your Honor, the point here is there are certain elements that want Mr. Patrick to step aside, identify his source of information so that government agents can then confront the source and force this source to cooperate directly with them, obviating the need for Mr. Patrick. Mr. Patrick would very much like to be out of this picture, but the problems are threefold. Mr. Patrick does not know the identity of the source, and has no knowledge of where the source is located. Moreover, to do what the government wants would require Mr. Patrick to affirmatively lie to the source by setting up a meeting wherein Mr. Bottom and his crew can jump out of the closet, so to speak, and cause a confrontation. Mr. Patrick declines to support such an effort."

"Your Honor, I object to Mr. Welby's characterizations of the government," Bottom said as he was jumping up to cut off Welby.

"I will sustain the objection and ask Mr. Welby not to characterize the government's intentions, at least until we get more on the record. However, it would now appear that if this source reads the Boston media, and after learning of this discussion today in court, I don't think an element of surprise will be at issue. The whole point will be moot. Please continue Mr. Welby."

"Next, Your Honor, Mr. Patrick believes that the government knows this source purports to be a member of a criminal group that is an ongoing criminal enterprise, and this is a criminal grand jury to which Mr. Patrick has been subpoenaed. According to current DOJ Guidelines for the handling of criminal informants, neither Mr. Bottom, nor any of assignees would be allowed by the DOJ Guidelines to handle this person as an informant. It is a violation of the guidelines to operate an informant known to be engaged in committing crime. Through Mr. Bottom, the Boston US attorney is seeking to force himself into contact with a person they cannot legally operate as an informant. Why should they be allowed to use a United States district court to force this contact in contravention of the guidelines?

Lastly, Mr. Patrick was told by the source that this current move by the government, presently championed by Mr. Bottom, was anticipated by the source. Mr. Patrick was informed that any effort by the government to identify the source would result in an immediate cessation of contacts. Mr. Patrick has explained this to the government. There has been discussion with the FBI as to options, and there are none at this point. Mr. Patrick has in the past and will continue to refuse to set up a meeting so the government can 'spring their trap,' so to speak. Mr. Patrick has provided the FBI with the bona fides of this source regarding information the source has provided in the past. The government confirms the value and accuracy of the information furnished by this source.

I have provided Mr. Patrick with certain legal advice. I can represent to this court that Mr. Patrick will exercise these constitutional rights before the federal grand jury and will refuse to answer any questions put by Mr. Bottom on this subject. If a decision is made to place Mr. Patrick in a contempt situation, I believe our position is subject to an immediate appeal to the First Circuit Court of Appeals."

Welby sat down. The courtroom was silent. It was a stunned silence. Judge West was not taken aback. He seemed to have understood what Welby was willing to do all along. Judge West was fixed on what the issues were.

"Mr. Bottom, would you care to give the court an overview of your position on Mr. Welby's objections?"

It was clear Bottom was caught short and did not think Welby would say this much in open court. He thought Welby would ask for a chambers conference with the judge, where Bottom could start negotiating to get Patrick into the grand jury outside of the public view. Bottom had told the US Attorney that this hearing would not get out of hand, and Bottom would force a negotiation to get Patrick to cooperate without any backlash on his office. Now Bottom was not so sure.

Bottom was up and began. "Your Honor, Mr. Welby's claim to our lack of jurisdiction is foolish. Mr. Patrick is in the courtroom today, and we believe he has had contact with the source within the Commonwealth or by phone while in the Commonwealth. It is premature to say we are not entitled to operate this person under the informant guidelines. There are always exceptions to the guidelines available for exceptional circumstances. Lastly, Your Honor, this investigation is a lawful function of the executive branch, which ought not to be limited by the judicial branch because of Mr. Patrick's insistence that he is in a better position to evaluate the needs of the Joint Terrorism Task Force."

"Mr. Bottom, do you agree that your superiors have all the information that Mr. Patrick has, and they have just chosen not to share it with your group?"

"I do not know what Mr. Patrick knows until I can make that inquiry before the federal grand jury. As to what he has told my superiors, I do not have the full picture and the US Attorney for Massachusetts has a duty to insure any crimes committed in the Commonwealth are fully investigated."

"And you think that will not happen with the FBI, the DOJ, and the other intelligence agencies as dictated by existing protocols?"

Judge West did not wait for a response from Bottom. He turned to Welby. "Mr. Welby, if the DOJ wishes to continue this process, will you seek an evidentiary hearing where you plan on calling witnesses?"

"Yes, Your Honor, I would."

"How many witnesses and how long would your examinations take?"

"Six witnesses, and I would say my time with all those witnesses would not exceed two hours."

"Are those witnesses in the Commonwealth and available today?"

"One witness is in the Commonwealth. I have no information as to that person's availability. I have not spoken to any potential witness. Some are in Washington, DC. I need to subpoena them. I have no idea as to their schedules. I only learned yesterday that Mr. Bottom would be opposing my motion. We are not prepared with witnesses today, and I would further advise the court that given the government positions held by some of these witnesses, they may have their own counsel who object to their being called by Mr. Patrick."

"Do you have those names on a potential witness list, and has it been shown to Mr. Bottom?"

"I do have a list. I have not shown it to Mr. Bottom. I am willing to provide a copy to him and the court if that helps move things along."

"Please do so, Mr. Welby."

Welby handed a copy of the list to Bottom and another to the clerk for Judge West, who then appeared to study the list. Bottom looked at the names, sat down, and made a few notes on his pad.

"I am going to recess for one hour to review the issues that have been raised. It is clear to me that Mr. Welby, and probably even the government, will be interested in having the First Circuit review whatever decision I make. Mr. Bottom, do you agree that Mr. Welby is entitled to call witnesses on behalf of Mr. Patrick?"

"No, Your Honor, I do not leap to that conclusion. If Mr. Patrick invokes his right under the Fifth Amendment before the grand jury, I am prepared to offer him immunity to compel his testimony. To me, this is a case of a witness who does not wish to testify. There is a straight forward process to legally require his testimony."

"So, it is your position that I have no choice in this matter Mr. Bottom?" Without waiting for a response, the judge rumbled on. "Is it not true, Mr. Bottom, that your agent told Mr. Patrick he would have IRS problems if he didn't cooperate with you? Did this statement originate with you? Why should Mr. Patrick not be allowed to plan a defense around that threat, which now even seems to be in the media reports? Lastly, is it your position that this court has no jurisdiction in a matter where the executive branch abuses its authority with the federal grand jury, which operates under the auspices and guidance of this court?"

"Your Honor, I can address your concerns."

"Not now Mr. Bottom. These are issues I want you to address when court resumes. During this recess I want you, Mr. Bottom, to personally speak with the US Attorney about what has transpired here. When you return, I want to know if you remain authorized by the US attorney to continue to pursue this course of action."

"Yes, Your Honor." Bottom knew the judge was going to put the US Attorney's head on the same platter as Bottom's.

"This recess also gives you two a chance to talk. I must say that I also read in the paper that this subpoena was about someone's bluff being called. I hope for your sake, Mr. Bottom, this is not a frivolous jaunt on your part. Common sense tells me that this country is not as safe now as it was when this hearing started." The last words were uttered, somewhat *sotto voce* but for the record, as the judge walked off the bench.

Patrick exited the courtroom and waited in the hallway for Welby. He was approached by the media for comment, which he gracefully declined.

Patrick, still waiting for Welby, was leaning over the railing looking out through the volumes of glass on the front of the courthouse, which offered a beautiful view back toward the city. He heard some footsteps behind him and turned to see a vaguely familiar face approaching him with an outstretched hand.

"Can't recall your friends from the organized crime conferences in DC?"

"Charlie Ward," said Patrick, "what brings an old, battle-scarred, retired agent like you into a courtroom in Boston? You still in New York?"

"Why should I ever leave the best city in the entire world?"

"I am surprised to see you here. What's up?"

"Since retirement I've been active with the Society of Former Agents and serve on a national committee that is looking into what we have found to be a series of injustices against former agents across the country. Since they are former agents, the current FBI leadership does not have the authority or jurisdiction to say anything nor to be involved. This tends to leave the agent out there alone, on his or her own."

"Like now you mean?"

Ward smiled. "The committee knows that former agents are frequently called back to testify in both civil and criminal cases. Often, as in your case, if they want the advice of counsel, they sometimes have to pay that cost themselves."

"I heard the society was interested in forming some type of committee to deal with these problems," said Patrick.

"We're setting up a foundation to raise money to be able to assist retired agents, like yourself, who are called back to testify and require legal advice for which the DOJ may not legally be authorized to pay. We are not operational yet, but I was asked to observe what is going on here today. Could I speak with you later to get some ideas of how we might help? What is going on with you here is what we are talking about at the Society," said Ward

"So what does this mean to me now, here, today?"

"All we can do right now is offer moral support. The Society chairman learned about your hearing on NPR news a few days ago. In a meeting with the Director, he asked what the FBI was doing to help you. The Director said he spoke with you and you were doing the right thing. There is a pissing contest in DC over who should lead certain types of terrorism investigations. Terrorism is where the budget money is flowing freely, so all federal investigative agencies are looking for a way to keep their rice bowl filled and remain relevant," said Ward.

"So what is behind this subpoena?" asked Patrick.

"From the little we know, and we are not asking you to comment, there is an element within DOJ that wants to make all decisions for any FBI investigation. Some DOJ attorneys are not satisfied with being prosecutors. They want to be the investigators, too."

Patrick nodded. He had seen that before.

"These attorneys have never developed nor operated a source. They are not trained or competent to do so. They have never sat across from an individual who could be killed if one made a mistake handling the often singular information that was furnished. It makes little difference if the person is called an asset, source, informant, or a cooperating witness if the person is killed. People sometimes forget they are dealing with human beings. They have no training or experience for this type of human interaction and have an inadequate understanding of earned trust."

Patrick just nodded slightly.

"Anyway, the Director can't control the problem and thinks you are getting nailed. He thinks this situation is a good first case for the Society to study. That's why I came to get a firsthand look and talk with you. I'll go back and suggest that they consider filing an amicus brief on your behalf with the First Circuit if it goes that far. In short, we want to shine a public light on what is going on here in Boston. We won't make it easy to pick agents off one at a time. The Society wishes to deliver the message that agents, retired or not, will not have to fend for themselves," said Ward.

"I must admit that it has been a little lonely lately. I appreciate what you and the Society are doing. The moral support is more important than anything."

"We know. Some of us have been there." Ward asked Patrick to call him later to discuss ideas. "Even if you want a safe place to vent, give me a call," added Ward.

"Thanks. I appreciate the offer," said Patrick.

At that point Welby walked up. Patrick introduced him to Ward. Patrick explained why Ward was there before Ward left.

"Ward is right. It's not so much about this case," said Welby. "From talking with Bottom there are factions at DOJ, and various US attorneys who think the FBI should disclose the identities of all their sources and informants to them so they can become part of the operational discussions. The FBI refuses to do it. Agents are refusing to have informants because of guidelines that are poorly drafted by DOJ, and under which the agent will almost be guaranteed to be found at fault, no matter what."

"Some just can't believe they should not be told everything all the time. The concept of a 'need to know basis' does not comport to Bottom's elevated self-image. What happens now?" asked Patrick.

"There can be no more discussion with Bottom. He has a clear intention to get you into the grand jury and make you give up the source. They want to bring the source into the grand jury and get operational control of that person," said Welby.

"But as you said in court, I don't know who the person is, and I don't have a direct contact."

"They don't care about the details. What will heat this up is the witness list I gave them.

Bottom says I'm not entitled to call witnesses. He may be right. They just don't want those names out. They tried to position you publicly, but I think that backfired. Bottom tried to manipulate the media and got caught. His credibility with them will soon be down."

"What's next?" asked Patrick.

"Bottom is going to say that you have no right to a hearing and should be ordered to appear immediately before the grand jury. I will say we need those witnesses and we are entitled to a public hearing. I will ask that the hearing be scheduled for next week," said Welby.

"What if I'm ordered into the grand jury and refuse to answer their questions?"

"Bottom will move for contempt, but that will not happen today. The judge will schedule a separate contempt hearing."

"What about a press conference?" asked Patrick.

"The media has a lot to chew on. Let the public and the rest of the world digest what was said today. The media will start probing the DOJ to see if there is a criminal or terrorist threat involved. I think we should just leave and let things percolate. We can have a press conference anytime. I hope this does not wind up causing people to take their eye off the ball. If there is a threat out there, it needs to be addressed. This is only a sideshow," said Welby.

"Thanks. Perhaps I was even beginning to lose sight of that," admitted Patrick.

Chapter 45

The Atlantic Ocean

The Engineer was in the lounge using the ship's computer to access the internet. He wanted to review the news in the US cities of interest to him. Afad was surprised when The Engineer was able to tell him that eleven million cargo containers entered the US each year and as yet there was no national program to screen these containers. He showed Afad the US news articles with comments by local and state officials in various cities as to how unprepared they were in case of a terrorist attack using any nuclear, biological or chemical agents. The deadline set by the government for a rudimentary system to examine ship's cargo containers had been postponed from 2010 to 2012. Homeland Security in the New York port was still experimenting with nuclear detection equipment for possible deployment.

Alpha particles are more easily blocked than gamma particles. Gamma particles require far more in containment to prevent their emissions from causing radiation sickness to the carrier. Greater containment would also make the material harder to detect. The Engineer intended to mix together his radioactive materials when making the bombs to maximize his desired effect.

The most serious health threat from alpha-emitting radioactive material occurs when it is ingested into the human system. When detected at the explosion site, the public would be warned and instructed on how to prevent ingestion. People would be in a state of panic and, he believed, as did Afad, such instructions at that time would only add to the panic.

The first responders would also learn that gamma emitting cesium-137 was present and dispersed into the air. The public would be warned that any physical contact with cesium-137 was hazardous and they must avoid contact. How this would be possible for people to do was of course unknown. This situation would create more panic among a populace eager to escape contamination. Later, the discussion would focus on the proposition that cesium-137 would be impossible to clean up and the entire contaminated area would be abandoned.

The Engineer could not wait to see a vibrant US city empty and devoid of human beings. It would be shown night after night on the evening news. By the time the arguing stopped about whether it was safe to clean up, the area would have lost any practical economic use. He wondered if even looters would choose not to enter the affected area to scavenge.

The credibility of the government among citizens would be non-existent. The Engineer wanted the world to see that Allah enabled him to punish the proud Americans. In doing this to one city, The Engineer believed he was instilling fear in every US city.

It was their al-Qaeda leader who came up with an additional twist to The Engineer's plan. Afad explained, "We will use a disinformation campaign to further instill fear and chaos in the American public after the detonations. The internet will be most useful and no one will know al-Qaeda has a hand in what is being said. I envision our people using quotes on the subject of preparedness from the federal political leaders to demonstrate that all of their security problems have been known, and no one in government seriously addressed them. The American public will be told they have been left to fend for themselves. We will say that Congress, the administration, and especially the intelligence community, have failed to live up to their duty to protect the American public from our jihad. These will be our themes."

"Do you have people in place in the US that can do this?" asked The Engineer.

"We have those eager to do our bidding. They do not have to physically be in the US, but they will appear as concerned US citizens worried about their own safety. We are in a position to engender conversations on the academic level also. We can do even more."

"How can we do that and not give our involvement away?"

"We can simply do it from here. We have access to computers. We can use blogs, Face Book, Twitter, as well as websites sympathetic to our cause. We will control the conversation. We get our message out first and aggressively. They will have to respond to what we say, and thus we get to control the conversation. We can physically move people to European and Asian cities of influence to promote discussions all over the world. After the events occur, we will assemble our disinformation group, give them the talking points, quotes from known leaders, and mix in less truthful material which will create more fear and confusion."

"Will the world turn on us?" asked The Engineer.

"How will they know it is us? We will deny it. They can only suspect as our confederates carry on these conversations," said Afad.

The Engineer continued his thoughts; "Even if any cell members are captured, they know next to nothing. They only know their particular assignment. They will not know we had the nuclear material to make the bomb dirty. They can talk about where their terror training took place, but those camps are not so vital. Loss of some camps or cell members would not be a serious blow. We can sow seeds of confusion and doubt about anything they may say, just like after 9/11. Where can the President strike? Who should he bomb? What can they prove? We will make sure the discussion stays on US failures and why they must agree to a serious dialogue with all of radical Islam."

The Engineer had to admit that as much damage could be done through a war of words as the bomb itself. Keep America on the defensive with its own citizens and the world of public opinion, and they would be begging to meet with al-Qaeda.

176

Chapter 46

Judge West returned to the bench in exactly one hour. He was a man of his word and thought it a public obligation not to keep the courtroom waiting on him. Not all judges thought that way.

"Mr. Bottom, if there has been no change in the positions of the parties, why don't you proceed with your argument for the government."

Bottom proceeded to state his argument much the same as he had before. This was a simple subpoena to a federal grand jury conducting a criminal inquiry. The person subpoenaed had information about an individual of interest, and the government had the right to require the testimony of this person. If this person felt so inclined to invoke any constitutional privilege not to testify, Bottom had already drafted an order of immunity for the court to impose on the reluctant witness. There was no need for the court to hold a hearing at this point, since witness testimony was not relevant at this juncture. Such witnesses might be called at a criminal contempt hearing if Mr. Patrick defied the court's order to testify once immunity was granted."

"Mr. Bottom, you have spoken with the US Attorney directly on this matter as I had requested?"

"Yes, Your Honor."

"Mr. Welby, do you wish to be heard any further?"

"Your Honor, this is not a normal subpoena. It is an abuse of process by Mr. Bottom and the US Attorney participating in a Washington power play that has spilled over to this jurisdiction. We ask the court to look beyond what the government represents to the court and look to the underlying problem. I need to call witnesses to the effect that Mr. Patrick's presence is not needed in a grand jury. The government already has his information. Mr. Bottom is being less than forthright with the court and wishes to direct the court away from the real issues at hand. It is Mr. Bottom who should be investigated for obstruction of justice. If Patrick is incarcerated for contempt, a necessary asset providing critical information to the US government will be lost and a critical investigation thwarted. I also disagree with Mr. Bottom's veiled suggestion that this court has no authority to monitor his use of the grand jury, alluding to some infringement upon the executive branch."

"We need not go to your latter two points yet, Mr. Welby," said Judge West. "However, I believe that Mr. Bottom is correct when he states you do not have the right to call witnesses at this particular juncture."

Bottom turned at this point and looked at Rickman behind him and smiled.

"Also the threat," continued Judge West, "that your client might be investigated for some possible criminal activity, as alluded to by Mr. Rickman when he served the subpoena, does not rise, at this point, to a level where this court is required to take punitive action against the government. For the purpose of this hearing I accept the representation that Mr. Patrick will refuse to testify even when offered immunity and ordered to do so. Thus, most of the legal territory prior to any contempt hearing has been staked out by the parties. The issue is whether the subpoena is void because the government already has the information it demands. Mr. Bottom argues that the information is not under oath and in front of his grand jury, and to that point I think Mr. Bottom is correct."

Judge West now looked directly at Bottom and continued speaking: "However, I am very concerned that the government is not being forthright with the court and that the government's position is somewhat disingenuous and misleading. I have given the parties time to work this out and they have not. My question now is whether this a local squabble, or one being directed from Washington? Is this a situation where the court process is being abused? While Mr. Patrick is no longer an employee of the FBI, I do question whether the FBI has a right, or even a duty, to claim informant privilege regarding this source of Mr. Patrick's. This point has not been raised by either party here. While it is not my function to argue the case for either side, I am going to continue this proceeding for two weeks. Mr. Bottom, you are directed to immediately file a memorandum of law as to whether the FBI has a duty to protect the identity of this source once the FBI accepted the information from Mr. Patrick. Mr. Welby, you have one week to respond. I invite the FBI legal counsel to submit their own brief."

Bottom looked worried again.

"Yes, Your Honor," said Welby.

"One more thing, if this court determines that any representations made by any counsel during these proceedings are disingenuous, I will impose sanctions on that counsel and any other lawyer involved in the promotion of that position. Lastly, I note for the record that my timeline is consistent with the needs of the case, as the government has not claimed exigent circumstances are present."

"Your Honor," said Bottom, "of course, as in any criminal investigation, time is of the essence and…"

"You better stop there Mr. Bottom. You have not argued that point so do not start now just because I have raised it. Are you saying you and your grand jury cannot wait two weeks while we try to uncomplicate what you have obviously complicated by your actions? The evidence is that the FBI knows what Mr. Patrick knows, and the FBI has shared the data with other agencies including the Justice Department. Do you want to argue that you do not have two weeks?"

"I withdraw that point, Your Honor."

"This hearing is adjourned for two weeks," said Judge West.

Patrick again declined comment to the media when asked after the hearing. He was joined by Welby and they walked to the far end of the hallway, where they had some privacy.

"What is the judge doing?" asked Patrick.

"He is giving DOJ a chance to drop the matter. In reality, he should order you in front of the grand jury, let you take the Fifth, have you refuse to answer, grant Bottom's immunity and allow Bottom to put you back before the grand jury. That way, if you refuse again, you would be in contempt. The stage would then be set for our appeal."

"So why doesn't he do that?" asked Patrick.

"The judge's guess is that Bottom will never get that far. This way there is a two week cooling-off period which is probably wise. Let's just play the turtle and go back into the shell. Let this thing work itself out in DC. The FBI now has a dog in the race. If they want to claim any informant privilege, the judge just opened the door for them to do so. If it turns out Bottom is intentionally misleading the court, his job could be in trouble as well as his ticket to practice law. He ought to be careful. Now, if you will excuse me, I have some important clients whose needs I must attend."

"Thanks, friend. If you need me I'll be fishing while you're working!"

Patrick left the courthouse and walked along the waterfront. He didn't feel like dealing with anything or anyone. He had the feeling that this mockery in the courthouse was not going to serve the public well. He questioned whether he was being hard-headed in protecting Vespa. It would make life easier for him if he didn't. Vespa had even told him that if forced, he could say what he knew because it would not lead back to Vespa. No, he knew what was bothering him. He was caught in the middle where he did not want to be. He retired, leaving this bureaucratic existence behind to those who enjoyed it. Turning it over in his mind as he walked along allowed him to regain a sense of balance and be a little less confused. He would continue on. He would not talk to Bottom and he would not set up Vespa. Vespa by now probably had a full account of the hearing. Vespa might never respond to an effort by him to contact her, knowing Bottom wanted Patrick to set her up.

What was really bothering Patrick was that The Engineer was still on the loose and had nuclear materials for a dirty bomb. If the shipment of arms was destined for New York, why wouldn't that also be the destination for The Engineer and his fire extinguishers? The two associates apparently knew little, and it would take time to put together the bits they did know to form some type of information mosaic. How could you stop one person with access to quality forged passports from entering this country? Whatever terrorists' supplies were recovered in Sicily could be replaced. Anyone who claimed success at this point was a fool, thought Patrick. However, he realized that he was out of the business and there were plenty of smart people to take up the chase. Like everyone else, he had to rely on others to protect him since 9/11. He would have to admit they had so far been successful. Perhaps he was sometimes jaundiced in his opinions because he knew too much about the system and tended to look at what did not work, rather than look at what was working.

"Hey Mark, you owe me a caffé."

Patrick turned. He realized he was in the North End and standing in front of Giovanni's restaurant. Giovanni was in the doorway pulling on his jacket as he walked out to meet Patrick.

"I haven't had a chance to say thanks for the other day," said Patrick.

"You can do so now while you buy me an espresso," said Giovanni, with a big smile on his face.

Patrick laughed as he thought of the "pervert" being stopped by the police and being forced to identify himself as an IRS agent. No wonder they still wanted to chase Patrick. They walked into the Café Strada arm in arm and laughing. It felt good for Patrick to just laugh at what his friend had done for him.

"The news is on the radio about your hearing today. No disrespect to your former job, but people are happy you are not throwing your source to the dogs. You'll treat the guy right. They will just use and abuse him."

"Are my friends still around?"

"Have not seen them," said Giovanni, "but I'll let you know if they show up. Everyone is on the lookout now. This is great. Instead of being a lookout for bad guys being chased by the cops, we are on the lookout for the cops chasing a good guy, one of their former colleagues, who is a friend of ours. Is this crazy or what?"

Patrick laughed as did some of the other patrons. Giovanni was not quiet and everyone in the café seemed to know what they were talking about. After he left Giovanni, Patrick went to the butcher shop and to the greengrocer. He wanted supplies to take to Southport tomorrow. People commented to Patrick along the way regarding the current news. They seemed to think the commotion was about a criminal investigation. No mention of terrorism. The media hadn't picked up on the nuances mentioned in court. This was further confirmed when he stopped to pick up some cheese at Felipe's.

"You're too old to chase crooks. Let the young guys do it. But don't give the person up to those people."

Felipe had spoken.

By the time he reached Franklin Wharf and saw Peter open the door to the attendant's booth, Patrick felt he had run a gauntlet just to get home. Peter stepped out of the booth, offered a handshake and said, "Well, you're not in jail yet and I bet you're wearing them down."

"Me! Wearing them down? I'm tired and they are fresh as daisies looking for another piece of me."

"They won't get it. Nobody is behind what they want you to do. It's just not right."

"What if it was about national security?" asked Patrick.

"Right is right. The feds have their information. They are just trying to put you in a terrible position that isn't necessary."

Patrick was amazed this was the public perception. The walk and conversations had done him some good. He was now going inside to sauté some pork cutlets in garlic and oil, with chopped red and yellow peppers. No pasta tonight. Have to watch the waistline. He bought some romaine lettuce and would rub a few pieces of anchovy in with the olive oil and a taste of balsamic. It would be something nice and simple. There was a Pinot Grigio that would go nicely in the refrigerator. Perhaps he and Liz could sit out on the deck with their coffee after dinner.

Before he started dinner, Patrick called John Peabody. He was out. He spoke to Joan about John's fishing schedule. There was an incoming tide on Saturday morning at the Bourne Pond's inlet. Patrick would be interested in fishing it with John. Patrick would get back to John tomorrow.

"You sound like you're okay."

"Thanks Joan. I am. It will get sorted out in the end."

"It's clear to me," said Joan, "that this guy Bottom is not being upfront. Seems to me like the judge called him on it today. If you tell the FBI and nobody tells Bottom, that says a lot about him. That much is clear."

"I must say you do have a perceptive analysis of things. Perhaps we can talk a little more this weekend."

By the time Liz got home, Patrick was all talked out. She was angry that his name was on the news associated with an adverse court action. She was afraid that was the only thing the public would remember. However, she did admit that her view as a lawyer was entirely different.

Patrick explained what people had said to him that afternoon. She reflected on the comments and they both decided the matter was eating up too much of their life. They would drop it for the time being.

The phone rang a few minutes later. It was Vincent Baker calling. "Sorry you had to spend another day in court. I can't say the matter is straightened out, but the judge doesn't seem inclined to rush anything."

"I know what went on. I was there. Are you calling to tell me the FBI is picking up the tab for my legal fees? It will be about $10,000 after Welby files the next response to Bottom's motions."

"Did you talk with Charlie Ward today?"

"Yes I did."

"All the ex-agents know what is going on."

"Oh, will that be on the front page of *The New York Times* in the morning? Are you and Carter Simms going to issue a press release to the world saying I've done the right thing and others are endangering the public, since I probably lost the source after today in court? We won't learn anymore now. But who cares? Look at the load grabbed in Sicily. Lots of credit to go around, is it? Is everyone happy?"

Patrick did not give Baker a chance to speak. He just continued. "The Engineer is still out there. He probably has some nuclear material with him for a dirty bomb. He can replace what was seized in Sicily. We can only hope he doesn't connect the loss in Sicily to an exposure of his plot."

Baker continued his silence, forced by Patrick's continuing monologue. "You know, I don't work for you anymore. I don't have all the great intelligence data you guys have from around the world. But I'm sure that our united anti-terrorism effort must have something in mind to replace Vespa, or you collectively wouldn't have blown it the way you have. Good luck."

"I can see you're really disturbed, so I'm sorry I bothered you."

"I'm not disturbed. I'm angry that there is such a vacuum of leadership. Good night." Patrick hung up.

Liz just looked at him. Then she turned her head back to the book she was reading without offering any comment. She was uncharacteristically quiet.

"Anything special on your mind?" asked Patrick.

"No. I can see you are all cranked up and that call didn't help. I guess I just want to remain calm so I might have a calming influence on you. We'll leave for Southport tomorrow afternoon and a change of scenery will do us good."

Patrick normally had no problem sleeping. He was now awake. It was 3:00 am. He had this feeling of unease. He could not name it or define it. It was just there. For some reason he was reminded of what a friend told him during an earlier, difficult period in the friend's life.

His friend found success for his problem at AA. He learned that he could not solve nor be responsible for all the problems around him. He could not always be the pillar of emotional support that his family and friends demanded. In the end, he didn't always try to figure out the answer to the problem at hand. Instead he learned to give it up to a "higher power." AA did not necessarily use a reference to God. He guessed that was to make the non-believers feel comfortable. However, his friend did believe in God and discussed how, when he could not sleep at night, he turned the problem over to God. He asked for His help with a solution, and the courage and energy to carry it out.

Patrick remembered his friend and tonight put this concept into action. He gave it all up and then went to sleep with no problem.

Chapter 47

The Atlantic Ocean

The Engineer had been aboard ship almost a week. He would arrive in New York City shortly. His first priority was to get himself through customs and immigration without any problem. He was traveling with his Italian passport, on an Italian ship, with nothing to declare. He expected no problem. Italy was an ally and friend of the US, and exchanged visitors at a very high rate. He was traveling as a tourist and would be in the US for no more than two months. He was scheduled to return home to Naples. He had prepaid tickets for his return trip on another cargo ship. His travel was consistent both ways. Many people did not like or trust flying these days.

The Engineer thought about various scenarios to get the fire extinguishers off the ship and around any potential US Customs inspection.

He had a pretty good idea of how to do it and not involve anyone on board ship. They could never talk about what they did not know.

He was up on the news in the three cities. He saw nothing to concern him. There was one thing going on in federal court in Boston which he noted, but it was a criminal matter. The Engineer was somewhat limited in his current research, as he did not want to leave too many search results and specific news articles on the ship's computer hard drive. Even when he erased them, they were still discoverable as a "deleted" temporary internet file. He would, however, make it difficult for anyone to see what he was doing.

The Engineer listed in his mind the first steps to take after getting into the city. He needed a cell phone. He already had his carrier and cell phone picked out. He would make it a cash purchase using a prepaid SIM card. Good luck to anyone trying to trace this phone.

The Engineer had enough cash to last a few months. He even purchased some American Express Travelers Checks in Naples. How unlike a terrorist was that? He could spend these like any tourist. The Engineer did not need to go to the Hawaladar until after he was settled and able to scope things out. He wanted to spend some time with his two team leaders to see how much they had accomplished. He would have to review everything himself to see if their observations were accurate. Only then would he finalize his plans.

If additional weapons or explosives were needed, The Engineer had the option to initiate a prearranged contact with the third al-Qaeda cell in the US, whose function was only that of supply. He thought it wouldn't be necessary. He didn't want this third team leader to physically know him. The Engineer's Naples container should arrive just after him. When the shipper offloaded the container and passed it through customs, it would be delivered to a location in the Bronx. Once delivered there, The Engineer would immediately transfer the container contents to a second location. No one could trace the shipment from the delivery in the Bronx, this second location known only to him and his New York cell leader.

The Engineer was quite content. He had been disturbed to lose the container in Sicily. But it was the Naples container that now held important equipment he could not afford to lose. He concluded his two associates made too many visits to the dock area and attracted the attention of the authorities. He didn't think informants could be involved. The Sicilians were noted for having an abject hatred of government and thought nothing of killing police, magistrates or journalists to continue their reign of terror. He didn't think they were the problem.

The Engineer slept well at night. He was excited that his plans and work were coming to fruition. He had no doubt he would enjoy success. Through his attack plan, which he fully-intended to survive, he would eventually be known worldwide and feared by the infidel. He would become the main warrior for al-Qaeda's jihad against the infidel. He reveled in his thoughts of personal glory. He did not bother sharing these thoughts with Allah in any form of prayer.

While he was impatient to get started, The Engineer had no timetable so he was only under pressure that he created for himself.

Chapter 48

New York City – Three Weeks Later

The surveillance agents set up several video cameras across the street from the used computer shop of the suspected money launderer. They had arranged for court-authorized telephone and microphone surveillance of conversations taking place inside the computer store. Inside, conversations were being picked up by microphones they installed during a nighttime break in.

The decision was made not to install cameras in the interior of the shop. There were too many cheap devices on the electronics market that made it very easy to find hidden video cameras. Video cameras were installed at key points to cover the front of the computer store and its immediate vicinity.

The computer shop was located in a partially restored area of Spanish Harlem on the East Side, south of the very busy 125th Street. Walking these streets was like walking the halls of the United Nations. One saw every shade of human skin coloring possible. The languages spoken sounded like word salad, unless you knew the various languages and the local dialects. It was a busy area with numerous local shops serving every culture represented in the area. It was easy to blend in as long as you were not a white male, American or European.

The signals from the video cameras, the microphone and telephone conversations, were digitally routed back to a central FBI monitoring office in lower Manhattan. There, more sophisticated electronic equipment and personnel were available. Agents on site had full access to the same information being routed back to Manhattan. The agents on site were calling the shots.

The shop was owned by Salim Bin Attash, an Egyptian by heritage but born in New York City of immigrant parents. Salim was a US citizen and entitled to all the benefits and guarantees the US Constitution conferred on its citizens. Salim was a devout Muslim who attended a mosque in an old, converted store front located five blocks away. He had attended a local community college, where he put his affinity for computers to work. Besides selling used computers and related hardware, he also gave computer classes at night in his store after closing. His parents had lived in New York for almost thirty years but decided to go back to Egypt five years ago to be with family after his father retired from his tailor shop.

Salim was unmarried, in his late twenties, and not known to be actively seeking a wife. He seemed content with his computer shop, his lessons, and his attendance at the mosque. Very few knew that Salim was a Hawaladar and an important cog in the American side of the ancient underground banking system, historically associated with the eastern trade routes. His family in Egypt had been Hawaladars for over a hundred years and his father, while a very good tailor, handled the family's money business in New York City for the years he lived there. Salim inherited the business from his father when he returned to Egypt. Salim was now a Hawaladar for the extended family in New York City.

Hawala was always a trusted money transfer system operated by those who chose not to recognize political borders or currency transfer regulations. Its origins were to prevent traveling merchants from being robbed. However, in more recent years, drug smugglers and terrorists found the system to their advantage after they learned the hard way that governments had ways of tracing money when dealing with commercial institutions.

Not so with the Hawaladar. No one had cracked this system yet. The best they ever had was just a glimpse here and there. Salim was a glimpse that had been picked up by both the CIA through rumors and from the NSA through electronic monitoring. Because Salim was physically located in the United States, the information was turned over to the FBI for investigation. The FBI wanted to determine the identities of those utilizing his services, and even more importantly, why. They had enough information to establish probable cause for electronic surveillance but not enough to arrest Salim. They had no idea that al-Qaeda was a customer of Salim's in the United States. If the truth be known, neither did Salim. His business was with people of certain tribes, not political entities.

Salim's shop was in an area that real estate agents described as "mixed" and certainly an area in which a sharp real estate mind would consider investing. Now was the time while the prices were still affordable, although the prices for remodeled units were starting to take dramatic leaps forward. However, despite the positive talk about the area's comeback, there was still a lot of space for rent at cheap prices. Salim's shop was one of these.

It was three weeks ago that The Engineer had successfully entered the United States. He recovered his container from the Naples cargo ship without a question or problem. He had the container delivered by pre-arrangement with the ground transport agent to an address in the Bronx. He and his New York team leader immediately transferred the contents of the container to yet another container, which was then taken to a second warehouse located in the area known as Hell's Kitchen. At this point, only two people knew the location of his armaments and they could not be traced by anyone from the shipping company to this location.

His New York team leader, Tariq Salah, had proven to be extremely competent. Salah was a US citizen by birth, born to Saudi parents who lived in Miami. Salah became a devout Muslim in Miami and moved to New York City seven years ago. He was later recruited and trained by al-Qaeda. He was now thirty-four years old and ostensibly worked as a cab driver. The family mosque in Miami had participated in fundraising for various Islamic charities but, unknown to any of the contributors, the money was really financing al-Qaeda.

The Engineer first spoke to Salah in London, where Salah was introduced to him by Mustaf ben Afad. Salah now had eight well-trained warriors under his command. Each had been recruited in the United States and was a US citizen. Each had been through an al-Qaeda training camp in Afghanistan via travel to Saudi Arabia. Some of their training had been designed and directed by The Engineer personally.

al-Qaeda wanted to have US citizens as trained al-Qaeda terrorists. It was easier than trying to smuggle teams into the United States to carry out the jihad against the infidel. American citizens had many legal rights that were regularly observed by law enforcement. Constitutional requirements made it harder for authorities to investigate its own citizens, as compared to a non-citizen. It would also be more politically meaningful for the jihad when the United States was attacked at home by its own citizens. The Engineer had at his disposal the first fruits of al-Qaeda's effort to recruit US citizens. The Engineer's plan would finally debut this long-term strategy of al-Qaeda.

The Engineer maintained total control of the two fire extinguishers. No one in America knew he had smuggled in radioactive material, much less what he intended to do with it. In the end, it was easy to get the fire extinguishers transferred from the ship safely ashore. When the ship docked, some workmen came aboard to make repairs before the ship departed for Lisbon and later back to Naples. The Engineer had a conversation with a welder who had come on board. The welder agreed, for a small fee, to put the fire extinguishers on his cart and take them off the ship. The welder was a regular on the docks. Although he had to go through a cursory examination going to and from the ships he serviced each day, no one paid much attention to him or the equipment on his cart. A couple of fire extinguishers could easily be explained as needed while welding in the ship's hold. In any event, an explanation was unnecessary because no one looked and no one asked. The welder was unconcerned about the small amount of "drugs" he was bringing past customs in the extinguishers. This was really nothing when compared to what was coming in via the large shipping containers that were never searched. What he was doing, he thought, was so small as to be of no significance.

The Engineer safely stored the two extinguishers before he met with Tariq Salah. The Engineer found a storage facility in the basement of an apartment building. The manager was glad to rent him an eight-by-twelve foot space for cash, no questions asked. This was on the lower West Side, not far from where the new container was now stored, and where the ever decreasing commercial port of New York City on the Hudson River was located. Most ocean cargo containers now came into the ports of Bayonne or Elizabeth City, New Jersey, where new facilities were erected to handle modern container ships.

On a Monday morning three weeks after arriving in New York City, The Engineer asked Tariq to drive him to a specific area in Spanish Harlem. They drove the FDR along the East River until they exited at 125th Street, turned west for a few blocks and then headed south. He instructed Tariq to drop him at a location about three blocks from his intended destination. He got out and walked a few blocks in the opposite direction to make sure he was not followed. He stopped at a local variety store for a quick soda and to get acclimated to the area and the people walking about. He saw nothing to disturb him so he proceeded to the computer shop.

The duty agent watching the video monitor immediately noticed The Engineer. He sensed that The Engineer was looking the area over. He did not seem to be walking directly to or from a point as others did. The agent brought him to the attention of the other two agents at the monitoring site. Neither could recall seeing him before. In addition to the video being recorded, they shot some digital photos to make sure they had some high quality images in the event he became of interest to their present inquiry. The photos had just been shot when The Engineer became more of an interest to them. He entered Salim's shop.

Salim was behind a counter replacing a hard drive in the bottom of a laptop. "May I help you?" inquired Salim.

"I am looking for a used Apple laptop. My friend told me to come see you. He said you often had used laptops for sale at a good price. He suggested a certain model and I had him write down the information, as I know little about computers."

The Engineer handed the piece of paper with numbers on it to Salim. It was a payment transfer code. Salim looked at the numbers and looked at The Engineer. "This is a good computer and I think I have one in stock." Salim then passed the paper back to The Engineer, said nothing, but handed a pencil to The Engineer. The Engineer wrote down on the paper a second series of numbers he had memorized from his meeting with ben Afad in Tunis. The Engineer pushed the paper back to Salim who looked at it. Salim put the paper in his pants pocket.

"I will go to the stockroom in back and see if it is still there." Salim disappeared behind a curtain. About three minutes later Salim reappeared with an Apple laptop and a power cord in one hand, and a brown leather computer carrying case in the other.

"Let me plug it in and start it up and I can show you what software is on the computer."

Salim did exactly that. While the computer was firing up, he reached into the brown bag, pulled out a money belt and motioned to The Engineer to raise his shirt. The Engineer loosened his shirt from his pants and Salim handed him the money belt, which he put around his waist. He secured it and tucked his shirt back into his pants. Salim put the computer bag on the counter and opened a very large interior pocket to show The Engineer it was filled with neatly packed $100 bills. The Engineer nodded.

Salim gave The Engineer a full demonstration of the Apple laptop and all its functions.

"I can sell you this computer for $800. It is a real bargain because I have practically rebuilt this computer from scratch, doubled the memory and even added a camera. It is set up with the Skype software if you want to use it for international calls."

"It is a nice computer but I was thinking of something cheaper, for a beginner, not so complicated."

"But this is what your friend recommended for you."

"But he told me not to pay any more then $600 for it."

"He did not know how much time I put into refurbishing this computer. It is like new. I am sure he would agree it is worth $800," said Salim.

The Engineer still looked unconvinced.

"I tell you what, call your friend and let me talk to him and I will explain what I did. He will agree $800 is a good price."

"No, he is at work and I can't disturb him. Let me propose to pay you $700. If my friend thinks it is worth $800, I will come back with the other hundred dollars."

Salim laughed out loud. "Somehow I doubt I will see you or this computer for a long time. I'll tell you what. I will sell it for $700 cash, no credit cards. I will write out a bill of sale and receipt for your business records. That way I don't have to give up 4 percent of the price to the credit card company."

"Agreed," said The Engineer as he reached in his pocket and took out his wallet. From the wallet he counted out $700.

"There is $56 dollars in city and state sales tax," said Salim.

"I don't have any more money," said The Engineer.

Salim let out a big sigh. "The next time you want to buy something for a computer, or buy a new computer, remember me. I will pay the tax and cut my profit but I hope you will become a regular customer after I have treated you so well."

"I will. Does it come with this carrying case?"

"Yes" said Salim. "I am putting your receipt in with the computer. You place the computer like this so it is padded all the way around. You close it like this."

The agents monitoring the transaction could even hear the zipper close.

The Engineer walked out to the street with his new computer in the brown leather carrying case. He now had the rest of his money from Tunis minus a service charge from the Hawaladar. He walked back to the area where Tariq dropped him off. The Engineer had asked Tariq to come back and pick him up in two hours. After walking for seven blocks, he was at the pick-up point with five minutes to wait.

The agents on the street asked the local monitoring agents if they should put physical surveillance on the customer. After a brief discussion, it was agreed that the transaction just overheard appeared to be a normal, negotiated computer purchase. The person was already on foot and they might not catch up to him. Besides, this investigation was in its infancy and they did not want to get caught following someone at this early point if there was no good reason to do so. There would be no surveillance. They would submit the pictures routinely to see if a hit came back on the customer.

Chapter 49

Boston

Welby filed an additional motion with the court, claiming that the informant information was privileged. Later that same afternoon, Welby called Patrick to tell him the government had just filed a motion with Judge West to dismiss Patrick's federal grand jury subpoena. The judge immediately granted the motion. The matter was over.

Patrick felt immediate relief, followed by anger. "As the saying goes, where do I go to get my reputation back?"

"If the press contacts me, I will tell them we think this was an abuse of process from the start. I will emphasize your cooperation with the FBI in an important criminal matter, and say there is no question that you are doing the right thing."

"Okay" said Patrick. "It sounds good to me. I just want the community to know it was all a sham and they were using the media to squeeze me with their allusion to tax violations."

"Well, that can be your addition to the media after I address the record."

"Agreed. Thanks so much. I really appreciate the time you took on short notice when I asked for help."

"Mark, I somehow expect I will hear from you again regarding a legal matter and, as always, it will be on short notice. That is always the way with you," said Welby with a smile in his voice.

"Send me your invoice. I will make every effort to pay it within six months. See, I'm practicing some long-range planning already."

They both ended the call laughing.

Patrick called Liz to tell her that her husband was no longer contemptible. She was not so sure. They would review his claim over dinner.

Within an hour, Patrick had a telephone call from Vince Baker at FBIHQ.

"I'm glad to hear your subpoena has been withdrawn," said Baker. "I hope you don't hold that against us."

"Vince, I said to you a couple of days ago what I thought. I don't intend to repeat myself."

"I take it you have had no further contact from Vespa?"

"None," said Patrick curtly.

"They've gotten nothing from the associates in Italy. Maybe they are more substantial players then we initially thought. We don't know. It bothers us," mused Baker.

Patrick said nothing. He had nothing to add.

"The airport cargo handler is a little more interesting. They have traced him to a Camorra family in Naples that does a lot of smuggling. There were telephone calls to Naples when The Engineer was with him. We're not sure what it means. The Italians are trying to shake the Camorra tree to find out if The Engineer shipped anything through them."

"Maybe the FBI legal attaché in Rome could go south to Naples and ask his Camorra informants about the cargo man and The Engineer. Maybe we could ask the CIA to check with their informants in the Camorra about the pair," Patrick said with an attitude.

"You don't have to drive that point home with me. You may like to know that discussions regarding the operation of informants have blossomed here in Washington the last two weeks. It's always a battle. Those who want absolute control over the FBI do not give up. The FBI wants specific and detailed legislation passed by Congress authorizing exactly what the FBI can and cannot do in developing informants. This takes it out of the DOJ guideline status, which is subject to the interpretation of whatever their immediate goals are. Anyway, the Director is ready to tell Congress that FBI agents are refusing to operate informants until they have all the I's dotted and the T's crossed by Congress. There is no trust between the FBI and the DOJ regarding informants, and it will stay that way until the matter is fixed."

"At least it's being addressed" said Patrick. "I can take some solace in that. I'll let you know if I hear anything."

"Okay, Mark. Thanks."

Patrick walked to the Café Strada. He sat alone enjoying an espresso. He was thinking about trying to contact Vespa to explain all that had happened. He felt badly for some reason about how things had been left. It just did not seem right. He could go home, move the chairs and see what happened. He vacillated back and forth. Finally he decided to wait and see. Why expose Vespa to possible danger for no reason. Maybe Bottom and crew had not given up.

When he and Liz talked that night, it was Liz who noted that no one from the press had contacted Patrick regarding the government's public filing, withdrawing Patrick's subpoena. Both previously thought it might take a day or two for the news to get out, at which point he would be contacted for comment. Both were wrong. No one from the media ever bothered asking Patrick for an explanation of what happened. The withdrawn subpoena was apparently not news worthy. As a result, if his name were "Googled," the last report would be that Patrick was an uncooperative potential grand jury witness who might be the subject of a government investigation himself.

Chapter 50

New York City

The Engineer spent hours touring the city in Tariq's taxi while Tariq explained the intelligence he had gathered. The Engineer really wanted to hit New York City again and again until it ceased to function. It was now time to make Tariq almost a full partner in the scope of the project being planned. The Engineer did not intend to tell him about the radioactive material.

"Here is the inventory list for the container I brought," said The Engineer. Tariq reviewed the list. His eyes widened when he saw there was 2,200 pounds of C-4 and Semtex plastic explosives. He had seen the boxes, but they did the unloading at night. He was not given any time to digest or analyze the contents. He recognized the other armaments as being weapons that were highly destructive and which had limited or no availability in their training camp. They were just too expensive and hard to get. Here, they were present in one container.

Tariq responded, "It is obvious to me that our friend who introduced us thinks very highly of you. He has provided you with substantial equipment for your operation. I have reported my observations to you about Wall Street as a target, as well as several key transportation facilities for both rail and ships. It seems to me that perhaps you have more in mind."

"Let me talk freely about my conversations with Mustaf ben Afad. After 1993 and 2001, al-Qaeda wanted to continue to hit New York City as it represents the economic heart of the infidel. For many reasons they have not. If we damage or remove this symbol we will shake the foundation of their economic system. We asked you to look at Wall Street because it is the symbol of what we want to destroy. We also don't think Americans

193

have the stomach to live in fear, which they will have to do when they see we can reach into their cities and kill without question."

"Is all this equipment for a single attack on Wall Street?"

"No," said The Engineer. "We also want to put fear into their rail and bus terminals, as well as their tunnels that are used daily to allow thousands to work in their economic machine. If the workers are afraid to commute, there will be no business left in the city."

"So your plan is for multiple, coordinated attacks?"

"Yes." They both sat silent for a few moments.

"But they will just clean up the rubble like they did after 9/11 and keep on going. If the World Trade Center destruction did not generate enough fear when seen all over the TV, what makes you think these multiple attacks will have a more lasting result?"

The Engineer recognized that Salah had an analytical mind and would not be easily fooled. So The Engineer made a tactical decision. He needed Salah's full commitment to make his plan work. He needed Salah to be eager about being part of a great moment in Islamic history. He felt he needed to tell Salah the whole story.

The Engineer explained to Salah he had the radioactive material in the two fire extinguishers, which he stored away from the armaments. He also explained how he wanted to use this material and how he thought it would enhance the overall objectives of his plan. He explained that he and ben Afad were in agreement about destroying an American city by leaving it largely intact and visible, but unusable because of radioactive contamination.

"Can you imagine the panic? The first responders will determine immediately there are alpha and cesium-137 emissions. They will have to warn the population to avoid contact with or ingestion of these materials. Imagine the dust and debris particles being carried as the wind blows. Think of how this chaos will wreak havoc on their great evacuation plans?"

Salah started to smile but was also frightened at what he was hearing.

The Engineer continued. "We want the world to see, moment by moment, the failure of the most powerful government in the world when they are unable to provide basic protection to their populace. Their intelligence leaders have referred to a dirty bomb as a weapon of mass disruption. They believe more deaths would be caused by the actual explosion and ensuing panic than from the long-term radiation effects. This may be what happens, but we want the world to see chaos, animal survivor behavior, and people killing each other to physically escape their great fear of radiation.

194

The government has failed to educate citizens about these possibilities. They are not prepared. After the attack, it will be too late. Chaos will rule. City, state, and federal governments will not be able to stop the panic. What can they say to the public? Do not come into contact with any radiation? Do not breathe? All of al-Qaeda will rejoice to see the mass hysteria as everyone tries to abandon a polluted city at the same time. Unlike 9/11, this attack will be ongoing every day for years to come. They will not be able to bulldoze and clear away this event. We will leave it standing but unusable."

"Will we have to die? Will this be a martyr's mission?" asked Salah.

"Do you still have all eight members of your team?" asked The Engineer.

"Yes. I have eight members. But I have listened to you describe your mission. There are two that I'm not sure have the heart for a martyr's mission."

"I will tell you this," said The Engineer, "I have no plans for you to become a martyr. I want you to be a live hero within al-Qaeda, to Islam, a symbol of this strike against the infidel. Let them try to hunt you down. They will have no luck finding you."

He sensed this was the answer that Salah wanted to hear. He observed Salah's shoulders visibly relax and straighten with pride. The Engineer did mean most of what he said.

"What is your timetable?" asked Salah.

"I don't have a strict timetable. It will be when we are ready."

"After seeing what I have shown you the last three weeks, do you now have the specific targets in mind?" asked Tariq.

Wall Street, Pennsylvania Station, Grand Central Station, the Port Authority, LaGuardia Airport, and the Holland and Lincoln tunnels are all on my list. I want no one willing to commute into this city. I want to contaminate every entry. I want to do the George Washington Bridge. While the bridge is hard to destroy and easy to repair, there are other reasons that make it a worthwhile target. We can discuss this later. The other targets cannot be easily cleaned up. They have no technology to do so, no workers trained or willing to clean up radioactive material, and no place to put it," said The Engineer.

"But do you have enough radioactive material to do all these areas?" continued Tariq.

"I have enough to make sure there is reportable and lasting radiation in all areas.

Tariq Salah's eyes locked on to The Engineer. "I am afraid that some members of my team may try and move family members out of the area ahead of time, and this in turn could cause information to leak out."

"I agree this is a possibility. If allowed to happen, it is a security threat to us. That is why your team members will never learn what I just told you about using dirty bombs. They will only know we are using plastic explosives and heavy armaments to rein our destruction. You must not tell them. Can you agree to that?"

Salah then again looked The Engineer in the eyes and said, "Yes." He added, "I have no family here in New York. They are all in Miami."

He believed Salah. This was good for Salah because if he had not, The Engineer would have killed Salah that night.

"We will spend the next days matching our equipment to your teams. You and I will draw up the detailed assignments, location by location, for each team. Then the team members will do reconnaissance before the actual event. You will have to tell me about the two men you question and whether or not we can even use them."

Chapter 51

Southport

Patrick and Liz had a great weekend in Southport. On Saturday, he and John Peabody went striper fishing from the beach and had some success. One striper measured thirty-four inches and was a keeper. The blues had returned. They caught three nice ones. They smoked the bluefish and filleted the striper. They put half in Peabody's freezer for later in the week. The other half got cooked over a charcoal fire after marinating it in olive oil, herbs, and a touch of soy sauce, and covered with lemon slices. Using a fish basket made it easy to turn the fish while keeping everything in place. A fresh garden salad with oil and vinegar, along with steamed wild and brown rice, rounded out the plate. The Pinot Grigio was cold and the after-dinner Grappa strong.

On Sunday, Patrick and Liz went on a two-hour hike. The day was a combination of late spring and early summer and many flowers were just starting to bloom. The woods were still damp but the fields were just starting to dry out, so what was in bloom depended on where you stood and how much sun was available.

As they walked along, they discussed some upcoming family obligations. Nieces and nephews were doing great things academically, playing great sports, and needed to be recognized for their successes. A Brennick family Fourth of July party was in the discussion stage. It was the time of year when people really wanted to slow down and enjoy those limited New England weeks of summer. They sat on a cedar bench overlooking a stream that was partially damned with huge stones. It created a pond and a narrow channel where the stream water raced through. It had partially disintegrated over the years but the original work, done two hundred years ago, was still visible. Patrick knew there were native brook trout in this stream but he never fished it. He didn't need them for food as much as nature needed them in the stream. They were too delicate for catch and release so they were best left alone to admire, which he was now doing.

"Should we move down here permanently?" asked Liz.

"On a day like this and on such a beautiful weekend my answer is yes. However, on rainy, cold days, I like the city. Sometimes when things get too quiet here, I look forward to going back to the city. We have a fireplace in both homes so we have the luxury of snuggling up in either location."

"I just like to ask you once in a while. I know how much you like it here, but I don't want you to get bored," said Liz.

"Being married to you absolutely prevents boredom, my love," smiled Patrick.

Patrick continued, "Besides, you haven't had to read or hear bad things in the news about me for several days now," said Patrick as he put a hurt look on his face.

"Nevertheless, I may have to regard you as damaged goods," said Liz.

"Can I sue Bottom for loss of affection from my spouse caused by his false and evil slings at me on the public record?" asked Patrick.

"Hire a lawyer and find out."

"But you are a lawyer."

"I'm not your lawyer!"

"You have little sympathy for your loving husband."

Liz answered by getting up and starting back on the trail without any comment or a look back. But, she was smiling.

Driving back to Boston Sunday night, Patrick's new cell phone went off. On the other end he heard a voice that was familiar.

"Tell your friends in Naples they must shake the Camorra tree as hard as they can for information. The Engineer was in contact with them and they helped him. They will know which Camorra group from the cargo handler's phone records."

The line went dead. Patrick knew it was Vespa. No use wasting time, he thought. He called Vince Baker and left a message requesting a call back. Before he reached Route 128 Baker was back to him. Patrick told Baker exactly what Vespa said.

Baker was silent for a moment. Patrick said nothing.

"Our people are still over there with the Italians. They have those phone records and were supposed to be running down all the numbers. We'll expedite the process. The Engineer is a critical factor still in play."

Patrick said nothing. He could think of nothing worthwhile to say.

"Let me know if you hear anything else?" asked Baker.

"Of course," said Patrick and the call ended.

Patrick and Liz briefly discussed the fact that Vespa was willing to call him after all that had taken place and was in the news. Vespa was still concerned about The Engineer running around now with the Camorra's help.

"Do you think they can get any cooperation from the Camorra?" asked Liz.

"The Camorra has a history of being part of the Naples shadow government. They got their start a couple hundred years ago by collecting taxes on behalf of the port of Naples from arriving ships. In recent years, there have been bloody scenes in Naples where the Camorra have viciously attacked other ethnic gangs trying to infringe on Camorra territory. I would guess the Camorra is presently not on very friendly terms with the Italian police."

"Okay, let me ask it a different way. What would you do if you were there?"

"The phone numbers and individuals contacted by the cargo handler should identify the specific Camorra family he worked for. I would go to the boss of the family and tell him I want him to find out exactly what his family did for The Engineer and everything they know about him. I would have him discreetly make available for interview those who dealt directly with The Engineer."

"And you think the boss would do this because of your wit, charm, and good looks?"

"No. I would explain there would be an easy way and a hard way."

"And what is the easy way for starters?"

"I would tell the boss that these are unusual times and hence the need for my request. Because of the effort he would have to put in to this request, I would be willing to pay him something for his personal efforts, which he could then disperse as he thought necessary. He also would have the temporary gratitude of the government for his exemplary civic behavior."

"I can't wait to hear about the hard way."

"I would explain to the boss that if I did not have his full cooperation on this most unusual matter, I would assign every available resource to investigate only his Camorra family, ignoring the other families. This would mean that each one of his ships and their cargo would be thoroughly searched before entering or departing the port of Naples. His crew and passengers would be subject to mandatory searches upon exiting or boarding the ship. Now, of course, I would suggest that he may want to refrain from carrying any perishable cargo as these new requirements may cause unavoidable delays in his schedule. From there, I would move to safety inspections by the Italian Navy on all his ships sailing in Italian waters. I would inform him that the Guardia di Finanza would be assigned to conduct a full tax review of this family business and all family members' personal bank accounts, which would probably take several years to complete."

"You mean you would bribe or extort the Camorra to get them to do what you want?"

"Well, I can't agree with your choice of verbs. I think I would need to pay a man for his time in helping me. In reality, our government extends offers to other governments all the time. It is called military aid, farm aid, debt forgiveness and so forth."

"Wouldn't it be extortion to threaten them with strict enforcement?"

"If they are doing nothing criminal, they should have no problem. It is the prerogative of any government to assign its limited resources against what is considered to be the greatest crime threat to society. In this case, I'm telling them ahead of time so they have the courtesy of advance warning and an opportunity to change their ways and amend their lives to be good citizens!"

"Do you really think it would work?"

"Yes. Remember the government let Lucky Luciano out of jail and deported him to Italy at the beginning of World War II in order to secure labor peace on the docks up and down the East Coast. Luciano wanted out of jail and the government needed to know it had peaceful and efficient docks as it entered World War II. It worked. Luciano remained in Italy and was never allowed back in the US. Therefore, there is precedent as they would say in the law."

"Why didn't you suggest any of this to Baker?"

"No. He can figure it out on his own."

"I don't think I would want you chasing me."

"Then don't become a terrorist or a member of the Camorra. As a lawyer, you are part of a somewhat naturally suspect group, but right now I think you are safe," said Patrick with a raised eyebrow.

Chapter 52

New York City

John Turco had been dispatched to Naples to find out more about The Engineer. From their phone company contacts in Palermo, they obtained the phone records from the cargo handler's apartment. Through these records Zio Vincenzo identified the cargo handler's contacts in Naples. These contacts were mostly individuals or places associated with the Renzotti Camorra family. Aldo and Zio Vincenzo knew the Renzotti Camorra family but had made no effort to make direct inquiry of them about the cargo handler or The Engineer. They sent John Turco to Naples to do a quick assessment, and now he was back.

Maria Torino stood with her father and John Turco in the basement garage of their office building. Maria reported her call to Patrick. They had debated beforehand what she should say. They had more information but were reluctant to say too much given the legal attention that Patrick had been under in Boston.

"So what do you think happened in Naples with The Engineer?" asked Aldo Torino.

Maria thought for a few moments then said "I think he was lucky in Palermo and saw the police following the two associates. He knew enough to get out of there fast. He already had contacts established with the Renzotti family through the cargo handler. You know the police were watching the flights out of Palermo. I suspect he was on the ferry from Palermo to Naples just as the police were making their move on the associates. The timing matches the departure time of the afternoon ferry."

"And from Naples what did he do?"

"He was shipping the Palermo container to New York. You assume he was going to Naples to further his plan. If he was smart, he did not have all his eggs in one basket. I believe there is another shipment of arms that went out of Naples and that he was with it or met the shipment when it arrived in New York."

"So what are the police doing in Naples?"

John responded. "Some of the detectives who worked the case in Palermo have been sent to Naples. They are looking for the same thing. The Renzotti family is big in the shipping business. Much of it is even legitimate. It makes sense he was using them."

"John, were direct inquiries made of the Renzotti family?" asked Maria.

"Not by us. I think the Renzotti family will shortly be having some difficult conversations with the Carabinieri on the subject of their cooperation. I checked with Zio Vincenzo, and we both thought we would not learn much from the Renzottis if we asked directly. Such inquiry would only serve to make our interest known."

Aldo Torino nodded in agreement.

"What are the Renzottis' interests here in New York?"

"Not much. They have a regular run from Naples to New York to Lisbon and back to Naples. They also have another regular run to New York, then Miami, then back to Naples.

Otherwise it is mostly in the Mediterranean or North Africa for their cargo ships. They do some more by plane, but not to the US."

"Passengers?" asked Aldo.

"There is room for a few on each ship. The accommodations are not fancy but nice. A lot of Italians, who dislike flying, use them to go back and forth."

"So should we have told Patrick more?" asked Maria.

"I think what you said was enough. They don't need a roadmap. They will do just what we've done except they will step on the Renzottis to get what they want," said Aldo.

"Will the Renzottis give it to them?" asked Maria.

"I think almost right away. He will get the point that this is irregular but very necessary," said Turco.

"What else are we doing now?" asked Aldo.

Turco responded. "We are on the docks trying to find out what we can about any passengers that came in on Renzotti's ships. That is easier to find than trying to figure out if they had a container delivered. But we are very low key for the moment."

"Okay," said Aldo Torino. "We must operate on the belief The Engineer made it to New York. That is where he wanted to go and he had the means to do so. We need to pick up this trail. The only chance we have is on the docks. This directly affects us. It is New York. I will have no qualms about being more direct and forceful with the Renzottis if that is necessary to protect us. I do not want this terrorist doing his work in New York!"

"Shall I check back with Patrick to see if they have figured it out?" asked Maria.

"Let's wait and see what develops," said Aldo. "I have a feeling things are going to pick up quickly in Naples."

Maria later sat at her desk reviewing the ships that had docked in New York City since the date the associates were picked up. She was looking for ships owned by the Renzotti family. She could see why John thought The Engineer was probably in New York. She would hold this data for her next conversation with Patrick. By then she hoped he would have the same information.

Chapter 53

Naples, Italy

Detectives Giorgio and Tomasso had been sent to assist their brethren in Naples. Since they discovered The Engineer in the Palermo airport video, their superiors hoped they could do it again for cameras in the port of Naples. They thought The Engineer could have come to Naples on the ferry. This time they had a lot of help and they were doing the organizing. The port was huge. The decision was made to concentrate the effort on docks utilized by the Renzotti family. They had been told not to approach the Renzotti shipping company for any information. They had not been able to identify all of the available cameras. It was not a matter of corruption, just incompetence.

Colonel Marco Bonillo was in charge of the Carabinieri organized crime unit stationed in Naples. His group had recently been concentrating on a series of murders between Camorra factions and a group of Nigerians trying to cut into their narcotics trade. Marco was a veteran of twenty years in Italy's war against the Mafia. He had friends that were murdered during this period. He didn't think he should be having conversations with the Camorra, but he was asked to do so. He followed his orders. Bonillo was accompanied by a short, compact, dark haired, middle-aged major named Michele Onessimo of the Naples Anti-Terrorism Police. Onessimo was new to terrorism work but well known as a homicide detective in Naples. He was rumored to have very good sources in the Camorra, who were always willing to identify the rivals shooting Camorra members. Of course, he often had a similar arrangement with some of the Nigerian gangs. He knew how to talk with everyone.

It was 10:00 am as they drove into the yard of the Renzotti Shipping Company. They had an appointment with Adolpho Renzotti who ran the company and was head of the family. Onessimo had previously met Renzotti and recognized the knarred, squat, grey haired man seated behind a desk smoking a cigarette that smelled as if it had been laced with oregano. Renzotti nodded to Onessimo and looked quizzically at Bonillo and then back to Onessimo. Onessimo introduced Bonillo, giving his full title and assignment to make it clear that terrorism was involved and not just organized crime. The only reaction from Renzotti to the introduction was that his half-hooded eyes may have blinked just a little. Renzotti called, "Luigi, I want you with me." At that point a younger version of Adolpho Renzotti entered the room from a door behind his father. Introductions were repeated for his benefit. Luigi was Adolpho's son. No handshakes were exchanged, but Adolpho Renzotti invited the police to be seated. He also picked up the phone and ordered four espressos from somewhere in the building.

Onessimo began the conversation by saying this meeting was somewhat out of the ordinary, but it was vital to the security of Italy and her allies. He stated that he expected the contents of their conversation to be private and not gossiped about. If that were to happen, Italy could be harmed. The hooded eyes blinked again. Onessimo then named the cargo handler and identified him as an associate of the Renzotti Camorra family. Then Onessimo got down to the meat of the conversation.

"Several weeks ago the cargo handler unloaded dangerous material from a small cargo plane that arrived in Palermo Airport from Tbilisi, Georgia. Shortly thereafter he picked up an Arab male, posing as an Italian, in his late twenties, from the airport hotel and took him to his apartment in Palermo. They remained together for several days. During that time they called you and some of your people a number of times. The police made a seizure in Palermo of deadly arms and explosives that this man and two of his associates were shipping to New York. The associates were arrested and this man escaped. We believe he came to you in Naples through prior arrangements made by the cargo handler. The Engineer murdered the cargo handler just before he left so he couldn't talk. We and our allies need to find this man immediately. Where did you take him?"

Adolpho Renzotti almost smiled. He had been bullied by more aggressive cops over the years. He had been beaten, thrown in jail, lied to, and tricked. He had managed to corrupt a number of important police officials to prevent this sort of questioning. The police had never made a solid case against him. Of course he was not one of the big fish nor did he pretend to be. But, these were men of rank. They were serious. They did not look hopeful but, they did look determined.

"We are a legitimate shipping company and you are welcome to all of our records for cargo or passengers. Of course my lawyers will insist you follow the normal judicial procedures to obtain them."

"We both know we can review all the records in the world and they probably won't identify this person or anything he might have shipped," said Bonillo. "We are asking for your cooperation as an Italian businessman who wants to serve his country."

At that point a bodyguard knocked on the outer door and opened it to admit a young boy bearing a pot of espresso and four cups. Luigi got up, poured the coffee, gave one to each of the police, along with sugar, and then prepared one for his father and himself. Bonillo and Onessimo were silent. They just looked directly at the elder Renzotti.

"And if I call my lawyer and address your needs with him, I gather you will not feel that I have been as helpful as you wish."

"You know that to be the case, Señor Renzotti," said Onessimo.

"You actually expect me to be a police informant. Did you drink grappa before you came to see me?"

"Señor Renzotti," said Onessimo, "We both know the ways of our worlds and what we expect from each other. We understand that you see our request as very unusual, and it is. Ordinarily we would expect to be referred to your attorney. However, our orders are quite clear. We are to obtain your immediate cooperation."

"And lacking that desired cooperation, you are going to threaten me with some kind of police action," said Adolpho Renzotti with half of a snarl on his face. That was all Onessimo was going to take.

"Señor Renzotti, we explained this was about national security. It is obvious that time is of the essence for us. You have information that we need. There is no exposure at this point to you. The man had perfectly good papers. You have no reason to look in any container from him. We are not looking to hold you responsible for transporting this man or his goods. You are not involved in this so my suggestion, most sincerely, is do not put yourself in the way of an affair that does not concern you. We are not to be taken lightly in our request."

"The security of my clients, their goods, and information is all important to me," said Renzotti. "I make it a point not to talk to the police about my business."

"This time we will ask you to make an exception," said Colonel Bonillo. Renzotti thought Bonillo was barely controlling himself and was a person under great stress.

Silence filled the room. Renzotti was taking the measure of the men sitting in front of him. He knew he did not need any police pressure at this time. The Nigerians were still pressing him and he needed to put them down. If he did not, the other Camorra families in Naples would view him as weak and they would start to move in on him. He knew Onessimo by reputation and thought Onessimo could also draw an accurate assessment of Renzotti's current predicament.

Renzotti looked at his son. "Luigi, take these men downstairs and show them the necessary records. I do seem to recall the cargo handler referring a client to us a couple of weeks ago for passage to New York City. I also believe he had a container dropped here that was loaded on the ship that went to New York and then Miami. I don't recall which city the cargo was to be delivered. Captain Adagio is in port. It was on his ship this person traveled. If they need to speak to the captain or any of the crew, please see that it is done immediately so the ship's departure is not delayed. Tell the captain and the crew their complete cooperation with this inquiry will be appreciated by me. "

Luigi appeared somewhat shocked but was cool enough to merely nod to his father and stand up.

Bonillo and Onessimo stood. This time they shook hands with Renzotti.

"Perhaps the day will be recalled when I was a loyal Italian citizen," said Renzotti.

"Perhaps," said Onessimo as they walked out of the office with Luigi to get the records.

Chapter 54

Washington, DC

By noontime in Washington, Vince Baker was giving an update to Assistant Director Bob Wilkins on the recent developments in Naples.

"Just hours ago, the Carabinieri and the Naples Police paid a visit to the Camorra Boss Adolpho Renzotti. It was his group that was contacted by the cargo handler. They managed to get his cooperation. The Engineer made arrangements for a second container to be delivered by truck to Renzotti's docks for shipment to New York. We have the weight, size and numbers, and it is similar to the one recovered in Palermo. The Engineer also booked passage for himself on another Renzotti ship that left for New York two days before the container was shipped. It looks like he wanted to get out as soon as he could."

"What about New York?" asked Wilkins.

"From the Naples records we know the name and phony Italian passport data under which The Engineer is traveling. He has a booked and prepaid return passage in two months on another cargo ship."

"Has his entry at New York City been confirmed?"

"Both Immigration and Customs have him entering New York City using the Italian passport. He has been here over three weeks," advised Baker.

"What about the container?"

"Shipping records verify the offloading from the ship to the dock in New York. Customs has it cleared as machine parts. It was not opened or inspected. The New York office is tracking down the trucking company that picked up the container from the pier for local delivery."

"So where are we and how well are we doing?" asked Wilkins.

"The Italians did a great job and saved us a lot of time. They have more video of him boarding the ship. We have the video of his processing into New York City. We have good pictures if we need to go public to find him. I'm not hopeful that the trucking company will lead us directly to him. These people are not stupid. Now, let me give you the bad news."

Wilkins did not blink. "Go ahead," he said.

Baker hesitated, cleared his throat and said, "The Italians interviewed the captain of the ship as well as the crew. The Engineer had two fire extinguishers with him. A crew member saw them when he helped The Engineer stow his gear in the cabin. He had them in a duffle bag. They looked heavy. The Italian police forensic team searched the Engineer's cabin. They got some prints. There was also evidence of radiation under his bunk. It's the same readings they got from the locker, the truck of the cargo handler's car, and his apartment. The Engineer has some radioactive material with him."

"Did he make it through customs with the fire extinguishers?" asked Wilkins.

"We really don't know what he did after his ship docked. The New York office is presently conducting interviews trying to establish his movements now."

"Anything else?"

"We have no evidence The Engineer possessed a satellite phone nor did he ask to use the ships telephone communications. However, he did use their internet service," reported Baker.

"Any leads there?"

"It's hard to tell because this computer was utilized by both passengers and crew members. Using the dates he was aboard, and his habits or schedule on the ship, the Italians think they can say with some certainty that he was reviewing news outlets in Washington, DC, New York, and Boston."

"Can we tell anything from the articles he was pulling up?" asked Wilkins.

"Not yet. This information is from a series of quick phone calls. They are trying to keep us posted as they go along. The legal attaché is in Naples with the CIA station chief and they are getting the hard copy reports to us as fast as they can."

"We need to start getting the Washington Field office and the Boston Division up to speed. Don't wait for paper, call them. Susan Crowley has been in contact with Patrick so make sure she knows what we are getting. Make sure the Joint Terrorism Task Force Center is getting this real time so the other agencies are updated. We need a lot of help to find this guy."

"I think we can assume he has a second container of armaments, some radioactive material, and a plan to do something that we will not like. We have to think about going public with his photo if we don't get some leads to find him," advised Baker.

"I agree," said Wilkins. "But let's wait until morning so we have the full reports from Naples, the analysts, and then all the other intelligence agencies. We'll have an update conference at 8:00 am tomorrow at the Terrorist Center and see where we go from there. I'll brief Carter before he goes home tonight. Thanks Vince. We will hope for the best."

Chapter 55

New York City

The Engineer wanted Salah to know what each attack was to accomplish and how it fit into his overall plan. He was going to share the mechanics and the philosophy of his operation.

"The death, destruction and shock of the 9/11 attack was more than anticipated. The results were far more glorious for al-Qaeda then anticipated by even our own engineers. However, human nature adjusts once the event is over. After the mourning and the physical clean up, they started to rebuild their lives, determined not to let it happen again. Admittedly, they have been successful. We have not had a meaningful attack on US soil since 9/11."

"So will striking these multiple targets achieve what you want?" asked Tariq.

"That is only part of the equation. After we execute coordinated attacks on their soil, they will be told al-Qaeda is bringing war directly to America. This will make them spread defensive efforts over a wide range of potential targets. Everyone will demand government protection for their business and personal lives. The government knows this is not possible. They cannot thoroughly protect everyone across the US. We will force the government to pick and choose what and how they defend against future attacks. This will anger those citizens left out of this protection sphere, when their fears are not addressed by the government response."

"So this is the start of a longer term effort?"

"Yes" said The Engineer. "It is also why you and I cannot make this a martyr's mission. We need to move to the next phase which will be attacks on a series of smaller cities. That will guarantee long-term negative economic impact and will cause fear in every small city resident in the US."

"So fear is more of an intended result then actual physical destruction?" asked Tariq.

"Yes. I envision," said The Engineer, "that, if Allah wills it, we can shut down New York City. No one will be willing or able to come to the city to work. The work will stop and the economy will reel."

"But how will this be better than 9/11?"

"Because," said The Engineer, "9/11 was an event that had a starting time and an ending time. After the World Trade Center buildings collapsed, the US cleaned up the rubble and treated the site like holy ground. They acted collectively. This time we want to change that and prevent any immediate cleanup. We will provide them a continuum of attacks, large and small. It will be a constant drum beat until their spirit is defeated."

"How?" asked Tariq.

"I want to shut down New York City as a hub of world commerce and trade. At the same time their financial system is weakened, there will be no end to havoc in their social and political institutions. Blame must find a home and it is that process of assigning blame that will be even more destructive to America," said The Engineer with certainty.

"How do our current targets accomplish that goal?"

The Engineer replied with patience "If we shut down and contaminate the Holland and Lincoln tunnels, the George Washington Bridge, how will the workers from New Jersey get into the city?"

Salah said nothing.

The Engineer continued. "If we add the Grand Central Terminal and Penn Station, we take out their commuter rail and the Northeast rail corridor that passes through New York City."

"How can we effectively destroy all this? I don't see that it is possible. The Lincoln and Holland each have multiple tunnels," noted Salah.

"That is what makes this effort different," said The Engineer. "We do not have to destroy them all. We just prevent them from using any of these facilities. The two forms of radiation released by our bombs will contaminate them. They do not have technology to clean up radioactive surfaces. It does not exist. Whatever is cleaned has to been contained, captured, and hauled away. But to where? Has anyone yet volunteered their town to be a radioactive dump? They will argue over this forever. Even if a decision is made, it will prevent any form of unity."

"You asked me to look at LaGuardia Airport as a potential target, and I told you I had no idea where to start. Have you dropped that in favor of the train stations?" asked Salah.

"No. I thought about what you said. I realized we only need to take out the control tower. I also know they are in the process of constructing a new control tower. Taking out the old tower will still serve our overall purpose. The old tower will probably serve as backup when the new one is completed. However, I believe no one will want to travel through LaGuardia after any part of it is contaminated by a dirty bomb. If we close down the other targets with contamination, who will want to come to New York via LaGuardia Airport?"

"But you only have forty pounds of radioactive material?" Salah noted. He was unable to comprehend how forty pounds of radioactive material could have such permanent impact at all the desired sites.

The Engineered replied, "It is not the degree of contamination that is significant. It is the presence of contamination, however slight, that will force them to adjust their response to the point of being ineffective. What can they say to the public? 'There is radiological contamination but it is somewhat spread out. Not so much as it could be.' What will that mean to a commuter?"

Salah nodded, somewhat knowingly, and The Engineer continued, "When first responders arrive, they will have to pull back, leaving those wounded and dying. The media will show their withdrawal, their inability and failure to help the injured. Those that have protective suits will also need breathing apparatus. It is impossible to work under these conditions, with that equipment, effectively for any lengthy period. All the money spent on homeland security equipment will come under attack as useless. Dealing with multiple targets under these conditions will for them be impossible. It is not the quantity we use, but the mere presence of nuclear material in multiple locations at the same time that will cause the panic. We are not trying to kill people with alpha or gamma emissions. We are doing what every terrorist should do. Instill fear. This is not fear created just at the scene of the attacks, but also fear created for anyone in a large city who participates in an economy that is reliant upon the mass movement of people to and from work."

"Do we have enough men for such an operation?" asked Salah.

"We have to review each site to see what it will take to achieve our goal. In some locations we may be able to use remote triggers for the bombs, which means we do not have to be physically present to detonate the devices."

"I know there is another team in Boston. We are not allowed to have any contact. Are they to join us here in New York City? Will they be available to help us?"

"They have a role in our overall effort, but it is totally separate from what you and your team will do here. I won't talk about them now."

Chapter 56

Washington, DC

The briefing for all federal agencies at the Joint Terrorism Task Force in Washington, DC, started promptly at 8:00 am. There were no smiles in the room. Each agency had already reviewed the hourly updates previously disseminated. The FBI, as the lead agency, had done most of the investigation. Vince Baker was to conduct the briefing. SA Susan Crowley from the Boston office was there, as well as terrorism managers from the New York and Washington Field FBI Offices. Carter Simms had Bob Wilkins sitting in for him.

Simms received a last minute notice to appear before a congressional committee, one of the sixteen or so the FBI reported to. He was required to answer questions about whether or not FBI agents were overusing administrative subpoena power in terrorist investigations. Simms would rather tell this committee what he should really be doing at this moment rather than answering their questions, but that was not how the game was played. The administration wanted its agency directors to immediately respond to any request for testimony by a congressional committee as a nod toward their authority to review the executive branch. The appearance was not to be negotiated. This was administration policy. How could he explain this terrorist investigation was getting to the point where all hands were needed on deck? He was not allowed to say this, at least not at the moment.

Vince Baker began: "The Italians have completed what needs to be done on an immediate basis. The two associates are lawyered up and not giving interviews. The Renzotti Camorra Family made available for interview anyone who interacted with The Engineer. We are calling him by this title as we still do not know his real identity. The Engineer used a phony Italian passport of the highest quality to enter the US. They and we are trying to trace the phony passport through known forgers. So far we have had no luck. It may not have come from Italy. The CIA is also working the passport forgery angle and trying to trace the suspects back in time to determine their origin. The most we know is what originally came from Vespa."

A hand was raised. "Go ahead," said Baker.

"Has there been any response from our allies to the photos of The Engineer and the two associates? Any hits?"

"Only what we have listed in the briefing memo. A photo in London and a reference to Afghanistan, but nothing we can build on at present."

Baker resumed. "Crew members reported The Engineer was on the computer in the shipboard lounge. Everyone aboard who used the computer was interviewed to find out what their usage was in order to determine what computer activity belonged to The Engineer. We conclude that The Engineer was regularly on various news outlets for the District of Columbia, New York and Boston. We do not see that he did any searches or used the email."

Another hand went up. "Can you tell what type of news article he was interested in? Was he looking at finance, local politics, or what?"

"It was just plain daily news for each city. Much like he was perusing through the local newspaper. He did click on an article about the fiasco in Boston where Patrick was subpoenaed by an AUSA, but he didn't do much more than read the article. He didn't do searches, nor did he click on earlier referenced articles. So we don't have much of a fact basis to conclude anything."

The DOJ attorneys said nothing. The story about Bottom was all over the place.

"We also learned that The Engineer had a conversation with a portside welder who came on board to make some needed ship repairs. Through dock area video coverage and interview of the welder, we learned that The Engineer paid the welder $500 to carry the two fire extinguishers off the ship on his equipment cart. The welder gave the two fire extinguishers back to The Engineer outside the terminal after he drove them past security. We can see this from a camera outside the front entrance. The Engineer is getting into a cab, but the picture is so bad we cannot ID the cab. The lab is working to enhance the photo, but so far no luck."

"Can you summarize the radioactive material information," asked someone in the front row?

"We found alpha and gamma particle responses under The Engineer's bunk, where he apparently stored the extinguishers. To a lesser degree, these particles were also detected on the welder's cart. These results are consistent with the results obtained from the cargo handler's apartment, vehicle trunk, and work locker. It is a trail of these extinguishers."

"Did anyone see him onboard using a satellite or cell phone?" was the question from the NSA rep.

"No. Not when he was aboard ship or immediately after the ship docked in New York. Every call from the ship's phone service is being traced anyway."

"Do we have any current leads that may tell us how to find him in New York?"

"The short answer is no. The New York FBI Office traced the container to an unused Hell's Kitchen warehouse where it was offloaded. We found the warehouse through the truck driver who delivered it. He gave a vague description of two men who received it. It is so general it could be anyone. We showed him a photo of The Engineer and he said he could not tell if it was him. The driver is a long-time union guy with some mob connections who does not like cops. We think he is not cooperating. We are going to polygraph him if he will agree. For the sake of argument, we are assuming one of the men was The Engineer, which tells us he has a partner here in New York."

Baker continued. "We found the container at the warehouse. It was empty. We sent lab examiners onsite to do the forensic examination and analysis. We do not have all the results but indications are there was C-4, or its kissing cousin, along with some freshly oiled armaments. For the time being we are assuming this container was similarly loaded to the one recovered in Sicily. We will update everyone as soon as we get the lab report back after they complete their chemical analysis."

A question was asked from the back of the room. "Was there any indication of radioactive material in the container?"

"No." said Baker.

There was a strange silence in the room.

"We have made some specific requests of each agency here. You can all see them in the briefing memo. We ask that you address these requests ASAP."

No one commented.

"In short, we believe we have a well-armed terrorist with radioactive material in two large fire extinguishers, and a supply of explosives, in New York City. We believe he has a partner who was with him on the Hell's Kitchen dock and who helped him unload the container and take the material someplace else. We have no leads from that neighborhood investigation. They chose their spot well. No cameras in the area. No witnesses. No physical or DNA evidence. We do have photos of The Engineer. We need to upload those photos into every system that has facial recognition software both in public and private sectors."

"We cannot go public at this time or we might drive him underground and he might not come out until it is too late for us. We do not want The Engineer to know we are actively chasing him here in the US. Any hit on

The Engineer via facial recognition may tell us at least in what section of the city he is active. Perhaps it might tell us something about his partner."

Another question, this time from the State Department representative: "Are the foreign intelligence agencies coming up with any informant information about a possible attack in the US?"

"There are no informants from any agency providing any data at the moment."

There was a total silence until a DOJ attorney asked, "What about Vespa? Isn't he an informant?" The smirk on the attorney's face was like an "I gotcha."

"Vespa is not a developed asset. Vespa is not the result of a human intelligence gathering program. Vespa is the result of luck. Someone with important information, who dislikes terrorists more than law enforcement, was willing to trust a former FBI agent to relay their information to the government. Of course, the existence of that source is now all over the media. We are unable to do a damage assessment and we don't know what Vespa's attitude is at present."

Bob Wilkins could see Baker was becoming agitated over the institutional ignorance and lack of interest in the room about the need for human assets. It was time for him to intervene and end the briefing. Everyone knew there were no terrorist assets in any agency providing information about this or any other threat. The agents had also seen the lack of administrative courage to get the asset ship back on course. There was a negative mood in the room and Wilkins needed to cut it short.

"We are all up to date on what we have. Everyone will start with every facial recognition database we have available. Homeland Security and local FBI offices will get The Engineer's photo into every airport and train station video surveillance system we can. Any system in the District, New York and Boston will be specifically targeted. That is as public as we will go for now. Let's give ourselves a chance to get a reference point on him through photo recognition. His phony Italian passport data is fully loaded into the computers. If he uses it again, we should know about it. I'm also going to ask the FBI agents who have relationships within the Muslim communities and mosques to keep those contacts current in case there is a scintilla of information out there we can use. Everything we get will be fed back though this center. If you receive any press inquiries about a possible terrorist threat, we have no specific information about an imminent terror threat here in the US at this time. Thank you."

The meeting broke up into small groups whose members were all trying to come up with ideas or possible new avenues of investigation. Baker and Wilkins were talking with Susan Crowley.

"What do you think Vespa's attitude is now? Will we get any more information from him?" asked Baker.

"I asked Patrick the same question. The last call was more of a short statement and then a hang-up. No time for any discussion. He does not know what that means for future cooperation. I guess we just have to wait and see," said Crowley.

"When you get back, would you meet with Patrick and give him an update on where we stand?" asked Baker. "For some reason, The Engineer is interested in Boston. See if he has any ideas. Review your resources in the Islamic community. We may have to start showing The Engineer's picture around to see if anyone knows him. We can talk later today."

Chapter 57

New York City

The Engineer met Salah at Salah's apartment. They were prepared to discuss the specific assignments for each target. They needed to discuss the form of each attack and what manpower would be required to execute each plan. From these details they could then determine what targets were feasible and what adjustments had to be made.

They sat at the kitchen table. Each had his own set of research materials for each of the proposed targets.

"We can take one target at a time, see what resources are needed and make sure it fits with our overall plan," said The Engineer.

"Okay," said Salah nodding his head.

"The New York Stock Exchange is the largest exchange in the world by dollar value of its listed companies. It is the great symbol of the infidel's greed and consumerism. Its self-interest ignores the starvation and poverty in the rest of the world. The trading floor consists of four rooms that are not as crowded as in the past, owing to electronic trading. My thought is a small bomb of say twenty-five to thirty pounds of C-4, some ball bearings or nails for personal damage, and one pound of radioactive material will make sure they cannot again use this space. The question is how do we deliver such a device? What did you see during your observations?"

"Security on Wall Street and Broad Street has picked up substantially since 9/11. There has been talk about a terrorist attack for the same reasons you want to do it. I have taken the tour and walked around the best I could.

I think it would be very hard to get a bomb to the trading floor unless you wanted to create a military style of attack, knowing you would never leave alive."

"You mentioned another possibility?"

"The place empties out quickly after 4:00 pm. There are cleaners in and out of the building for the next eight hours. There are a limited number of custodial people on duty during the day. I think the best way to get the bomb in is by someone who works there."

"Have you found anyone we could use?"

Salah smiled. He was waiting for The Engineer to ask this question.

"I started driving the area in my cab around 11:00 pm to see if any of the cleaning crew needed a cab at the end of their shift. There are no cabs down there at that time of night. I picked up a young man a few times when it was raining. I give him a ride to the bus station. He does not like his job and thinks he is being victimized by his employer. It is the only job he can get. He is a very angry person at present. The man has a wife in Mexico. He is trying to get her into the country but Immigration is questioning the validity of his Mexican marriage and will not grant his wife temporary US residence. He needs money to pay coyotes to smuggle his wife across the border. I also think he might be a little crazy."

"How many times have you talked with him?" asked The Engineer.

"We have spoken six times over the last three months. The last time we stopped for coffee. I asked him questions about how he got hired. At first I thought he was an illegal, but he is not. He was born in New York. He fell in love and married in Mexico. His social security number and driver's data are valid. I asked him about the hiring of custodial workers at the Exchange."

"You thinking of getting someone hired?"

"I didn't know. I was just trying to learn what I could. They are not hiring right now, and besides, they do a full background check on whomever they hire."

"So where do you come out?"

"I have hinted to him I want to go on a secret tour at night. He says a good time is after the supper break. When everyone returns to work, the guards slack off for the night. He could walk me in then with no ID or borrow someone's who is not coming in that night. The guards really don't look at the faces on the IDs. I could use that visit to see if there is a spot where I can plant a bomb overnight that would not be discovered."

"Are there any other options?"

"We could bribe the guy to carry the bomb for us. We have it set to go off the next morning with everything else. The guy needs the money and he will not be told what we are doing."

"What if he guesses?"

"What does he care? He won't be there when it goes off."

"What if you ask him and he refuses?"

"Then I'll kill him."

The Engineer thought for a minute. While he was thinking, Tariq Salah got up to make some Arabic coffee. He filled his special copper pot, with a long copper handle, with water and put it on the lighted stove. When the water was warmed, he put in four tablespoons of ground coffee with cardamom and four teaspoons of sugar. As the brew started to boil, Tariq removed the pot from the burner to allow the boiling to subside. He returned the pot to the still lighted burner. He repeated this procedure two more times and brought the pot to the table with two cups. Tariq filled each cup with coffee and foam on top. He served The Engineer a cup. Both sipped their coffee without talking."

"Meet him again and ask about a 'tour.' I think it is worth the risk. You'll see how far he is willing to go. You can get some idea about how desperate he is for money, his wife, and how much he hates his employer."

"Okay. So for Wall Street we can keep that on the list and see what we can work out."

"What have you done on the transportation targets?" asked The Engineer.

"I have been to all of them and made physical observations. I also researched each site on the internet. It really depends on which ones are important to your plan, what type of damage you want to do, and how much effort you want to put into each one."

"I want to do them all. I want to shut down all commuter and business travel into the city. If there are no workers, there will be no work. Other world capitals will move in like jackals and soon New York will have no relevance."

"What about LaGuardia?" asked Salah.

"I am applying our maximum strength against their weakest points. I want to take out the current control tower and its equipment at La Guardia. Contaminate the general area with radioactive material and they will not quickly be back in business," said The Engineer.

"One of my men has been to LaGuardia with me. Why don't I have him go out and see what the control tower situation looks like? We could even consider kidnapping one of the controllers to get in. We will see how secure the place is and how we might get the bomb in, or near, the tower. Whatever way we do it, we will need a willing martyr for this location."

They stopped talking to enjoy their coffee and to muse over what they had just discussed. Salah picked up a pen and started jotting down notes of their discussions and follow-up questions he needed to address for each of their targets.

Salah started with his next review. "The George Washington Bridge has two levels. The upper lever has four lanes in each direction, plus two pedestrian paths. The lower level has three lanes in each direction. This is for a total of fourteen vehicle lanes. If you take this bridge out of operation, that traffic would have to travel another half hour to reach the Tappan Zee Bridge and then, after crossing the Hudson, reverse direction for another half hour just to enter the city. Closer to the tip of Manhattan, the Holland and Lincoln Tunnels won't be available either. The George Washington Bridge handles 100,000 cars a day. This traffic would not be easily transferable to another route. There would be no direct bridge access from the city to New Jersey."

"Is there any chance the bridge could fail entirely?" asked The Engineer.

"You have the expertise to answer that question. You would know better than me. One of my team members with extensive training in explosives does not think it would fail because the open space would rapidly dissipate the energy of the blast."

"What about detonation from the lower level?" asked The Engineer.

"We talked about it but are not sure about the blast dissipating. I also thought about the entrance and exit areas. If they were contaminated, wouldn't that render the bridge useless?"

The Engineer thought for a moment. "We have to think of our overall objective. It is not the damage at one site that will make us effective. It is the total package of attacks executed at the same time and witnessed by the media immediately thereafter. The bridge attack will cause the desired chaos.

"So you want to continue with this target?" asked Salah.

"Yes," said The Engineer. "One car or SUV transported bomb packed with shrapnel material and three pounds of radioactive material will cause paralysis of travel over the bridge. We will have one martyr to drive the vehicle. We will have him drive the route to know exactly what time he has to enter the bridge in order to be exactly in the middle when the bomb is set off."

"So you don't want to use an entrance or exit?"

"No," said The Engineer. "I want the news helicopter cameras to show that first responders can't get to the scene. The bridge and the roadways will be full of vehicles. After the explosion nothing on the lower level will move. There will be physical destruction and wounded within camera sight. The reports of radiation will create further chaos extending to river traffic on both sides. Cars will be abandoned and roads will remain impassable. This is just part of the overall attack, but it creates the best media piece. The police may be able to block the media from the other sites, but not this one. Eventually they may get this bridge working again, but will anyone take it?"

"By using the lower level we will get whatever compression is available for structural damage."

"There are limitations on truck use of the lower level, so a car or SUV bomb is better suited and will pack enough explosives to achieve our goal. Regardless of the structural damage achieved, it is a worthwhile target when considered as a whole with the other targets and the overall objectives of the day," said The Engineer with growing satisfaction.

"You know they refer to the lower level of the bridge as the Martha Washington," said Salah with a smirk, knowing the sexually crude reference intended.

The Engineer said nothing. He just stared at Salah. Then he said, "I am not interested in their deviant sexual humor."

Salah nodded, but at the same time still thought the reason for the name humorous.

"Why don't we continue this later? I need to review the inventory from the container."

They agreed to meet later in the evening at Salah's apartment to continue their discussion of targets.

Chapter 58

Boston

When Susan Crowley returned from Washington, she called Mark Patrick for a meet. The weather was splendid so they agreed to 4:00 pm at Christopher Columbus Park on Boston Harbor. The dog owners were also gathering at the park with their charges on the large expanse of green grass that went down a slight incline to the water's edge. Dog ownership was another way for city people to meet and make new friends. It was the time of day dog owners looked forward to, and it was often their first act, albeit of necessity, upon returning home to an eager pet. Dog owners who lived near city parks were a whole subset of the civic and social body.

Patrick was seated under the rounded trellis that extended from one end of the park to the other. It was a cool spot for the elderly to gather on hot days. He had stopped for coffee and was drinking it while watching the interactions of dogs and humans. Crowley walked up behind him.

"Thinking of getting a dog?"

"I would love to get a West Highland white terrier. Had one years ago. They're great dogs. I told Liz I'm getting another when I'm fully retired. I can't see keeping a dog confined in a city apartment all day. A dog should have more freedom than just this event at the end of the day. Now that I have expounded on my theory of dog ownership in the city, how can I help you?"

Crowley explained the meeting earlier at the terrorist command center and how Vince Baker and Bob Wilkins asked her to give him a briefing. They wanted to be sure that if Vespa contacted him, Patrick was able to make the most of the contact.

After the initial talk, they spent a few quiet moments watching the dogs. Then Patrick said, "This is really getting serious. Explosives and radioactive material for a dirty bomb are not good news. We may be headed for a first in this country and the world."

"We have a lot riding on locating The Engineer," said Crowley. "If the photo recognition effort doesn't work, we may have to go public. The potential harm in doing this is clear. If The Engineer finds out about our interest before we find him, he goes underground and we have no assets in place to find him."

"What about the news articles he was reading on the ship?" asked Patrick.

Together they reviewed the articles that The Engineer accessed for the Boston area. Patrick then noted, "He read an article where Bottom was laying out his argument against me, yet he wasn't curious enough to click on and read the earlier articles?"

"Maybe he had already read them before he got on board," said Crowley.

Patrick thought she might be right.

"Okay. He has an interest in Boston and DC besides New York City. So what is the FBI's plan to get ahead of him?"

Crowley said, "We're checking every facial recognition system we can find in all three cities, without going public. This limits the databases we can search but we don't want to risk our inquiry becoming public. We also hope to get more cooperation from the truck driver who delivered the container to the Hell's Kitchen pier, but he's an old union guy who doesn't like talking to cops."

Patrick made a mental note of this in the event he talked to Vespa again. He had an idea.

Crowley continued, "We're reaching out to our established contacts in the Islamic communities in all three cities. There is little information we can give them. But, we can tell them that we are in a dangerous period and ask if they hear anything, no matter how small or inconsequential, to contact us right away."

"Isn't Maha Soufan part of that group in New England?" asked Patrick, knowing the answer.

Crowley knew Soufan was a friend of Patrick's. A few years back, Patrick aided the mosque in setting up a program to prevent unwanted donations from terrorist organizations to the new mosque building fund. Patrick first met Soufan through Liz. She knew Soufan for years as a person active in the greater Boston community. Patrick and Soufan became good friends and it was from Soufan that Patrick learned about Islam. Soufan presented Patrick with a Koran for Patrick's help to the mosque, and to Liz, a prayer rug that Soufan had brought back from his Hajj. When the FBI was setting up a program to establish positive relationships in the Muslim community, Patrick was not surprised when they asked Soufan for his help.

"Yes. In fact I am meeting with him in the morning," said Crowley.

"Would you tell him we have spoken? I would like to speak with him after your meeting. I'm not trying to do your work, but we are friends and I want to offer him my point of view," said Patrick.

"Not at all. I'll ask him to give you a call," said Crowley.

New York City

While Patrick and Crowley were talking, Maria was meeting with John Turco about his effort to locate any new information around the docks about The Engineer. Turco did not have much to report. The FBI had found the welder. Turco was assured by a friend in the welder's union that the welder told the FBI everything he knew. Turco reported the truck driver who hauled the container to the Hell's Kitchen pier was only somewhat cooperative with the FBI. He had not identified a photo of The Engineer, and was very vague in his description of a second person who was present.

"I would like you to get to our union friends. Tell them my father would appreciate whatever cooperation this driver could provide the FBI. He should make an effort to do his best. Provide no further explanation and answer no questions. They will get the point."

"I'll do that right now," responded Turco.

Maria and her father were both concerned. They knew The Engineer, the container and the material for a dirty bomb were either in New York City or had transited through the city to yet another location. No matter what the scenario, it was their worst dream come true. This was the reason for their extraordinary cooperation with the FBI, which now might go for naught. They concluded that continued contact with Patrick was still in their best interests, if it was reasonably safe to do so. They had made the inquiries back to the original source of information on The Engineer. The effort did not result in any new information. People on that end continued to be in the dark as to the specifics of what al-Qaeda and The Engineer were up to. However, they were still trying.

Chapter 59

It did not take long for the FBI to get a break. When the New York Office entered photographs from the surveillance of Hawaladar Salim Bin Attash into terrorist databases, they got an immediate hit. The passport photo used for The Engineer's entry into New York matched the photos taken during the surveillance of Attash. The photos of the unknown male visiting Attash's shop also matched photographs that had been identified as The Engineer in London and Afghanistan. It was a clear trail of travel based on photographs alone. Now they knew there was more to The Engineer's visit to Attash's computer shop than a laptop computer.

Agents were dispatched from the field offices in Washington and Boston to provide additional manpower in New York. Attash had been an exploratory case regarding money laundering. Now the Attash investigation had every available resource the FBI could offer.

Three surveillance teams, with supporting aircraft, were on duty around the clock. Anyone in contact with Attash would be identified and subject to a full background investigation. Each of these investigations was a priority. Other FBI field offices were instructed to send agents from their offices to New York. Another group of agents was assigned to review the money laundering case from day one for fresh ideas and to initiate inquiries on every person known to Attash.

All foreign contacts were being handled through the FBI legal attachés and the CIA jointly. Additional electronic surveillance "ears" abroad were now targeted by the NSA to pick up any traffic from a foreign country in contact with the Hawaladar Salim Bin Attash. All data developed was simultaneously furnished to the JTTF Center in Washington. Nothing was to be missed because someone did not share information in a timely manner. In less than twelve hours after The Engineer's identification at the computer shop, the FBI and other federal agencies had in progress one of the largest federal investigations ever undertaken.

It would not be long before the NYPD would add its own unique talents and resources to the project. They at least had criminal informants in many areas. Money laundering within immigrant communities was one area that often provided them intelligence about a larger criminal problem. The NYPD often provided key intelligence to the FBI. The NYPD would continue to delve into their street sources for any information relating to Attash. They would expeditiously build a complete profile of Attash and his local contacts in an effort to find out what he was up to.

At the same time, the attorney for the union truck driver contacted the FBI and asked that his client be re-interviewed. The attorney said his client was thinking more clearly now and wanted an opportunity to view the photograph previously shown him again. Agents were dispatched immediately.

The agent laid ten photographs on the attorney's desk. The union driver reached over and picked out a photo of The Engineer. "When I got to the Hell's Kitchen pier, this man came up to my truck and had copies of the bill of lading. He asked me to unhook the chassis carrying the cargo container. He didn't have the equipment to offload the container. I checked with dispatch and they told me it was okay. They had a deposit to cover the use of the chassis. I left the container on the chassis and came back in a few days to pick it up. The man knew the office had enough money to cover the delivery this way. I did what he asked, and when I got unhooked he signed for the container and the chassis. I left."

"Was there anyone else with this man?" asked the agent.

"Yea," the driver said. "There was a guy with him the whole time. He seemed to act like an assistant."

Upon request, the union driver provided a detailed physical description of the second man. He would be able to recognize either one if he saw them again. The driver agreed to work immediately with the FBI and the NYPD to create a sketch of the second man.

The driver saw no one else except for these two individuals. He thought the area was largely abandoned. The driver then added the observation, "That's why I thought it was strange when I saw the cab parked on the side of the building."

The interview pace picked up. The driver was able to provide a very detailed physical description of the cab, but could not provide the license plate or cab number. The driver volunteered to take a polygraph examination to confirm he was fully cooperating. They accepted the offer. The test was immediately administered. He passed. The truck driver was truthful.

When the agents reported the results of the second interview with the truck driver, their veteran supervisor could not figure out the driver's change of heart. The supervisor was unaware of John Turco. The truck driver did not want to do anything to require a meeting with John Turco. He cooperated as asked.

Now the FBI knew The Engineer had a partner in New York who might have access to a cab. When the sketch was finished, they would decide whether or not to make it public or keep it restricted to law enforcement for the time being. While they could use the public's help, they also would be warning the opposition about what they knew. It was not an easy call.

Agents reviewed the audio tapes of The Engineer's transaction that took place in the computer store of Salim Bin Attash for any new information. They could find nothing. Without a video camera in the store, the audio reflected just what was said. The Engineer purchased a used computer. Another team of agents discreetly canvassed the neighborhood looking for outside video cameras that might track The Engineer's path after he left the store. They found a few possibilities and had the NYPD getting copies of the tapes using a local robbery as an excuse. So far they had discovered no new information.

The Joint Terrorism Task Force Center for New York City was now up and fully staffed by the participating agencies. The FBI was the lead investigative agency but fully sought collaboration with its colleagues. They would continue the electronic, video and physical surveillance in hopes of additional contact between The Engineer and Attash, but worried that time could be slipping away. Was The Engineer ready to strike? Were they wasting time sitting on Attash when The Engineer's business with him might be completed and he had no need of ever returning?

One group argued they should just arrest Attash and rely upon the interview process to crack him. The opposing side thought this was a high-risk option with low potential reward. They preferred to maintain the surveillances for a couple of days before deciding what to do. All agreed that if The Engineer was located, they would arrest him as a fugitive on the Italian arrest warrants regarding the seized container of armaments. In the United States, he would be a fugitive from Italy traveling under false documents. He would not be admitted to bail, and they would have him where he could not cause harm.

No one wanted to create public fear about a potential terrorist attack with the few facts they had. In the end such a decision was made. The surveillance continued in hopes some new leads would soon be produced or they would soon get another hit from the photo recognition effort in place.

Chapter 60

Boston

It was Thursday morning and Patrick needed to get some errands done. He stopped to see Peter in the attendant's booth. Patrick wanted to know how Peter had done babysitting his grandson. Peter reported that all went well, but a two-year-old was physically hard to keep up with. Patrick asked Peter if he was considering a diet to improve his staying power. Peter ignored him. Patrick continued on his way.

Felipe was grinding some parmesan and pecorino romano cheeses for Patrick when he said, "I heard they have a good lead on the guy attacking the women."

"Who told you this?" asked Patrick. He was interested in the potential reliability of Felipe's information.

Felipe ignored his question. Patrick looked at him quizzically.

"I'm just not used to repeating names," said Felipe. He wanted to offer an explanation. "It's all over the street," said Felipe.

"Oh," said Patrick not knowing what else to say.

Renaldo was standing in front of the Pharmacy when Patrick walked by.

"I hear they are about to arrest the rapist," said Renaldo.

"Oh," said Patrick. "Anyone I know?"

"Won't know until they arrest him," said Renaldo.

"Makes sense to me," said Patrick, as he continued on his way up Hanover Street.

Patrick saw Giovanni in the Café Strada so he joined him for an espresso. They talked about the neighborhood, the tourists beginning to pour in, and the increase in traffic. In other words, it was their usual conversation.

Patrick went to the greengrocer Arturo to see if he had any fiddleheads.

"They're all past now" advised Arturo. "I still have fava beans, great broccoli, and young, fresh spinach."

Arturo also mentioned that an arrest was expected of the man attacking women in the North End. He didn't bother reciting a source for his information, and Patrick didn't ask.

Patrick took the spinach and headed up to the butcher shop where he talked with Mario. After getting some freshly ground hamburger, Patrick went to the cleaners to pick up his shirts from Hien.

"I heard they are about to arrest the rapist," said Hien. "I hope they do. I worry about that man in our neighborhood. The mayor was in the neighborhood last week and told us the police are working overtime to catch this man."

"I also hope they catch him soon," said Patrick, convinced that the rumor of an imminent arrest was fully spread in the neighborhood even though no one seemed able or willing to quote a source for this optimistic outlook.

As Patrick stepped into the Franklin Wharf parking lot, Peter came out of the booth. "They just arrested the guy who was attacking the women," he said proudly as if he, and justice, had finally prevailed.

"You mean they have a lead on who he is and may arrest him, as I heard up on Hanover Street?"

"No, that's old information. I just heard on the radio they arrested him coming out of his apartment in Charlestown. They were waiting for him. The police had a victim with them who had a good look at her attacker. When the man came out, the victim identified him immediately. The police arrested him. Before the police made an effort to interview him, the man started babbling about how he could not control himself and how sorry he was to have bothered all those women in the North End. That is what they just reported."

That was a lot of news for the police to put out immediately after an arrest. Patrick could understand why the police wanted to communicate to the public they had the right person. Women could again walk about with confidence in their safety. Patrick thought that he should not disregard generally accepted community rumors in the North End. What these people seemed to know as a group was often beyond him.

"Agent Crowley is waiting in her car over there for you. I told her you were out running errands but would be back shortly."

Patrick had to laugh. His lived in a fishbowl. Peter seemed to speak as if Crowley was his mutual chum and they had known each other for years. Still, it was an efficient process.

"Good morning Susan."

"Good morning Mark. I didn't mean to barge in but Peter said he thought you might be back shortly so I thought I'd wait."

"Just part of our excellent concierge service here at Franklin Wharf," said Patrick as he sat his parcels on the sidewalk.

Crowley looked around to see if anyone was within hearing distance. She got out of her car. "Let's walk over to the docks." They did.

"Since we spoke there has been a new development. We're pretty sure The Engineer has a partner in New York and access to cash." Crowley explained how the union truck driver was more cooperative, had positively identified The Engineer's photograph, and described a second person with him at the Hell's Kitchen pier. She had a digitally produced portrait of the second man and showed it to him. She put it back in her pocket.

Patrick noted he was not offered a copy of the digital portrait.

"We also know one place The Engineer has been in the city. We also think we know why he went there." Crowley explained how The Engineer was identified as going into the shop of the Hawaladar Salim Bin Attash.

When she finished Patrick said, "So he has armaments, explosives, radioactive material, a partner, and possibly a lot of cash. Would it be too

228

wild to speculate he probably also has a plan that we know nothing about?" offered Patrick with a critical edge to his voice.

"That is just about where we all come out," said Crowley, not responding to Patrick's tone. "Baker asked me to update you in the event you hear from Vespa. They want you to see if Vespa has any knowledge of the Hawaladar without providing all of the details, if you can."

"Have the Boston authorities been notified of the threat yet? Has Mayor Corso been notified that Boston may be a target?"

"No. The powers that be have not concluded that Boston is actually under threat."

"And who, pray tell, has looked into the crystal ball and concluded this?"

"ASAC Phil Kirby," said Crowley rolling her eyes.

Patrick said nothing, but a visible curtain came down over Patrick's face and, it seemed, his entire physical being. Crowley could not miss this change.

"There's more. Kirby wants me to tell you that he has responsibility in this matter now that there is a potential threat in Boston. He wants you to call him directly and immediately with any new information you get from Vespa."

Patrick's eyes narrowed and his jaw muscle tightened. "Is that an order?" asked Patrick.

It was Crowley's turn to say nothing.

Patrick continued, "Tell ASAC Kirby that I have been asked by Baker, Wilkins, and Director Simms to contact the JTTF in DC with any new info. I thank him for his interest. It will take a personal call from Carter Simms to ask me to report to Kirby. Before I even consider such a request from Simms, I can tell you the answer will be no. He's a complete idiot who has survived the promotional trail due to luck. I expect that will run out soon. I'll call him right after I call Harvey Bottom."

"I'll tell him. By the way, how did you know Bottom and Kirby were friends?"

"I didn't. But thanks for completely scaring me. Kirby is the last person I'd have running this investigation in Boston."

"I did speak with Maha Soufan. However, prior to the meeting, I was instructed by Kirby on exactly what I could and could not say. I was not free to have an intelligent discussion. I told Soufan that you and I are speaking, and he will call you today. Of course you are not under the same restrictions that Kirby put on me. Let your judgment be your guide."

"I understand," said Patrick.

As they parted, Crowley knew that something had changed with Patrick and it was not good.

Patrick went back to the sidewalk and picked up his bags. Peter leaned out of the booth and said, "I was watching them for you," as he broke out laughing.

"You'll probably expect a Christmas card from me this year. Don't get your hopes up."

Peter looked at Patrick. What Patrick said was humorous. The way it came out was not. Peter closed his door.

Chapter 61

After putting his packages away, Patrick left the apartment and walked to his office. When he passed through the parking lot he didn't say a word to Peter. As he walked by the aquarium, his cell phone went off. It was Vespa.

"The truck driver of the container should be more cooperative."

Patrick laughed. "I was just told a few minutes ago that he was. He identified The Engineer and described a second man with him at the Hell's Kitchen dock. He's even volunteered to take a polygraph to show he is cooperating fully. We owe you one for that."

Vespa continued without acknowledging what Patrick said. "So far, we have been unable to develop more information from the original sources out of Afghanistan. We are told the two associates are well trained and not bothered by the Italian police interrogations. They believe they cannot be connected with the actual contents of the container and will be released. Whether this is true or not does not matter. It is what they believe, and we do not see any cooperation from them."

"I think the people here have concluded the associates did not know what The Engineer was going to do, or possibly even where he was going," said Patrick.

Patrick asked Vespa directly if she could find out about the Hawaladar Salim Bin Attash. He gave the name and address and explained that The Engineer was identified going into the shop and buying a laptop computer. They feared The Engineer was there to pick up a supply of cash.

Vespa said the she would check to see if any of their connections knew this person. She hoped to be back to him today with an answer. Vespa continued: "It seems that things are getting worse rather than better. With his equipment, and what you have told me, he must have a specific mission. It could be very ugly. We want you to know that despite Mr. Bottom, we are totally committed to seeing this matter through. Our resolve is the same as originally explained to you."

Patrick was touched by what Vespa said, and with the tone of how she said it. Vespa's sincerity came through over the phone.

When he got to his office, Patrick made his call to the terrorist center in DC and was immediately put through to Vince Baker. He provided the details of his call with Vespa. Baker seemed relieved that Vespa was still willing to help. The fact that Vespa's resources had no more information in Afghanistan about The Engineer's plans mirrored the lack of success the CIA had in gathering any data from the same region. It also matched the NSA's inability to pick up any significant electronic chatter from that area. al-Qaeda had no electronic footprint they could intercept. Whatever was happening was being closely held, which to Patrick's thinking lent even more credibility to the seriousness of the threat at hand.

Patrick had been thinking about what Crowley had told him and decided it was time to clear some air with Baker.

"I thought you told me that Kirby wasn't involved with this investigation."

"What do you mean?" asked Baker.

Patrick explained what Crowley had told him a little while ago.

"I don't know where he got the idea he could insert himself like that. We did discuss whether we should brief Boston authorities at this point. Kirby thought not, saying we should wait a little longer until we could make a more intelligent analysis of the facts. I agreed to that because it seemed to make sense at the moment. But Kirby has nothing to do with the management of this case."

"Well, it seems at a minimum you have a serious communications breakdown. Is Boston under a possible threat from The Engineer?" asked Patrick.

"We don't have a specific answer yet."

"I was not asking for your official description of the current status. I asked you a simple question and got bureaucratic jargon for an answer."

Baker was taken aback and did not respond.

Patrick continued, "So even if a threat to Boston is a possibility, a decision has been made not to tell the Boston authorities what you know. No one is giving them time to prepare and organize for the possibility?"

"What makes you say that?"

"Crowley told me it was Kirby who made the decision not to allow Boston agents to inform the local authorities of a potential threat."

Baker said nothing at first, but then said: "Mark, I am not required to report to you."

"So, have you already returned to your recently renounced bureaucratic bullshit? Telling me only what you think I need to know. The need-to-know basis? Is that how we are again?"

"You are making too much out of this. It is a very temporary decision until we get things sorted out."

"Does the Director know that Kirby does not want the local authorities notified?"

"I don't know. We just don't know exactly what to tell them the threat is."

"Kirby is a fool. How can you let him have anything to do with what affects public safety? Perhaps I take the decision more personally since I live in downtown Boston and probably close to anything The Engineer wants to attack or blow up. You think I want my safety, that of my wife, my friends, my neighbors, in the hands of that pompous ass Kirby?"

"Look Mark, Kirby also doesn't have a lot of good to say about you, Vespa, the Mafia, and I don't have time to get involved in a pissing contest between the two of you."

"I told you back at the start that I did not have a dog in this race. I don't want to know your secrets. I did not want to be part of your investigation. I said I would stay in contact with Vespa and report what is told me. But you forgot what else I said."

"What is that?" asked Baker with a weary voice.

"I conditioned my statement by saying unless they planned on attacking Boston. That now appears to be a very real possibility. Kirby seems to be trying to climb into your saddle and that seems to be okay with you. Since I don't work for the FBI, you, Kirby or anyone connected to government, I am free to act as a citizen and I'm telling you that is what I will do from now on."

Baker wanted to continue the conversation, but when he started to speak Patrick was no longer on the phone. Baker had been forewarned by

Crowley that Patrick appeared to be really upset about Kirby exercising any form of decision-making authority. Crowley went out on a limb and told Baker that agents in the Boston FBI Office felt the same way. Baker thought he should put Director Simms on notice as Patrick would probably call him to complain. Upon further reflection, Baker decided not to do this, as his last conversation with Simms about Patrick did not go all that well. He would wait and see.

For his part, after speaking with Baker, Patrick called Boston Mayor John Corso and set up a meeting in Corso's office for the next morning. Corso would have Boston Police Commissioner Ed Blake present at Patrick's request. Corso knew this call was about a problem, but he was willing to wait for Patrick to explain it fully the next day.

Patrick then put in a call to Maha Soufan and they decided to meet after Patrick's meeting in the morning with Corso and Blake.

Chapter 62

New York City

Tariq Salah was using no notes. He was speaking from memory as he and The Engineer sat in a park two blocks from his apartment drinking a soda.

"The Lincoln Tunnel is one-and-a-half miles long and has three tubes, for a total of six lanes. One of the lanes in the center is called the XBL and is used only by buses during the morning commute. Seventeen hundred buses every day, to be exact. That's sixty-two thousand people a day just using the buses. We have the same problem with the Holland Tunnel. The Holland Tunnel has a pair of tubes, each with two lanes. Each tube is twenty-feet wide and twelve-feet, five-inches high. We can get good compression, but there are four lanes."

"What is the problem that you see?"

"There are only eight people besides us. How can we attack all these lanes to shut down the tunnel commuter use?"

"Anything else bothering you about these tunnels?" asked The Engineer.

Salah was not sure if The Engineer even understood him. "Look, The Holland Tunnel connects Manhattan to Jersey City. There are physical restrictions on a full attack. And, they have taken further steps to protect this tunnel."

"That is an indication of its importance to them and, therefore, also of its importance for us," said The Engineer.

"Just after 9/11 they did not allow single occupant vehicles in the eastbound lanes. After another threat in 2004, they do not allow truck traffic in the eastbound lanes. They allow trucks going westbound but not eastbound. I am not sure exactly what the security precautions are today. We need current data for the Holland Tunnel."

The Engineer had done the same research and had the same questions. However, he just nodded to Salah as if he were more knowledgeable.

"In 2005, they turned off cell phone use in the tunnels. I heard it was turned back on more recently. Since I would not believe what they say, we need to test cell phone coverage in each tunnel, so we know for sure."

"What did you learn about ventilation systems for the tunnels?" asked The Engineer with the hint of a smile on his face.

"I think I remember the Holland Tunnel was the first tunnel to have an exhaust fan system designed to remove automobile exhaust. I think that was in 1927."

"Yes," said The Engineer. "Those fans are eighty-feet in diameter and carry a lot of air in and out of the ventilation system. If that air is contaminated with both alpha and gamma radioactive material, will the entire ventilation system be compromised?"

"So you don't want to destroy these tunnels, just contaminate them?"

"Let me put it this way. After all is done, how long would it take you, as a commuter, to be convinced that all of the radioactive material was removed and you no longer had to fear contamination? How long before you would be willing to drive through this tunnel? Would you sit comfortably inside this tunnel in traffic? Do you even believe it is possible to clean it up? Would you be afraid the terrorist would do the same thing again, when that is exactly what we will promise to do? Will the pictures of death, destruction, chaos, inability to evacuate, and a general lack of confidence in government lead you to conclude you should look for work outside of New York City? If so, then we will have accomplished our first objective in a program of fear that we want to carry to other US cities, both large and small."

"So the number of attacks aimed at commuters, the contamination, and the fear created must all be taken as one. Physical damage is not as important as contamination that challenges all commuters. It is long-term damage because of the radioactivity. The government will be seen as not being able to prevent it happening again," Salah reminded himself.

"Yes. It is that simple, said The Engineer. "So we don't want to make our planning too complicated. Our attack is about numbers, creating visuals for the media, and disruption of the status quo. It is not about one event that begins to fade away. We want the discussion to be new every day, for a long time. This is terrorism at its core, in action, and we have not finished with our target list."

"Okay, so give me the short version for the Lincoln Tunnel. How would you do it?" asked Salah.

"A bomb will be planted in the belly of a commuter bus. The bomb will be detonated by cell phone or a preset timing device. When we know the bus is in the XBL lane, either or both can be used for ignition. It will take out that lane and possibly the other half of that tube. The rest will be done by the ventilation system."

"And the Holland Tunnel?" asked Salah.

"We need to update our information through personal observation and testing. Then we will know if we need one or two people for that mission. I would prefer not to waste two valuable martyrs because time has been invested in training them by al-Qaeda. I would prefer to find two fools who are willing to "deliver" a car into the city for a handsome reward. Hire them strictly to make delivery of a vehicle into the city. They will have an ignition valet key that will start the car but will not open the trunk. If we are using unknowing martyrs, the vehicle and its bomb will be in an eastbound lane and set off by cell phone or a preset ignition device. Part of the plan is subject to cell phone coverage inside the tunnels."

The Engineer continued, "If we use a knowing and willing martyr to drive the vehicle into the tunnel, he can directly detonate the bomb. Should he fail to do so, we also will have as backup a preset ignition device as well as a cell phone triggering device available."

"There are ten of us all together. Do we have enough men?" asked Salah.

"Right now, if our current plans stand for the tunnels, I am sure we do."

Chapter 63

Boston

Patrick, Mayor John Corso, and the BPD Commissioner were seated at a conference table in the mayor's office. They had all known each other for years and, besides friendship, there was a great deal of mutual respect between them.

"I am going to tell you a story from the beginning so you will know exactly what I know as I sit here this morning. When I finish, I will answer whatever questions you may have." Patrick then began to describe the events and conversations since his first meeting with Vespa, continuing through to his last phone discussion with Baker late yesterday afternoon. He did not describe Vespa.

Corso looked at Blake. "Do you know anything about this?"

"No," replied Blake, with some embarrassment at having to admit he had been stood up by his counterparts and FBI partners in the Boston Joint Terrorism Task Force.

"Do you know this guy Kirby?'

"Yes, we have met but have done very little business together. I deal more with the SAC."

"What is Kirby's reputation?"

"A self-serving asshole looking for the next promotion."

Corso laughed. "Look Ed, I need you to be honest with me." Then they all laughed.

"What do we need to do now?" asked Corso.

"Start getting your mind around the potential for a problem," said Patrick. "Think about your resources and what you want to do in anticipation of a developing threat. Right now the focus is New York, but there were two containers and there are two fire extinguishers. Corso agreed to think about how he might address a lack of federal cooperation with the senior US Senator and FBI Director Simms. Patrick said he felt better knowing that they knew. He could not in good conscience agree with Kirby's position. They agreed to have another conversation at the end of the day to review where the matter stood.

When Patrick left the mayor's office, he met with Soufan. They exchanged the Muslim greeting and the kiss of peace. Patrick had no problem with this custom, noting it was not much different from other greetings within Mediterranean or European cultures. Some people, even in a cosmopolitan city like Boston, would look quizzically at men exchanging this greeting. Yet, if they walked four blocks to the Italian North End, no one would even notice.

Soufan began, "I met with Susan Crowley who wanted some help. She appeared greatly concerned but unable to say exactly what the problem is. They were looking for us to report anything out of the ordinary. This is not the type of thing we can practically pass on within our community, but we can try to be aware within the mosque leadership."

"Crowley was ordered to say only what she did. I have no such restrictions, but I must respect information considered to be on a need-to-know basis."

"Does this have anything to do with your recent court appearances?"

"Yes. It's all about the same thing. Let me explain."

Patrick explained in general terms how he had gotten involved. Now it appears there is a terrorist in the United States who is well-financed, well-equipped, with a network, and with access to high quality, phony documents. This person is an Islamic extremist who has a history of terrorist bomb training, and known to be active in Afghanistan and London.

"They know this person was reading news articles regarding Washington, DC, New York City and Boston. There was no common thread to the articles, but the fact they were about the same three cities over a period of days is a pattern by itself. He was in New York City, but his present location is unknown. They have no good leads to find him."

"Do they think he is connected or has contacts at our mosque?"

"No, nothing that direct. You and I both know that not all Muslim terrorists are religious."

Soufan laughed.

"Look, the FBI has no informants or assets in place to cover Muslin terrorist groups in the US. We all know al-Qaeda wants to use US citizens in their terrorism program on our soil. I don't have any great belief the federal government knows much about what al-Qaeda is doing to recruit US citizens. It's possible that some information could be generated in or around a mosque that is not thought to be significant. They want you to know this is a very dangerous time and to treat anything you might hear as important."

"What you have told me certainly puts Crowley's visit and conversation into perspective. I will go to the mosque and do what needs to be done to insure the problem is appropriately understood. I can assure you it will remain confidential. I will pass on anything that seems potentially relevant."

"We will continue this conversation as needed. You have my cell phone number."

It was only early afternoon and Patrick felt like he had already done a full day's work and then some.

Later, Patrick was seated in the condo living room, deep in thought, when Liz walked in. She chose not to speak to him immediately and just let him go with his thoughts. Finally she said, "Hello. Is there anyone home?"

Patrick smiled. "I'm always home for you." She decided not to contradict him.

Liz proposed, "Why don't we go to Giovanni's for a quick plate of pasta? I'm hungry but I have to do some work tonight."

They left and walked to Hanover Street. "So what's up?" asked Liz.

"I talked to Vespa. Her people don't know the Hawaladar Salim Attash and they don't have anyone to ask. It seems the Mafia has also failed to keep up its informant development in the Islamic community."

Liz smiled. She was glad Patrick could at least attempt a little humor under the circumstances. "What about Vince Baker?"

"I told him what Vespa said. They have nothing going either. He thinks they will soon arrest Attash. They want Attash to talk about The Engineer's visit to his computer shop. The feeling is whatever they had going is over, and The Engineer won't be back. They are trying to figure out how to hold Attash incommunicado so word can't get back to The Engineer."

"Good luck. They arrest him and his constitutional protections kick in. They can't hold him incommunicado. He has a right to counsel. He needs to be arraigned."

"They're thinking about having him declared an enemy combatant. They're not worried about a criminal prosecution down the road. If they lose the case they will worry about that later. The present problems are just too compelling."

"Didn't you say he's a US citizen?"

"I did."

"They are in a bind. If they hold him incommunicado, they might be charged with kidnapping."

"I thought lawyers were supposed to help their clients and create ways for them to do things."

"A first duty for every lawyer is to provide a client advice that will keep him or her out of jail."

"Well, if you have any positive ideas about how to proceed, I would be curious to hear them."

"Right now I can think of none and that is probably why they have not moved yet. They can't think of a legal way to do this to a US citizen."

"Perhaps this is why al-Qaeda wants to recruit US citizens. They travel within the US with few questions and enjoy their constitutional protections wherever they go."

Patrick then told Liz about his conversation with Baker yesterday afternoon and his follow-up conversations this morning with Corso and Blake, followed by Soufan.

"No wonder you were deep in thought when I got home. If it is any consolation, I agree with what you have done. The thought of my safety in Kirby's hands does not fill me with confidence. In fact, it causes fright."

Patrick smiled. It felt good to smile.

"Let's leave this problem out on the sidewalk and go enjoy the company of Giovanni and Carmella. You've been doing nothing but worry of late. Learn to change what you can and recognize what you cannot," said Liz, completing her line of thought.

"Is my lovely bride paraphrasing Saint Anthony?"

"It's Saint Francis, you heathen. Learn your saints."

Giovanni broke out in a huge grin when they entered the restaurant. They were glad they came.

New York City

Maria Torino sat with her father in a small park behind their office building.

"We have done what we can. Things may be at the point where we have no means to further help them," said Aldo Torino. "I reviewed this with John. He has some solid contacts in Boston and wants to know if he should pay a social call to see what resources we might tap up there. We cannot alert the family in Boston because they have been decimated by prosecutions and riddled with informants. I doubt if they could be of much help. They would probably listen more to Patrick's former colleagues than to me."

Maria laughed.

"We have no family presence in DC. There is nothing we can do there."

"Patrick knows how to use the signal to contact me if they have a question. Otherwise we are out of it for now," said Maria.

"I really think you and I should take off for a few days with John. Go to the mountains for some fresh air."

"You want to make sure we are not in the city. You believe some type of radioactive bomb will be set off by these people?"

"Yes."

Maria nodded. "You don't think the FBI will be able to stop The Engineer?"

"They seem to be at a dead end. They indicate they have no means to know where he is. They don't know any of his associates except the Hawaladar. That relationship probably involved the transfer of money, not information. It looks to me that absent some piece of luck, some *buona fortuna* delivered by God, they can only wait and react to what The Engineer does."

"Let's go up to the Catskills."

"Agreed," said Aldo Torino. "But first let's have John do a little reconnaissance in Boston. We may have some union contacts and a few contacts outside the family we can call upon."

Chapter 64

Washington, DC

Vince Baker stopped by the office of AD Bob Wilkins to provide a late afternoon update. "Salim Bin Attash has given no sign that he does anything other than operate a used computer store. We did not find bank accounts or suspicious communication systems. If he is moving money or serves as a Hawaladar, it will take time and a thorough investigation to establish that. As of now, he cannot move without us being with him and hearing him, at his store, apartment or even in his car. We have court orders for microphone and video surveillance at each location."

"Is there anything we can do to speed this up? We may not have the luxury of months of investigation to put this together," said Wilkins.

"There is plenty of sentiment that we should just arrest him. Convince him how serious this is for him and his family, and get him to talk. That would be a short-cut."

"Not one that you like?" questioned Wilkins.

"Not at this point. We really have little on him. Let's assume he is a Hawaladar. We do not have him on tape doing a transaction. We have no stash of cash. We have none of his records. We don't know his customers or how he gets his instructions."

"So what makes others think we should arrest him and he will talk?"

Baker sighed. "Some feel the pressure from on high to do something, whether it is a good idea or not. I asked the Psychological Profile Unit to take a look at Attash, not based on a formal study, but to informally advise me. Specifically, I asked their opinion on the chances of getting him to talk given what limited information we know about his activities and his background."

"What are their thoughts?" asked Wilkins.

"They have too little data to make any formal recommendations. However, informally they point out he would have to be pretty dumb to believe our bluff. We have nothing serious to say about what he is doing other than some generic money laundering allegations. The only real meat is The Engineer, and we have no idea as to their relationship. If it is just about delivering money, then Attash may not even know The Engineer's name or where to find him, much less what he is doing in this country. If he is smart, which they conclude he is, Attash can sit quietly and leave the burden on us, knowing we don't have the evidence. If you try to interview him and don't arrest him, he can take off. If you arrest him, we don't have enough evidence to survive a probable cause hearing. We just don't have the cards to confront him right now."

"So what is the plan?"

"I've made the decision to keep the surveillance ongoing. We are still hoping for a return visit to Attash by The Engineer, which is probably unlikely. We're entering The Engineer's photo in every database we can find in Washington, DC, New York and Boston. Maybe we can get lucky again."

"Is there no intelligence on possible al-Qaeda operatives in New York that we can monitor in case The Engineer contacts them? Can't we try and locate him that way?" asked Wilkins.

"I will say it again knowing that no one wants to hear it," said Baker with frustration.

"This is where the rubber meets the road. Cases like this are advanced when we receive electronic or human intelligence. We have no electronic intelligence on this matter. The CIA, NSA, DIA and our foreign colleagues have picked up no signal intelligence that even hint at what we now know. This is where the government has put its money and its effort for the last twenty years. The only problem is our adversary has regressed to stone age communication to avoid our strength in intercepting all forms of electronic communications. He is not going to play into our strength."

"What about all our recent work on the human intelligence side. Don't we have resources in the Islamic communities in these cities?" countered Wilkins.

"We have resources in the legitimate Islamic communities. These people are good US citizens. They are decent Americans and they want to help stop radical Islam from doing bad things to their country. The thing is, they don't know anything about radical Islamic terrorists. What is it you think they can tell us?" replied Baker.

Wilkins continued his questioning, "Does the CIA have informants in any radical Muslim groups that may be operating in the US?"

Baker was now out of patience as he replied brusquely, "You know the CIA is not supposed to conduct operations inside the US. If they were operating a radical Muslim source inside the US, I don't think they would tell us and admit they were working outside their charter. They would pass the information on and make it look like a non-US source. Outside the US, I cannot say what they have. They don't tell us. In any event, they are silent at present."

Wilkins looked at Baker, saying nothing. It was not a look that Baker appreciated. Ignore the message and shoot the messenger. Baker was proceeding from frustration to outright anger.

Baker continued, "Certainly CIA management conveys to the administration they have made 'great' progress in preventing another 9/11, but they have no intelligence to provide us on this case. They sit there and say nothing. So, perhaps when you meet with more senior management at the CIA, you might ask them directly. Perhaps they will be more forthcoming with you. From what I hear among my CIA friends, whom I trust, CIA agents and FBI agents have one thing in common. Neither is operating any assets that could be described as radical Muslim terrorists. All guidelines seem to prohibit this, either directly or indirectly, through burdensome and foolish administrative practices. The agents know there will be no administrative support for them if something goes wrong. No agent is willing to put his or her neck on the line to operate a top level al-Qaeda informant inside the US."

"So do you just want to sit back and complain? What do I tell the Director you're doing with all our resources to insure our citizens are not victims of a dirty bomb?"

Even though Wilkins and Baker had been friends for years, this discussion had taken on an edge. It offered all the possibility of harming their friendship. Their voices now had an edge to them, suggesting more than was being verbalized. Baker wanted Wilkins to know that management's failure to address the concerns of FBI agents about the practicality of operating terrorists as informants and long-term assets was a chicken that had come home to roost.

It did no good to take pictures from a drone of a man and a mule climbing a mountain deep inside Pakistan. It could not hear what that man murmured into the ear of another, deep inside a cave. It was not possible to electronically intercept the return message carried on the back of another mule to a village or city, where Western intelligence had no influence, and local authorities had no desire or intention to cooperate with outsiders. Mules never made good informants. These were the realities that Baker described, and these were the realities that Wilkins didn't want to hear.

"You can tell the Director I am continuing the surveillance of Attash. Others will say I am wrong. They will ask you to overrule me and order an immediate arrest. Do what you think is necessary. I have made my best judgment. It could be that you put handcuffs on Attash and he will start babbling uncontrollably. However, I don't believe that will happen, and we will then have a greater problem with even less of a solution."

Wilkins was silent for a moment. He said nothing.

Baker continued, "There are those who want to have a voice, to be heard, to be in the picture, to be consulted but who don't want to be accountable if the shit hits the fan. They will insure they are not connected to any decision that goes wrong, but will be on the podium if it goes right."

"Do you realize how cynical you sound?" asked a disconcerted Wilkins.

Baker responded, "We should have had this discussion a long time ago. We've had it in bits and pieces but apparently that didn't work. We have declared a war against terror. The administration too often only allows people into their decision making circles who tell them what they want to hear. I'm not privy to what goes on at these levels, but I do know that serious issues have gone unaddressed. We have almost no human intelligence on terrorist groups within the US. We are using the same skills we used to chase bank robbers. Let them rob the bank and after the robbery we collect evidence and do interviews and hopefully develop enough evidence to make an arrest. Of course, they may rob twenty banks before we get the evidence to make one arrest, and we may only be able to convict them for one of the twenty robberies they committed."

Wilkins sat there speechless, so Baker just kept on going. He decided he might as well put all his cards on the table. "Our Evidence Recovery Teams, lab experts, and agents doing interviews in foreign countries have done a great job putting together forensic evidence cases after the fact. People responsible have been arrested and charged. However, we have developed little capacity to learn what the terrorist is going to do before he does it. We only respond after the bank is robbed. This works, perhaps for traditional criminals, but not so well for a well-armed, nuclear-equipped terrorist."

"So what are you doing with the cards we have left?" asked Wilkins.

"I told you about searching The Engineer through every photo database we can find. We can continue to monitor Attash and hope for a break, or we can arrest him and roll the dice. We have re-interviewed all the witnesses. The truck driver described a cab and some damage to the right front fender of the cab he observed parked nearby the warehouse in Hell's Kitchen. It had a temporary repair using two different colors of tape. We know the year and make of the cab. Crowley talked to Patrick. Patrick told us of an agent in the New York office who works with the NYPD on international, high-end car theft rings. Patrick said we should talk to him, as Patrick was sure this agent would be a great source of ideas on how to locate this cab.

"But we don't even know if that car is related to this case. There are thousands of cabs in New York," said Wilkins, continuing his rude tone of speech.

"Well, you may be right, but we have a lot of manpower available and no new leads and nothing for this manpower to do. We might as well try it," replied Baker.

"I'm surprised and disappointed by your negative attitude."

"If there is anything that I have said that is factually incorrect, please tell me. Otherwise, I challenge you not to be one of those who ignore reality just because everyone else around you is. No one wants to see, much less discuss, the large, grey elephant lurking in the living room." Baker walked out.

Now Baker was really cranked at Wilkins' attitude. Wilkins was actually pretending not to understand the problem, hinting it was only Baker's incompetence at issue.

But as soon as Baker left his office, Wilkins picked up the phone and called his counterpart at DOJ. "Okay, run by me again why your people think Baker is wrong and we should arrest Attash immediately?"

Chapter 65

New York City

The Engineer spent five days looking over the target sites he and Tariq Salah discussed. They needed to agree on manpower assignments, allocation of explosives, and other needed weapons. Part of his training stressed the importance of the decision maker actually viewing the target site and participating in a dry run to insure all critical facets of the operation were acknowledged and being considered. The Engineer had taken several buses, made cell phone calls from the tunnels, and was driven over the George Washington Bridge going in both directions. He did not spend much time around the control tower at LaGuardia. It would be a difficult target but, perhaps for a dedicated martyr, a worthy one. He knew what the current security arrangements were for the Holland Tunnel.

"What is your plan for Penn Station?" asked The Engineer.

"Everything is below ground and very busy. It handles the East Coast Amtrak trains and some commuter rail. With Madison Square Garden above it, there will be added media value. It has two levels, and I think we need two martyrs and two large suitcase bombs set to go off at the same time. I am not sure we have enough martyrs."

"Did you notice how low the ceilings are for a train station?" asked The Engineer.

"Yes. I read it is because it was built in the 1960s when they tore the old station down, after they sold the air rights. I read no one wanted to spend the money to make a monumental structure, as done years ago."

"Well, the low ceilings will help increase the devastation caused by our bomb. It will keep the force from quickly dissipating. On an average day, six hundred thousand people use that station. I think we can do the job with one bomb and without a martyr."

"How?" asked Salah.

"Fifty pounds of plastic in a large roller suitcase would blend into the scene very well. I sat at a table drinking a cup of tea for over an hour, and no one paid any attention to me. Several times I noticed someone ask a person nearby to look after their bag while they went to the bathroom. They seemed to ask older couples or people dressed nicely. There does not seem to be the same concern for bags in Penn Station as there is at the airport. We can exploit that weakness."

"Remote detonation?" asked Salah.

"Why take the chance on an error. We can use both. The timer on the bomb can be preset. When the bomb is properly constructed, we can activate the detonation timer, leaving plenty of time to walk away. I think five minutes is enough for our man to get out. One man, one bomb and no martyr. We will have cell phone detonation as backup to the timer." The Engineer smiled as he finished outlining the plan. He was proud of its simplicity and efficiency.

"The media will report the bomb exploding. The bomb will kill many when packed with metal fragments. The first responders will report radioactive material present," Salah said, somewhat out loud as he was imaging the scene in his head.

"That's the picture," said The Engineer. "We do not have to totally destroy the terminal. We just make it unusable. There will be no one in Penn Station for a long time."

"The same plan for Grand Central?" asked Salah.

"There are different problems at Grand Central. It handles less traffic than Penn Station. It is a much greater physical area to impact. It is the largest train station in the world when counting platforms. They have sixty-seven tracks on two floors; both floors are below ground level. Its significance is its rich history and size, as well as the fact that it serves many of the commuters who come into the city by rail on a daily basis. There is a dining concourse with lots of small food shops. While not as much baggage is seen as in Penn Station, nonetheless, it would not be out of place. The main concourse is just too large. I think we can do more damage by going to the dining concourse one floor below."

Salah asked, "How many men needed for Grand Central? The same as Penn Station?"

"Exactly," said The Engineer. "The beauty is in the simplicity. One person, one suitcase, and a trip made to the restroom. We can control the timing of the event to coincide with the others."

"So far we have two bombs and two men to deliver them at the same time?"

"Correct."

"Let's add up the others."

"Okay. After our last conversation, I viewed LaGuardia Tower. We need one martyr, one bomb."

"Have you figured out how he gets into the secure area?" asked The Engineer.

"My thought is that since this position is definitely going to be for a willing martyr, he actually wears the bomb. He can take a hostage to gain entrance to the tower, kill a number of people, and cause a standoff. The bomb is detonated at a pre-arranged time with the other bombs while he is 'conducting negotiations' with the authorities. One martyr and one bomb should work."

Salah volunteered, "At the Stock Exchange, I can get my contact to get me in the night before. Even if I can't, I can steal his identification and get in myself. I have no doubt I can plant the bomb in a suitable container. The bomb will be equipped with a delayed timer to detonate the next day. We'll back that system up with cell phone detonation capability. This means I have to be personally dedicated to this site."

"I agree. So that is another man and one more bomb."

"Are we agreed on the George Washington Bridge?"

"Yes. We need a martyr, but the martyr need not know of his status ahead of time," said The Engineer.

Salah was confused. He had a quizzical look on his face.

"This is an open area. We need to pack a car or SUV with as much explosives as we can get in it. If we have a reliable martyr, fine. If we don't, then we can 'hire' someone outside the group to drive the vehicle for 'delivery' into New York City from New Jersey. He will think he is being hired just to deliver the vehicle. To him it is just a driving job. What he will not know is that the van will be detonated while he is on the bridge. One large car bomb and one martyr ignorant of his status is what will be required for the George Washington Bridge."

Salah was somewhat startled to hear The Engineer's callous attitude in discussing the life of another Muslim. However, he remembered how hard it was training in the mountains and how they were told they would have to undergo depravation and make hard choices in order to defeat the infidel. Perhaps this was the way it had to be. He said nothing.

"We have the Holland and Lincoln Tunnels left," said Salah.

"In both cases, we should use inbound lanes. This is what will cause the commuters to say 'I don't want to commute into the city again.' The Holland Tunnel will either take one martyr, or an ignorant 'driver,' and someone else to detonate the vehicle when they confirm the driver is inside the tunnel. If we do not have a martyr then we can find an individual we can 'pay' in advance to deliver the car to an address in the city. In fact, we can dry-run this a few times so they get use to 'delivering' cars into the city. When we decide the time of attack, we will give this driver a car loaded with the bomb that we can remotely detonate via cell phone. We can follow him, to make sure he goes into the tunnel, and then detonate the vehicle."

Salah added, "Just before entering the Holland Tunnel going into the city, there are two stoplights for cross streets. One of our team members can be in the vehicle and exit it at the last stop light, before it enters the tunnel. This way, with the traffic of eight lanes being compressed into the two eastbound tunnel lanes, we can make sure the vehicle actually goes into the tunnel. Our team member will rely on a cell phone device as the primary detonator. Again, as backup, we'll use a preset timer activated by the team member when exiting the vehicle before it enters the tunnel. He can remain in the area to insure the vehicle is detonated, one way or the other."

"I think you've added some valuable detail to this part of the plan. Make sure your team member understands the changes," said The Engineer.

"What about the Lincoln Tunnel?" asked Salah. "Do you have a final plan for it?"

"I was in New Jersey looking at how they loaded the commuter buses that use the XBL Lane. The driver opens the bus luggage compartment and then goes inside the terminal to collect the passengers' tickets. As he collects the tickets, passengers go through the door onto the loading dock. If they have a bag, the passenger puts the bag into the bag storage area under the bus and then boards. If there is no bag, the passenger just boards the bus. Our person will present his ticket, go through the door to the loading dock, place the bag in the bag storage area, and not board the bus. He will walk back into the terminal using a different loading dock door. The bus driver will have his back to the bus while collecting tickets and will not even notice what our person does. After collecting all the tickets, and after the passengers have boarded, the driver will shut the baggage container door and the bus will depart. The bomb will be set for a detonation at a prescribed time, with a back-up for cell phone detonation. Again, we can follow the bus until near the tunnel and then detonate by cell phone once we think it is well into the XBL Lane.

"Do we have enough men?" asked Salah.

"We need one martyr or person to drive the car through the Holland Tunnel. If just a hired 'driver,' we need a team member to follow the vehicle, make sure it enters the tunnel, and detonate the bomb. We need a team martyr for the vehicle on the GW Bridge, or a 'driver' to 'deliver' the vehicle. If using a 'driver,' we need a person as backup to detonate the van when it is on the bridge.

The Engineer continued: "We need one competent and true martyr for the La Guardia tower, as we discussed. You will handle the Stock Exchange the night before. Penn and Grand Central Stations will each require one person to deliver the bomb, set the detonator, and walk away as we discussed. So we need one to three martyrs. We need from your team those who will detonate the respective bombs where a true martyr is not being used. I also intend, in the case of a true martyr, to rig the bomb with a remote detonation device to insure the martyr does not weaken at the last moment. No matter what the mix and match is, we have enough people. There are the assignments for seven of your eight people, and possibly only one is a martyr. You and six others remain alive to continue the fight."

"We have plenty of material?" noted Salah.

"We need to build six bombs, each containing fifty pounds of plastic explosives, and one large van bomb. We could triple the number of attacks and still have material left over. No, we have enough to continue the war after this action. Now, I need a ride to Chinatown. Can you give me a lift?"

In the cab going to Chinatown, The Engineer said, "I will call you in a day or two to meet me at the storage facility. In the meantime, I want you to purchase six large size roller suitcases, all from different places. We also need boxes of nails, screws, nuts, bolts, and ball bearings for the bomb projectiles. We can use plastic containers to hold the projectiles while in the suitcase. Maybe you can take a run across the river and visit some hardware stores in New Jersey. When I get back, I will bring the cell phone detonation devices. We are ready. Start assembling the bombs."

Salah was waiting for The Engineer to tell him where he was going, but The Engineer said nothing more. Sometimes he felt like The Engineer didn't trust him. Other times he realized he didn't have a need to know. If something were to happen to Salah, he could not tell what he did not know. Still, it was hard to feel like a brother toward The Engineer. There was something missing in this man.

When giving The Engineer a ride to Chinatown, Salah realized The Engineer wanted to be dropped off at an intersection where the China Express Bus stopped for passengers going to Boston. It was the cheapest transportation between the two cities. It was started in the Chinese community, but now it was used by college students and older people. There was no bus terminal. You waited on the street, the bus came by on a regular schedule, you gave the driver twenty-five dollars in cash, and four hours later you arrived in Chinatown in Boston. Salah figured The Engineer was going to Boston to meet with Talat Mehmood.

Chapter 66

New York City

New York City Police Detective Tony Bernardo had been on the job for twenty-one years, fourteen of them as a detective. His specialty was stolen car and truck rings. For the last five years he had worked with FBI Special Agent Cameron Jones, who had advanced training in the smuggling of high-end vehicles out of the United States into foreign countries. The vehicles were stolen, or given away for insurance money by owners deeply in debt, and placed on ships destined to countries where there was no effective inspection of incoming luxury vehicles. Other times the vehicles were dismantled and sold as parts, which were equally in high demand by those not wishing to pay the exorbitant list prices of the luxury car manufacturers. Bernardo and Jones found that foreign police cooperation could be difficult. Once the cars were physically removed from the United States, the evidence was outside their criminal jurisdiction.

Susan Crowley called the New York City Joint Terrorism Task Force after Patrick reminded her of the expertise of agent Cameron Jones and his NYPD partner regarding vehicles. Both were asked to immediately come to the JTTF. They were told of the problem, given the reports of the truck driver's interviews, and asked how they would try to find the cab. Bernardo responded with his sharp New York humor that they were "car guys" not miracle workers. However, as Patrick believed they might, the two came up with a plan.

Bernardo told the Task Force, "There are about ten thousand cabs in New York City. About a third of them could fit the make and model description. However, there are some distinguishing characteristics of the cab, observed by the truck driver, which will be helpful in locating it. The truck driver described an eight-inch tear, or rip, on the top side of the right, front fender. Several pieces of black duct tape were placed over the jagged edge. The right front hubcap is missing and the right passenger mirror is taped into position on the door with gray duct tape. It looks like it was pulled away at some point, and rather than buy a new mirror, the owner just taped it back into place. Probably not a lot of cabs in New York City have this combination in place on the right front end."

Special Agent Jones continued: "There are forty-thousand New York City Police Officers. About one third or more are on duty at any given time. You can put out a bulletin with the car description and ask every officer to be on the alert for this vehicle. If the vehicle is spotted, they need only to get the cab number and registration number and report it. Do nothing more. They don't have to stop it or identify the driver."

"You don't have to tell them why you want the vehicle and you don't have to say it's for the JTTF," added Bernardo. "You don't want this leaking to the press. We can put it out with homicide or our auto theft unit. Let the word out it is important. The officers will read between the lines, and if the cab is moving on the streets you have a shot at finding it."

A flyer describing the cab was sent to every precinct electronically. It was the main item at every roll call and brought to the attention of every shift coming on duty. The "word" was out. This vehicle needed to be found quickly and quietly. Any reports were to go to Bernardo or Jones at the Auto Theft Task Force, until further notice. There was no snickering or jokes among the officers as the request went out. There was an aura of serious business. There was nothing to attract the attention of the press. They would try this approach. If it didn't work, they would extend the circle to include the eyes of other public servants. All bus drivers, firemen, and public works people were potential eyes and ears. It was better than doing nothing.

Back in Washington, Vincent Baker was spending his Saturday afternoon in his office following the arrest of Salim Bin Attash. The decision was made by Bob Wilkins to overrule Baker and arrest Attash. Wilkins sided with the faction that wanted to arrest Attash and confront him with his money laundering activities, and force his cooperation regarding The Engineer. The agents and detectives knew that Attash was in his apartment alone, as he had been under full surveillance. They had, in addition to an arrest warrant, search warrants for his apartment and place of business. If they got his cooperation, they would have time to debrief him before anyone noticed he was absent from his normal routine. At least that was their plan. If they arrested Attash on a federal warrant, agents had the obligation to bring Attash before the nearest available federal magistrate for a preliminary bail hearing. This would, of course, be a public matter and an attorney would be available to represent him at this proceeding. However, if arrested by New York City PD on local warrants, Attash could be held in lockup until Monday morning. So instead of federal warrants, they applied for and received state arrest and search warrants.

Bob Wilkins flew to New York to personally oversee the next critical hours. Wilkins did not have any desire or affinity toward field work, but he thought it necessary that a senior decision maker be present. After the arrest of Attash, Wilkins called back to the JTTF to report the results. Baker was included on the call.

"The arrest team got him out of bed. No problem. We have an Arabic speaking agent on the arrest team. Attash is refusing to speak with them, in English or Arabic. It is not what we expected. They have searched the apartment and have found some records, which may be coded financial data. The lab will have to examine and tell us what is there, if anything. Otherwise, he seems to lead a very simple existence. The initial report from the search of the shop is much the same. However, with all the computer equipment seized, it will take forever to examine all the potential electronic hiding places. They already found some encrypted files on one computer, but our knowledge level has not increased."

"Has he been shown the photographs of The Engineer yet?" asked Baker. Everyone was waiting for the answer, which was slow to be delivered.

"He was told this could be a very simple matter if he cooperated and would tell us about the man in the photograph. He looked at the photograph, showed no reaction, and looked away. There is no conversation taking place. No small chatter, no questions except that he asked to call his attorney. We have not allowed that yet. That is all we know, and we will call back as soon as anything changes."

Baker was not angry. You don't know how someone will react until you ask them to cooperate. The decision was made, over his objection, to make the arrest in order to make things happen. Baker's experience, combined with the results or lack thereof from the physical surveillance, told him they did not have much leverage on Attash. If he did not panic, did not try to explain, stood his ground, then the law and available facts were on his side. This is what he was doing. Sooner, rather than later, they would be dealing through an attorney who would want to see a lot of cards on the table before suggesting any form of cooperation by his client. Who knew at this point? Maybe Attash had no information to give that would help find The Engineer. Baker also felt that this arrest action ignored the centuries of Hawaladar history and their code of privacy regarding their clients' interests. A Hawaladar would make a Swiss banker look talkative.

By late afternoon, nothing had changed. Despite his request, Attash had not been allowed to make a phone call. The processing procedure seemed to be moving at a very slow pace. Attash remained stoic and not flustered. It was as if he could tell that it was his captors who had all the pressure on them. If he thought that, he was right.

At the same time late Saturday afternoon, Officer Maria Gonzales was on foot patrol, standing in front of the Jacobs Javits Center, which was just east and a little south of the area in Hell's Kitchen where the container had been delivered. What Officer Gonzales first noticed was that the cab had the duty light off, indicating it was not in service. She observed no passenger and thought it was an off-duty cab headed home. Then she looked at the right front fender and saw the black duct tape. She looked at the mirror and saw the gray duct tape. Her head snapped forward and she saw that the right front hubcap was missing. She motioned with her head to her foot patrol partner, Alex Carver, to look at the cab. He did. He nodded back to her as they both wrote down the taxi number and the registration. Gonzales was in a position to get a quick look at the driver. Carver could not see the driver, but was on his cell phone calling the Auto Theft Task Force. While the cab was still in his general line of sight, Carver was on the phone with Detective Bernardo. Carver was told he and his partner should wait there. A sector car would arrive shortly to pick them up and everything would be cleared by their sergeant. Carver relayed this information to Gonzales.

"Can you believe this shit?" said Gonzales. "I never see anything. At first I said it can't be, but there it is. I wonder what this is about?"

They compared notes and both had the same cab number and registration number. Gonzales starting writing down her memory of the face she saw behind the wheel. A few moments later Carver received a radio call from his sergeant, saying that he and Gonzales would be picked up shortly for a temporary special assignment.

Gonzales and Carver were surprised when they were picked up by an FBI agent rather than a sector car, and delivered to the JTTF rather than the Auto Theft Task Force. It was explained to them that it was a terrorist investigation they were trying to shield from public view. They were separated and debriefed individually. It did not take long before records were being pulled regarding the cab. A NYPD computer sketch of the driver was being generated with Officer Gonzales' help, based on her brief view of the driver. When done, it looked very similar to the one generated of The Engineer's helper, based on the truck driver's description. There was a positive charge of energy going through the JTTF. These developments held the possibility of being hardcore information.

Chapter 67

After speaking with Vincent Baker, AD Bob Wilkins returned to the New York JTTF Office for the evening briefing. Attash was in the custody of the NYPD on local criminal charges, but it was only a technicality. Local authorities were working so closely with the FBI that federal standards would have to be applied to Attash. If they did not let him call his attorney or continued to hold him incommunicado, no matter how necessary to the inquiry, they would be violating his rights. Both the lawyers from the US Attorney's Office for the Southern District, and the FBI's own lawyers, were in agreement on this point. Attash, who had not spoken one word since his arrest, was now on the phone with his attorney. A short while later Wilkins was informed that the attorney had visited with Attash in a police holding cell, and now wished to speak to the FBI person in charge. Wilkins advised that he would speak with the attorney.

Attorney Raymond Bielski appeared to be in his early fifties. He was about six-feet tall, medium build, dark hair graying around the edges, dressed in khakis and a blue button-down. He gave the initial impression of being a serious person.

"I'm Ray Bielski and I represent Salim Bin Attash. While I understand he was arrested and is being held by the NYPD, those actions are in conjunction with and at the behest of the FBI. So my question is, what do you want with my client?"

Wilkins responded, "Your client is a suspected money launderer who has been in contact with someone in whom the FBI has an investigative interest. We've asked him about this person, but he declined to answer and requested to call you."

Bielski responded, "While it seems to have taken a long time for you to find an operating telephone, let's move on to the why behind the what. Why do you think my client has any knowledge of the person in whom you have an interest?"

"I'm not going to sit here and detail our evidence against your client. You can deal later with the AUSA and the court if you want to conduct discovery, but you won't do it through me."

"My client's position at present is that he will remain silent and put you through the steps necessary to prove he has committed a crime. The only reason why I'm even having this conversation is to prevent events from going out of control because of any misunderstanding. It is my duty to defend my client in court. It's how I make my living. But it's also my duty to extricate him from any situation where assumptions are being made that may not be correct."

"Are you saying your client is not a Hawaladar?"

"I am not saying anything. I'm asking you to tell me what you think my client knows. Something is causing an Assistant Director of the FBI in charge of the Counterterrorism Division, to be in New York City on a

Saturday night talking to a criminal lawyer. I don't even get to talk with agents I know in the New York Office that I've had cases with over the years. They know me. I know them. Let's cut to the chase and see what we can straighten out. Tell me what you want to know or we stand pat and go to court Monday morning, when my client will be released on bail. If you turn around and arrest him on a federal warrant after he makes bail, you have to take him directly to a US magistrate judge for a bail hearing. No screwing around like you've been doing here. He will make bail again and you will have to show your cards publicly at a court hearing. Why not save the intervening steps and discuss it now."

"I suggest your client make a proffer of what he would like us to hear and we will consider it," said Wilkins.

"You never served in the New York office, did you, Mr. Wilkins?"

"No," said Wilkins somewhat testily. He didn't like answering any question from Bielski, much less one that implied his FBI service was less than perfect because he had not served in the New York Office.

"You showed my client a photograph. You could at least have done the same thing and shown it to me. But you chose not to. That ends this conversation. Say hello to Vince Baker for me. I know he served in the New York office."

Wilkins sat there after Bielski walked out. He realized he was at a disadvantage in speaking with Bielski. He had not taken the time to find out if the agents knew him and what his reputation was in the New York Office. It was not unusual for agents to have informal discussions with defense attorneys who wished to minimize damage to their clients before things got too far. This was one of those times. Wilkins realized he should not have been the one talking to Bielski. Did Bielski know Baker? How did he know Baker might be involved in this case?

After a few brief conversations around the JTTF Office, Wilkins knew Bielski was regarded as a competent defense attorney in federal and state court. He was known to be direct and reliable in his dealings with law enforcement. When Wilkins told them he demanded a proffer from Attash as a prelude to further discussion, even about the photograph already shown Attash, they said nothing. They didn't have to. Wilkins knew he had taken on more than he was prepared to handle. But at least he had an idea as to how the conversation might be resurrected.

Wilkins telephoned Vince Baker, explaining the details of his conversation with Bielski. He concluded by saying, "Would you be able to call Bielski and see if the conversation can be put back on the table?"

Baker worked political corruption cases when assigned to New York. Bielski was involved in two that went to trial. They had a mutual respect for what each other did. Baker would make the call and see what could be done.

By 9:30 pm, Officers Maria Gonzalez and Alex Carter had been completely debriefed. The owner of the independent cab they observed was determined to be Tariq Salah, with an apartment address in Chelsea. Chelsea was next to Hell's Kitchen, where the container was delivered. Using basic computer research of government and private databases, they knew that Salah was a US citizen born in Miami. He had a valid New York driver's license and cab license for the last five years, and no record of any arrests. His name was searched through the FBI indices and every terrorist database they could access. No records were found. He did hold a valid US passport, but travel records under that passport were not immediately available. They also searched records for Salah's parents in Miami and came up with almost no information, other than they existed and were not the type of people to come to anyone's attention. There was a photo of Salah available in the taxi records, but no one had yet gone outside with this name until an investigative plan was agreed upon.

Chapter 68

While the information about Tariq Salah was being distributed throughout the New York JTTF, the group leaders huddled to cobble together a strategy as to the next investigative steps. Back in Washington, Vince Baker had reached Attorney Raymond Bielski at his home. After some updating about each other lives in recent years, Baker asked: "So why were you busting Wilkins' chops? He was trying to talk to you."

"We weren't speaking the same language, so I thought I needed to push the conversation along. I figured you would be involved since I know you are working terrorism, and that is what I heard this was about. I thought if I provoked Wilkins somehow, I would get a call from you. What do you want with my client other than harassing him because of his cultural, religious, and ethnic background?"

Even though Baker could not see Bielski, the smile on his lips was evident. Baker could hear the clink of ice cubes in the background. Baker laughed out loud.

"Short and sweet," said Baker. "Your client has been laundering money for terrorists that may want to do great harm in this country on a very near-term basis. The matter is utterly serious. If we don't get immediate cooperation from your client, and harm is done to the public, your client's lack of cooperation will be remembered and addressed to the greatest degree possible."

"That sounds like a threat," said Bielski.

"It is what it is. Take it however you wish, but I cannot be more clear or concise."

"And what is my client offered for his cooperation?"

"As usual, I have no authority to negotiate terms. However, if your client tells us what he knows and successfully takes a polygraph, and the facts are borne out by further investigation, he is not a serious problem to this country and would be treated accordingly."

"Will he be required to become a Hawaladar tattletale and asked to report on his clients, who are doing nothing but acting as families helping each other out?"

"No. Not our battle right now. If you are looking for guarantees in writing with bells and whistles and fancy ribbons, we don't have the time. If he does the right thing, he won't get screwed, but he won't get a complete pass."

"I'll present exactly what you said to my client first thing in the morning. Will you be in New York?"

"If you tell me you are going to recommend to your client that he speak with us, I will come up tonight. If you plan on dragging this out, I have other things that need doing."

"Why don't you meet me at the police lockup where they are holding my client? Bring one of those general immunity letters with your authority to sign along the lines of what we just discussed? Then we can see what happens."

It was agreed they would meet at 9:00 am at the lockup.

Back at the JTTF office, orders had already been given for the surveillance teams to conduct a survey of Salah's neighborhood to determine what type of fixed and moving surveillance the area could accommodate. Subpoenas were being served on telephone companies and wireless carriers for call records of Salah. They wanted to learn who he was and what his assets were before they started surveillance in the neighborhood. If they got too close, too soon, they could disclose their presence and Salah could turn into a rabbit and be gone down the hole. At the same time, they had the immediate need to find him and whomever he was with.

A photograph of Salah was obtained from the New York City cab license file and from the Department of Motor Vehicles. A photo was put into a spread and shown to a rather sleepy truck driver and his attorney. He picked out Salah as the person present with The Engineer when he dropped the chassis in Hell's Kitchen. The search for duct tape on a cab had paid off. What started out as a wild shot in the dark was turning into hard core evidence. A team of agents and lawyers were now reviewing data to submit an affidavit in support of an application to a federal judge to authorize electronic surveillance on Salah. This would be a roving wire enabling them to monitor any location he was present. Such interception authority was harder to get, but necessary in this case. Who knew where Salah would be going, or with whom he would be speaking? They were still desperately seeking some telephone records of phone calls made by Salah. Who did he know? Where had he been? They still didn't have any records from his passport, so his travel history was still unknown.

Tariq Salah was busy trying to decide if he should keep the receipts for six roller suitcases and the hardware items he had been told to purchase. He had dropped these items off at the storage facility. He decided to throw the receipts away. The Engineer did not like anything written lying around. So Salah dumped the paper in a street trashcan on the way home from parking his cab in the garage. He did not like to see litter on the streets. Salah had done a lot of running around over the last several days and he was ready for a good night's sleep.

Salah was excited as he thought about the immediate future. He would be a hero in al-Qaeda and to Islam. He would be honored in fundamentalist mosques around the world. Salah now expected he would survive this operation and later would be personally recognized by those who shared his faith and beliefs. Salah thought he may have to go into hiding for a period of time. While there might be some talk about his name being associated with this operation, there would be no proof of his involvement left behind. Salah's friend at the Stock Exchange would not be alive to talk about him. Salah would make sure of that as soon as he got the necessary entry into the Exchange to plant his bomb.

Chapter 69

At 9:30 am, Attorney Raymond Bielski and Special Agent Vincent Baker sat down at a gun-metal grey desk, bolted to the floor, in a police interrogation room just down the hall from the cell where Salim Bin Attash was held. Bielski spent a half hour speaking with his client before meeting with Baker.

After a few moments of small talk, just to get things going, Bielski finally said, "You have the letter?"

Baker pulled out a signed immunity offer to Attash from a manila folder. There was not a lot of dress up for this meeting. Bielski read the letter, got up and left. A few minutes later he came back with the letter countersigned by Attash and witnessed by Bielski.

"My client does not know the fellow whose photo you showed him."

Baker remained silent.

Bielski continued: "Money was transferred to my client within the Hawala system. The transfer originated in Tunis. It was to be delivered to a person appearing at his shop who could provide the correct introduction followed by a complex delivery code. Your man gave the correct introduction and wrote down the required code. My client gave him $250,000, all old money and none of it from any one particular source. My client thought this person might be back to buy some computer parts, but he never saw him again. He didn't see a car. The man appeared to be on foot. He has no contact information for this person."

"Is there anyway your client can help us identify or find this person?"

"My client feels that if he were to ask about this person, or the source of the money back in Tunis, he would not get an answer. Such inquiry would call attention to him as probably having been exposed. In fact, he thinks his family may already know of his arrest and the word may already be out. Neither my client nor those with whom he does business are in league with any known terrorists. Like other world bankers, they do not consider political affiliation to be any of their business. Having said that, they do not consider drug and terrorist groups to be worthwhile business affiliates. My client avoids them if he learns that either the individual or the money is drug-related."

Although Baker had anticipated these answers, he still felt deflated. His shoulders even started to round for a few seconds. Then he collected himself and started to engage his brain again after it had digested what he had just heard.

"I have an interview team standing by for the formal interview. Can we get it started now?"

"Sure, why don't we both take them in and introduce them to Attash. I'll have to remain with him at all times while he is being questioned. He cannot be questioned unless I am present."

"I understand," said Baker. They got that part of the process started. Baker went back to the JTTF to provide an initial briefing of what Attash had said through his lawyer. The interview team would come out to give periodic reports, but no one had any high hopes the answers would change.

When it came to doing joint physical surveillances, the agencies did not break up their teams. Surveillance teams that worked together over a period of time were able to read each other so well, and their procedures were so well developed, they required little communication to get the job done. However, all the agencies would share a common communication system. This is the way surveillance teams from state and federal agencies could work together in seamless fashion. Like any other operation, it needed to be tightly led. This was left to the FBI.

By midday, the scouting report was available outlining what surveillance activity could be set up in the neighborhood around Salah's apartment. One team was already on site, using an apartment across the street. It was owned by a firefighter who was the brother-in-law of one of the surveillance team members. They had direct eyes on the front of Salah's apartment building. They were still trying to get coverage on the rear of the building, which led into an alleyway. They needed to record and identify every person entering and leaving the building. Other teams were set up to follow people from the building to determine their identities for later interview.

It would be a great help when they could get a microphone planted in Salah's apartment. They could then narrow the surveillance to just those people having contact with Salah. Otherwise, they were going to burn a lot of manpower and risk too much activity, which might alert an astute eye. They were still working on the affidavit of probable cause to support the application for electronic surveillance, so they were flying blind while getting set up. The difference was they all thought they had a good lead. They were right. Now they needed a little luck. That they would not get.

Chapter 70

Boston

Talat Mehmood was born in Boston twenty-eight years ago to devout Muslim parents who emigrated from Jordan thirty-five years ago. They were originally natives of Palestine who immigrated to Jordan when they could no longer take the daily violence in Palestine. All of the Mehmood family members were now proud US citizens. Mehmood's father worked in a small accounting firm in Dorchester. He was not a CPA but had been trained in general accounting. He was able to achieve a sustainable wage over the years, sufficient to raise his family. Talat graduated from a city public high school and later attended a local community college, receiving an Associate's Degree in general business. He moved to the Allston section of Boston, where he did odd jobs and drove a cab part-time. About four years ago, he purchased a small convenience store in Allston with money his parents saved to help him start a business. Talat worked seven days a week until the store started to make money. Then he slowly hired others to help so he could have some time off.

Talat's parents attended the mosque in Boston for many years. It had changed very little during the period they attended. The Imam was theologically moderate and was well respected among Boston area religious leaders.

Talat grew up going to this mosque, listening to this Imam explain Islam, the Prophet, and the Muslim way of life. Since his parents were devout Muslims, Talat knew that his parents fully expected him to make the Hajj at his first opportunity. It was a very important event in the life of any true Muslim. Talat knew his parents had made their first Hajj while living in Palestine, and later a second Hajj when living in Jordan. They had not traveled to that part of the world since coming to the United States. They knew little about the hardship, and sometimes danger, facing those today seeking to make their Hajj.

One of Talat's Muslim friends from youth moved to Bayonne, New Jersey, because he landed a job. He later told Talat and other friends about the mosque he attended in Bayonne. The friend explained that he was attracted to this mosque because the Imam's preaching had opened his eyes and allowed him to see the world as it really is. It was not the same as Boston. The Imam educated them about the problems of Muslims in other parts of the world, and how certain political and religious groups sought the suppression of Muslims. The Imam told them how the clearly expressed words of the Quran were being ignored. This Imam was the first one to explain to these young men the nature of jihad and their personal obligation and duty to insure the words of Allah, as revealed through the Prophet Muhammad, were respected by all. They were introduced to Islamic Fundamentalism without the words ever being used. Talat Mehmood was invited to join with his friend and others for private meetings with the Imam, who further explained his teachings. Talat soon fell under the Imam's spell and, after a number of visits, started viewing non-Muslims in a completely different way.

Talat's parents were very happy when he announced he was making the Hajj. He was given the names of distant relatives and former friends in both Jordan and Palestine to visit if he could make it to either area. Talat was eager to see Mecca, to be able to walk the same ground, see the same space, breathe the same air, which played such an important role in the life of the Prophet. The Imam in Bayonne also gave Talat some names of individuals he should meet after the Hajj. Talat was excited to think he might meet distant members and friends of his family. He felt it gave him some connection to the true Islam. He also was anxious to look up the people the Imam wanted him to meet.

In the end, Talat never made it to Palestine or Jordan. He spent two weeks with friends of the Bayonne Imam. After that, the records would show, he remained in Saudi Arabia for four months studying Islam. The truth was, he was given a new identity and transported to an al-Qaeda training camp in Afghanistan. When he emerged from his training, Talat returned to the United States to begin his present mission.

When The Engineer stepped off the bus from New York in Boston's Chinatown, Talat Mehmood was standing nearby, next to his parked car. He was directly across the street from the entrance gate to Chinatown. Another group of people were lined up on the sidewalk ready to board the bus for its return trip to New York City. In the unloading and loading of the bus, people did not pay much attention to each other. Talat nodded to The Engineer, who walked over to Talat's car. They embraced and performed the Muslim greeting. They drove to Talat's apartment in Allston to eat and to talk.

Chapter 71

New York City

The FBI agents in New York were doing what they did best. Working with bits and pieces of information, they were compiling a detailed history of Salah's life. They knew his childhood in Miami was uneventful. His father worked for the city bus company as a mechanic for over forty years and was now retired. His mother had done part-time work as a maid at a local hotel, but basically was a stay at-home mother. They lived in a very modest neighborhood that also housed other families of Saudi heritage. It was a simple life, not much by US standards, but by average Saudi standards, it was luxurious.

Like many young people these days, Salah relied on a cell phone and text messaging. Computer usage was more likely wireless than cable. Still, they could not find his Internet Service Provider. They were beginning to worry he could be using cash to pay for cell phones purchased under any name, as well as internet cafés. Still he probably had an email account. They needed to find his electronic persona.

The surveillance teams were still getting situated and receiving instructions. The first thing they needed to know was whether they should break off the surveillance if they thought they were made. This was a difficult question. "Don't get made but don't lose him," was an instruction that used to be given. That didn't fly anymore. It was very difficult, or next to impossible, to follow someone who is looking to see if they have a tail. Quite often, the surveillance had to be done in progressive segments just to prevent this. You had to build your knowledge base of the target a little at a time. Staying anonymously with a target that was on full alert was next to impossible. That raised the next question. If they were made, do they arrest Salah? The formal process would be to detain the person to determine if an arrest should take place, or if the person should be released to go about his business.

In this case the answer was hard, but simple. There was insufficient probable cause for Salah's arrest. They needed to follow Salah to gather probable cause of his criminal activity and to determine his accomplices. Where was The Engineer? They needed Salah to find The Engineer and his radioactive material. On the other hand, they did not want to spook Salah. He needed to think he was free to carry out his mission. Don't burn him. Don't get made. Drop the surveillance if you have to. They would put a transmitter in his cab as soon as they could find it. They already had a court order for that. As soon as they could get a court order for electronic interception of his communications, and a microphone in the area of his person, it would be easier to conduct physical surveillance. Hopefully, they could learn in advance from a microphone where he was going. Right now was a tough period. Back off and don't get made were the clear instructions given.

The next issue was simpler. What if Salah took them to The Engineer? He was a different story. The orders were to arrest The Engineer. He was not to be lost for any reason. There was sufficient evidence to arrest him as an illegal entrant into the United States. There was also an Italian arrest warrant in effect. He was far too dangerous. They needed to get him off the street no matter what. Arrest him if seen and detain Salah. We will figure Salah out later. The orders were clear and the agents and other JTTF members knew exactly what was expected of them.

These instructions were still hot off the press when the spotter across the street thought he saw Salah walking down the front steps of his building. It was a difficult call for identification purposes. All they had was a full-facial photo of Salah, of poor quality and several years old. The person exiting was wearing a baseball cap and had his head down. The spotter asked for some help, but there was no one close by to get a good look. They still were not in place. Rather than go off ill-prepared and uncoordinated, the decision was made to get the rest of the surveillance set up properly and not to run after this first individual in question. If it was Salah, they would just have to hope he was off to buy the Sunday paper, get some coffee, and be back shortly. They could then be set up for a proper start. It was a good procedural call, but bad for the case. It was Salah.

Salah completed his needed night's sleep and was anxious to start assembling parts for the six suitcase bombs. Salah decided not to take his cab to the storage facility, as the cab was now conveniently parked in a local garage. It was easier to take the fifteen minute bus ride over to Hell's Kitchen, where the storage facility was located. It was less than a mile from where the container was originally delivered. The Salah surveillance teams would not find the storage facility today. This opportunity was gone.

Chapter 72

Southport

Patrick and Liz were in Southport. The weather was nice and there were signs that summer might occur this year. Both had spent the day on the deck, reading and listening to the sounds of nature. Liz was reading a book by Eleanor Roosevelt concerning her views on post-World War II and causes she wanted to bring to the world's attention. Patrick was reading a mystery and enjoying every minute of it. It was just plain entertainment, with no pretensions of being anything else. Liz offered to make tea. Patrick accepted. When Liz served the tea, Patrick questioned why there wasn't something sweet to accompany it. Liz countered that her offer was only for tea, nothing else. She further pointed out that Patrick was not yet in bathing suit form, and that he needed to get working on it. She wanted to help him. Nothing sweet today with tea, thank you.

Patrick grumbled. He lost before the battle even started.

Patrick's cell phone started to vibrate. He answered. It was Joan Peabody calling to see if they wanted to come over for baked striped bass, which John caught that afternoon and was now in the process of being cleaned. Patrick did not consult Liz. He immediately accepted.

"You have no idea how meanly I have been treated this afternoon. I was served tea with nothing else. No sweet of any kind," Patrick grumbled.

"Liz already told me that you were not ready to model a bathing suit and needed to trim down just a little. I promised to help. So with the fish you get rice and salad, with fruit for dessert."

"This is a female plot to violate my rights to an enjoyable life."

"No, it's a female plot to keep a man approaching his senior years in good physical condition and still attractive to the opposite sex. I don't think you will pass away from hunger on my watch. Oh, and bring some white wine." Joan hung up before he could even respond.

Patrick looked at Liz. She had a smile on her face but did not look up from her book.

"You knew and approved of this attack on me."

"Why do you think she called your cell phone and not the house phone?"

"You knew John caught fish already?"

"Not exactly. Unlike you, I knew there was a high probability that John would catch a fish and that we would be invited for dinner. The white wine is chilling in the refrigerator. Make sure we don't forget it." Liz never took her eyes off her book while speaking.

Patrick's cell phone vibrated again. He opened it. "No doubt you have called to apologize and offer me something more than fruit for dessert."

Patrick heard a laugh. "Hi Mark, this is Susan Crowley. What's wrong with fruit for dessert? They do it in Italy all the time. I thought you liked the Italian way of eating."

"If I were playing chess I would reach across the board and knock my king over to indicate surrender. What's up?"

"Vince Baker wants you to know things are active in New York City. They have some potential leads in progress. They found someone who might be able to take them to The Engineer. They are keeping Boston and Washington Field Offices up to date on the briefings in the event the direction of the inquiry turns to us. I cannot go into more detail."

Patrick cut her off. "I've told Baker the terms of my contact with the FBI have somewhat changed. There appears to me to be a threat to the City of Boston. I'll do what I can for you but you have to recognize my personal interests in protecting my home, family and friends from these inglorious bastards. I don't intend to see Boston attacked."

"Baker told me exactly what you said. If we provide you with information to help us, understand that we trust your judgment as to how you use that information for the good of the overall inquiry. Baker thinks Vespa may have something to do with New York. It is the only reason he can think of as to why the truck driver turned so cooperative. In fact, the truck driver has been able to identify someone of great interest. Baker is concerned we may need Vespa again. To keep you up to date is in our interest."

"So there is a motive for your call. You want me to do something. And I thought you were calling because you missed me."

She laughed. "I knew you were mature enough to understand. I should also mention that they made an arrest in New York of someone who delivered funds to The Engineer, but he is not in a position to help further, even though he wants to. Somehow *The New York Times* got a tip that this money laundering arrest is connected to a terrorism investigation. The New York office gave them the 'cannot confirm or deny' and blew it off. It may have worked only because it is a weekend, but the *Times* owns *The Boston Globe.* Given your recent news history from Boston federal court, you could get a call from a reporter trying to put this together. We didn't want them to catch you off guard."

"I appreciate the heads up, but you know I would not answer their questions anyway."

"Just so, they may go fishing. You never know. We're at a point where we need to find The Engineer and we don't have a lot of time. We can't have him disappear on us."

"I'll let you know if I hear from anyone."

Patrick thought about what was not said. New York is now in play. Baker, for whatever reason, thinks Boston will also be in play. Patrick had to admit he had been thinking about potential targets in the Boston area. If they were going to use a dirty bomb, that meant close confines for maximum damage. That, in turn, probably dictated a city environment. Boston was rich with potential targets of symbolic value. It is where America's experiment with democracy started. Virginians might wish to disagree, but Boston always got the credit. If you wanted to attack American democracy, Boston had lots to offer. There was one potential target that had been drifting through his mind for days. He had not verbalized it to anyone, and would not at this point. He did not even want to think about it. It came into his mind again and he immediately put it out, choosing to think about the baked striper. He was trying not to worry about things that presently were beyond his control and influence. He was not good at it, but he was trying.

Patrick and Liz had a lovely evening with the Peabodys. The fruit compote for dessert was delicious, and Patrick didn't feel stuffed. He had to admit, the ladies were right.

On the way back to Boston that night, Patrick realized that his friend Maha Soufan had been on his mind. He thought he should give him a call just to check in.

"Hi Maha, its Patrick."

"As Salaam Alaikum"

"Alaikum as Salaam"

'Where are you?"

"Liz and I are driving back to Boston from Southport. I have been thinking of you. Things are still the same, if you know what I mean?"

"I do. I understand. We have nothing to discuss from this end, but we have done what we can to be informed if the circumstances dictate."

"I will be around all week if you want to talk."

"Okay, Mark. Thanks for calling."

Patrick felt better after making the call. Even though he had nothing to say, he wanted Soufan to know he was thinking of him and appreciated what Soufan and his colleagues were willing to do.

Patrick next called Mayor John Corso at home and gave him an update, with the agreement Patrick would stay in touch and Corso would keep Ed Blake up to speed.

"What do you have tomorrow?" asked Patrick.

"Not much," said Liz. This is going to be a paper week. I have a lot of motions to answer and a few to write. I am flexible and available if you need any help."

"You think I might need help?"

"I'm thinking about what you are not saying out loud. This thing is heading to Boston. We both can just sense it. It's why you called Soufan. You don't want him to feel alone."

Patrick did not respond. It wasn't necessary.

Patrick was not the only one on the phone. Harvey Bottom and Phil Kirby were following up on what they had discussed over the weekend.

"Baker was pissed at Patrick for getting on Baker's case about not notifying the locals in Boston. It worked just like you thought. Patrick got pissed and dumped on Baker, who is up to his ass in alligators down in New York," said Kirby.

"Over the weekend I've been talking to some people at DOJ and Homeland Security. I've said the FBI is way out of order, letting Patrick run with Vespa and cutting everyone else out. I've hinted there may be something not quite right about Patrick's 'friendship' with the mob. Patrick is another sad case of someone who can't retire gracefully and accept the world no longer needs him. We need to move on and he needs to stay behind."

"What kind of response are you getting?" asked Kirby.

"They accept he's protecting Vespa too much. They were not happy about the media coverage of Judge West's hearings. They think it makes the US Attorney look petty. So I came up with another suggestion."

"What's that?"

"They should immediately initiate a DOJ Inspector General's criminal investigation into Patrick's relationship with the Sicilian Mafia. They can use administrative subpoenas to get the bank and phone records, and the IG's staff to start doing interviews."

"Will they?"

"The people I'm talking to think it's likely once I make the formal complaint. I've asked them to nudge the idea along with the IG down there. This way we don't have to worry about anyone filing a motion to suppress a federal grand jury subpoena before West."

"When will you know," asked Kirby?

"Soon. My request officially goes in tomorrow morning, but I've spent the weekend on the phone greasing the skids. They agree with me that if we can just put a little more pressure on Patrick, he will fold and do whatever we want. He can't afford to be spending his own money to fight us. There is no one willing to step out for him against us."

Kirby laughed. "Patrick told Baker the last hearings cost him $10,000. We will see how much of his own money he wants to spend before he caves in and does what we tell him to do."

Chapter 73

One of the agents assigned to gather background on Salah's apartment building noted that the building was owned by a realty trust. Those holding a beneficial interest in the trust were not disclosed. The agents were looking for a connection with the building whom they could approach for information and not alert Salah to the inquiry. You cannot investigate without asking questions, but asking questions of the wrong person can alert the subject. The agent noted that the attorney who filed the deed and the trust was a law school classmate at New York University fifteen years ago. The agent had seen him a few times over the years and knew his practice was in real estate. The agent asked his supervisor if he could contact this attorney to feel him out as to who owned the beneficial interest in the building, and whether they may be reliable to ask for background on Salah. The agent was experienced and permission was granted.

A few hours later the agent called his supervisor to report that he had met with the attorney. After being given assurances that his client, the owner, was not the subject or target of any investigation, he was willing to cooperate. The attorney knew the building superintendent and had his client's permission to provide whatever information might be helpful. The client did not even ask which tenant the FBI was looking at. Neither had the attorney, but now it was crunch time.

The agent identified Salah as the person of interest and asked for any records that existed for the five years Salah had been renting. The attorney did not ask the exact nature of the investigation, nor what earned Salah the right to be called a "person of interest." Things being what they are, the building manager's records were online and the attorney had access to them by computer. Salah's file was called up and a hard copy of his application and current lease were printed out, as well as emailed to the agent. While the application had not been updated for over two years, it contained a cell phone number and an email address that the FBI did not have. From this information, the JTTF was trying to leverage additional background information.

The agent spent some time with the attorney discussing the apartment building, its history and management. The building super was onsite before Salah's tenancy. The attorney volunteered to call the super to see what he knew about Salah. The agent thought this approach too direct for right now. The attorney suggested an easier way to get some information from the super without alerting him to an investigation regarding Salah.

"The super is a retired Irish railroad conductor. His wife died about eight years ago and he has been with us since then. He rented from my client at another building before he came here. I talk to him periodically about contractors we hire and whether they have fulfilled the contract, so we know when to pay them. He likes to talk. I could suggest some questions about contracts and delinquent tenants, and see if I can work Salah's name into the conversation."

The agent ran the idea by his supervisor and was given the go-ahead with the proviso that nothing would be direct.

The attorney called the super. "Charlie, I'm sorry to call you on Sunday, but I'm in the office closing out some items for the bookkeeper. We have to start on the report to the realty trust tomorrow. Has that furnace and boiler work been inspected by the city? I need to see the inspection certificate before I authorize payment."

"The work was completed over a month ago and I sent the inspection report into the office," was the reply.

"I'll look again. You watching the ballgame?"

"Yea. The Yanks are clobbering the Sox. I love it."

This engendered a few moments of sports discussion, followed by a few more contractor issues.

The super then told the attorney about the cops coming to the building a week ago to handle a loud party on the third floor. The super tried to quiet the party down but they ignored him, so he called the cops. They broke up the party and sent people home. The attorney asked who the tenant was, and the super told him. That started a discussion about some good and bad tenants.

"That reminds me," said the attorney, "this guy Salah has been with us over five years now. I was looking through the leases and saw that he has renewed the lease, but his application is several years old. Do we need to update it?"

"If you want to we can. The last time I talked with him there seemed to be nothing new. He's still driving his cab. He seems to be doing okay. Never makes a fuss and is very pleasant to everyone."

"Well as long as we have his current, contact data and email I guess we don't need the extra paper."

The super volunteered to check his address file and came up with another phone number for Salah.

"I know this is his cell number. He gave it to me a few weeks ago. He was waiting for a friend to visit and wanted me to call him if the friend came by while Salah was working. I never had to call him because he showed up with the friend. He never said who it was. I just assumed it was the friend he was expecting, because he never had any visitors until this friend showed up."

"Is he sharing his apartment now?" The lawyer made it sound like a legal question that had to be asked.

"No, the guy has been visiting off and on for a few weeks now. I got the impression he is visiting from a foreign country. I've not seen him for a couple of days now."

"No, we have enough paper in the world. We don't need any more. Get back to the game. Thanks Charlie."

The agent was allowed to listen to the entire call. They learned a few things and gave up nothing. Arrangements were made for the agent to obtain the building's master key from their locksmith. It was offered and accepted, with neither party having to explain. The attorney knew whatever was going on was important, and neither he nor his client had any reason not to fully cooperate. Whatever the problem was, it was not theirs. Helping out could return a favor to them down the road. It was the New York way.

Immediate inquiry determined the phone number on the original application executed by Salah was for a cell phone not currently in use, but last listed to Salah. The email address listed on the same application was shut down by the ISP for lack of use. The telephone number that Salah recently provided the super was for a cell phone in current use, purchased with cash, and using prepaid cards for minutes. The phone was not listed to Salah. It could have been obtained by him or anyone else using a phony name and address. They would pull additional records and start looking at whomever this phone contacted. Now the agents had some facts to work with, some hard data, and it was beginning to feel like an investigation of real people, not ghostly, shapeless figures.

Chapter 74

Salah was in the storage facility preparing the suitcases and the plastic containers to hold the metal fragments. He had removed all the tags from the suitcases and was laying out the plastic containers when The Engineer arrived with Talat Mehmood. The Engineer did not call ahead. He just showed up. Salah hadn't seen nor spoken with Mehmood since they departed their al-Qaeda training camp. They greeted. Salah had a small camping stove he used to boil water for tea, which he now did.

Mehmood and The Engineer arrived from Boston in a smaller size rental truck. Salah, in response to some questions from The Engineer, explained how he had purchased the suitcases at various stores as well as the nuts, bolts, screws, and ball bearings from a number of hardware facilities. Salah discussed with The Engineer how to fill the plastic containers with what would be the shrapnel for each bomb. Salah's job was to put all the components together and assemble the explosives. He was to wait for The Engineer to hook up the detonators to the explosives, which in turn would be connected to the cell phone and other triggers. However, The Engineer said he still didn't have the triggering assemblies. He offered no explanation.

"Can I see your cell phone," asked The Engineer?

Salah looked quizzical, but took it out of his pocket and gave it to The Engineer. The Engineer examined it and put it in his pocket. He reached into a white canvas bag he was carrying and took out two cell phones with chargers and gave them to Salah. He pulled out another cell phone from his coat pocket and made a test call to each of the phones he had just given Salah. They both worked.

"I have turned off the GPS feature on each of the phones. Each has a prepaid card for five hundred minutes. We will be replacing them again but that is enough for now. Otherwise the phone is empty. Keep it that way. Until our mission is complete there is no one you need speak with using these phones, other than me."

The Engineer then gave Salah two cell phone numbers written on a piece of paper. "Memorize these two numbers now and destroy this paper. I will be back shortly. Please help Talat load the truck with what he needs. He has a list."

Talat told Salah what armaments and explosives were to be loaded into the rental van. It was clear to Salah that Talat was taking over one half of the explosives and less than half of the serious firepower. While Salah was not privy to Talat's mission, it was clear to him that it was big and possibly as important as Salah's. He felt a pang of jealousy at sharing glory with Talat, but quickly corrected himself. They were all doing the will of Allah.

They had just completed loading the truck when The Engineer returned carrying a black duffle bag. Salah had not seen this bag since he picked The Engineer up at the docks. He was sure it contained the nuclear material that The Engineer had stored elsewhere, and apparently nearby. It looked like this material was also going to Boston. Talat's thought was confirmed when The Engineer put the bag in the truck's cab.

Salah fixed another pot of tea. They sat quietly with little to say. Each seemed to be in their personal thought world about what lay ahead.

The Engineer broke the silence. "Complete what you are doing. When I come back, I will call you. We will meet here and finish the remaining assembly and arming. Insure that from now on each member of your team is constantly available and ready to move on short notice."

Pulling an envelope from his pocket The Engineer said, "Here is $10,000 for you and the members of your team. I know they are not working regularly right now. They have families. Use this to insure their availability. You know how to reach me if necessary."

Without further comment, The Engineer got up and informed Talat it was time to go. It was an abrupt departure.

Salah, sitting alone, finished his tea and went back to work. Rather than going back to his apartment, Salah decided to work until he got tired and just sleep in the storage facility. He would let tomorrow handle itself. He would not drive his cab for a few days. Salah needed time to be in contact with the rest of the team. He needed to confirm that each member was attending to his duties. Team members were supposed to be visiting their assigned target areas to insure no changes had to be made to the existing plans. Salah wanted to confirm that they had a driver to deliver the vehicle using the George Washington Bridge. Mostly, he needed to insure the fervor of each team member remained intact for the mission. Salah generally used a communication chain within the team to avoid unnecessary exposure, but now he needed to increase his personal contact with each member to know there was no failure of wills, or mistakes.

Chapter 75

New York City

Vince Baker sat in the Justice Terrorism Task Force Office in New York listening to the morning summary. Court orders had been issued to intercept conversations of Salah at his home, in his vehicle, or on any cell phone used by him. Permission also was obtained to monitor any of Salah's email accounts when located, as well as any text traffic discovered. Execution of these court orders was in varying states of progress. Since they had a master key to the apartment, they could move more freely and quickly and not arouse suspicion within the building. The court order also included roving authority because Salah appeared to be a moving target, with no fixed base of operations. The door was left open for the government to notify the federal judge when Salah was located away from his home or car so that location could also be bugged to pick up his conversations. Baker's immediate problem was that he didn't know where Salah was at present. They had not found his cab. They didn't know enough to make an educated guess as to how or when they might find him.

The agents didn't need to explain to Baker how impossible it was to investigate someone when you couldn't ask questions for fear of talking to the wrong person. It was even more difficult when the person was a loner, with no obvious family or social life. The call between the super at Salah's apartment building and the attorney was reported to Baker by the agent who overheard it.

The ongoing discussion among the agents was how to find Salah, his vehicle, and how to stay with him to see who his accomplices were. They desperately needed to find The Engineer, and Salah was their only lead to him.

"What about interviewing the super directly?" asked Baker.

"I'm all for it," replied the agent who talked to the attorney. "It's not an unreasonable chance. There is no indication the super has any more than a landlord-tenant relationship with Salah. I'm sure he could tell us a lot about Salah, his associates, and the recent visitor who may be The Engineer."

"What if the super tips off Salah?" asked Baker, playing the devil's advocate.

"We have to establish an information base for Salah. We need it yesterday! We don't have the luxury of time. From what we know about the super, he appears to be a reasonable risk. If we just wait and do nothing, it could be a long time. If we find the cab, we can put a GPS tracking device on the vehicle and we won't lose the cab again. It appears to be their main source of transportation right now."

"Is there any objection from anyone about contacting the super? We will say Salah is a person of interest to the FBI regarding an investigation, and solicit the super's cooperation."

The room was silent. It was clear that this reasonable step needed to be taken now.

Baker turned to the agent: "I'd like to have the attorney call the super and tell him that he's sending someone to see the super, and that he has the owner's full authority to cooperate. Run a quick background check on the super. If events go badly with him, we can consider getting a material witness warrant for the super and arrest him to limit any immediate damage."

Instantly, the room was energized. This decision meant they were going on the offensive. The agents knew that is how cases are solved. Time does not often favor those who sit and wait. It favors those who are on the move and making things happen.

As the agents were leaving the meeting, one said, "I didn't think there was anyone from Washington with balls. This guy has two."

The Assistant Director for the New York Office, who technically outranked Baker, asked Baker if he was going to call Assistant Director Bob Wilkins with an update on this morning's meeting. Baker said, "No, we have no new information to report." Translated, these words meant "I don't intend to have each decision I make approved by someone else." Baker suspected that a call would be made to Wilkins anyway.

The attorney made the call to the building super, as requested. The agent went immediately to see the super. The agent told the super the FBI was conducting a criminal investigation and that Salah was a person of interest. The FBI needed to learn about Salah, what he did, and with whom. The super responded that he had clearance from the owner and that he did not need to know why the FBI was conducting this inquiry. In fact, he didn't want to know anything about what they were doing. The super was of that vintage where one did not feel compelled to question an authority that had earned his respect over the years.

"Where is Salah now?"

"I don't know. Normally this would be a day he takes off, but I haven't seen him since noontime yesterday. I saw him go out but did not see him come back, not that I see him all the time anyway."

"Where is his cab?"

"He parks it in the brick garage two blocks south and one block east. It's called the old ice house because that's what it was years ago. Sometimes, when he's not working, he will take a bus."

While the super was being interviewed, another team of agents determined, using thermal imaging, that there was no body heat inside Salah's apartment. They entered the apartment with the master key and started a thorough search. Other agents installed covert microphone and video equipment for each room. Another team had the building under surveillance from the outside in order to warn those inside should Salah return.

Two hours later the agent was still interviewing the super. The agent was not in a hurry. He was developing a relationship with the super, which would enable the FBI to have an asset inside the building. He could keep them informed as to Salah's comings and goings and be alert for any changes in his schedule or behavior.

"He hasn't been working his cab that much the last several weeks. He's had a visitor, and I think he was showing his friend around the city."

The friend of Salah's, he thought, was a fellow Muslim. He recalled hearing Salah say he was taking his friend to the mosque he attended in Bayonne. The super did not know the name or location of the mosque, but the agents thought they did. They knew the Imam at the Bayonne mosque and he was not a friend of America. Now they knew of another place to start looking for Salah confederates. FBI databases immediately began to spit out information about the Imam, his contacts, recent travels, and the identification of others at the mosque known to support jihad. Coverage of these people would now intensify.

Salah lived in this building since he came to New York from Miami. As far as the super knew, he had always driven a cab. He knew of no girlfriends, or friends for that matter, and had never known Salah's parents to visit. As far as travel, Salah had mentioned going to see his parents a few times, but not much more. After a few moments silence, the super said: "He did go on his big pilgrimage a year or so ago. He was gone for a while, too."

This new line of discussion established that Salah had made the Hajj and had been in Saudi Arabia. He traveled with members of his mosque and was gone almost four months. The agents knew the Hajj did not take four months, but the super knew nothing else about this trip so they said nothing more. Efforts to get Salah's passport records were expedited.

While the super's interview was still ongoing, agents located Salah's cab in the garage. The vehicle was entered and searched. A GPS tracker, a video transmitter, and an audio transmitter were installed. Now the FBI could hear and see whatever transpired in the cab. They could locate the cab anytime electronically. One very disconcerting but positive piece of information came from the cab. Radiation traces were detected in the trunk of the cab. They were much the same measurements as found in the cargo handler's apartment in Rome, and The Engineer's room aboard the ship. Now they knew for sure the radioactive material had made it into the city and Salah's cab. Salah would now be arrested before he was allowed to slip from anyone's sight. That order was immediately given. If you think you may lose him, arrest him.

The FBI had full coverage of Salah's apartment building, as well as his cab. A full surveillance was now on the mosque and the Imam in New Jersey. Passport records for Salah confirmed a four-month visit to Saudi Arabia two years ago. Efforts were now being made to check the passport records for other known members of this mosque to identify who might have traveled with Salah at this time. The key was who stayed four months, and not two weeks. While Saudi Arabia was supposedly an ally of the United States in the war on terror, no one was going to ask their intelligence service any questions at this point. It was common knowledge that some members of the royal family supported various forms of radical fundamentalist Islam. It was also quite possible that Salah traveled to an al-Qaeda training camp from Saudi Arabia under another identity.

The search of Salah's apartment did not reveal a landline telephone, a computer or any internet service. He had a television, but only the most basic cable service. A monk's cell might be more revealing. However, the lack of material one normally expected to find about daily life told the agents this was an apartment for someone who did not want even that limited information readily available.

The current cell phone number Salah had recently provided the super was another story. It used a prepaid card purchased eight weeks ago at a major electronics dealer. A name and address were given, but it was not Salah's name and the investigation so far indicated it was phony data. Copies of the calls made to and from this phone were immediately obtained and were presently being analyzed and searched through all terrorism databases. The FBI made arrangements for any future calls to or from this phone to be digitally routed by the service provider, under the court order, to the FBI electronic communications interception center. Now they had some meaningful possibilities to determine Salah's recent and current activities. They did not know that this cell phone was now lying at the bottom of a storm drain just outside the storage facility, where The Engineer had thrown it after providing Salah with two new, clean cell phones. There would be no current telephone calls to intercept on this discarded phone.

The super had one more piece of information. He often saw Salah in the evening at an internet coffee shop where young people in the neighborhood hung out after work. The super passed by the café on his way for a few beers each night with his buddies at a local tavern. He never really saw Salah with anyone, but he always seemed to be on a computer in the back of the café. The super did not know if Salah realized the super had seen him there, as they never spoke about it.

Within the hour, another team of agents was at the coffee shop with administrative subpoenas to review security camera coverage of the coffee shop maintained by the owners, as well as records of all computer usage and methods of payment. It was not unusual for owners to receive these requests from police, so they paid little attention. The agents intended to use the video history to see when Salah was using the computers, and exactly which computers in the shop he accessed. Next, the records for those specific computers could be obtained from the hard drive and the ISP for the exact times Salah was observed using the computer. Once they identified the computer or computers he used at this coffee shop, they were confident they could get a good look at his internet activity and also determine what email service he used.

Next, they would find his email contacts and what they were saying. Even if Salah tried to delete his data after each computer use, they thought they stood a good chance of recovering the stored electronic data. The agents knew that delete does not always mean delete. The café owners were not told the exact reason for the investigation. This was New York. They didn't even consider asking. While rumors around the neighborhood as to the FBI's presence were possible, they would not be mission specific. From the time agents stepped foot in the internet café, another team of agents set up an outside surveillance in the event Salah showed up. They still didn't know where he was, and until he was found, they did not want Salah finding them in action by accident.

Chapter 76

Vince Baker updated Bob Wilkins on the progress the agents were making regarding Salah. Wilkins had an evening briefing with the Director. After Baker finished, Wilkins patched Baker into an ongoing briefing that Deputy Assistant Director Gerald Oates, from NSA, was giving to the JTTF in Washington.

"What I am laying out for you are not facts. It is not the product of one interception. It is from a compendium of information we started to pick up about three days ago and augmented by some other interceptions picked up by the Defense Intelligence Agency. Our analysts have collaborated, and it is their joint opinion I am sharing with you."

A question was asked: "Are the intercepts from one specific country?"

"No. That is what initially triggered the monitoring computer's interest. They are from a number of Mid-East countries, some from Western Europe, and a few from Africa. It appears to be a group of individuals who are prepared to go on the internet at some common time to start, generate or lead discussions to affect public opinion in the United States. The plan specifics are not being discussed. We are picking up chatter about a plan that was previously communicated to them. They are talking about this plan amongst themselves, but very quietly. We do not know where the plan comes from or when the activity will commence."

Oates could see the baffled looks on the faces of the participants.

"I know this doesn't sound like much, but I know what you are working on. I cannot say the matters are related. It is our shared opinion that whatever these people are talking about, their assignment or roles on the internet are to take place in the immediate future. That is why we wanted to share this with you. All of the specifics have been uploaded to the system here. Your analysts are free to poke about the data as they wish."

"What do you consider the immediate future?" was the next question.

"We are talking weeks, not months. It is all very sketchy but it fits a pattern. The chatter picks up as the event gets closer. We are doing everything we can to come up with a subject matter, and we will let you know if and when we do."

"Tell us again what you think these people are doing?"

"They are preparing to act as a group to use the internet, such as blogs, public discussion forums, and contact with the media, to influence public opinion in the United States about a subject which is not known to us. We think this effort will occur in weeks and not months."

"Can we electronically remove some of their ability to use the internet when they start, if we find it is part of what we are investigating?"

"Basically, no. It wouldn't be effective for any period of time. We can't stop blogs and social networking sites. We might disrupt them, but we can't stop them. Any effort to do so generates another story and tends to add credence to whatever is being postulated."

On that less than high note, the briefing ended.

Baker had a copy of Oates' report sent up to the New York JTTF for all to read.

al-Qaeda had shown an efficient use of the internet to promote its recruiting and to keep its message and opinions fresh on the Arab street on an almost daily basis. It was known they had even explored committing acts of terror against infrastructure sites using computers. But for the present, they seemed committed to explosives and mangled bodies that could be shown on the world's evening news.

That evening, when Wilkins was with the Director, they called Baker to discuss the current status. They had not yet found Salah but as soon as they did, they would stay with him until they took him down. They were starting to get some data back from the internet café. Salah used only one computer, in a back corner of the café, where the screen was not visible to other patrons. However, it was in front of a concealed security camera. They were working on enlarging the video so they could actually view what he had on the screen. The hard drive had been copied and a number of computer forensic specialists were combining efforts to expedite the process. They had several email accounts already identified and subpoenas were presently being served on the ISPs. By morning they hoped to know a lot more about what Salah was doing on this computer, and with whom.

While Baker, Wilkins and the Director were still on the phone, word came to Baker that Salah had just shown up at his apartment. He had taken a shower and was now fixing something to eat. The video cameras and microphones were all working. A monitor had seen Salah take two cell phones out of his pocket and put them on the kitchen table as he went to change his clothes. Arrangements were made to monitor any cell phone calls that were from or to any cell phone in that apartment. They may not yet know the vendor or the name on the account, but they would hear what Salah was saying from the apartment microphones and, if all went well, they might intercept the transmission from the other party participating in a call with Salah.

They would not learn any more that evening from Salah. After Baker had showered and eaten, he went to bed. While he slept, the FBI was increasing its knowledge of Salah by leaps and bounds.

Boston

Agent Susan Crowley briefed her supervisor, George Fisher, and ASAC Phil Kirby on the information from the JTTF in New York. The JTTF in Boston still was not activated. Crowley and Fisher reviewed this decision with Kirby to no avail. The Washington, DC, JTTF had been activated on even less information and all the local officials were briefed.

Crowley and Fisher could not understand why Boston was not thinking the same way.

Kirby said, "I have reviewed all the data with Harvey Bottom and we both agree it is premature to notify the locals. We don't want to hear about a potential but unconfirmed terrorist threat via the news. We know these Boston politicians are not sophisticated in handling sensitive information like their counterparts are in DC, and they might tip their friends in the media."

Later in the evening information began to come in from the FBI computer forensics experts. It was not good news at all. Salah had been doing research on the internet for months on many historic, business, political, cultural and sports venues in New York City. No one thought he was interested in learning more about New York City. If he was looking at potential targets, the list was just immense. The data was sorted by the actual dates and put into a chronology. A more specific outline was discerned. Many of the venues he initially researched did not show up in later searches. As time went on the circle got smaller. Within the last three months he paid more attention to a smaller number of venues. They could see very recent internet activity relating to seven different locations. The New York Stock Exchange and LaGuardia Airport were two sites that had the least activity. The Lincoln and Holland Tunnels as well as the George Washington Bridge had a high volume of searches for the longest period of time. A substantial amount of recent activity focused on Penn and Grand Central Stations. The list was astonishing in scope and staggering to the minds of the agents. The analysts were furiously checking and cross checking data to see if they could refine the analysis or pinpoint his final interest as the potential target. It was not working. There was just not enough data.

Into the night, the agents and others assigned to the JTTF were driving themselves crazy trying to divine what Salah was up to from the existing data. Theories and counter theories abounded. They were argued and reargued. Finally Baker thought he needed to put things into perspective.

"We don't have enough information at this time to know what he has planned. That is okay. Look where we were this morning and where we are now. We have him located, covered like a blanket and can, unfortunately, tell whenever he passes gas." That drew a few smiles. "Let it go for now. Get some rest. The forensic people will have more in the morning. We have another team from the laboratory on their way up so we can have ongoing analysis overnight. We are doing okay folks. Let's not kill ourselves second guessing what might happen. Let's stay with the facts and see where they take us. The NYPD are quietly assessing the sites in which Salah has shown the most interest. We don't have the best case against him yet, but I don't think it will be very long before we do. We now have standing orders that he is not leaving our presence. It has been a productive day. Rest up. Get some sleep. I'm sure tomorrow will be very busy."

Chapter 77

New York City

Salah was awake at sun-up. After a cup of tea he left the apartment and walked to the garage where his cab was parked. The GPS and the microphones were working perfectly. This was good news. Such was not always the case with electronic gear.

Traffic was light. Salah drove from the garage directly to the storage facility in Chelsea. Salah parked his cab in front of the large metal rollup overhead door. He got out of the cab, took a leisurely look around in all directions. He walked to the right side of the building and entered the facility by unlocking a smaller side door. Salah wanted to finish all the preliminary bomb assembly for the roller suitcases. Later, he needed to meet his Wall Street contact.

From the storage unit, Salah unloaded blocks of plastic explosives. Fifty pounds were allotted for each bag. The fragmentation pieces placed inside each bag weighed another ten pounds. He would add one or two canisters of the nuclear material at The Engineer's direction. Salah was also building a bomb for The Stock Exchange. It would be slightly different from the others. Salah wanted to make it look like a technician's repair case. It would be small enough to place on a cleaning cart or in a large trash receptacle. He would be there as the cleaning ended and long before anyone came into work in the morning. A half hour undiscovered was all he needed to plant the bomb. If the cops showed up before the preset timer went off the next day, he would remotely detonate the bomb. It was not absolutely necessary that all the bombs go off at exactly same moment. In fact, some small separation of time between detonations would add stress to the city's emergency response system. Chaos and confusion would further deteriorate the performance of the first responders.

Salah also prepared a suitcase for the martyr at LaGuardia. It was a natural for the airport. It had rollers and soft sides with long straps so it could be mounted and carried like a backpack. The martyr would have his hands free for weapons use if he had to force his way into the tower area.

Salah had the detonators out and ready to insert into the plastic explosives. He was waiting for The Engineer to complete the construction of the triggering devices and bring them to the garage. Salah did not know how to construct a triggering device using a preset timer, nor how to assemble a switch permitting the martyr to cause immediate detonation. In addition, The Engineer wanted each bomb to have a remote detonation component. This three-way system would have to be set up by The Engineer. Salah hoped to learn from The Engineer how to do this.

Salah completed what he could do with the devices. He needed to check on his team members and make sure each was clear on their final instructions. He had to make sure he could deliver the devices the night before the scheduled attacks. Security dictated that he use his team chain of communication. However, he was also concerned that he needed to speak to each person directly so there were no misunderstandings, no failures of will. The need to manage the coordination, he thought, outweighed counter security measures. This group had trained together in the al-Qaeda camp. Many worshipped together at the mosque in Bayonne. They all knew what each other was doing with his assigned target. They were not security threats. He could meet with them as a group this one time. He really felt the need for the team to assemble to quietly reinforce each other with the importance of their assignments and the necessary sacrifices they were making for Allah. Salah would do what The Engineer did not seem inclined to do. He would minister to the psyche of his team.

Salah knew that The Engineer wanted the storage facility to be totally secure from everyone other than Salah and himself. But The Engineer brought Talat to the facility when it was convenient for him. It occurred to Salah that he could use the facility to meet with his team. Before the attacks, Salah and The Engineer would move the remaining equipment to another location anyway. So there was nothing to lose. Even if one of the team got captured and talked, there would only be an empty facility. Besides, Salah thought of himself as a leader of this great Islamic jihad act and, accordingly, he had the right to have others come to him. Salah used his communication chain to instruct each team member to meet him at the storage facility address at 7:00 pm.

The FBI could not hear the telephone call Salah made to gather this meeting. They did not have coverage on Salah's two new cell phones and did not have enough time to target all cell phone calls in the geographic area of the storage facility. The FBI could not hear or see what Salah was doing inside the building. They had no microphone or video coverage there. When he finished packing the roller suitcases, Salah left the building. He drove his cab to lower Manhattan. While driving, Salah telephoned his contact at the Stock Exchange to meet for a cup of coffee and discuss Salah's "tour" of the Stock Exchange. The FBI could not hear what the contact said to Salah because Salah's current cell phone was not bugged. However, from the microphone inside the cab they could hear Salah's end of the conversation. They would soon know a lot about Salah's contact at the New York Stock Exchange. Salah's call fueled the initial belief that the Stock Exchange was The Engineer's target.

The JTTF leaders dispatched more agents to set up a fixed surveillance targeting the newly found storage facility. The FBI was obtaining a search warrant to enter and search the facility. They desperately needed to know if this could be the location where the armaments, explosives, and radioactive material might be stored.

The surveillance continued following Salah into lower Manhattan. He parked the cab in an off-street parking garage and walked to a street level café in an older office building about two blocks away. At the café, Salah met his contact from the Stock Exchange. At the moment, the surveillance teams didn't know the person Salah met. They would soon. They were prepared and would immediately put this person under constant electronic and physical surveillance.

While Salah was having coffee with the contact, a parole search warrant was obtained based on oral representations made by an agent under oath to a federal judge. Authority was needed before the standard affidavit and application for search warrant could be completed. Now that the FBI had the oral authority, the agent was hastily converting the oral representations into a written document.

A team was prepared to make a discrete entry into the storage facility, mindful that the opposition could have it booby trapped or under counter surveillance. Vince Baker was with the agents when they entered the storage facility. An entry team picked the locks. Bomb techs checked for booby traps. There were none. There were no alarms. It made sense. Why alarm the building so that the police or private security would respond to a possible malfunctioning alarm and expose everything? Better to have no alarm. Baker and a few agents went in. Baker was shocked beyond belief at what he saw. This was the gold mine. It was not the six nearly completed suitcase bombs that shocked him; it was the amount of plastic explosives and the variety of powerful armaments that were present. Rocket launchers, anti-tank thermal missiles, light and heavy machine guns, mortars, grenades, communications equipment, night vision equipment, anything and everything an army would need. Baker thought to himself, how can this be? How could these people get this stuff here and we don't know about it. He thought of what could have gone wrong to prevent them from finding this place. His thoughts were interrupted.

"We don't have any trace of radioactive material. That stuff is not here," reported the agent.

Baker spoke with the SWAT team leader. "Give me an assessment of how much danger there is for the immediate area if this place goes up.

What explosives can we take now? Can we replace it with inert material and use the same wrappers so they won't know? Can we disarm some of the weapons to make them inoperable but not noticeable to the naked eye? How long would this take? In short, what can we do in a very brief period to reduce danger to the public and not alert the subjects that we have been here? Salah can turn around and come back at any time."

"Give me about fifteen minutes and I'll let you know."

Baker had a conference call with Wilkins and Director Carter Simms. He quickly described what they had found and what he thought the issues were. It was not just about capturing all the bad guys. It was also about public safety.

"Salah was meeting with someone in lower Manhattan as we entered the storage site. It would appear we don't have to guess which of the seven suspected locations the intended target is. Each of the locations appears targeted for a bomb. We have at least six powerful bombs waiting for their detonators. We don't have any trace of the radioactive material. The only thing that doesn't fit is the George Washington Bridge. A suitcase bomb wouldn't do much there. That target may not be active, or they may have some type of car bomb for that. Lord knows they have enough material."

"Where do you stand for manpower?" asked Simms.

"Can you send me two hundred more agents and two more SWAT Teams from Newark and New Haven? I also need the Hostage Rescue Team up here. They have all trained with the NYPD, and we may need all of them."

This was not a hurried conversation. All of the participants were turning these facts over in their minds and no one was rushing or being rushed.

The onsite SWAT leader approached Baker to report. Baker put his cell phone on speaker so the others could hear.

"We think there is over one thousand pounds of plastic explosives here. We can't change it out in a short period of time. There are a lot of different wrappings we would have to replicate. However, all the detonators are the same manufacturer and have the same label. The plastics, under most circumstances, won't explode without the detonators and the triggering devices. The triggering devices are not here. We use the same detonators for training purposes. Ours are inert. With a few minor changes in the markings we can make them appear the same as what they have here. I have ours on the way here now. We will replace all the detonators they have exposed with ours. We will empty the unopened boxes of detonators and fill them with some ammo for weight and seal them back up. We will have cameras in here to see what they are doing after we leave. If we have done anything noticeable, if our efforts spook them, we move in and take them. Either way we move in. We will leave some tear gas and flash bang grenades behind, which we can detonate from the outside to slow down their response time to us if we have to make a quick entry."

"How long to do all of this?" asked Baker.

"One hour from the moment the detonators get here. While we are waiting we'll start removing or damaging the firing pins, starting with the biggest weapons first. We will get done what we can with the time we have. These weapons will not fire when we finish. This greatly reduces the danger, but there is still a lot of danger here."

"Did you get all of that?" Baker asked those on the call.

All did. Wilkins was next to speak. "Is there any way to video the disabling of the weapons? It would be helpful to show they were operable weapons and how they were rendered inoperable to provide immediate safety. We want to avoid someone claiming we were tampering with the evidence."

"Okay," said Baker.

The final decision to implement what they discussed resided with Simms. "This seems to be the best we can do with the time we have. We need to identify the people involved to find the radioactive material. I'll notify the AG and Secretary of Homeland Security and insure they advise the mayor of the plan."

The SWAT leader put everything in motion. They made every effort to keep the outside quiet. They worked inside with the minimum number of people needed. They were expert at leaving a site exactly the way they found it. They would make sure there would be nothing to indicate their presence. Within minutes, concealed video cameras were transmitting a signal to a nearby building set up as the onsite command post. It had a line of sight to the storage site. It amazed Baker how quickly and quietly these people worked.

Chapter 78

One hour and twenty minutes later, the SWAT leader informed Baker they had done what they could. Salah was on the move again and they needed to vacate. They did. As they were leaving, Baker had to smile. They had an opportunity to mitigate the now obvious and very aggressive plans of this terror cell. To his eye, there was no telltale sign of their presence. Hopefully, Salah would enjoy the same opinion.

Salah initially intended to return to the storage facility, but realized there was little he could do until The Engineer returned. He needed to get some cash ready for his team so he decided to go home. Once there, he looked look over the expenses owed each team member and decided how much cash each member needed for their families. This way he could give each one a sealed envelope with the cash he predetermined they needed. He did not want team members second guessing his judgment as to how much money he had given the others. They would not open their envelope until after the meeting, and after they had separated from their team members.

After his meeting with his contact from the Stock Exchange, Salah was even more convinced his plan would work. The contact would take him in carrying a silver, hard-sided case that looked like what technicians use to carry equipment. Once inside he would conceal the bomb and leave. He did intend, after planting the bomb, to kill his contact at the first opportunity. The contact would not have an opportunity to later change his mind and talk.

The agents viewing the video from Salah's apartment observed Salah reviewing pieces of paper and doing calculations. Salah took an envelope from his jacket, opened it, and started to count out cash. Salah took eight letter-size envelopes from a drawer and put cash in each one and sealed them. When he finished, there were eight envelopes in front of him. On the face of each envelope he appeared to write a number. He put these envelopes back in his jacket pocket. The remaining cash he put in his pocket.

The monitoring agents immediately sent word of what they observed. Was it possible that Salah would be giving money to eight different people the next time out? They considered different options. He could have any combination of meetings, from eight different meetings to one meeting with eight people. They needed enough manpower for a potential of eight different surveillances.

About 6:30 pm, Salah put on his jacket, went downstairs, and walked to the bus stop. He took the bus to the area of the storage facility and walked the block from the bus stop to the facility. The agents knew it would be the test when he walked in and looked around. Would he notice anything amiss? Would he see something to tell him his space had been violated? They held their collective breaths.

Salah, after entering the storage facility, went over to the camping stove, fired it up, put on the tea kettle, and took out some loose tea and put it in a holder. He looked around as the stove was doing its job. He took the envelopes out of his pocket and put them on a table. The agents' hearts pounded. Could it be that his associates would be coming to him? They needed to be ready for this. The word went up the chain of command. This possibility was discussed. If The Engineer came they would have to go in. Everyone would be arrested. That part was easy. What if others came to join Salah but not The Engineer? Could they afford to let anyone walk out of that facility? The answer was no. The contents of that building were a great danger they could not control. If people came to meet with Salah and were present with all the armaments and explosives, there was sufficient evidence to arrest them. If they took an envelope of money from Salah, the case got even better.

Director Simms wanted Baker to augment the number of SWAT teams present to cover the possibility of nine potential terrorists meeting at this site. The FBI and NYPD teams were working out the specific assignments for each of the participating SWAT teams. Speed was essential in entering the building, and an absolute necessity for the immediate takedown of each person present. Action time is less than reaction time. The first move would be theirs and they had to make the most of it. By the time the terrorists realized what was happening, the SWAT teams needed to be inside the storage facility and in physical control of each person there. They would have gas masks and, if needed, would activate the tear gas and flash bangs they had left behind.

Everyone realized the situation was fluid. New facts could require that their plans be altered in a moment. The most they could do was be prepared to change as needed.

Baker was back at the JTTF office, which now had a camera feed from both the inside and outside of the storage facility. They could hear inside the facility from the microphones left behind and could monitor all the surveillance traffic. Baker had a separate channel to communicate with the SWAT team leader. He was prepared to wait, but it did not take long.

"One unmale (unknown male) approaching from the direction of the bus stop."

"Got him," was the reply from a nearby spotter.

"He's checking a paper in his hand. He's approaching the small door. He's knocking. The door is opening. He's inside."

"We have him inside. You all have the visual. Sound quality is good." There was no disagreement. Everyone could see and hear inside the storage facility.

The man entered, exchanged the Muslim greeting with Salah. They went over to the area around the camp stove and started pouring tea.

"Another unmale approaching from the bus stop area. He's up to the door. He's in."

Another visitor exchanged the Muslim greeting with Salah and guest number one. They began to speak in Arabic. Translators in the monitoring room were providing instant translations so nothing was lost.

Not everyone came by bus. About half were dropped off by cabs in or near the bus stop area and walked to the facility. Each knocked. Each was admitted. Within twenty-five minutes there were eight men plus Salah inside the facility. Each of the newcomers looked around doing a visual inspection of the weapons that were in view. Salah made some references to the power they now had, and how they were better equipped than in training camp. It was clear Salah was comfortable inside this facility and, as a result, so were they. It was Salah's headquarters and he was saying, as their leader, they were safe from outside forces.

After a few moments, Salah told the group that he wanted to speak to each of them individually. After that he would speak to the group, they could have a cup of tea, and then be off. Salah asked the first man to join him near the table by the stove and they began to talk. They picked a good spot. One of the technical agents earlier had seen the tea setup and thought it a potential gathering and conversation area. He was right. The microphone he placed there allowed the monitoring agents to hear the plan unfold. It was terrifying to overhear Salah review specific plans with each of the visitors to his tea station.

While the group inside was having their conversations, SWAT teams started moving much closer to the facility in a variety of guises. They didn't want to alert anyone who might be keeping an eye on the building for Salah. They had not seen anyone yet. However, they had to be prepared for counter surveillance on the building. They need not have taken any precaution. The Engineer and Salah had not considered counter surveillance on the building. The Engineer did not imagine that Salah would ever bring his team members to the storage facility.

The first unknown male discussed how he would take the suitcase to Penn Station. He would leave it there after asking someone to watch his bag while he used the restroom. He would leave the station and remain outside until the bomb detonated. If it did not, he would use the remote detonator to set off the bomb.

The second unknown male reviewed the plan to take a suitcase bomb into Grand Central Station at the restaurant level, where he would ask someone to watch his bag while he went to the restroom. He would leave and later utilize the remote detonator, if necessary.

The third man was the individual who would put the suitcase on the inbound bus using the Lincoln Tunnel. He had watched the bus load a number of times. The driver opened the luggage bay of the bus before collecting the tickets. Passengers could put their suitcase in the storage compartment under the bus after giving the driver their ticket. Instead of getting on the bus, he would walk to the next dock and re-enter the terminal. This could be done without the driver seeing what transpired because he kept his back to the bus while collecting tickets. This person would have another team member waiting for him outside with a car. They would follow the bus to make sure it was in the correct lane for tunnel traffic. If any kind of problem developed, they would use the remote detonation.

The next unknown male described the SUV he had rented and how he had "hired" a driver to make deliveries into the city taking the George Washington Bridge. This would be a martyr who did not know his status. This member of the group would follow the van and insure it got onto the bridge. He could detonate the bomb from the west side. Another team member would be in a position to detonate the SUV bomb from the east side of the bridge. They would not be able to see the van, but from timing the practice runs, they knew how long it would take for the van to be approximately in the middle of the bridge under normal traffic conditions. Salah told this team member that he intended to bring the plastic explosives for the van bomb to him in one trip, and the detonators and projectile material in a second trip. The Engineer would come and finish the bomb assembly and provide the remote detonating devices.

The next two people meeting with Salah seemed somewhat different. They were quieter in overall demeanor, spoke in a barely audible manner, and showed no outer emotion. They did not gesture with their hands as did the others. They also spoke in Arabic with Salah. As the translation came through, they were different. One was definitely on a martyr's mission. The first man talked of forcing his way into "the tower." The second team member would be within sight to throw a smoke bomb if a diversion were necessary. If not, the second man would take no action and leave after this man made the tower entry. If the man forcing his way into the tower became disabled before he made entry, the other team member would remotely detonate the explosives carried by his fellow team member. He would see that his teammate killed as many of the infidels as possible so that Allah could reward the strength of his devotion.

The last man to speak privately with Salah did so in an unemotional and very factual manner. Once Salah and The Engineer had prepared the car bomb, this man would drive it into the Holland Tunnel and detonate the bomb when halfway through. It did not matter which lane he was in, as long as he was eastbound. The man would not consider hiring someone to "deliver" the car into the city. He wanted to be a martyr for Allah. No one tried to talk him out of it.

From the conversations overheard, there were either two or three martyrs that would be involved in the attacks. It was hard for the agents to make out immediately all that was said while passing through immediate translations. At the same time, the final arrest plans were being put in motion.

Salah handed an envelope to each man. As he was doing so, Salah quietly expressed to the group, and by eye contact to each man, the importance of their individual and collective actions. He told them that Allah would reward each of them with eternal paradise. If the action required one to be a martyr, their families would be forever under the protection of Islam and made financially secure. He did not fail to mention that Islam would hold their names among the greatest of warriors since the Prophet himself walked the earth. This is what they had trained for and committed themselves to. Salah started to explain the envelopes of money for temporary expenses. He never completed the sentence. Salah never got the words out of his mouth.

Nine men stood in utter shock and stunned silence as they tried to absorb what was happening. They could see the large, metal, roll-up garage door just seem to evaporate before their eyes. The smaller door on the right side of the building seemed to mysteriously vanish. There was a hole in the cinder block wall where none had been before. There was a loud noise and a bright light that caused their very beings to momentarily freeze. They could observe, but nothing seemed to register. Salah looked up to see what he thought was a strobe light pointed at him, and when he looked at the light, he felt sick and was unable to stand. Salah and his team could not even begin to react to this assault.

The action time of the agents entering the facility was much shorter than the reaction time required by Salah and his group to respond. Salah and his men had experimented with flash bangs in training, but this was real life. Training was much different when you knew what to expect. Salah had no idea what the light was or why he was sickened by it. Here, surprise truly favored the SWAT units. It was impossible to react in time when the flash bang was used against someone comfortable in their environment and not alert or prepared for immediate danger. They were under attack with many guns pointed at them. Each of Salah's men had at least two agents physically putting them on the ground, securing their movement. It was arrest, cover, and removal techniques working together flawlessly. The hands of each man were secured before they even realized it. None of them was armed. It was too dangerous for them to carry an illegal gun in New York City. They didn't know that the meeting location was their own armory. They were just not prepared.

As some of the terrorists came to their senses and began to realize their position, they became angry and started yelling, screaming, and thrashing about. It did them no good. More and more people seemed to fill the room. The lights went out for all the terrorists when hoods were placed over their heads. They felt themselves being physically carried out of the building into some sort of vehicle. The SWAT teams were taking no chances in case there were any self-destruct devices that one of these clowns could reach and detonate. The plan was to remove everyone from the building as soon as they were secure. It took less than sixty seconds from the first breach maneuver to the time all of the subjects were removed from the facility. They never had to use the tear gas they left behind.

Baker returned to the site. He did not enter the facility until the subjects were removed and the area fully secured. Teams were set up, each with an Arabic speaker, to process and make some effort to identify each subject. This would take some time. The building was searched for booby traps. All the material needed to be recorded, examined in detail, and inventoried as evidence. Only then would they start tracing the origins of the seized material. Trained ordinance personnel came on board to safely handle the removal of the weapons and explosives to a military storage facility.

Baker's attention was drawn to the table with the camp stove. On it were two cell phones. They were exactly where Salah was observed placing them earlier. If anyone called him, Salah would not be answering. All cell phones within one quarter mile were temporarily jammed during the assault, but that ended as the building was secured. These two cell phones now represented the hottest lead they presently had to find The Engineer and his radioactive material. The phones were immediately secured by an agent. Tracing their purchase and usage had already started. An effort would be made to identify any telephone trying to contact either one of these cell phones. They needed a bit of luck for this phone trace to work. They just had some luck with the arrests. An operation such as this could not be executed without planning and competence. Even then it was always better when competence and planning were augmented with a little luck.

Chapter 79

They would have liked more time before news of this raid hit the media. But it was just too big an operation to keep quiet. The media flood gates had opened. A press conference was needed to address all the immediate inquiries and to establish an update schedule. The media beast had to be fed. The feeding was in direct competition to the investigators' need to quickly identify other participants before they became aware of the arrests and could escape or go underground. It was decided by Director Simms, the Attorney General and the Mayor of New York that Washington, DC, would be the site of the news conference. They wanted to take some pressure off the inquiry now going full bore in New York City. It would help but only briefly. A delicate balance had to be maintained to satisfy the media's need to print, report, discuss and analyze but not disclose critical evidence that would jeopardize the investigation. It was always a difficult balance to achieve, and imperative that it be done well.

The scheduled news conference in Washington gave Baker some room to maneuver. They needed to find the radioactive material. It was not stored with the weapons and munitions. Wilkins arranged to have the Department of Energy Nuclear Emergency Support Team (NEST) for the East Coast be on standby. This group had been in existence for over thirty-five years. After 9/11, its' mission was taken more seriously. Government research to create smaller and more portable nuclear detection equipment had resulted in hand-held devices that were in common usage. NEST also had nuclear search equipment mounted on helicopters and fixed wing aircraft, and mobile labs that could be driven through neighborhoods. They also developed backpacks that could be worn by technicians to search inside large buildings. The problem was any of this equipment could pick up false positives caused by naturally occurring radiation not connected with any type of bomb. Still, thought Baker, the next step was worth the effort.

After locating the storage facility in Hell's Kitchen, and noting Salah's apartment not less than a mile away in Chelsea, one could reasonably argue that the nuclear material might be stored in an area around either of these two points. There was no indication that the material had been in Salah's apartment, and so far no indication of the material in the warehouse. Baker thought it was reasonable to search concentrically from each of these two points. He thought first effort should concentrate on the overlap area between Salah's apartment and the storage facility. A mile in the city is a lot of space to search. They could start with the helicopter, then mobile units, and then do more detailed searches with handheld or backpack equipment. The NYPD had long ago acquired computerized building plans for most of the structures in the city. Using these plans they would first concentrate on buildings that offered any kind of temporary storage rental. They had found Salah's cab looking for duct tape repairs, so this was no less a reasonable effort. Besides, they had nothing else at present to help find The Engineer or the radioactive material.

A discussion to release the photo of The Engineer resulted again in a decision not to do so. A release could swamp them with leads that would take their resources and energy away from inquiry, directly resulting from the evidence at hand. Now was not the time.

The media was provided a joint press release from the NYPD Commissioner and the Assistant Director of FBI New York. It said little more than nine individuals were arrested on weapons charges at a warehouse in Hell's Kitchen. Further details were to be released at the press conference in the morning.

It was decided that the identities of each person arrested and last known addresses would be given out at the press conference. Arrest photographs would not be given out until later. The press conference would reveal those arrested were being charged only with illegal weapons possession. The media would be told the investigation was presently directed at whether or not these men were part of a terrorist organization.

By only charging weapons violations, they were conservatively staying within their evidence. They had placed enough serious charges to hold them without bail. This also gave investigators time to gather more evidence about the terror plot. Everyone was being very guarded about any great pronouncement of success in preventing a serious terrorist attack. They knew The Engineer was still missing and the radioactive material could still be in the city. From the evidence and the conversations intercepted at the storage facility, they had a pretty good picture of the magnitude of the attacks planned for New York City. What was the connection between these armaments and those found in Palermo? One had to wonder how big their supply of armaments and explosives was. How much of that supply was present in the United States? How many terror cells were they dealing with? What about Washington, DC and Boston? None of these possibilities was ignored. The media would be given just the basic facts followed by the worn but accurate cliché … "the investigation is continuing."

The leaders of the JTTF in New York met shortly after the arrests to review the new data and determine the next investigative steps. The NEST resources had been initiated. The defendants were being processed. All had initially declined to be interviewed and sought lawyers. There was no effort to aggressively change this status. They wanted to give the cell members time to reflect on their surroundings and adjust to their current predicament. After this brief period, the interview effort would start through the lawyers. One should not appear too anxious to interview. It could raise the value of negotiating chits. Sometimes poorly thought out questions could tell the opposition more then you intended or wanted.

"What about Salah's cell phones?" Baker asked the agent with that assignment.

He was not going to like the answer.

"They were purchased at a warehouse store in Boston last week. The purchaser paid cash and set up five hundred minutes prepaid on each phone. The information recorded by the clerk handling the transaction for name and address is bogus, it doesn't exist. We are looking for the store video to see if the transaction was caught on tape."

"Were these the only two phones purchased by this person?"

"At this store, as far as we can tell right now, the answer is yes."

"Any data in the phone contact list?"

"No."

"Any call history to the phone since it was purchased?"

"No."

"If they have not been used, were they purchased to be used as part of a detonation system?"

"We don't know yet."

"Then what was Salah using for a phone?"

"He could have just obtained these two and disposed of the cell phones we thought he was using. These look like the same ones he had in his apartment earlier this afternoon. He could have been in Boston before we started the surveillance, we just don't know."

"Is there anything at all from Salah's apartment or from the storage facility that gives us any idea as to where to look for The Engineer?"

There was silence for a few moments. Agents looked at each other. Finally one said "No."

"What is the status of the phones right now?" asked Baker.

"They are on and being monitored. We have decided not to answer any calls. Not answering leaves open more possibilities that favor us over the wrong person answering. If The Engineer calls, we may get to trace the call to him. He will not know why Salah is not answering, at least not until the news breaks. We have everything in place here with the service provider to try to identify any telephone number that calls either one of Salah's phones."

A short while later Baker was on the phone with AD Wilkins and Director Simms.

"We need to start shifting some manpower to Boston. I don't have any indication Salah was in Boston to buy those phones, but my fear is The Engineer or another group is there. The magnitude of what they planned for New York is so bold that I think we need to think more aggressively to match their mindset. The evidence suggests they are planning multiple attacks in more than one city."

Wilkins responded: "Intelligence has indicated for months an al-Qaeda desire to utilize multiple, coordinated attacks to demonstrate our vulnerability and to increase fear. What about DC?"

"These phones are from Boston and very recent. DC can still be possible. Can we have someone take another look at the articles The Engineer was reviewing on the internet for both Boston and DC? Maybe another look might tell us something we hadn't thought about before."

Wilkins would see to it. Simms and Wilkins requested updates throughout the night.

Chapter 80

The agent assigned to monitor the two cell phones belonging to Salah did not have to wait long. At 10:07 pm one phone activated with an incoming call. The caller's number was restricted and did not appear on the telephone screen. The agent did not answer the call. It ceased after six rings. Salah had no voice mail on this phone. A few moments later, the second phone sounded an incoming call to mirror the first. It also ceased after the sixth ring. It was clear someone was trying to reach Salah. They were able to trace both incoming calls back to the same cell tower, located atop the John Hancock building in Boston..

The Engineer knew that something was wrong when Salah did not answer the first phone call. When he called the second phone and got the same response, he switched his phone off. He walked to the nearest storm drain and dropped his two phones into the black abyss. Somehow, he knew Salah had been compromised and it would be only a matter of time before his phones were compromised. He would have Talat Mehmood get him a new phone in the morning. The Engineer was not concerned for his immediate safety because Salah did not know where he was.

The Engineer was standing in the North End of Boston when he dumped his cell phones. He walked immediately to a coffee shop on Hanover Street to watch the eleven o'clock news. The lead story was the arrest of nine men in New York City on weapons charges. The media speculation was they were terrorists. The news information was limited. A news conference was scheduled at the Justice Department in the morning. Names of those arrested were not yet available. The Engineer was in shock trying to figure out how the authorities could know about Salah and his entire team. His immediate fear was that there was a traitor in the group that could expose him. But that didn't make sense. All of the arrests took place at a building in Hell's Kitchen. All nine were in the same building when arrested! The Engineer was shocked at the incredible lack of security displayed by Salah. No one, including the team members, was to know the location of the storage facility. Salah must have used it as a meeting spot for his entire team!

The Engineer's head was spinning. He needed time to figure this out. He walked from the coffee shop down Hanover Street, across Haymarket, up Tremont Street to Park Street at the Boston Common. He took the Red Line train south toward Quincy. He got off near a non-chain motel that catered to cash more than credit cards. Alone in his room, he began to review what he knew, and what he needed to find out. Whether or not he had to abort his current plan with Mehmood needed to be resolved. He watched more news at midnight but learned nothing new. About 1:00 am he went to a payphone in the motel lobby and called Mehmood.

"I am without a cell phone. Get me one. Don't call me here. I'll call you in the morning." The Engineer hung up.

Mehmood had also seen the news. He said nothing. He concluded The Engineer must have dumped his phones. If they got Salah and his team, would he be next? Would the FBI come for him tonight? He thought about leaving his apartment but decided against it. He would wait for The Engineer to call in the morning. He thought it would be a long, sleepless night. He was right.

New York

The NEST teams had been roaming the designated New York City streets all night. They tried first with the helicopter but got too many false positives. They were now using mobile units along with technicians on foot to rule out potential hits. All indications were that this was going to take a while and it would be more difficult when the morning traffic picked up.

Vince Baker was back in his hotel room trying to get some sleep. There were no hot leads to find The Engineer. He was debating whether to give The Engineer's picture to the media and ask for the public's help in locating him. The FBI and the JTTF members were collecting evidence, developing witnesses, and gathering facts that in the end would result in a case that no one could beat. By making the arrests they had made their move and there was no turning back.

The evidence would be there for the ten they had arrested, which now included the person from the Stock Exchange. The media had not been told about his arrest. In the morning it would become obvious that this was a terrorist cell. Slowly, the scope of the plot would publicly emerge. Their time to work without overwhelming media interest was limited. The person who had the nuclear material was not keeping it with their explosives and armaments. Why not? Maybe the people in the cells didn't know about it? Maybe the leader didn't trust them? Maybe it had already been moved somewhere else in the country? Baker finally chided himself for this random, disorganized thought process doing him no good. He needed sleep so he could start with a clear head in the morning. Both he and The Engineer recognized rest was necessary to enable one to keep going efficiently.

Boston

Liz and Patrick ordinarily did not watch the eleven o'clock news, but tonight Patrick tuned in to see what the Red Sox did against Baltimore. He hadn't watched the game. They sat in silence as they watched the same news The Engineer was watching less than six blocks away. When the lead story was over, Patrick turned off the TV.

"Do you think they have the whole thing?" asked Liz.

"From your lips to God's ears," said Patrick.

She cocked her head to one side.

Patrick continued, "It sounds like they hit the jackpot. They got people and hardware all in the same place. I think that's really unusual. It's really great work plus some luck I would guess. Both are always necessary."

"It sounds as if the media knows only a little. They held them off overnight by scheduling the big press conference in the morning. They're buying time. They don't have it all," opined Liz.

"As usual, you are most insightful."

The phone rang. It was Baker. "You see the news?"

"Yes" said Patrick.

"I think we don't have it all," said Baker.

"Is Boston in play," asked Patrick?

"I'm almost sure it is, based on what I know. I'm leaving New York and coming to Boston."

"That special material?" queried Patrick.

"No sign of it here. We have reason to believe The Engineer was or is in Boston. Things are coming in fast and furious. Let me sleep on this tonight. I'll get a report in the morning. If things are the same, I'll be up there and we can meet."

"Okay," said Patrick.

Chapter 81

"There's no doubt about it," Susan Crowley told Baker. It was 7:35 am and Baker had not gotten a cup of coffee to his lips even though the coffee pot sat in front of him in his New York hotel room. The phone calls started off fast and hadn't slowed for half an hour.

"The Engineer took fifteen to twenty minutes to look over and complete the purchase of the cell phones. The security video is high quality. The facial recognition program confirms the ID of the earlier known photographs of The Engineer to this video. Besides, it is obvious to the naked eye. You can tell just looking at both the pictures and the video. It is probably the best image of him we have yet," Crowley finished her report.

Baker reviewed out loud what he just heard. "We have The Engineer buying the phones in Boston last Wednesday. We have someone trying to call Salah late last night in back-to-back phone calls to each of his new cell phones. Both calls passed through the same cell tower in Boston. What leads do we have to find The Engineer in Boston?"

"Specific leads? None that I know," said Crowley.

"I put in a request earlier for another review of all articles The Engineer called up on the ship's computer that concerned Boston. Have you heard anything back?" asked Baker.

"I'm told it was mostly general news and not site specific like it was for New York. The sites were the same ones any tourist coming to Boston would call up. I've not heard any lead value coming out of them," said Crowley.

"The NEST Teams are still at it here. They're getting a lot of false leads. It's more time consuming then we thought. It will be a slow go. Let me get updated and I'll get back to you. I'm going to get more manpower up to Boston. It looks like we may have to shift gears," said Baker.

So far each individual under arrest declined interview. Efforts were underway to secure their requested free, legal counsel. There was nothing further the agents could do. They could not speak to the men, much less try to convince them they needed to help themselves now. Investigation into the backgrounds of each was proceeding rapidly. It was clear at this point they were probably a cell recruited through the mosque in Bayonne. The passport records were mirror images. Each traveled to Saudi Arabia for the same Hajj period as Salah, and each was recorded as remaining in "Saudi Arabia" for four months. Everything was being done to see what other American citizens were supposedly visiting Saudi Arabia during this same period of time. More than one cell may have been trained at the same time. It would make sense to train the Americans together, out-of-sight and unknown to anyone else. Having a cell or cells of Americans ready to serve al-Qaeda was in itself a worthy secret.

Baker was now on the phone with Director Simms, who wanted to hear case details first-hand from Baker before the press conference. There could be no errors in the information he provided to the media.

"The main focus, after recapping who was arrested and why, is going to be whether or not this group was acting alone. Are there other groups poised to strike? The AG and I both think we need to stay with the facts and not speculate. The usual comments about the ongoing investigation seem paltry in light of what is known, but we may have no other choice. My question to you is, what are we up against?"

Baker paused for a moment before answering. "From strictly an evidentiary point of view, it could go either way. This group could be acting as a single cell and there are no others. The alternative is there are other cells and a bigger plan. We do not have it all. If we had some additional pieces of critical information, we might be able to make a more educated assessment."

"What information is that?" asked Simms.

"What have we learned about the source of weapons recovered in Sicily? Finding where these materials came from in the supply line might tell us something about who got them. Were they forcefully stolen or pilfered? The supply line is an avenue of inquiry where we have no results. Now we have a second cache of weapons and explosives. We need to know ASAP if they have any commonality to the first."

Simms dialed Wilkins into the call with Baker. "Where do we stand with tracing the weapons and explosives?"

Wilkins responded, "The last I heard it was still a work in progress. Some US equipment was provided to the Iraqi military and disappeared from their supply system. I will get this expedited."

"What else?" asked Simms.

Baker continued, "We need to know what other American citizens listed travel to Saudi Arabia during this same period. They could refine the search by using the four-month period rather than the Hajj period. That might tell us about another possible cell."

Wilkins said he would contact the State Department about the status of their prior requests to State for this information.

"We are being told that The Engineer's computer research onboard the ship regarding Boston was far less specific then it was for New York. He seemed like a tourist checking out the city. We need to have the best view our analysts can give, and we need to know if there are any dissenting views," said Baker.

Neither Simms nor Wilkins responded, but it was being added to the list of items to be expedited.

"I was talking with one of the ordinance technicians," said Baker, "who helped remove the weapons and explosives from the warehouse. He had seen the pictures taken by the Italians of the material seized in Palermo. He reviewed their inventory in detail. He pointed out common elements between these two recoveries in content and manufacturer. The ordinance person wanted to offer an opinion, if someone was willing to listen, noting his opinion was not backed up by empirical data. I listened."

"And?" said Wilkins, interrupting Baker, as if the conversation was turning too pedestrian for the Director's immediate needs.

"He opined that when the Palermo container was recovered, it appeared to be efficiently packed and undisturbed. In contrast, the container in New York looked as if someone had rooted through it, pulling out items and doing some restacking in less than artful way. It appeared rummaged. Items were stacked haphazardly and not as tightly as one would do before shipping. He also noted the size of the container versus the actual contents found. He thinks we may be looking at only half of what was originally in this container."

"What do you think?" asked Simms.

"We don't have The Engineer. We don't have the radioactive material, for which we have evidence made it into this country. The

Engineer was also looking at Washington, DC and Boston. Last week The Engineer was in Boston buying at least two cell phones that end up immediately in Salah's possession. We have the two calls to Salah's phones last night that came through the same Boston cell tower. We have an al-Qaeda cell of US citizens recruited out of a mosque in Bayonne, New Jersey. We have an Imam known to be an al-Qaeda supporter and probably now a conspirator. It looks like a duck, it quacks like a duck, I think it's a duck. We still have a very serious problem."

"The Director cannot be speculating with the American public. They need to have faith in the FBI and believe we can successfully defend them against al-Qaeda," said Wilkins.

Baker responded immediately to Wilkins, "We have been very lucky so far. One agent and one NYPD detective figured out a way to find Salah's cab. Salah made the mistake of taking us to his storage facility and then broke all rules of security by having his cell gather in one place. Remember the theory that the war is not won by the better equipped and trained army, but rather by the army that makes the fewest mistakes. They are down one container of armaments thanks to Vespa, and another thanks to some luck on our part. Beyond that we should not delude ourselves by any success to date. We need to be open to thoughts that do not originate with us. Had it not been for the original tip from Vespa, we would not know any of this until six suitcase bombs went off. As far as the FBI is concerned, Vespa is a fortuitous event having nothing to do with our counter intelligence efforts."

Wilkins started to respond to Baker's negative attitude when Simms cut him off. "We will see you get the updates on the items you have listed. We are so limited by law as to what we can say about those under arrest that our limited comments should not be an issue with the media. The press will be doing its own investigation of these people for the next several days. Anyway, I cannot promise what I cannot deliver. We are in a time of uncertainty and I think the public understands that. They will have to share that uncertainty with us. Knowing that we are being as direct as we can be is what will give us credibility, and them confidence."

"Those two hundred agents I asked for in New York, will you redirect them to Boston?"

"Wilkins will see to that" said Simms. "Do we have any leads there yet?"

"Not many. My fear is that if we wait for the leads we may not get the manpower there in time when we need it. The AD here can continue what needs to be done. I need to go to Boston because I think that's where The Engineer is. I also think he has another plan and we need to figure it out fast. Given Salah's arrest, I think he will act sooner rather than later," said Baker.

"What do you think about that, Bob?" Simms asked Wilkins.

"I think it's a good idea. The SAC of Boston is on a temporary assignment doing bomb investigations in Iraq. His senior ASAC, Phil Kirby, reportedly has a close working relationship with the JTTF in Boston."

Simms just grunted at this statement by Wilkins. Wilkins and Baker did not know what Simms had learned earlier in the morning about Kirby. It would have to wait for right now. There were more immediate and important matters.

"Baker, you go to Boston. We will reroute those agents to you. Do you need the Hostage Rescue Team?" asked Simms.

"They are available from DC on short notice so there is no need for them to be physically located in Boston right now."

"I expect that things will operate as smoothly in Boston as they did in New York. If that is not the case I am to be informed immediately. Is that clear?" asked Simms.

It was.

Chapter 82

Boston

Patrick just finished surfing his computer for the morning news. There was no new information about the arrests in New York. Liz had gone to her office but was available if Patrick needed her. They said nothing more about why. Each seemed to understand without saying. Patrick was tempted to put a call into Susan Crowley but decided to wait. He wanted to hear from Baker. The phone rang and broke up his thought process.

"Hello Patrick, it is Maha."

"Hello my friend, what's up?"

"I take it you have followed the news in New York?" asked Soufan.

"Yes"

"What do you think? Is this what the problem is?"

"Maha, I think these arrests are part of it. I don't know how large the problem is. I only know a little more than what was reported. The names of those arrested are not given nor have they said exactly what was recovered in the raid. The news conference should be starting soon. I'll listen to the conference to see what comes out. After the news conference, I'll speak with Baker and call you later."

"Can we talk after the news conference? The Imam is looking for some advice about how to handle possible media inquiries that come to him at the mosque."

"Sure. I'll give your cell a call after the news conference."

"Good. Thanks."

While Patrick was speaking with Maha, The Engineer was meeting with Talat Mehmood at a coffee shop in Government Center. The morning commute was done. People going to their offices had already picked up their coffee. Things were quieter. The Engineer had taken the Red Line to Park Street and walked the two blocks to Government Center. Talat had a small notebook computer and used the coffee shop Wi-Fi to hook up to the internet. Together they watched the DOJ press conference being broadcast live.

Prior to the start of the press conference, the reporters were given packets of data that outlined all the available hard facts necessary for their detailed reporting. It contained the names, ages, addresses of those arrested as well as the specific charges against each. At the same time this information was also released electronically to the wire and internet services. It was a level playing field for the media. The press conference was used to present a couple of "talking heads" for TV and radio, and to create an opportunity for questions and photographs. The AG led the press conference. He was not new to this process. When the questions started about the continuing investigation and other possible suspects, Director Simms was called to the microphone.

"Is this an al-Qaeda terror cell of American citizens?"

"Those arrested are all American citizens. At present, these men are charged only with weapons violations and not with any act of terror. So to call it a terror cell at this point may be premature."

"We understand that some of these men are affiliated with a mosque in Bayonne, New Jersey, that has been linked to al-Qaeda in the past. If this is true, aren't we looking directly into the eye of al-Qaeda?"

"The arrests are based only on their presence with illegal weapons and explosives. Those are the facts we can present. I cannot discuss the current path of our ongoing investigation. That will have to wait for another time."

"Do you think they had these weapons and explosives with the intention of using them against American citizens?"

"That is where the investigation is focused at this time. We can only address that question publicly if and when additional charges are filed."

"Do you believe these arrests have removed a terror threat or prevented a terror attack on US soil?"

"We do believe these men were gathered together with these weapons and explosives for reasons not in the best interests of the American public. This is just common sense. The investigation is ongoing and we cannot say with certainty at this time exactly what these people intended to do. I can say that we are giving this investigation top priority. We have assigned all the agents necessary. The NYPD is addressing this in the same manner as are other agencies in the Joint Terrorism Task Force. Simply put, we are moving full speed ahead with as many resources as necessary. This will not change until we can tell you that we feel confident there is no further immediate threat to report."

"And you don't feel you can say with confidence there is no immediate threat at this time?" asked another reporter.

"That is correct," said Simms.

The last comment was what the media needed to know. The press would report that Simms was still concerned about a potential threat to the American public, and that threat was being actively investigated. Simms thought it needed to be said. His comments might put political pressure on the administration about the state of the current threat alert across the United States. There would be demands to know exactly how the administration was responding to them. There was nothing Simms could do about it.

The press conference ended. The media had many questions that could not be answered. However, the media beast had been well fed and was satiated for the time being.

Talat closed his computer. He and The Engineer walked outside and sat down on the brick wall at the Government Center T stop.

"How did they find Salah and the storage facility?" asked Mehmood.

"I don't know. I think one of the group, or Salah himself, led them there recently. If they knew about the facility when we delivered the phones and picked up the weapons and explosives, they would have arrested us. They must have just found it. I don't know how."

"Apparently no one is talking?" said Mehmood.

"So far that appears to be the case. Praise Allah for the training. Except for the contact Salah had for Wall Street, they are all good and well-trained men. I do not think there is a traitor among them. Tracing them back to the mosque in Bayonne is unfortunate, but it could not be changed. It is where their recruitment started."

"Do you think they will be looking for me?"

"You are not connected in recent time to the mosque. There are a lot of people in and out of there. I don't think so at this time. However, I think we need to step up our time-table."

"So we are going ahead?" asked Mehmood.

"Yes," said The Engineer firmly. "Both Palermo and New York could have been caused by operational mistakes. We will make sure that going forward there are none here. When we're successful here, they will realize that we can strike at will, despite setbacks. We are resilient. This is also a message we want them to hear."

"What do I tell my group?" asked Mehmood.

"It is unfortunate, but now all the responsibility falls upon their shoulders. At the same time, all the more glory will come from their success. We will overcome all obstacles. Let's take a walk so you and I can review the plan again."

Chapter 83

Boston

As promised, Patrick called Maha Soufan after the press conference.

"What do you think?" asked Soufan.

"I think it's an al-Qaeda terror cell of US citizens. al-Qaeda has at last been successful in recruiting resident US citizens to their cause. I think the materials from the storage facility will turn out to be related to those recovered in Sicily and part of the same overall plot. I don't think they have the most dangerous materials. The Engineer isn't in custody. There is a continuing problem. Help from your mosque is more important than ever given the recruitment from the Bayonne mosque. These people appear to have a continuing interest in Boston but we don't know why."

"But Mark, they cannot put us in the league with that Imam in Bayonne. Everyone knew he was al-Qaeda. We are nothing like that."

"Everyone knows that Maha. Law enforcement is in contact with many Muslim US citizens and groups across the country in the hopes that if something relevant comes to their attention, they will report it. It won't do any good for the FBI to go to St. Paul's Cathedral with the same questions. The Episcopalians there won't be in a position to help."

Soufan laughed. "I guess not Mark. Now, the Imam wanted to hear what you thought he should say if contacted by the media?"

"He should be himself and say what he thinks, as he has always done. He has an excellent relationship with the media and has a way of putting this conflict in perspective for everyone."

"What if they ask him if he has been contacted by the FBI?"

"He has an ongoing relationship with all law enforcement in New England. He knows nothing about the events surrounding the people in New York. He does not publicly discuss conversations between mosque leadership and law enforcement. After that he can continue to educate the public about what Islam is and how it is not represented by the actions of terrorists. He does this very well and it could be helpful for the public to hear his words again to balance some more aggressive opinions coming from other quarters."

"Thanks Mark. I'll let you know if he is contacted for comment."

By noontime, Baker had shifted his desk operation from New York City to the Boston FBI Office located in Government Center, just across from the T-stop by the same name. He was meeting with ASAC Phil Kirby, Supervisor George Fisher, and Special Agent Susan Crowley.

Crowley gave Baker an update on what was done in Boston since their last conversation. Kirby seemed to be put out that Crowley had conversations with Baker that did not go through him. Baker picked up on his attitude but said nothing. Crowley ended by recounting her conversation with Maha Soufan and her request for any information that could be of relevance, no matter how small it might seem.

It was clear to Baker that Crowley's conversation with Soufan had been a one-sided request with Soufan being told nothing about the potential problem. He probed a little.

"So all that Soufan knows is that there could be something they might hear around the mosque. This is a dangerous time and we ask them to contact us if they hear anything?"

"That is what he would conclude from our conversation," said Crowley.

George Fisher pointed out that Crowley, and to some extent himself, had invested time developing a relationship with this mosque. The mosque later established relationships, not only with the FBI, but with other federal and state law enforcement across New England. The mosque contacts were well liked and respected by all.

"I instructed Agent Crowley how to phrase her conversation with that guy Soufan so she didn't give away the shop," said Kirby.

"Do you know Soufan personally?" asked Baker.

"No. I let these two handle those contacts. I try to keep a management perspective."

Baker let the subject drop.

"The Director is sending two hundred agents to Boston. We will need an off-site location. Do you have one available?" inquired Baker.

"We have an arrangement for some emergency space in a building at the old Charlestown Navy Yard that we can call upon. We can have it set up in twenty-four hours," said Fisher.

"Make it twelve hours and we have a deal" said Baker with a smile.

Since the SAC was out of the country, it was suggested that Baker use his office. Kirby introduced him to Rose Phillips, administrative assistant to the SAC, who would be sitting outside his door. Baker invited her in and, with Kirby present, gave her an overview of his present assignment and identified the people he was in contact with regularly and who might be calling him. When he finished, Kirby cautioned Phillips that everything she heard was highly confidential and she should not discuss the matter with anyone. Phillips ignored Kirby, and his comments, and asked Baker if there was anything he needed done immediately. There was not. She gracefully excused herself.

Baker was waiting for Kirby to do likewise so he could get some work done. Kirby didn't.

"I have a close working relationship with the JTTF here in Boston and Harvey Bottom who is the AUSA assigned to that group. He expressed an interest in meeting with you. If you have time, we could pop over to his office this afternoon. He is mostly up to date but would like a briefing from you. He has some thoughts and ideas he would like to share with you."

"Well thanks. Let's see how the afternoon progresses?"

"What do you want me to tell Bottom?"

"I'll see how my afternoon goes. Now thanks for your help. I don't want to keep you from your duties any longer."

Baker and George Fisher went over the data from the cell phone purchases by The Engineer. Efforts were being made to see if The

Engineer had been in any other stores that sold cell phones in the immediate downtown area. So far this survey had turned up nothing.

Likewise, there was no further data available from the cell tower atop the John Hancock building. Cell phone, home landline phones, email accounts of those arrested had all been initially reviewed and no links to Boston could be found. They had begun interviewing those affiliated with the New York subjects, at least those who were willing to open their doors, but nothing indicated any travel to or contact with Boston. Baker could not escape the feeling that The Engineer had another Salah in Boston, and he had no idea how to identify and find him. Was it time to put The Engineer's photograph all over the news?

Rose Phillips put through a call from Bob Wilkins.

"There are some developments tracing the weapons. The Semtex was traced through its taggants. It was sold to the Russians and later became excess to Moscow's needs, so they sold it to the Syrians for hard currency. The Syrians won't answer any questions, including whether or not they even know the Russians. This stuff could have been kicking around the terrorist market for a few years. The important point is that the Semtex in Palermo and New York are part of this former Russian stockpile."

"Then Palermo and New York have some common supply?"

"Yes. It gets deeper. The C-4 is from good old US of A. It was missing from its last known storage point at a weapons dump outside of Bagdad. If you believe a US Army inventory, it was there less than a year ago. So if the bad guys got it, it was recent. C-4 from this location is present in both Sicily and New York. Some of the lighter weapons can be traced to losses on the battlefield by the US military, as well as other allies, over the last several years in Iraq."

"So there are two indications of a common denominator."

The laser guided 50-caliber machine guns were shipped by the US to the Pakistani Army as part of the deal for them to go after al-Qaeda in the tribal region. The Pakistani Army has no record of them missing, but has no records of where they are. You figure that statement out."

"I have met the enemy and he is us," Baker dryly observed.

Wilkins continued paying no attention to Baker; "The rocket propelled grenades are mostly Chinese. They work pretty well and are sold to anyone with cash."

Wilkins continued without waiting for any response from Baker; "The laser guided anti-tank rockets are older US technology. I think they are called Dragons. The US manufacturers have been selling these missiles to US allies for years. These came from shipments to the Northern Alliance

James Ring

when they were helping to kick the Taliban out of Afghanistan. Apparently, the sales were arranged through some CIA affiliated companies. It seems that the Afghan warlords who bought these things at great discount with their poppy proceeds did not bother to keep any inventory records. They have no idea who had them or what they did with them, if they ever had them.'

"So does it appear to the weapons analysts that we have a common source of supply that was responsible for both containers, Palermo and New York" queried Baker?

"Pretty much, but there is more. Found on the floor in the New York storage container was a small metal plate that contains safety instructions for storing a carrying case for an FGM-148 Javelin."

"I don't know anything about military hardware, so clue me in."

"I would suggest you look it up on the internet to save time. It surprises me there are no secrets about the capabilities of many of our military weapons. The information about them is readily available. Anyway the Javelin is the anti-tank weapon that replaced the Dragon. It's really bad. One man can aim it at a target, fire it, forget it and move on before the target is even hit. Laser guided. It locks on and that's it. You can fire it directly at a building or a moving helicopter. If you want to take out a tank, it has a top attack profile that allows the missile to go high in the air and hit the tank from the top where there is less armor. The Javelin was used in the 2003 Iraq war and effectively demolished T-72 tanks into very small piles of scrap metal."

"So how many of these weapons are floating around?"

"Each of these units, consisting of a launcher, a missile, and a case, costs about $125,000. A missile alone costs about $80,000. So they seem to be a rich terrorist's toy. A few probably went missing in Iraq. However, the US manufacturers have been selling these things abroad. Some of these Javelins have been sold to Jordan, Bahrain, United Arab Emirates, Oman, the Czech Republic, and a fairly large supply to Mexico. Until we get our hands on a specific Javelin, we won't know its origin."

"So we have to assume that some of these Javelins might be in possession of The Engineer?" asked Baker with noticeable tension in his voice.

"Remember that ordinance technician who thought the New York container may have been disturbed or rooted through? Perhaps they took out the Javelins?" said Wilkins.

"How do you figure? The evidence shows they are building suitcase bombs with fragmentation and possibly augmented by dirty bomb material? What we see in the warehouse indicates bombs to murder and maim. What you are describing with these Javelins is a whole different type of attack."

"That is exactly what our analysts are suggesting," said Wilkins.

"Anything new regarding the review of the internet activity by The Engineer?"

"No."

They agreed to talk later in the evening.

Patrick left his office at Counting House Wharf to get some fresh air and a bit of lunch at Sal's. He normally cut through the King's Wharf Hotel rather then walk around to reach the waterfront on the other side. As he exited the hotel on the north side he saw Claudia Bell and Harvey Bottom sitting on a bench near the commuter boat dock. They didn't see him. They were too engrossed in their conversation to notice him. Patrick thought Bell might be pumping Bottom to find out if there was any connection between the arrests in New York and what Bottom was trying to do with Patrick in Boston. Patrick thought he might get a call from Bell asking him directly. Patrick just noted what he saw and kept on moving. He was hungry.

Patrick thought Bottom a fool for meeting a known reporter in a spot that had no connection with either of them. Bottom could give up all the state secrets to Bell standing in a hallway inside the federal courthouse. It was common ground where they could be talking about anything. Even though they were in full public view, away from the courthouse like this, they looked secretive.

Patrick sat down at Sal's and ordered a hamburger with lettuce, tomato and onion. A glass of iced tea was added to the lunch. He was set until later in the afternoon. Sal had the TV on so Patrick watched the early afternoon news and learned nothing new. The media had expanded the story. They identified again all those arrested and where they came from. No new facts were introduced for Patrick to consider.

Chapter 84

Boston

The Engineer and Talat Mehmood took the Silver Line bus to the fast-developing area known as the South Boston Waterfront. This area would be the new Boston over the next twenty years. The land here had formerly held fishing or commercial warehouses, trucking terminals, and general industrial buildings. This area contained a vast amount of land for any East Coast city to have available for re-development. Efforts were being made to learn from the past and to develop this land well for future generations. The new federal courthouse was one of the first buildings to locate there. Now several hotels and commercial buildings had been completed and were occupied. More were on the way. The area was designed as mixed use to include residential. It would be occupied and used all hours of the day and night, just the way a city should be.

Facing Boston Harbor, The Engineer and Talat Mehmood sat on a bench in front of the modern Institute of Contemporary Art. They had a beautiful view back to the city center or across the harbor to Logan Airport and the open sea. They could even see north up the harbor to Charlestown and beyond to where the Mystic and Chelsea Rivers entered Boston Harbor. Mehmood pulled a slightly dog eared chart of Boston Harbor from his jacket pocket. He and The Engineer also had their plans to alter the landscape and functionality of Boston Harbor on a permanent basis. What The Engineer really liked about his plan was he did not have to do all the work. An energy company, aided by the federal administration that ignored all local opposition, was bringing the key ingredient into the Boston Harbor for The Engineer to use. The United States Coast Guard would escort The Engineer's bomb, a Liquefied Natural Gas (LNG) tanker, into the heart of the city. All the Engineer had to do was set it off.

Talat Mehmood began briefing The Engineer. "I have been studying the LNG tankers coming into Boston Harbor for over a year. They are very predictable. On average they unload about two tankers a week. Given that they have to come in at this frequency, and given the time it takes to unload, and that they require specific high and low tides for coming and going, their transit schedule is quite predictable. The LNG tankers are quite visible before they even get close to the harbor. I can take the schedule I have established for prior deliveries, look at the tide chart, and tell almost exactly when the next one will arrive."

"Are there fluctuations in security depending on day or night deliveries?" asked The Engineer.

"Day or night does not seem to matter," said Mehmood. "What does matter is any recent adverse media attention to the LNG tankers. When some public group makes another demand that these tankers should not be allowed into the harbor, the media carries the story anew. Then you will notice an increase in visible security. It's not more effective security, it just seems the energy company and the Coast Guard put on a better show for the public. They say they have security under control and there is no unaddressed danger."

"What is the floating security arrangement at present?" asked The Engineer.

"A small Coast Guard cutter leads the entourage. I see no heavy weapons on this boat and if there is a machine gun or cannon on the bow, I have never seen it manned. Following that boat, about three hundred yards back and off the port and starboard bows, will be two police boats. Generally one is from the state police and the other from the Boston Police. Amid ships and close to the LNG tanker is one Coast Guard inflatable boat on each side. These have machine guns mounted in the bow. I have never seen them manned and do not know if they are loaded. Off to the stern, on both port and starboard sides, is stationed another police boat. One is the Environmental Police boat and the other can be from any of the above groups. They are small and have no observable heavy weapons."

"What is the role of the police boats? What can they do?" asked The Engineer.

"I don't know what to tell you. Other than for communications and for control of civilian boat traffic in the harbor, they really cannot contribute much to the physical defense of an LNG tanker. The police do not carry military type armaments. They are civilian police. Some officers may have military training in their history, but it is not like they have Navy Seals protecting these tankers."

"Any more boats involved in the protection?"

"About 250 yards astern of the tanker is another Coast Guard vessel. It can be a small cutter around eighty-seven feet or, periodically, I have seen the larger cutter about two hundred feet longer. Generally it is the smaller one."

"What does their function appear to be?" asked The Engineer.

"The larger cutter has a substantial amount of electronic gear mounted over the bridge. There are antennas and electronic pods and other structures we don't know. We assume they use this cutter and its electronic equipment to monitor the harbor while the LNG tanker is under escort. They do not use these larger craft to escort a departing and empty tanker.

The cutter may monitor boat transponders to identify boats in their immediate vicinity. We also think they have the ability to jam radio signals for voice and electronic communication if an attack started. There is a cannon mounted on the bow of the larger cutter but they cannot fire this weapon into a civilian environment."

"I was led to believe," said The Engineer, "that boat traffic was not allowed in the harbor while the tanker was coming in or going out."

"That is only somewhat true," said Mehmood. "There are all kinds of regular harbor boats that just pull off to the side of the harbor while the entourage passes by. Once passed, they resume their activity. The Coast Guard can identify these boats using transponders just like is done with airplanes. The Coast Guard can identify these boats and whether they belong in the area."

"On the boat we're using, there will be such a transponder to make us look normal in the area?" asked The Engineer.

"Yes," smiled Mehmood.

"Have you determined what you want to use as the point of attack?"

"Yes," said Mehmood. "We will fire on the tanker just south of City Wharf. This will allow for the drift of the tanker to the site where the two automobile tunnels cross beneath the harbor. They have carried vehicle traffic since 1927 between downtown Boston and East Boston, and forward to points on the North Shore. After the attack and the fire, whatever is left of the LNG tanker should sink over these tunnels. The pressure created by the ship hulk will rupture these tunnels or at least make them unusable. Of course, the entire harbor will be impassable and unusable as the hulk sinks at the harbor's narrowest point. If the sinking hulk destroys the two vehicle tunnels, East Boston will be directly cut off from downtown Boston."

"How far is the point of attack from the Coast Guard station?" asked The Engineer.

"It is about six hundred yards south."

"In essence the attack will take place almost in front of the Coast Guard station?" noted The Engineer.

Mehmood smiled with The Engineer as he continued his briefing. "I could say we are doing this to add even more disgrace to the failings of their security plan. However, it is one of the narrowest points of the harbor, so the weapons we are using cannot miss, and the harbor will be totally blocked by the sunken hulk. Additionally, ground security is almost non-existent until you get near the company docking area under the Tobin Bridge. Around the firing area we selected, ground security consists of perhaps one or two Boston police officers sitting inside their cruisers with the blue lights blinking. It is more an advertisement for the public than an effective security measure. They have no weapons other than their individual sidearms."

"Do you expect different security arrangements with the additional LNG tankers now scheduled to be loaded in Yemen?" queried The Engineer.

"Without a doubt," said Mehmood. "After 9/11, when the public and the city fought against the federal government in court for allowing these tankers into the harbor, the energy company and the Coast Guard made a big show about security. They put on more boats in the defensive perimeter but they were smaller craft with no military fire power. Instead of eight boats, they had twelve. They brought the largest tugboat on the East Coast in from New York and hooked a line from that tug to the stern of the tanker. The company claimed that if anything happened to the tanker the tug would tow it out of the harbor. Of course, others familiar with tugboats said this was nonsense. A jammed or inoperable rudder on a stalled LNG tanker could prevent the tug from towing it backwards. If there was a fire on the tanker, no one near it would survive. The tugboat and its line would melt. This large tugboat eventually left and they use a smaller one for the same designated purpose. It is like a lot of their security. It looks good to civilians but it will not be effective in stopping our plans."

"What about the helicopter?" asked The Engineer.

"We don't see it relevant to what we are doing. Our plan is to be in a public place at a time of day or night where the public is expected. If at night, and the helicopter has thermal imaging or infrared devices, they will see lots of images of citizens about the Harbor Walk, hotels, parking lots, and coffee shops. This tanker is passing through a very active public area. There is nothing they can do about it. We will be part of the populated scene," said Mehmood.

"Should we avoid the first Yemen tanker as a target because of increased security?" asked The Engineer.

"The last time they increased security they put up two helicopters instead of one, used twelve boats instead of eight, and added more ground security in East Boston near the water and at the Tobin Bridge, which they often close to the public as the tanker docks. None of this would impact us where we will be. Our idea is to be present, be part of the public scene, and the majority of our attack is land-based, not water-based. Our presence on the water will appear legitimate. We fully expect three teams to escape the police after the attack. Whether they will escape the fire and destruction is another question. The fourth team consists of two dedicated martyrs. You and I will be outside the immediate fire area, far enough away, as we execute our part of the plan," explained Mehmood.

"I have to agree with you." said The Engineer. "Let them increase their security. We will take them on. It will make no difference. Their protection system will not be effective in a populated civilian area. Who will they fire their canon at? Where can they point a 50-caliber machine gun? They will only see civilians until it is too late. It will be over so quickly they will not be able to do anything."

Chapter 85

Baker needed to have the JTTF in Boston functioning at the same level as in New York. He now regretted listening to Kirby's advice not to notify the local authorities of the potential threat. Time was not on their side and he wanted it done right away. He called Kirby to set up the meeting and to make sure the Boston Police commissioner and the Massachusetts State Police colonel were personally asked to attend. He was in the process of getting an update from the JTTF in New York when Kirby walked in.

"I called Bottom to get his thoughts and he suggested we hold off getting the JTTF going full blast. He's reluctant to have agency heads discussing this with the mayor and the governor."

Baker now had to force himself not to lose control. "Why?" asked Baker using great restraint.

"It may get leaked to the media."

"Doesn't Bottom think the mayor and the governor have a right to know what we know since they are in charge of the public safety for this community?"

"He thinks it's better to hold things a little tighter to the vest until we get some idea that The Engineer is really in Boston."

"So purchasing the cell phones does not count?"

Kirby said nothing but looked at Baker with exasperation and contempt in his eyes. Baker was controlled enough not to let his thoughts be obvious to Kirby.

Baker continued. "Well you have gone to great lengths to tell me what Mr. Bottom thinks. Now tell me what you, as the Acting Special Agent in Charge of the Boston FBI Office, have to say."

"I just want to do whatever is best."

"That does not answer my question. So I will take it you do not wish to go on record with an answer. So much for your leadership. Why didn't you call the people I told you to call?"

"You don't know how I have things set up here. You're stepping on my working relationships. You are not doing what I suggest."

"And what is that?"

"You need to meet with Harvey Bottom. You should have done that first thing, like I asked."

"And what makes Mr. Bottom so necessary to this terrorism investigation? Why should I clear things through him as apparently you feel you have to?"

"He has a lot of pull at DOJ. You are pissing people off there. There are some at DOJ just waiting to nail you, and I don't want to be standing next to you when it happens. Bottom could help you but you won't pay him any respect by going to his office and giving him a personal briefing."

"Ah, now I get the picture. Sorry, I am a little slow sometimes. It must be my preoccupation with this case." Baker called out to Rose, "Would you ask George Fisher to step in please?"

While waiting, Baker called up his email and started clicking away.

Fisher walked in, nodded to Kirby, and said to Baker, "You wanted to see me?"

Baker directed his comments to Fisher. "We need to get the managers of the JTTF together at 6:30 pm. I want the Boston Police commissioner and colonel of the state police personally invited so there is no miscommunication about the seriousness of the matter. You will speak to each of them personally and let me know if they can attend. Mr. Bottom is perfectly welcome to attend, but the FBI is charged with coordinating this investigation. We have not turned that control over to anyone else, no matter how much pull they have in Washington. Mr. Kirby does not seem to understand that, nor did he do what I asked a short time ago. So I am relieving him of any responsibilities regarding this Boston terrorism investigation and putting you in charge. Are there any questions?"

A sneer came over Kirby's face. "We will see if you can pull this off."

Baker continued to type on his keyboard. He finally hit enter. "I just sent an email to AD Wilkins advising him of what I just told you, Kirby. You can appeal to whomever you wish, but as of now you have nothing to do with terrorism. Don't get in my way again. Now let's all get to work."

What a time to run into an idiot, thought Baker. They are few and far between, but since the FBI is inhabited by human beings, there are some. He could not afford distractions or petty thinking right now.

Rose came in. "I just took a call from Claudia Bell looking for you. She wants to know why the head of the FBI's al-Qaeda desk is working out of the Boston office. I told her you were in a meeting and I would take the message."

So someone was keeping a news reporter posted on him. He was in Boston less than six hours and had made no outside contacts. Someone inside was posting her. He was thinking of her articles regarding Patrick and the source Vespa.

"Would you ask the agent assigned to press inquiries to return her call for me? Tell her that I am not available for media questions. The agent should note that the SAC is in Iraq on temporary assignment and I have been asked to come in and lend a hand. Otherwise, there is no further need to comment."

Rose smiled. "While you were in here with Mr. Kirby, the JTTF duty agent in New York called. He asked that you call him as soon as you were free."

"Thank you, Rose. If Mr. Kirby wants to know anything about what I am doing, tell him I have instructed you not to reply to such questions as he has been relieved of his duties in terrorism matters."

"Yes sir." She turned and left.

Baker called Mark Patrick, got his cell phone voicemail, and left a message for Patrick to call Baker ASAP.

Baker then called the JTTF in New York and got the duty supervisor.

"Would you like some good news, Vince?"

"If I had to kiss a frog to get it, I would. What have you got?"

"Let me put this on speaker so you can also talk with NEST JTTF representative Bernie Williams at the same time. Can you hear us?"

"Fire away," said Baker.

"The end of the story I give you first. We have one thirty-inch red fire extinguisher that is spewing alpha and gamma particles. Same readings from Palermo and from the bunk room of The Engineer aboard ship. It weighs about forty pounds. We are removing it from where it was found, and getting it properly shielded. We can get people with protective gear to fingerprint it. We want to see if the welder's prints are on it, since he handled both canisters when he took them off the ship for The Engineer. That would definitely make it one of The Engineer's."

"Just one, not two?" asked Baker.

"Yes."

"How and where are my next questions?"

"Excuse me if I run on, but I need to give you the picture so you know what works and what doesn't. The entire West Side is an area where the bedrock is over two hundred feet below the surface. That is why the buildings in Chelsea and Hell's Kitchen are generally no more the six or seven stories tall. The ground won't sustain higher buildings. There are docks on the nearby Hudson River. The area used to be noted for shipping cargo, storage and commerce. Container shipping put these smaller docks out of business. After the demise of these docks, many of the buildings were converted into tenements. The famous Irish gangs, that worked the docks before they lost their jobs, were followed by immigrants from Puerto Rico. In recent years, buildings have been upgraded and converted into condos or apartments to house the white collar work force in the city. However, many of the area buildings still serve the storage needs of businesses in midtown as well as local folks with small apartments. With me so far?"

"With you."

"We had a helicopter run this area because the building heights let us get close to the ground. The results were not good. We kept receiving false positives. We put out the mobile units but kept getting similar results. Then we got the idea to start targeting buildings that offered any kind of storage. We asked ourselves what The Engineer would see if he were walking around the area looking for a small storage space on a less then formal basis. We did this using backpack and handheld equipment between the warehouse and where Salah lived. We started looking for small storage accommodations like cubicles offered to apartment dwellers. Bingo."

"I think I like the sound of that," said Baker.

"On 11th Avenue near West 47th Street, a building super had posted signs in a nearby laundromat for storage cubicles to rent. We went to his place. He had converted some cellar space into twenty small cubicles made of plywood and chicken wire, and was renting them out for a little extra income unknown to the building owner. It's a cash business with no records. Less than a month ago The Engineer walked in looking for a place to put some boxes. He said he didn't have room in his apartment, or so the story went. The super saw some boxes in the cubicle after he rented it to

The Engineer. Inside one of the boxes was a black bag containing the fire extinguisher."

"What are the contents of the extinguisher and how bad are they?"

"We can't tell yet. This happened less than one hour ago. We are in the process of trying to discreetly remove the cubicle contents and evaluate what clean-up is necessary. We don't think leakage is an insurmountable problem in the short term, but we have to make sure. We will get it to a secure location and our technical people can start the examination."

"We have agents present with the fire extinguisher for evidentiary and chain of custody purposes," said the duty agent. "We also are bringing in the welder to see if he thinks it is one of those he brought off the boat. We will get back to you as soon as we get further results."

Baker thanked the NEST representative and the duty agent profusely. He was elated.

Rose came into Baker's office as soon as he hung up. "Mark Patrick is returning your call. I have him on hold if you are ready."

"I am. Put him on, please."

"Hello Vince," said Patrick. "I would normally say how nice to have you in Boston but since you are here working, I'm not all that happy."

Baker smiled. "I still believe The Engineer is in Boston. I want to make sure we are doing everything we can with Vespa. We can't let any possible opportunity go by. Would you be able to come by the office now?"

"I will be there in one-half hour."

"Great. Just ask for Rose."

Chapter 86

The Engineer and Talat walked west on the Boston Harbor Walk towards the new federal courthouse and then crossed the Fort Point Channel using the old turning bridge now restricted to pedestrian traffic.

"Explain to me, what is this Harbor Walk?" asked The Engineer.

Mehmood responded, "The Harbor Walk was created by a legislative act to give all citizens the right to access the harbor waterfront. It means all property owners on the harbor have to allow the public to walk or bike on their property. In some cases, where there was no place to walk, the city built boardwalks. They are beautiful."

"Is it well used?' asked The Engineer.

"Very much so, both day and night. It is a refuge for people living in cramped apartments, which are what you have in the North End. The property owners question no one on the Harbor Walk. I have spent hundreds of hours on the Harbor Walk and it is the perfect environment for us to use," said Mehmood.

The Engineer commented, "When this is over, perhaps we should thank them for allowing us to get so close to the LNG tanker that we cannot miss, and for providing us with adequate cover before the attack."

The Engineer and Mehmood turned north walking around the edge of Counting House Wharf, passed Bay Towers and up to the Harbor Cruise and MBTA commuter boat docks at King's Wharf. The Engineer went over to the MBTA ticket booth and picked up a small map of Boston Harbor.

Instead of cutting through the King's Wharf Hotel as Patrick earlier did, they turned right and walked down to the water's edge, around the tip of King's Wharf and back on a boardwalk to the north side of the hotel. Here was the outdoor waiting area for the commuter boats to Salem and the water taxi stop. Had they been a little earlier they might have seen Claudia Bell and Harvey Bottom in their secret talk on one of the benches.

Just around the corner on the water side of Christopher Columbus Park, they sat on a bench at the harbor's edge facing the water. They watched the ferry from Salem slip into a live docking maneuver to permit the disembarking of the passengers aboard, and to allow the return passengers to Salem to come aboard. The ferry quickly pulled out for the return trip out of the harbor and back to Salem. The Engineer did not see anything useful in the ferry's operation insofar as his mission was concerned. The water taxi he saw dropping off a few passengers at an adjoining dock held some possibility as a small craft they could hi-jack and use in their attack. He noted that boat's movements with interest.

"I still think the water taxi can hold 1,000 pounds without a problem for a short ride" said Mehmood.

"You're right. I think it is a good option. We can look at the other one in a few minutes."

Mehmood and The Engineer continued walking north on the Harbor Walk past more of the old warehouses now converted to high-end condos. After walking past the City Wharf parking lot, they turned right into Franklin Wharf. They walked by Peter in the attendant's booth as they followed the Harbor Walk to the edge of Franklin Wharf. They continued north to Merchants Wharf, where they sat on a bench to view the narrowest part of the Boston Harbor through which the LNG tanker passed.

"I was concerned because it takes the Javelins seventy-five meters of travel before they arm. I was concerned there might not be seventy-five meters between the shore and the tanker. Sitting here, it appears to be plenty of room," said The Engineer.

Talat took a small device used to measure distance on the golf course and held it up to his eye. "There is enough room for them to arm. The tanker is so huge in this confined area, it appears closer than it really is."

"When we get back, we will check the available satellite maps on the computer and review the entire area in detail. They have a distance-measuring capability on these maps. We can make sure we know the exact distances for all of our critical points. We can get a good overview of the Coast Guard station at the same time."

They both looked across the water to a wharf on the East Boston side. A tugboat was exiting a pier into the harbor. "The tugs that move the tanker are docked in a wharf area that you cannot see from here. Tugboats are not active all the time and are easily accessible from East Boston." Mehmood had considered hi-jacking a tugboat as part of one plan.

The Engineer nodded as the tugboat approached them and passed by. The Engineer took out his chart of the harbor to coordinate the position of the Sumner and Callahan Tunnels between East Boston and Boston with the surrounding buildings. The tunnels were almost under where he was sitting and ran slightly in a Northeast direction. Sinking the LNG tanker in this area would have the desired effect on the tunnels. What a bonus this might be, thought The Engineer. If the tunnels were breached, any drivers and passengers inside would surely drown.

Talat and The Engineer got up from the bench and continued walking north on the Harbor Walk. They walked between the two Merchants Wharf buildings passing the small Boston Fire Department Marine Station on the first floor of the northern building. Moored on the north side of the BFD Marine Station was the primary City of Boston fireboat. Its more common use was to welcome vessels of some importance with spray from its water cannons. There were not many fires on the harbor. Moored behind the large fireboat was a smaller one about forty feet in length and powered by twin 250-horsepower outboard motors. This fireboat had a small water cannon mounted in the bow. Both Talat and The Engineer paid substantial attention to this boat. They also tried to see the interior of the fire station, with little success. The windows that were not shaded were darkened by material to keep out the bright sunlight.

The next complex of buildings north of Merchants Wharf was North Wharf, with its new hotel and condominium complex. This was now the most expensive real estate on the waterfront and not all the units had been sold. The area, while open, was still undergoing final construction. This was important for Mehmood and The Engineer to observe. Workers and trucks might be part of their plan.

After walking through North Wharf, they followed the Harbor Walk back to Commercial Street. The Harbor Walk did not go through the next set of buildings, which were part of the Coast Guard station. They walked past the Coast Guard station on Commercial Street. The entrance was secure and required identification to enter. Here were stationed the various Coast Guard vessels with which they had to contend. They would get a look at them from the water in a little while.

The Harbor Walk returned to the water's edge after passing the Coast Guard station. It took them past the neighborhood swimming pool, two baseball diamonds and three bocce courts, all located in Cosca Park. Adjacent to the park just before the Charlestown Bridge was an ice skating rink and tennis courts. Instead of walking over the bridge, they walked under it on platforms constructed for pedestrians. They continued walking over the Charles River locks and eventually to the Charlestown side of the harbor.

The Charles River locks system controlled the water level in the Charles River by holding back the ebb and flow of the harbor tides. Back Bay was renowned in early Boston history for the foul smells from the river flowing through a city that did not have a sewage system. Creating the locks allowed the water level in the river to remain at a higher level permanently and covered the odor with water, no matter what the tide.

The next stop on their walking tour was just past the Charlestown Yacht Club. It was the National Park at the old Charlestown Navy Yard. Everyone who visited Boston toured this park, home to the U.S.S. Constitution, more commonly known as Old Ironsides.

Mehmood and The Engineer viewed Old Ironsides from a parking lot at Charlestown Plaza, between the Yacht Club and the Navy Yard. The lot was used by tenants and visitors to a nearby commercial building. The US Navy had installed barriers preventing any vessel from entering the dockage area by water where Old Ironsides was berthed. However, this parking lot, which had no government security, was less than seventy-five yards away from Old Ironsides.

Next, Mehmood and The Engineer entered the Charlestown Navy Yard Park just north of the parking lot. There was no security to pass going into the park, but visitors seeking to board Old Ironsides passed through a building with security apparatus where individuals and bags could be screened. Old Ironsides' berth had a security fence extending from the security building south, ending at the stern of the vessel. At the end of the same pier, on the east side, was the U.S.S. Cassin Young. It is a WW II vintage destroyer now serving as a public museum. From here Mehmood and The Engineer had a direct water view south through the harbor, where they could observe the narrow portion that was of interest to them.

The Engineer addressed Talat. "You did an excellent job of putting together this plan. As I walk through the whole area and think of your outline, I see a very thorough and creative scenario that has every chance of success. Each component is based on fact and careful analysis. The ride back will give us a better sense from the water side."

Mehmood and The Engineer waited for the MBTA commuter boat that ran every half hour between Charlestown and King's Wharf. It would give them a water view of the entire attack area. They would see it as the enemy would when they had to respond to their attack. Allah willing, the attack would be all over before they could even begin to respond.

Earlier, they saw the boats of the Massachusetts State Police moored at the locks for the Charles River. The boats of the Massachusetts Environmental Police were docked in Charlestown near the MBTA Wharf. What they saw matched their expectations. They were not impressed. None of the police boats was armed with weapons necessary to repel a military style attack. These were civilian boats for police use.

As the MBTA boat left the Charlestown dock, it slowly passed the Coast Guard station. They got a good look at the inflatable boats the Coast Guard used, and the various cutters available to escort an LNG tanker.

As the MBTA boat passed North Wharf and Merchants Wharf, Mehmood and The Engineer observed the distance from their position on the water. They did the same for the wharf on the east side where the tugboats were moored.

As the MBTA boat pulled into King's Wharf, The Engineer felt he should thank the MBTA and the Harbor Walk officials for making the Boston Harbor so accessible to the public. Their so called freedom represents their sin of pride, he thought. It will be their undoing. The Engineer intended to be the one to point that out to them!

Chapter 87

Patrick walked from his office to the FBI office at Center Plaza. He gave Rose a hug and was escorted into Baker's Office. Baker asked George Fisher and Agent Crowley to come by. While waiting, they discussed the Red Sox versus the Yankees this year for the World Series. There was not agreement but there was common ground. Neither one was a Yankee fan.

When Crowley and Fisher were seated, Baker started. "The protocol here is from the Director. I can discuss with Mark whatever I want about this case and so can you. We need to seize every opportunity to maintain Vespa's cooperation. We can pick Mark' brain about his knowledge of Boston and how we can best communicate with those at the state and local level. Has anyone brought you up to date on what has transpired in New York?"

"No," was Patrick's simple reply. Baker spent the next five minutes recounting the recovery of the armaments and explosives and the arrest of the individuals now in custody. He asked Crowley to summarize the investigation in Boston. Baker recounted his recent conversation with the NEST agent in New York about the recovery of one fire extinguisher that appeared to still have its evil contents and the fact that a second one may still be loose.

"Is there anything recent from Vespa" asked Baker?

"No contact since my last report."

"Is there anything Vespa can do for us in Boston? Can you contact Vespa and ask?"

"I can try. How much can I tell Vespa and exactly what am I supposed to ask?"

Baker looked at Crowley and Fisher. "We can use any help we can get. None of us thinks we have the luxury of time, and I doubt that Vespa is the one talking to the press," said Fisher.

"Tell Vespa we have arrested The Engineer's crew in New York and recovered what may be half of the weapons and armaments. We now have evidence that The Engineer is in Boston. He may have another crew here with more arms, explosives, and radioactive material. We have no idea what the target is. This place is rich with history and potential terrorist targets. The usual target analysis does not help. Does Vespa have any ideas or resources that can be used? Please use your own judgment. I don't intend to limit you on what should be said."

"I have pressed before about going back to their original sources in the mountains. If anyone knows what The Engineer is doing, that person is probably in the mountains. Maybe we should ask Vespa to try again there now that we know New York and Palermo are connected" said Patrick.

Baker noted a different look on Patrick's face. "What are you thinking?" asked Baker.

"What is your press problem?"

Baker told him about Claudia Bell's call, adding: "I was going to mention this anyway. She seemed to have inside information relative to your matter in court."

"At noontime today I was walking out of the King's Wharf Hotel and I saw Bell and Harvey Bottom in deep discussion at one of the tables in the commuter boat waiting area. During the court hearings, I observed what I thought was Bottom giving Bell his extended version of the government's position. Shortly thereafter Bell called looking for me to respond. It was obviously inside information slanted to make me look bad in the public realm and force my capitulation."

"Bottom has been using Kirby to pimp me this afternoon to be one of his minions. So don't feel badly."

"You had better button this up. Bottom is just enough of an ego maniac to tip the press to The Engineer being in Boston. If that happens The Engineer can panic and do something stupid or make a run for it."

"I have relieved Kirby of his duties in terrorism matters."

"Not a bad start" said Patrick, "but I think you need to get both of them physically out of here, perhaps to Washington. You can have them both fully interviewed and given a polygraph. That's the only way you can do a damage assessment and prevent them from getting any more information."

"Both?" asked Baker.

"You are going to make me say it? Where is Bottom getting his information? Kirby is giving it to him blow by blow. Kirby may not know what Bottom is leaking, but he probably has an idea." Patrick was not happy having to say what he did. He felt it necessary to for the good of the case.

Baker responded, "Now I see how and why you view Bottom as you do. Let me move on. Do you have any ideas or opinions, based on your local knowledge and experience, regarding potential targets?" asked Baker.

"Look, you have all kinds of potential target ratings. These assessments are done by people who are paid to sit around and evaluate these things," said Patrick.

"Are you going to answer the question?" asked Baker.

Crowley and Fisher laughed. Patrick had been called.

"I am prejudiced but you can hear me out, if you want."

"Go ahead," said Baker.

"The 9/11 Commission was critical of our intelligence gathering, saying that we were not bold or imaginative enough in our thinking and analysis of al-Qaeda. On this point I would agree. I also think we continue to make the same mistake."

"How so?" asked Baker.

"Terrorists have been hijacking airplanes for years. We know al-Qaeda wants to kill four million Americans in retribution for their claims against the infidel. We know in 1993 they did not just try and bomb the World Trade Center, they tried to knock it down. If their truck driver had selected a different garage parking space, they might have succeeded."

"What has that got to do with Boston today?"

"al-Qaeda looked around for material in place to help them do what they wanted. They had no trouble imagining what a huge aircraft fully loaded with fuel could do if rammed into the higher floors of a very tall building. They imagined it and then did it. We did not see that as a possibility. There has been a public debate going on for years in Boston about a way to destroy everything for a mile around the harbor, and no one has mentioned it to you?"

Baker looked at Fisher. "Does this mean anything to you?"

"No, not since I've been in Boston."

"Crowley, you have been here longer. Do you know what Patrick is talking about?" asked Baker.

"Probably the LNG tanker," replied Crowley.

Baker said to Patrick, "You have the floor."

"Let me give you the bottom line right from the start. I know of no other potential terrorist target where the United States government brings so much combustible material to the scene. The terrorist only needs to bring an ignition source."

"Give me as many details as you can so I can understand the scope of the problem," requested Baker.

"An LNG tanker is over nine hundred feet long, twelve stories high, and can only fit through Boston Harbor under tugboat power and direction. Twice a week, and on only the highest tides, LNG tankers come up from Trinidad, enter the Boston Harbor under the auspices and protection of the Coast Guard, and are taken by tug to an offloading site just under the Tobin Bridge. The harbor theoretically is shut down while the tanker is in transit. Most LNG tankers have five cargo holds, each containing 25,000 cubic meters of LNG for a total of 125,000 cubic meters. This is twenty times more than the amount of LNG that destroyed one square mile of

327

Cleveland in a 1944 LNG accidental explosion. Looking at it another way, an LNG tanker has more than five times the energy contained in the bomb dropped on Hiroshima."

"How do you know all this? I take it you have some prior history with LNG tankers and Boston Harbor?"

"The City of Boston after 9/11 sued the Coast Guard, claiming this program was not safe. They got nowhere. The federal court ruled that only the US Coast Guard had authority over traffic in the harbor and the City of Boston had no say at all. The Coast Guard for years maintained the shipments were perfectly safe and the matter was well under their control. No questions need be asked. Those were their marching orders from the administration and it was their only position for years. No matter who produced an expert as to the dangers, the Coast Guard or the energy company produced their experts who just happened to arrive at the opposite conclusion."

"So that is why you are prejudiced?"

"I am prejudiced because these monster ships pass within 250 yards of my front door. My research led me to conclude that, originally, the Coast Guard science and security assessments included assumptions that were not fact based. It was and currently is the position of the Boston Fire Department that the LNG tankers are a serious threat to the public and they are incapable of putting out an LNG tanker fire. Now, the Coast Guard says things a little bit differently than they did a few years back. Now they tell the neighborhood they have mounted the best security plan possible, but if citizens are displeased they should take it up with their elected representatives, not the Coast Guard. This is a political problem. I personally have heard them say they have "mitigated" the potential dangers to the LNG but there are, of course, no guarantees. You might ask if allowing the LNG tankers to transit Boston Harbor is such a great idea, why is Boston the only place in the country where these ships are allowed to traffic in such a dense, confined, and populated public space?"

"You mean blow up?" said Baker.

"Well that is a word some would use. But that may not be exactly what happens. If only one ship hold is breached it might not blow up, to use a general term. What can happen is the lighter than water LNG would float unmixed, and if ignited would burn very quickly at immensely high temperatures. These high temperatures would prohibit any type of fire suppression. No one will get near the ship. Once ignited, the floating LNG fire would reach to the surrounding docks and buildings. If one hold is breached with a ten square yard hole above the water line, the hold would be mostly emptied and the LNG portion of the fire would be over in three-

and-a-half minutes. No one would have a chance to react. It is the incredible heat from this initial fire that will cause surrounding incineration.

Multiply this effect by five times if all five holds are penetrated. You can imagine why the fires would incinerate everything for a half mile around and additionally ignite anything or anybody within its range. No one knows what impact the escaping LNG at a minus 260 degrees would impose on the rest of the ship. How would the rapidly leaking frozen gas interact with an existing fire? Would the ships metal structure be corrupted by the frozen LNG and become brittle? It is all theoretical science at that point but I will tell you now, if that ship gets breached and a fire starts, it will not be good for anything within at least one mile.

Baker looked at Fisher. "Where is the LNG on the potential target list?"

Fisher answered, "Well it is always there. All the cities in North America that I know of have LNG tankers offload away from populated areas. Not here in Boston. I know they were trying to get permission to bring LNG tankers into Fall River. That effort is being blocked successfully by various state and federal politicians as well as multiple government agencies, including those on the federal side that have approved or supported the LNG transiting Boston Harbor. That makes no sense to me, but I have heard no explanation for the same people holding opposite positions for two different locations."

"Where is it on the list of targets?" Baker repeated with less patience.

"Same place it has always been since 9/11. The Coast Guard says the shipments are safe, one has never blown up, and they have a security plan. They claim to be the experts in this area, not us. The EPA, DOE, Justice, none has raised the issue except for the City of Boston and the local public that live in the area. They got no place. Now it seems everyone has agreed it should not be allowed in Fall River, and that is certainly much less populated than Boston Harbor. I guess it is who you want to believe."

Baker was not satisfied with Fisher's response. He asked Patrick, "If these LNG tankers are so dangerous, why are they allowed in the harbor?"

Patrick answered, "When the general public is told their homes will go cold in the winter for lack of gas or the cost of heating will skyrocket, whether true or not, they listen through their pocketbooks. If they do not live within a couple miles of the harbor, it is not their fight. The thought of an area for a mile or two around the harbor lying in ashes is the type of thought one tends to push to the less active side of the brain for later consideration."

What about the elected officials? Where do they stand?" asked Baker.

Patrick responded, "The mayor has vociferously opposed and even sued the federal government to halt the LNG tankers. He lost. The governors since 9/11 have been of the same party as the sitting President, and that is so today. They do not seem eager to go against the administration or to opine on a controversial issue where neither the public nor the media demands they take a position."

"Where are the US senators and congressmen on the issue?"

Patrick sighed a bit and then answered. "I don't recall a sitting senator taking a position on the LNG tankers in Boston Harbor. When it comes to the new project for LNG in Fall River, somehow they are opposed. A few congressmen whose districts could be negatively impacted have spoken against the LNG tankers in Boston Harbor, but none has sought the mantle of leadership necessary to keep this issue on the front burner to stop them. You tell me how federal and state agencies can oppose Fall River and at the very same time remain silent on Boston Harbor?"

Patrick paused, and then continued. "What really seems to have happened was after 9/11 the President got whatever he wanted when the words 'national security' were used. He said that tankers were needed for the national energy policy. He said the Coast Guard could and would protect these tankers from terrorists. At the time, the LNG pipeline and offload facility at sea had not been approved. Now it has not only been approved, it has been constructed and is now in use by other LNG suppliers. We are left with a unique situation where one foreign company owns an energy plant they converted to gas, they own the ships that bring in the LNG and own the gas production. They control that entire process from production to delivery. They don't seem to want to lose profits through a shared pipeline. Lastly, it is to their economic advantage to use gas supplied exclusively from their own source of production. In effect, it seems to me, the LNG tankers are protected and sponsored by the US government. The Coast Guard is not reimbursed for its costs in protecting the LNG tanker. Little wonder the company is not anxious to spend corporate profits to construct a dedicated LNG gas line from an offshore site, across sea and land, to their current offload site."

"I guess I don't understand that if a tanker creates a danger of destroying the heart of the City of Boston, why isn't there more vocal opposition?"

"Neither do I" said Patrick. "When things have gone wrong, like a couple of LNG tankers have lost power at sea and had to be rescued from drifting by the Coast Guard, the media will revisit the dangers of the LNG tankers. Then the news cycle shortly changes to another topic and the situation goes on. There is no staying power to the story without political leadership and an identifiable threat. It is like changing a piece of bad legislation. Often it takes an emergency to activate the collective will to make the change necessary. In Fall River, it is clear that a number of federal agencies and some of the same politicians have in fact opposed LNG tankers crossing under the Braga Bridge and entering the city to unload. No one seems willing or interested to apply that same thinking to what already exists here in Boston, where the unloading takes place under the Tobin Bridge."

Baker just shook his head.

"Don't worry," said Patrick. "It's human nature in action. Until there is a fire or terrorist attack on an LNG tanker, the public will won't be able to overcome the political and economic resistance to change. If the heart of Boston lay in ashes, people will ask why their leaders allowed this to happen. We can't just walk away and say 'Let's see if The Engineer wants to blow up an LNG tanker in Boston Harbor.' We need to stop him whatever he is planning. It may be ironic that in doing so we protect the status quo."

"I am meeting with the JTTF at 6:30 pm and specifically asked the heads of the state police and the Boston PD to come. Hopefully the mayor and the governor will have their own representatives present. I will see what the view is towards an LNG tanker as a possible target."

"If you decide you would like to hear a viewpoint other than from the status quo adherents, I will set up a meeting for you with the mayor. If you determine the LNG tankers do not merit any additional discussion or planning, would you let me know? It is an issue I intend to discuss with the mayor. I realize there are many possible targets in Boston. Some in the JTTF will feel strongly about other possible targets. The mayor may wish to put his own security plan in place until this threat is resolved. Meanwhile, I will see what can be done with Vespa."

"I will ask Crowley to call you after the meeting. Thanks for coming by Mark."

As Patrick walked across City Hall Plaza, he could not help but think about those in science and government who pronounced nuclear power plants to be completely safe. Their historical safety record "proved" the point. Plant age did not matter with modern and well documented maintenance plans. All was well and any voice of dissent was mocked. Then Chernobyl happened. Fukushima Daiichi happened in Japan. Were humans even capable of learning from their past experiences? Patrick wondered.

Chapter 88

Baker wanted a few moments alone to gather his thoughts, but that was not to be.

US Attorney John White was calling. "Harvey Bottom was just in complaining that you've relieved Phil Kirby from his terrorism duties. He questions your action as I do. I thought I'd ask you why?"

"What did Bottom say were my reasons?"

"He says you don't like Kirby. You hold Kirby's friendship with Bottom against him because Bottom challenged your friend Patrick in court."

"I see. Did he mention that within a few hours of my arrival in Boston a news reporter called asking why I was here? Did Bottom explain to you that he thought the governor and the mayor should not be told of the current state of the threat against this city? And while you mention Patrick, did you discuss with the DOJ or the Director how Bottom's actions in subpoenaing Patrick negatively impacted the entire investigative process that was in place. And since Mr. Bottom seems to like going public, without coordination with anyone else, does he understand how critical it is for there to be no public discussion at present about the recent events in New York and Boston. If The Engineer knows we are active in Boston, he may take off and we will have nothing. Lastly, is Bottom really your employee or does he report to someone else in the Department?"

"What are you getting at?"

"Ask Bottom with whom he was meeting early this afternoon on the north side of King's Wharf Hotel. Ask Bottom if my name came up in that conversation. Also ask Bottom where this same reporter got inside information that appeared in print during the court hearings involving Patrick. After you have your answers, call me back. We can decide if we need to call the DOJ Inspector General and the FBI Office of Professional Responsibility and request an immediate investigation. If word leaks out and The Engineer gets away, someone will go to jail for that leak," said Baker with a voice that carried even more depth than his words. "I promise you that. Kirby suggested I should accommodate Bottom's desires because he has friends at DOJ that can help my career. Has Bottom made that offer to you?"

White agreed to speak with Bottom immediately.

Patrick walked from the FBI office to Franklin Wharf and went up to the condo. He opened the patio door and moved both chairs to the left side of the patio. "We shall see," he said to himself.

Patrick went to his desk and started writing out his thoughts while fresh in his mind. One sheet contained his ideas for when he talked with Vespa. Another sheet was for a discussion with the mayor about what the City of Boston might do about the LNG tankers. The third sheet was for conversation he wanted to have with Maha Soufan. He did not like to interfere, but he had his own ideas about tracing The Engineer in Boston. If the FBI chose not to put more confidence in Soufan, that was their choice. He realized his focus had narrowed because of his beliefs about the LNG tankers, but he also believed in exploring all possibilities. That was what he was willing to do with the help of others. Writing out his thoughts helped Patrick to focus his thinking.

Liz came home. She stuck her head in the door. "Would you like a cup of tea?"

"He would, thank you. Perhaps you could find a wayward cookie to go with the tea?"

A few minutes later Patrick emerged from his desk and sat at the dining table with Liz. They had not caught up in a while and he wanted to run some things by her. They started talking over tea and Patrick brought her up to date. The more he talked, the more of a concerned look she had on her face.

"How many times have we sat out on the deck when the LNG tanker came through and talked about how it could be attacked? Now, maybe, it's for real. If al-Qaeda is looking for raw materials in place to boost their ability to destroy, there could be no better target."

Patrick just nodded and munched his cookie.

Baker started the 6:30 meeting with the JTTF. He was informed Bottom was not there. The governor and the mayor sent their chiefs of staff. Both the governor and the mayor had earlier in the afternoon requested and been given their own briefings by Crowley. Tonight they sent their chiefs of staff for the details. Baker asked Crowley and Fisher to give the group an update on tracing The Engineer to Boston and the recovery of armaments in New York. While the meeting was ongoing he called the JTTF in New York and spoke with the duty agent.

There was another development regarding The Engineer. The agents and detectives from NYPD went through the neighborhood where the fire extinguisher was recovered looking for security video cameras. They found one that showed The Engineer walking the street carrying a black bag that appears to have some weight in it. This was only a brief exposure and they were still checking more cameras. Right now it looked like The Engineer carried the second fire extinguisher out of the storage cubicle."

"When?" asked Baker.

"It was less than forty-eight hours before we raided the storage facility. We just missed him."

"But it was after he purchased the phones in Boston. He must have presumably delivered the phones to Salah. I'll guess he took some other things with him when he left. Let me know if you learn anymore."

Baker was almost convinced that the second fire extinguisher came to Boston. He could not prove it, but in his heart he knew it.

Within two hours of Patrick moving the patio chairs, Vespa called Patrick's cell phone.

"You wished to speak with me?"

"That was quick. Your eyes on me are pretty good." Vespa did not comment. "Have you seen the news from New York?"

"Yes. Did you get any radioactive material," asked Vespa.

Patrick thought for a moment, then said, "Yes, but not all."

"Where's The Engineer?"

"We don't know. Now can I play the investigator for a minute?"

Vespa chuckled. "Sorry. I was just curious."

"We think your city is safe for the time being."

"So, you assume I am in New York?"

"The thought has crossed my mind," said Patrick.

"How can I help?" asked Vespa.

"I'm not sure. The FBI seized a lot of explosives and weapons. We think there could be more weapons that are missing including some radioactive material. We have evidence of The Engineer's presence in Boston. It is very probable there is another terror cell here. We do not think we have a lot of time. Is there any way you can press your resources here or across the way? We would be looking for any form of a status report The Engineer might be sending back to the mountains after what happened in New York. I only emphasize the mountains because if The Engineer were to provide an interim report, especially after New York, that is where the report might be going. We are running out of time. We need to be aggressive. If there is any 'chatter' out there, we need to hear it now."

"There is always the chance that our affirmative efforts may raise more questions than we get answers. If you understand and can accept that possibility, we are willing to try."

"My former colleagues realize that risk and think it's the time to accept the risk."

"I will get back to you as soon as I can."

"Thank you."

Chapter 89

After Crowley and Fisher finished their briefing, Baker told the participants they would have two hundred more agents by morning. They would work out of the site in Charlestown. There was not enough room in the downtown office and it would avoid conversation about the sudden influx of agents.

Baker switched the subject to potential targets. The whole room came alive. Boston was full of historic sites that any terrorist would love to blow up in order to carry the attack to the American infidel and his government. There were a number of high tech companies in the area that contributed greatly to national defense. There were educational institutions that trained many of the country's leaders. It was the city that started the American Revolution, so why not take the fight directly to the foundation of American independence? A target list was available but the suggestion was you could throw a dart and where it landed would be as good as any other form of selection. Baker mentioned the LNG tanker and the groans started.

"That has been around for years. One has never been attacked. The ship will not blow up it will just catch fire. The Coast Guard has a net around that one. No one can get close to the ship. They shut the harbor down when the LNG comes in." The Coast Guard representative sat there without comment. which struck Baker as strange so he directed a question to him.

"Does the Coast Guard believe that these ships are safe to pass through the harbor? Do you regard the LNG as a high probability target?"

"One has never been the subject of a terrorist attack. We have a full security plan in place, including closing the harbor, a flotilla of police and Coast Guard boats surround the LNG, and we use the latest technology to monitor the shoreline from a chopper even during the night time. Besides, the federal court ruled in our favor years ago."

Baker thought the last comment was meant to end the discussion by the Coast Guard. "Didn't the court rule that the City of Boston had no jurisdiction over the LNG tankers and they were within the sole purview of the Coast Guard," asked Baker?

"Seems to me to be the same thing," the officer said smugly.

"Did you ever read the court opinion to know exactly what the court said? Has anyone in this room?"

No one answered, for no one had. Baker continued.

Did the court say the public was not in danger from these shipments?"

Again, no response. He took another tack.

"Is the helicopter armed?" asked Baker.

"That's classified," was the answer.

"What type of helicopter is used?"

"A two-seat observation copter." The answer was spoken before it had been thought out.

"Not much room for heavy firepower in that two seater, is there?" observed Baker.

"The security has a small cutter leading the parade and another larger one five hundred yards behind the LNG. There are two Coast Guard inflatables with 50 calibers mounted in the bow," countered the Coast Guard rep.

"Let me cut to the chase here. Would your current security plan cover one or multiple FGM-148 Javelins being fired on the LNG tanker from shore or from a boat in the harbor?"

Those in law enforcement turned towards those with a military background awaiting the answer. No one volunteered an answer. The room was silent. Baker looked at the Coast Guard officer with a raised eyebrow.

"No water craft traffic is allowed in the harbor during the LNG passage."

"I understand the rules but the harbor is narrow. It would only be 250 yards or so from the LNG to the shoreline on each side, Boston and East Boston. At the narrow points of the harbor, could a swift boat pull a surprise attack in such short distance? What would happen if multiple Javelins were fired from shore at the same time? What if they were on a boat docked or anchored? What are your orders about firing your military weapons in a civilian environment?"

"Look, no one has ever said there was no danger. The answer is we believe we have the potential danger reduced to within reasonable limits. We prefer to say we have done everything possible to mitigate any potential attack. That does not mean we can absolutely defend every form of possible attack. We have done what we have been asked to do. Whether it should be done at all, or not, is a question to be directed to those in the administration who gave the Coast Guard this mission."

"Is the Coast Guard LNG security plan regularly reviewed against new intelligence?" asked Baker.

No answer.

"I am just trying to understand the facts," said Baker. "I am not looking to point fingers. We have some indication this group has access to Javelins. I am told they are pretty nasty and can turn a T-72 tank into a hole in the ground with a little scrap metal scattered here and there." Heads in the audience nodded. "If they had one, or more than one, and fired it or them broadside at an LNG, what would it do to the vessel? Blow it up? Cause a fire? Freeze the ship's deck metal to a brittle point? What?"

No answers were forthcoming. Baker thanked everyone for their attention.

Baker went back to the Boston office. There was a message to call USA John White. He didn't have the time or the inclination to be distracted by this baloney with Bottom. Baker put in a call to Wilkins who was at home. He in turn patched in Director Simms. Baker gave them an update about the second fire extinguisher possibly being in the black bag. He thought they should assume that The Engineer had more radioactive material, more C-4 or Semtex, some heavy duty machine guns, field arms, and anti-tank weapons such as the older Dragons or Javelins. Baker passed on Patrick's concerns about the LNG tanker. Baker explained in detail the conversation at the JTTF meeting. Simms picked up on this immediately and said he would put in a call directly to the Coast Guard commandant to get an update on the LNG security plan and have that run by others in the FBI and DOD for another view. They needed to know what the Javelin could do to an LNG tanker. They might need to ask the President to order a stop to the LNG deliveries at least for a short period.

Wilkins then said, "I had a strange call from USA John White about you standing down Kirby and questioning that Bottom might be leaking to the press."

"What was the point of the call? What did he want you to do?" asked Baker.

"He did not say exactly which struck me as odd. He seemed to hint everyone should kiss and make up in this time of need."

Baker explained what Kirby had told him about Bottom and what Patrick observed at King's Wharf. "I asked White to let me know if he would join in a request for an OPR and DOJ inquiry. I'm waiting for his answer. I also told him I want Bottom to take a polygraph about conversations he may or may not have had with Bell. We cannot afford a leak now, and I do not have time for dealing with ego maniacs."

Wilkins said he would have Kirby summoned to FBIHQ first thing in the morning for an interview. Wilkins would also call White back about a formal inquiry on the news leaks. If that effort produced no useful results, Wilkins would speak with the DOJ Inspector General tonight to have Bottom formally interviewed in the morning.

At this point Simms stepped into the conversation. "Over the weekend, the DOJ Inspector General notified the AG that Bottom was instigating at both DOJ and Homeland Security to have the IG conduct a formal criminal investigation of Patrick and his relationship with the Sicilian Mafia. The IG heard this from a number of people within DOJ and even some at Homeland Security. The commonly expressed fear is that Bottom is acting irrationally and may be having some sort of breakdown. Bottom is calling these people constantly, ostensibly, to update them on The Engineer investigation even before their formal briefings here in DC Each time Bottom harangues the recipient about Patrick's contact with Vespa. Bottom will be addressed today and Kirby will be ordered to FBIHQ immediately by me for interview and polygraph. The AG and I have no intention of letting Bottom or Kirby remain anywhere near the investigation. They will be under 'house arrest' so to speak until this investigation is resolved. There is no more either of you need to do regarding Bottom and Kirby and I don't want you discussing this with anyone. Is all of this clear?"

It was.

When the call ended, Baker realized how tired he really was. The phone rang. It was

John White. He immediately started talking about how people should get along especially in difficult times. Kirby was a good man and should not be shut out of the ongoing process. Certainly White would rely upon Bottom's advice.

Mindful of his just concluded conversation with the Director and Wilkins, Baker said nothing and just let While ramble on about everyone getting along. Baker then excused himself from further conversation saying he had a slight emergency to address.

Now Baker was more than just tired, he was also pissed. He also had a great deal more respect for the complexity of the job Simms was required to perform.

Chapter 90

Talat Mehmood and The Engineer were in The Engineer's motel room off the Southeast Expressway. They had a detailed map of Boston Harbor spread out on the bed.

"Let's review the assignments given to each two-person team starting with team number one," said The Engineer.

"Team one has a passenger van that has been loaded with one hundred pounds of Semtex surrounded by projectile material. They do not have the special canister yet. They have the detonators and the cell phone to trigger the detonators. They will make the final connection of the detonators just before they park the van at the airport. One team member will drive the van, park it, and activate the timer. That member will be picked up by the second team member in a car. I have the cell telephone number to detonate the device if the timer should fail.

'What are their parking instructions at the airport?"

"They will use the garage closest to the airport tower and park the van as close to the tower as possible. They will back the van into the space to direct the blast back toward the airport tower. They will put your canister next to the Semtex."

"What will they do next?" asked The Engineer.

"They will drive to the designated area in East Boston between the old, unused piers and the park. They will take the two Javelins from the trunk along with two MP40 automatic pistols and proceed to the area previously selected. The tanker should be at the desired location shortly after they arrive. They will be ready to launch the two Javelins when the LNG tanker reaches the location just south of the tunnels under the harbor. Each will bring a radio and cell phones to be in contact with us."

"Describe their specific point of aim?" asked The Engineer.

"The missiles are set for a top-attack flight profile and will rise above the height of the tanker when first fired. They then turn and descend onto holds three and four, striking them from the top. Immediately after firing both Javelin missiles the team will leave the launchers and return to their vehicle to make their escape on Route 1 North."

"What about the vehicles?"

"They stole the wallet of an acquaintance, used his license and credit card to rent the vehicles for two weeks, and then returned the wallet before the owner knew it was missing. They intend to drop the vehicle in Revere upon leaving East Boston and pick up their own vehicle at that point."

"It is unlikely they will ever leave East Boston. The Javelins will ignite the LNG tanker and the team will be consumed by the heat from the fire. They will be martyrs."

Mehmood merely nodded agreement slowly.

"Do you have any concerns about their ability to properly launch the two missiles?"

"No. Both have military training and have fired various anti-tank weapons. They have reviewed all the firing instructions. The lock-on before launch infrared automatic self-guidance system is familiar to them. They have also met with the other firing teams to review the firing procedures. There is agreement on how to do it. Like 9/11, they can do it on the first effort."

"How will they sequence the firing?"

"They are prepared to fire at the same time. These missiles fire with a 'soft launch arrangement' meaning the rocket motors ignite after they reach a safe distance from the operator. This makes it harder for anyone to detect the location of the shooter. They will just drop the launchers and walk away before the missile even hits the target."

"Are we using the top-attack flight profile with the other teams?"

"No. Per your instructions, only the two missiles fired from East Boston will use the top-attack profile. The other shooters will use the direct-attack profile aiming at the holds above the water line."

"Okay. We will get to them in a few moments. How will they get the missiles to the firing point without the weapons being seen? They have to walk across the park?"

"The missile and case together weigh about forty pounds, are forty-eight inches long and about six inches wide. They are being carried in duffle bags of that size."

"Where are they now?"

"The missiles have been distributed to each team. It is their responsibility to safely store them. I do know this team stored theirs in the trunk of the car, but I don't know where the car is. The ignition in the car has a kill switch."

"Tell me now about the instructions to team two."

"Team two examined various firing positions starting with the park at the end of King's Wharf. That is a location where the Boston Police park a cruiser when the LNG tanker comes in. I have seen it staffed with one or two officers. It makes little difference, as they only sit inside the police car with blue lights on. They don't even get out to look around. We could neutralize them quite easily, but it is not worth the effort. There are plenty of other good firing positions that require no special action."

"So, what did you decide?"

"Well, we had planned on using the yacht club just south of City Wharf. They could use the Harbor Walk to the rear of the club and fire from there. We could also use a boat on their docks as a firing platform. There are some rooms at the top of the club for rent. We thought it a perfect place until we realized we need to account for the forward motion of the tanker after it is hit. When at sea under full power, it takes five miles to bring an LNG tanker to a halt. Of course the tanker, while in the harbor, is under the control and power of the tug boats. It still requires some time for it to stop. It we want to have it sink over the tunnels, we needed to move team two slightly north so we are using the parking lot at City Wharf. It will put them a little closer to team three, but in the end we think the missiles fired in unison will cause so much destruction the tanker will stop its forward motion or run aground over the tunnels."

"Tell me about City Wharf."

"It is now used as a parking lot. It is bound on two sides by the Harbor Walk. The main entrance and egress is on Commercial Street. There are people around all hours of the day and night. If the helicopter has infrared detectors to pick up human images in the dark, this is a place where people will not stand out. They will operate out of a van with side sliding doors parked parallel to the water. They can open the opposing doors and fire from inside the van, or they can step out and fire. There is minimal back blast with these missiles especially if they open the doors on the other side of the van. The distance from where they will park to the side of the tanker is less than three hundred yards. This is the narrowest part of the harbor and the distance is the same for most of the firing area from both sides of the harbor.

"What is the point of aim for team two?"

"One team member will fire at hold number one, just forward of the stern at a point just above the water line. The second team member will fire amidships just above the water line. Since team one will be firing top-attack profiles, we wanted to make sure we had another round in the middle at the water line. This will create a tremendous stress on the middle structure of the tanker. We have been advised that missiles in this sequence may cause the entire ship structure to fail. The real unknown is what happens to the metal of the ship when it comes into contact with the leaking LNG at minus 260 degrees. If the metal turns brittle, the whole structure might fail, but no one can tell us for sure. We will just have to wait and see."

"What is team two's escape plan?"

"They will drop the launchers, get back into the van and exit the parking lot. They intend to drive south on Commercial Street away from the fire. They will take Commercial Street to the Surface Artery, then to a parking lot in Chinatown where they will abandon the van. The van is stolen, but has license plates not yet reported stolen. They will have one of their own cars at the parking lot in Chinatown."

"They also will probably not survive the fire," said The Engineer flatly and without emotion.

Mehmood this time just looked at him.

"Are they carrying small arms?"

"Each team carries the same small arms."

"How will the Coast Guard defenses negatively impact teams one and two?," asked The Engineer.

"We have reviewed the defenses together and individually by team. The results are the same. We do not think they are in a position to hinder us at all. We think that all the teams can get their missiles off and move out before or just as they are hitting. The helicopter does not appear to have any armaments. If it is using infrared at night, our people will be in places where people are normally found at that time of night. Night vision equipment will not help them for the same reason."

"What about the Coast Guard boats guarding the tanker? Are there any changes? Let's go over that again."

"There will be anywhere from eight to twelve boats accompanying the LNG tanker as part of the Coast Guard flotilla. None is of any real consequence to our plans. The formation is always the same. Four hundred-fifty yards ahead of the tanker is a small Coast Guard cutter as the lead ship. It has a small cannon but we have not seen it manned during the mission. Just ahead of the tanker are boats of the Massachusetts State Police and the Boston Police. Neither of these boats has any observable outside weapons. You just saw them on our trip to Charlestown. I will say more about that in a minute. These boats can be fifty to seventy-five yards away from the tanker. Directly on the bow of the tanker on both the port and starboard are two tugs each providing the control and forward motion."

"Are there any other tugs?"

"There is a third tug off the starboard side that does not appear to be involved until they turn the tanker around just before the Tobin Bridge. There is a fourth, larger tug just astern of the tanker that holds a line to the stern of the LNG tanker. This appears to be the brakes of the operation, so to speak. This accounts for all the tugs."

"Go on."

"Amidships on both the port and starboard sides and immediately next to the tanker is one Coast Guard inflatable, which appears to have a 50-caliber machine gun mounted in the bow. Again, we have never seen the weapon manned during the operation. Even if it is loaded, they still need time to get to it."

The Engineer thought about the arrogance of not manning these weapons and smiled.

"About seventy-five yards from the tanker on the port and starboard sides, just after the tanker's stern, are two more police boats. They are small craft, again from the state police, Boston police or environmental police. These boats have no observable weapons. We do not see the four police boats having any impact on the teams firing missiles."

"What about the large Coast Guard cutter. What about that one?"

"It is about 287-feet long and has a large cannon mounted on the bow. More importantly, it seems to be the only craft with a lot of electronic gear. We are assuming they may be able to shut down our cell phones, but only after they realize they are under attack. We still have our radios. I personally think our attack will be over before they even get a chance to start jamming communications. This ship is always behind the flotilla by at least four hundred yards. By the time it sees the smoke, or hears the noise, it will be too late."

"What about local police along the shoreline?"

"We have walked the Harbor Walk and followed the tanker coming in by foot. We have seen the Boston police sitting in their car with the blue lights on at King's Wharf Park. We have seen lights on a police cruiser in East Boston on a road that goes near the water. Sometimes there is a cruiser parked just south of City Wharf, but we have seen this only during daylight hours. We have never seen any undercover police or signs of police in unmarked vehicles. It seems they park their cars with the blue lights on so people will see them and assume they have protection. From our standpoint they are not even a factor in our planning. We feel free to roam the area as our needs dictate."

"Why do you think their security is not up to the task of protecting the tanker?" The Engineer had heard the answer before but knew it gave great courage and comfort to Mehmood and his teams to repeat their explanations. It did them good to have their confidence at a high level just before the attack.

"The Coast Guard is a quasi-military force operating in a very dense civilian area. What are they going to do? Fire their cannon into civilian, residential or business areas, at a target they will never see. The Coast Guard inflatable boats will require someone to leave the pilot cabins to activate the weapons, assuming they are loaded. Now what are they going to fire at? People walking along the Harbor Walk? Will they shoot at people in their apartments looking out the window? They cannot fire into a civilian population. No, it will be over and done before they realize the attack started. "

"The police boats must have a role that perhaps you don't see?"

"We think they are only for show and to keep civilian boats from interfering with the harbor transit of the tanker. To the uninformed, it may look like security, but it is not. They have no weapons of substance and they cannot fire at civilians! They will never see a terrorist. They never fire their guns except in extreme circumstances and only when they have a well identified target that is recognizable as an immediate threat. Their first notice of attack will be when they hear or see the actual missile strike, and by that time all missiles will have been launched. Their electronics will not give them any real advantage in responding. That part of the attack is over. By the time they begin to understand the attack is taking place, and get over the flash bang effect, team four will be in motion. If there is not already a fire of immense proportions, there soon will be."

"Okay, we need to review teams three and four."

Chapter 91

When the phone rang, Patrick thought it was the middle of the night. He looked at the clock and it was 6:30 am. He had slept well.

"I do have some news but I don't know how valuable it is," said Vespa.

"That was quick," said Patrick.

"As it turns out, our contacts had enough curiosity to act on their own. After hearing the news about the recovery in New York, they anticipated a call from me. They decided to ask the poppy people, who originally contacted them, if there was an opportunity for more shipping business.

They were told that while they understood some adverse activity to the interests of their friends had occurred both in Palermo and in New York City, their friends did not have any immediate needs. They implied that the person receiving the material was out of contact but that, if needed, he has a means of re-supply, which he has not made any effort to access. The poppy people, however, wanted to insure that the door remained open for future business. They admitted it was al-Qaeda doing the shipping and they expected some important success in the immediate future, which would trigger further shipping needs and business for all."

"Translated, using what we know, it appears your friends think The Engineer still has enough equipment for his mission and people to use it?"

"Yes, but you missed something. While not entirely clear, it seems the possibility exists that The Engineer has another source of weapons supply inside the US to call upon if needed."

"You're right," said Patrick. "I missed that. It could be just another underground arms dealer. However, it holds the possibility of another al-Qaeda cell. Wonderful. Why is The Engineer out of contact? Do you have any idea?"

"My friends speculate that it is for security reasons. The plan has been approved. The Engineer has what he needs. To give status reports only endangers their security. There is another piece of information I want to bring to your attention."

"Please, go ahead," Said Patrick.

"We have some friends in the European financial world who study their markets to advise us on potential investment opportunities. I told you we were mostly almost legitimate."

Patrick chuckled out loud. He could not help it.

"You may have heard that just before 9/11, there was divesting of airline stock by some believed to act on behalf of al-Qaeda investment interests."

"Yes," said Patrick.

"We previously asked a financial advisor of ours to keep an eye on the European stock markets as those are the markets they used before 9/11. We requested they report any significant movement by anyone that might be tied to al-Qaeda financial movements given the 9/11 history."

"You got something?" asked Patrick.

"First thing this trading day in Europe, several investment entities started shorting the stock of a European conglomerate that ships LNG from the Caribbean to the US. We also hear this company just got another big contract to ship LNG from Yemen to the US. This is not a stock one would think of shorting given the strength of their existing contracts."

Patrick was stunned. Could it be this obvious, he asked himself?

"Are we talking big numbers?" asked Patrick.

"Let's put it this way, they had a very sizeable bet on this company going long, which they just totally reversed with this short move."

Vespa gave Patrick the details of the transactions so US investigators could view the data themselves and monitor the stock for further changes.

"Do you have any friends that might be able to help us locate The Engineer if he is in Boston?"

"I am afraid not. None of our friends want to have dealings with any family members in Boston. They feel it would be like talking directly to the FBI. Who knows what would get out if they were asked to do a favor?"

"If you hear anything more, please let me know. We are assuming The Engineer is in Boston with an active cell and equipment at his disposal. We just don't know the target or when they may strike. Your information helps a lot, though."

"If this matter concludes in a way not made public, will you let me know? We have people to thank," said Maria.

"Yes, I will," said Patrick.

"Was Vespa helpful?" asked a not fully awake Liz.

"Yes. There is a belief The Engineer is still going forward despite his losses. There could be an al-Qaeda supply cell in the US. The Engineer has explosives, possibly some Javelin missiles, and radioactive material. He was last known to be in Boston and I would say the situation is far from good. Someone may be shorting the LNG company stock on the European market for no good reason. We need something good to happen for our side, and soon."

Patrick set up coffee with Vince Baker in Government Center for 7:30 am.

Vince Baker was on the phone getting a morning briefing before his meeting with Patrick. The added manpower was on duty and available in Charlestown. The JTTF in New York had no new data. The trail was going cold and no one under arrest was talking. The great electronic surveillance mechanisms for the US government still were not picking up any information of value. He wondered how many ways the electronic intelligence community had to say the same thing. We hear nothing. We have no information. The less they heard, the more they wanted to tell you how good their equipment was, what areas they covered, and perhaps ask if you could be wrong in your threat assessment because they are not hearing about it!

Baker's call with Bob Wilkins did not help much. The Coast Guard was standing by their protection plan for the LNG tankers and saw no need, based on current available data, to halt LNG shipments. They did not claim their protection could not be penetrated, but cited the lack of a specific threat and again noted the fact no tanker had ever been attacked. As far as what damage a Javelin missile, or multiples thereof, might do to the structure of a tanker, they suggested the FBI conduct its own engineering and damage assessment study. As far as being able to put a fire out on an LNG tanker, the Coast Guard said that would be the responsibility of the Boston Fire Department. Wilkins said it was like going in circles talking with them. Maybe Patrick would have something to tell him?

Patrick and Baker met at the coffee shop on the mall behind One Center Plaza. Each had wanted to meet without others in attendance so they could speak their minds and do a little brainstorming. Patrick passed on what Vespa had to say. The Engineer was not in contact with his own people. It appeared that only a few at the top of al-Qaeda knew of The Engineer's plans.

Then Patrick told Baker about the LNG tanker company having their stock shorted by investors purportedly tied to al-Qaeda.

"Post 9/11 there were some who believed al-Qaeda had their investment arms short the stock of US passenger airlines. When the records were reviewed it was supposedly not clear at all that this was the case, but the rumor never died. I'll get this to FBIHQ immediately so they can get a full market analysis done and see if other agencies have any resources that are aware of this movement."

"What about finding The Engineer in Boston now?" asked Patrick.

"I have two hundred agents in Charlestown. We have willing partners in other agencies. I have no suggestions of what to do next other than flood the airways with The Engineer's picture. You have any ideas?"

"Raising the public threat assessment level is a waste of time. No one even talks about it except the anonymous voice at the airport. It's always the same. Orange. Without intelligence it is impossible to be proactive. You almost have to wait for them to attack. But before making The Engineer a wanted public figure, and giving him a chance to lead from a bunker, there is something else I would consider."

"I'm listening," said Baker.

"If you're buying I'll take another coffee and a doughnut."

"This is blackmail," said Baker.

"No, it's extortion. You have your crimes mixed up."

"Okay. I'm buying. Fire away."

"In New York, most targets were related to transportation. An airport tower, two tunnels, two train stations, and the GW Bridge were on the menu. Suppose we continue that same thinking in Boston. You had good results from using facial recognition software comparing The Engineer's photo to security camera recordings. It even worked for his purchase of cell phones in Boston. Boston is not London where they have cameras all over the city specifically dedicated to police use. Here, we have to physically find relevant security cameras, contact the owners, and get permission to download their data. Why don't you start collecting security camera images from all the transportation centers in Boston? Download them to a common database and see if you can get a hit? You have South Station for Amtrak and MBTA. South Station is also a major bus terminal. North Station is commuter rail for everything going north. The state police can help you with internal and external cameras at Logan Airport. The transit police can be helpful for the MBTA system to see if he is riding it."

"Keep that thought going. Why are the targets transportation-related? What does it mean?"

"The whole point of 9/11, and choosing the World Trade Center as the target, besides instilling fear, was to attack the American economy through its symbols. Our economy requires our citizens to move about. They have to commute to work. After 9/11, the majority of businesses in lower Manhattan had to move to alternate locations. Just think, if they had been successful in New York last week, no one would be commuting there to work this week."

"That's for sure," noted Baker.

Patrick continued, "When economists talk about the health of the American economy, they all predicate their comments by saying 'if there is no terrorist attack'. They understand how an attack can derail a rebounding economy. Apply those same thoughts to Boston. I keep thinking how al-Qaeda needs to reassert itself as the biggest badass around. They need to make a statement now. They need a big score. They need to rally their troops worldwide. For years now they have done nothing and have been getting their butts kicked. Their leadership is being marginalized. Perhaps their benefactors want more for their money than supporting a group hiding in caves in remote corners of the earth. Those bastards are introducing radioactive material into the fray. That is a big step. We need to think big!"

"So we start pulling video at the transportation hubs in Boston," Baker asked to confirm Patrick's suggestion.

"I would do it for any location connected to public transportation. You have nothing else to do. It is a potentially productive way to occupy your agents until something better comes along."

Baker nodded affirmatively.

"Can you imagine al-Qaeda's reaction when The Engineer explained that twice a week the US Coast Guard actually escorts a vessel into Boston Harbor that contains energy equal to five Hiroshima bombs? You think that would interest these delusional excuses of human beings? They have a lot of time to sit in a cave and think about how to achieve their goal of killing four million Americans. These people are not dumb. They have calculated with more certainty than we have just what a Javelin can do against an LNG tanker. Maybe that is why they wanted the Javelins, but not in New York. They needed them in Boston."

Patrick finally stopped talking. His second doughnut was in front of him uneaten. His coffee was getting cold. Baker said nothing at this point. He was deep in thought.

Patrick's reflection turned inward during the present silence at the table. After he finished his last words, spoken in a rush, Patrick suddenly felt awkward. He had no proof or evidence to back up what he was thinking. He was not a trained analyst who reads worldwide intelligence reports to mine them for significant data nuggets. He was just a retired FBI agent from a different epoch. He thought he was beginning to sound like what he never wanted to be, an old fart, out of his place in time, but who could not let go. He always said that when he retired he would never be that way. No claw marks on the wall for him. A clean break it would be. Why was he doing this? A moment later he began munching his extorted doughnut with a slight smile.

This was his backyard and he knew it well. This was his neighborhood. These were his friends, his co-workers and associates who might be subject to attack. It was getting personal, very personal. Patrick was not inclined to listen to bureaucratic bullshit passing for intelligent analysis. His mind was not cluttered with all the current theories and administrative baloney. He didn't have a dog in the intelligence race. He was not looking to protect or improve a career. He had spent a lot of time since 9/11 thinking about this potential problem. He was not winging it. He did know what he was talking about. He always had the ability to think like an opponent. One of the biggest compliments ever paid him was from a mob boss, who said regretfully, "You think like we do."

Baker finally told Patrick what the Coast Guard had to say about delaying the LNG tankers.

Patrick responded "I believe their thinking is lazy. Almost any defense can be penetrated. They seem only now to acknowledge this. I could sit on my balcony and fire a Javelin into the side of this tanker that is less than 250 yards from my face and no one can stop me. A terrorist could commandeer any number of apartments along the waterfront and do the same thing. All the police and Coast Guard boats cannot stop this type of attack, so any discussion about helicopters and cutters and police boats is simply not applicable to the potential at hand. In fact, they are irrelevant to the discussion. If one or more Javelins are fired at the LNG tanker, they will hit their target. Right now the Coast Guard has not told the FBI what will happen to the tanker if that occurs. Will it blow up? Will the ship's metal fail? Will there be a fire that will ignite everything for a mile and no one can put out?"

Baker shifted the subject by returning to the original subject and asking, "Should we put The Engineer's face on TV and start the manhunt?"

Patrick responded, "You can do that. It may be the right thing to do. You have a lot of manpower to chase down all the sightings that will come in. Of course The Engineer may well be able to crawl into his hole. If you miss him, and if he has an active cell in the Boston area that you know nothing about, he may still be in a position to go forward with his plans using just the unknown cell members. He had a failure in Palermo, and now one in New York. He may be a little less patient about the next time."

"So then you would hold public display of the picture for now?"

Patrick paused and thought a few moments. "I would use that photo on a selective basis?"

"How do you mean?"

"I'm thinking about Crowley, me, and a BPD detective from Area A, taking a walk along the Boston waterfront from the Fort Point Chanel to the Charlestown Bridge. We have a picture of the engineer. The BPD detective and I know the people and places along this route. Crowley represents the FBI. We show the photo to some people who are around the waterfront and see a lot. There are parking lot attendants, concierges, condo building managers, coffee shop managers, people in the sailing centers and boat docks, for starters. Many of these places also have security cameras that could be checked. We show it and move on. That way there is no photo floating around for the media to pick up. We don't have to give a specific reason why we are looking for the individual in the photo. This will peak people's curiosity even more. We just show the photo. This is a person of interest in an investigation, whatever that means. Perhaps we mumble something about the recent attacks on women in the North End. We leave contact data for Crowley and the detective and request an immediate call if they see or recall anything."

Baker thought for a few moments as they each sipped their coffees.

"I wish there was something more we could do," said Baker.

"Of course you do, but the reality is the trail has gone cold. You have no leads and you have no intelligence about what these people are planning. You are left with creating your own leads in hopes of stumbling onto the trail again. The alternative is you do nothing and just sit and wait for them to act. Then you react. You will always be a step behind them because you have no informants among these terrorists. I hate to keep beating a dead horse, but that is really the sum total of the problem. It also will not be solved in the immediate future," said Patrick.

Baker agreed with Patrick's idea and arranged to have Crowley call him as soon as she returned to the office. Patrick again prodded Baker to check out the stock shorting activity that Vespa had detailed.

"This could really be indicative of and a precursor to a major attack. If the shorting is confirmed, perhaps even the Coast Guard would interpret the shorting as being evidence of an impending LNG attack."

Chapter 92

The Engineer and Mehmood finished their cups of tea and were ready to resume their review of the attack plans.

Mehmood started. "Teams three and four have been furnished all of the information we obtained from an asset we developed. He works for a company that services the outboard motors for the small Boston fire boat. He has access to the Marine unit. We know how many men are in the station for each shift. We know where the keys are kept for the small boat. We know how to operate the boat, and we know how to use and answer the fire department marine radios. We have monitored their channel for a while."

"How will you get in?"

"We have a copy of the key to the front door from our source. One of the team members will approach the station door dressed as a Boston police officer. If the door is open, he will walk in. If not, he will knock. If there is no response he will use the key. This team member will be armed with a silenced weapon and will immediately kill the two firemen we expect to find on duty. We will then control the Boston Fire Department Marine Unit at Merchants Wharf."

"When I walked by the other day, the door was open."

"Sometimes it is. At night it is closed. It is the best firing position on the waterfront at the narrowest part of the harbor. It is less than three hundred yards south of the entrance to the Coast Guard yard and only three buildings away."

The Engineer had seen this and was impatient for Mehmood to move on with the review.

"As soon as they control the space, one will monitor radio traffic and the other three will unload five hundred pounds of Semtex into the fire boat. To that they will add five of the canisters of your material. They will be wearing Boston Fire Department t-shirts and pants and will look like any work crew. The fire department personnel are often out of the station and walking about during good weather. The movement will not be suspicious. When the boat is loaded, team four will be ready to go at a moment's notice."

"Will they keep their uniforms on?"

"Yes, we want to keep up the illusion that they are firefighters right to the end. Neither the police nor Coast Guard boats in the LNG escort will fire at the fireboat on suspicion alone. Our fire boat will be emitting an electronic identification signal registered to the Boston Fire Department. It is a legitimate transponder giving off the correct data. When the boat comes out its docking slip, they will notify the Coast Guard they are heading to a reported boat fire by the Moakley Bridge. There should be no suspicion until they make the turn going toward the LNG tanker, which will be less than two hundred yards away! The Javelins already will have been fired and this boat will appear to be appropriately responding to assist the LNG tanker after the missiles have struck. By the time anyone can react and get permission to fire on a Boston fire boat, our martyrs will have completed their mission."

"Give it to me again in the actual sequence. You have jumped ahead," said The Engineer.

Mehmood summarized the situation again: "Once the boat is loaded, the martyrs of team four are on stand-by awaiting the order to start the engines, turn on the lights, and make the call to the Coast Guard that they are coming out of their slip. They will be passing by the LNG tanker enroute to a reported boat fire near the Moakley Bridge. Team three will be in the Marine unit station with the small overhead door open. They will have two Javelins ready to fire. When the LNG tanker is in front of City Wharf, all teams will fire a total of six Javelin missiles. There will be enough room for the LNG tanker to drift to a halt and sink over the tunnels. The fireboat with team four will already be out of the slip, but it will now detour to 'assist' the LNG tanker under missile attack. The stolen fireboat driven by two martyrs will deliver five hundred pounds of Semtex and five canisters of radioactive material into the side of the LNG at the waterline, directly amidships."

What is the firing point of aim for team three?"

"Their point of attack is the two forward holds with the missiles delivered just above the waterline.

"When does the fireboat make its turn toward the LNG tanker?"

"As soon as the first missile hits the LNG tanker, the fireboat will turn sharply east, and go to full speed as if going to service the explosion. It will take only a few moments to cover the distance to the tanker. It will look like firefighters doing their job. There will be chaos and they will have no reason to fire on team four."

"What does team three do after firing their two missiles?"

"Abandon everything and go to the van. If they can make it past the fire, they'll drive south on Commercial Street to Atlantic Avenue and vacate the area.

"Do they know they may be too close to the fire to escape?"

"Not really."

The Engineer looked at Mehmood as if he were expecting more of an answer.

"I have told them the tanker will not ignite until team four strikes the tanker with the fire boat setting off the five hundred pounds of Semtex, and they should be clear by then," said Mehmood.

"We both know that won't be the case," said The Engineer.

Mehmood did not stop the team three members from deluding themselves about their chances of escaping the firestorm. If fact, he assisted them in that delusion. He did not intend to correct their wishful thinking. When the fire started from the first hold ruptured, it would only last three-and-a-half minutes or so. They could not get a half mile away in that time. This is why he and Mehmood would be in Charlestown, over one mile away, on their own assignment.

The Engineer thought it best not to continue this line of conversation with Mehmood. The Engineer did not care how it happened as long as it did happen. He continued, "That is an excellent plan. You still don't think we need the machine gun?"

"No, firing the machine gun from inside the Marine Fire Office is really of no value and would only attract unneeded attention. We would do better to use stealth and mimic legitimate activity until the first explosion. Then it will be too late for them to do anything. We don't need it."

"I didn't agree with you at first about the machine gun but now I do. We don't need to waste effort on the escort police boats. They are not any threat to our plans."

Chapter 93

Baker took a call from Mayor John Corso when he got back to the office. Baker volunteered to walk over to the mayor's office in City Hall, which was just across the street from the Boston FBI Office.

Baker and Mayor Corso talked alone for over an hour about the current state of affairs. Baker was direct and forthright and the mayor could tell. They liked each other. The mayor could tell that Baker was concerned about doing what was needed consistent with his assignment to locate and apprehend The Engineer and his cell members.

"I understand the problem about the multiplicity of targets in the city," said Corso. "We have been over this hundreds of times. Presidents come to Boston multiple times a year. We are constantly either doing or being provided threat assessments. The one factor that can't be ignored is the great amount of energy that could be unleashed upon this city by exploiting an LNG tanker. Why take the chance? Quietly hold the ships outside the harbor for a few days."

"The Coast Guard does not think that is necessary at this point, based on the available information."

"Please don't quote the Coast Guard without telling me what the FBI thinks. I want to know what you think should be done. What will you recommend?"

"To be frank Mayor, even Patrick would admit he is operating on a hunch, a feeling. There is as much a chance the terrorists could be involved with some other target."

"So am I, on the hunch part," said Corso. "That does not make what we think wrong. You can't argue with the logic. We are fighting a done deal that has been foisted on us by people who won't be here to answer the questions. Understand, around that harbor are not just my voters, but my and my wife's family, our friends, things that we hold near and dear. Why should we even remotely endanger them if there is something we can remove to reduce the danger, even for a short period of time?"

Baker said he would speak immediately with Wilkins and Director Simms and carry the mayor's request for a cessation of the LNG tankers until this could be cleared up. If they could work this out without the media being all over it, Baker would also be in favor of the cessation. It made sense. The mayor would wait until he heard back from Baker and if something was not done, the mayor would make a formal request to the secretary of Homeland Security. If that did not work, his next stop would be a press conference. Corso said he was telling Baker all of this so everyone would know what Corso was thinking and willing to do. That way there would be no misunderstandings.

Baker did not tell Corso what he had just learned from Patrick about the LNG company stock being shorted in Europe by al-Qaeda. Baker believed this information was a very bad omen. He also believed Vespa's information was probably accurate and would be verified, but he could not bring himself to give this information to Corso before he had it verified by FBI analysts.

They shook hands and parted. Baker went back to the office. It was only midmorning and he felt like he had worked a full day.

Chapter 94

"You and I are team five. What are we doing and when?" asked The Engineer. He had reviewed their assignments before but now action time was getting closer and there could be no mistakes. He did not think the plans needed any changes. Now it was time to execute.

"I will be driving the rental van," said Mehmood. "In it will be two suitcase bombs each containing 40 pounds of Semtex, some shrapnel material, and two canisters of your radioactive material. I will drive you to South Station one hour before the attack. You will buy a ticket on Amtrak for the night train to Washington, DC. You will check this bag with the porter. The porter will put the bag in a room just off the main lobby separated only by a dark glass wall. You'll exit South Station. I pick you up and we drive to North Station. That bomb will be in a bag inside a suitcase. You can either leave the bomb in the suitcase and place it in one of the two areas we discussed or, if necessary, remove it from the suitcase and place it in the trash can located just off the platform. It will only take five minutes to drive from North Station to the parking lot at Constitution Wharf. We will wait there until we see the attack starting."

Mehmood continued. "We will be in position the same time as the other teams. In our rental van, there are two Dragon anti-tank missiles and two machine pistols. We'll park in the lot at Charlestown Plaza. On the east side of the parking lot is the Harbor Walk. Across a short distance of water is the old Charlestown Navy Yard. Within seventy-five yards from where we are parked, and within an unobstructed line of sight, is the USS Constitution. We will park the van in the commercial parking lot, open the side door, and fire two anti-tank missiles into the side of the USS Constitution just above the water line. These rounds will cause substantial damage to the ship and set it on fire. It will sink at the slip and be a visible reminder that Islam does not forget."

The Engineer had to admit that the attack on the USS Constitution was a good political strategy. The USS Constitution was completed in 1797, a few years after President George Washington authorized its building. The new United States had no navy. Its merchant ships were constantly being attacked and seized by pirates off the Barbary Coast in North Africa. The fledgling government had no choice but to pay ransom to get the ships, the cargos, and the crews released. In 1803 and 1804, the USS Constitution, a now mighty and modern war ship, was on duty in the Mediterranean Sea with a particular eye on the pirates operating out of Tripoli and Tunis. The first shots fired from the USS Constitution were in 1804 at pirates in Tripoli. Shortly after this brief engagement, Tripoli entered into a treaty with the new United States. The treaty was negotiated and signed aboard the USS Constitution.

After the Tripoli action, the USS Constitution led a squadron of vessels into the Bay of Tunis. It did not take Tunis long to figure out that a treaty with this new country, wherein Tunis promised to avoid any further contact with pirates, was a good idea. They had never seen so many cannon on one ship.

The American government of 1804 used its newly created naval capability to stop the Barbary Coast pirate attacks. The pirates were called "Turks." They were Muslims. As part of its present day disinformation campaign, al-Qaeda was not afraid to "adjust" history a bit to increase the ardor of its members and recruits. They made no reference to the pirate activities during this period and referred to the USS Constitution as a tool of a Christian country waging war on Islam. This new country did not respect Islam then and this lack of respect continues to the present day. After The Engineer finished with the USS Constitution, the al-Qaeda disinformation campaign would proudly maintain to the "Arab street" that worthy Muslims never forget insults against Islam! The firing on the USS Constitution would make the LNG tanker assault into an extension of this religious act of retribution. The Engineer would fire one of the two Dragon missiles.

"At what point do we fire?" asked The Engineer.

"We'll be looking down the harbor at the bow of the LNG tanker. We can see when teams one, two and three fire their missiles. When we see their missiles, we fire."

Would a cell phone jam prevent us from setting off the bomb in North Station?"

"We don't think so but we are using backup timing devices on all the bombs to make sure we do not rely only upon cell phones for detonation."

"And after we have fired the dragons, what do we do then?"

"We exit the parking lot at Constitution Wharf, get on the McGrath Highway, and drive north away from the city. We will drop the van about two miles up the road and pick up my car. All of the teams, except team four, expect to meet at the location in Lawrence."

The Engineer had in truth been discouraged after his team in New York had been captured with all their supplies. He greatly wanted to have the New York and Boston attacks coordinated to demonstrate al-Qaeda's ability to commit multiple simultaneous attacks of major proportions. He would feel greatly accomplished when the Boston attack was successfully carried out. He had paid over two million dollars for the six Javelin missiles. Some balked at this expenditure. The Engineer got what he wanted and now he would give al-Qaeda what they needed. America would be in turmoil for years. It would destroy itself with blame and recrimination.

Chapter 95

When Baker returned to the office, he called Bob Wilkins and Director Simms to relay his conversations with Patrick, followed by that with Mayor Corso. Fisher had already called in the information about the stock shorting and that inquiry was in progress. Simms agreed it was more than reasonable to hold the tankers out of Boston Harbor for a few days until they had a better idea about what The Engineer might be up to. He would try again to speak with the Coast Guard but thought that line of conversation already exhausted. He would raise it with the Homeland Security Director, the Attorney General, and the President at the morning briefing.

Simms added that he was afraid the public discussion could be started sooner than desired. Baker asked him what he was talking about.

"We had Kirby interviewed this morning. He has been a puppet on a string being controlled by Bottom. The whole thing with Patrick was a power play to discredit the FBI and to allow Bottom to get direct control over Vespa and this investigation. USA John White did not stand up to Bottom as he should have because Bottom does have friends at DOJ."

"What about the interview of Bottom? Did he lie?" asked Baker.

"Bottom has refused to be interviewed. The Inspector General at DOJ was not pressing the issue. I think he wants us to act against Kirby and make Kirby the problem, not Bottom."

"Have you talked to the AG? What does he say?"

"I did a few minutes ago. It seems that Bottom has contacted the House Committee on Government Reform and is trying to sell them the story that he is being hounded by the FBI because of his federal court action against Patrick. He is claiming the FBI is screwing up the investigation of The Engineer, is not following the informant guidelines, and has left a great public safety exposure owing to our ineptitude."

Baker was stunned. "How could anyone have the audacity to try and sell a story like that?"

"Because he knows there is always some audience for any negative story alleging an FBI performance failure," said Simms.

Now both Wilkins and Baker were stunned.

"What is going on? Something is not right here. What am I missing?" asked Baker.

Simms explained. "After Watergate, Congress did not want a powerful FBI and CIA talking to each other without their knowing all about it. They did not trust the President not to abuse his executive power. After 9/11, some members of Congress did not want to discuss the limitations they imposed on the FBI that prevented us from doing what the public thought we should be doing. Dilution of power and more legislative control over the FBI was their goal. So what these members did after 9/11 was to change the public discussion. Rather than discussing the handcuffs put on cooperation between the FBI and the CIA after Watergate, and the damage these restrictions did, they recited the "failures" of the FBI and CIA to cooperate. Some members of Congress suggested that the US should not have its primary criminal investigative agency be responsible for maintaining the internal security of the country. It was their position that the FBI should not be involved with thwarting terrorism because it did not fit with their mission of upholding the Constitution in the process of catching criminals. It was even suggested that another new agency needed to be created. This new agency would be responsible for internal security like the MI-5 in England. The police chase only criminals. MI-5 deals with internal security. If arrests need to be made, MI-5 turns the facts over to the police who press the criminal charges."

"But in the end, the argument got no traction," said Wilkins.

"Not quite," said Simms. "It had a lot of traction for a long time. It's always easier to shuffle the chairs around on the deck than it is to repair the ship. All this committee wanted to do for its TV face time was to hold hearings on what was not done, never addressing why it was not done. Believe me, the 'what is wrong' question' never comes back to Congress when they control the microphone and the questions asked."

"So where do we stand?" asked Baker. "We do have a rather critical matter up here."

"Bottom has told the Chair about the current threat in Boston, according to his delusional view, and offered to appear immediately before the committee to discuss the current investigative failures of the FBI."

"Where is the AG on all of this?" asked Baker.

"He knows what is going on. He's not a fool. The Committee Chair also sensed that dealing with Bottom could be like touching the third rail. While this chair doesn't like the FBI, he is not looking to let someone like Bottom publicly embarrass him especially where he could be accused of interfering with an ongoing investigation that may allow terrorists to do their damage and escape."

"So where do we stand at this moment?" asked Wilkins.

"FBI agents are on the way to interview Bottom right now. If he refuses to fully cooperate, he will be suspended, his credentials taken, and he will be escorted out of DOJ and put on unpaid administrative leave until a full criminal inquiry can be completed."

"What about Bottom's friends at DOJ who have bailed him out before?"

"Bottom's behavior down here this morning has even them convinced that Bottom may have temporarily taken leave of his senses and is a danger to anyone who listens to him."

That is what they needed to hear. They did not need useless distraction, or worse, actions that could harm the investigation.

At 12:30 pm Maha Soufan arrived at Patrick's office. At the same time Liz showed up with sandwiches. Patrick had asked her to bring some food so the three of them could talk in privacy. Just as they were starting to eat, Mayor Corso called Patrick to talk about his conversation with Baker.

Patrick told Corso he was there with Soufan and Liz, so the mayor asked Patrick to put them on speaker phone so they could talk together. At the end of the call, the mayor said he was willing to wait a little while but he did not want any LNG tankers in the harbor until this could be resolved. Stopping the LNG tankers briefly would greatly reduce danger to the city.

"One other thing," said Corso. "Is there anything else the mosque can do in all this?"

"Like what?" asked Soufan.

"I read the people arrested in New York were connected to a mosque in Bayonne, New Jersey. Do we know of any people in Boston who had anything to do with the mosque in New Jersey?"

Soufan responded. "I don't know of anyone. I talked to the Imam this morning and he didn't either, but he was going to check around and get back to me. When the FBI initially talked to me, they wanted to keep it all hush-hush and really told me nothing. It was Patrick who told me what the problem is. I don't know what the FBI is doing to look into our mosque."

"Why don't we just start anew," suggested Patrick. "Can't you make sure none of the mosque leaders are aware of any connections to New Jersey? Maha can be a little more open with the leadership and tell them there is some concern about a Muslim terrorist cell in Boston. It is not much of a leap after what they have heard about the arrests in New York. Everyone wants to make sure that if a clue presents itself it is not lost through ignorance or neglect."

Soufan agreed he would return to the mosque for more detailed conversation with the Imam. Patrick would be hitting the waterfront with Crowley and the BPD. They would all talk later in the evening after the day's efforts and after the mayor had a chance to get a briefing from the police commissioner.

Chapter 96

The Engineer and Talat Mehmood sat at a lunch counter in a diner near South Station. They had little conversation while they ate. There were other people close by. That was not what limited their conversation. Mehmood realized the only thing he had in common with The Engineer was the planned attack. So while in public they had little to discuss. The Engineer did not want to know about Mehmood's family, friends, or discuss their Muslim faith. Being a Muslim was not only important to Mehmood, it was the essence of his life. To be anything other than a Muslim living in full accord with the Quran on a daily basis was not acceptable to him. Mehmood wanted the eternal reward promised by Allah through the Prophet, and he was willing to do whatever he was told was necessary to obtain that reward.

The Engineer did not want to know about the strain placed on Mehmood's relationship with his father because of his belief in a radical and fundamentalist version of Islam. Mehmood was excited when he first met some of the people his age from the mosque in Bayonne. Their discussions were alive. The Imam had vision for a full Muslim life in the United States with Sharia law as a guide. He had not told his father where he had been or with whom he had spoken because his father thought that Muslims in America needed to live in harmony with respect for other religions. While he loved his father, Mehmood thought he had become weak and was under poor leadership at the local mosque.

After they had walked outside, Mehmood asked, "Do you plan on meeting with the entire team before our work begins?"

"I want to but I am not sure after what happened in New York." said The Engineer. "If I knew why they were together in New York and how the police found them, then I might know what to say. I have been putting off that decision."

"If there is any way you could meet with them, I would do it. The men look up to you. They are all well prepared but they could use a meeting with you to discuss our common cause to bolster their enthusiasm. You represent all of al-Qaeda to them. They want to hear from you again about the importance of this mission in the eyes of Islam."

"Do these men not have the faith?"

"Of course they do. But they lack an Imam here in Boston to refresh their minds that this action is the will of Allah. If they risk their lives for Allah's work, Allah will give them eternal paradise."

The Engineer knew that this was the first combat action for this cell and it would be an ambitious project for even an experienced cell. No doubt they would be nervous. He might have to risk the security issues to insure his team was operating at their highest level of motivation.

"I accept what you say and will think about it. The next high tide to accommodate a regular LNG shipment is Thursday at 10:00 pm. Tell the teams that is when we will act. They shall remain quiet and available at all times between now and then."

"Allah Akbar," replied Mehmood.

Patrick called Baker. "We have shown The Engineer's picture along the waterfront with no immediate results. Crowley had agents gather a lot of video from the North End waterfront. The East Boston side does not have as much video owing to its more industrial nature. They are checking for what is available. The agents in Charlestown will do a search running only the photo of The Engineer against the data collected. That is a shorter search designed to find only him. After that we will run a search of all the video collected against the entire known terrorist database. This search will take far longer."

"Anything else we can do right now?" asked Baker.

"What about the Coast Guard and halting the LNG?" asked Patrick in return.

"I just got off the phone with Mayor Corso. I explained the Coast Guard is adamant that they cannot disrupt shipping just because there is a possible threat in the general area. We have no specific facts to offer the Coast Guard that point to a direct LNG threat."

"So when is the mayor holding his press conference?" asked Patrick.

"Wise ass," said Baker. "The Director just told me the Coast Guard has agreed to consult internally tonight to determine if they are willing to hold up the next tanker due in Boston absent a specific threat against that ship. They maintain a specific threat against a Boston bound LNG tanker still does not exist. They are willing to think about it overnight and get back to everyone in the morning. They only agreed to this overnight review after the Director said he would support the mayor's need for a press conference as being within his duties and responsibilities as mayor of Boston. The Director also told the Homeland Security Secretary that he would discuss this matter with the President at the morning security briefing if this did not get resolved beforehand."

"So when will you know?" asked Patrick.

"Not until I talk with Wilkins in the morning."

"It just mystifies me how intelligent people can be so adamant and stubborn and demand proof of a specific threat before they will act. Such proof rarely exists. It means they would almost never delay one of these tankers," said Patrick with a note of frustration and disappointment in his voice.

"It has been a long day. Let's wait until morning," replied Baker.

Chapter 97

Patrick was at the kitchen counter stuffing the calamari when Liz arrived home.

"What are you fixing?" asked Liz.

"I heard a rumor you had a light lunch. I thought I would make my stuffed calamari. In forty-five minutes, I will be ready to serve you."

"Want me to pour you a glass of wine?" asked Liz.

"If you insist you sly, silver-tongued fox."

Patrick told Liz of his call with Baker.

"Well at least it puts a little breathing room in place. Maybe by Thursday the FBI will have more information and get the shipment scrubbed, period."

"Since when were you willing to be rational on this subject?"

"'I am a well trained lawyer capable of viewing the many sides of the same set of facts. Besides, I can afford to be that generous when I have you around to growl at everyone. I'm going to change."

The phone rang.

"Mark, it is Maha. Can we get together? Something has come up."

"I'm just ready to have dinner with Liz. Please join us. We can talk over dinner. You like stuffed calamari?"

"I am about fifteen minutes away. Is that okay?"

"See you then."

Liz returned to the kitchen. Patrick asked her to set the table for three. Maha would be joining them for dinner to discuss something that had come up.

Vince Baker just finished his evening meeting at the JTTF. Most of the two hundred agents sent from other FBI offices to help were still at the site in Charlestown addressing the security videos gathered from around the harbor and various large electronic stores downtown. They were dealing with much disparate data. It was proving hard to set up a common search system. Baker hoped showing The Engineer's photograph along the waterfront might generate some leads, but so far nothing. In reality, they were doing busy work to keep the troops moving in the hope of generating new leads. When you are out of leads and have no intelligence on your opponent, it is all you can do.

Liz had the table set and Patrick had the food prepared by the time Maha arrived. Maha was too excited to eat. After he spoke a few sentences, Patrick and Liz also forgot about dinner.

"I met with the Imam late this afternoon," said Maha. "I wanted to follow up to see if he knew of anyone from Boston that had a connection to the mosque in Bayonne. The Imam recalled that one of our members complained to him some time back about his son going on the Hajj with Muslims from another mosque. He recalled the father seemed irritated that his son would make the Hajj with strangers. The Imam recalled counseling the father that in this day and age, he should be glad that his son wanted to go at all. It was a minor conversation as the Imam recalled. In fact he cannot even recall with whom he had this conversation. He asked me to relay these events to you and tell you he will help any way he can."

Liz looked at Patrick and then back to Maha.

"I and the Imam ask you receive in confidence what I am now going to say to you. The Imam needs you to help him work through how to give some information to those people who need to have it, while, at the same time, preserving his agreement with a fellow Muslim. Can this be done?"

Patrick looked at Liz. "This sounds like Vespa all over again. Maha, are you saying there is a conversation to be protected on religious grounds?"

"Our Imam has spoken with a member of the mosque who cannot be identified at this point for family and religious reasons. This person wants to follow the advice of the Imam and see that the information, regardless of the value, gets to the proper authorities. Our Imam, as you know, has stressed that we are Americans living in America and we have the same duty as everyone else to protect our country regardless of religion, ethnicity, or country of birth."

"Why not start this way," said Liz. "Tell Patrick and me the story without identifying anyone. That way it gives us an idea of what the legal ramifications may be. Also we cannot say any more than what you have told us. As the facts come out perhaps we can do more to protect this person."

"Agreed," said Maha. "An FBI agent, a Boston police detective, and another man showed a photograph of a person around the harbor today. One of the persons shown the photograph may have recognized the man. This person is a legal immigrant but comes from a country where the police are feared. She said nothing one way or the other and just shrugged her shoulders and pretended not to speak good English."

"Is this person just afraid of police or are there more reasons why she was reluctant?" asked Liz.

"This person is a young, married woman whose husband, a US citizen, is in graduate school. She works at night to financially support his schooling. The problem is her father. He is a strict Muslim and would not agree with his daughter working in public at night without a male guardian. Since she is married, it is no longer his right to say anything but the woman does not want to flaunt Western ways in front of her father. She does not want to tell him about her working at night."

"Has she witnessed a crime?" asked Liz.

"No, not to her knowledge," said Maha. "But I think what she saw may have a bearing on what you are investigating now. On the other hand, the Imam saw Mark brought before the court against his will, subject to public ridicule, and he does not want that to happen to this woman."

"I can say to you Maha that if you do not tell me the person's name, and do not tell me how to identify this person, they cannot demand of me what I don't know. However, and more importantly, my being called into court was an aberration that I do not see happening again."

"The Imam is concerned that responsible government officials allowed it to happen to you at all."

That brought a moment's silence to the table and also some reflection on what was said.

"Let's put it this way, tell me what you can and we will work it out," said Patrick. "If we cannot, the information will not be repeated by me in any way that will identify this woman. It will be my problem only. I must also tell you, I was the third person showing that photo today around the waterfront."

Maha just nodded and started with what he had to say.

"Several years ago the mosque offered computer courses, which this woman attended for a number of weeks. In the class was the son of a mosque member. This son attended prayer infrequently. The woman did not socialize with this man and this is the only context in which she knew him. His name is Talat Mehmood. They are about the same age. She thinks he is around twenty-six. She sees the father periodically at the mosque but has not seen the son for a long time. She knows nothing about where he lives or works, other than she thinks he had gone to college. The Imam knows the father."

"What does this have to do with the photograph being shown around?" asked Patrick.

"She has periodically seen Talat Mehmood on the Harbor Walk at City Wharf since early last winter. He seems to like to come to this area with male friends and walk. She has seen him there anytime from late afternoon to midnight, when she gets off work. More recently she thinks she saw Talat with the man in the photograph she was shown."

"Wow, talk about close to home," said Liz.

Patrick nodded. The table was again quiet while this information was being processed by those present.

"Will she speak with the FBI and tell them this much?" asked Patrick.

"Will the FBI call her to testify or will they agree ahead of time never to call her?" responded Maha.

"I don't speak for the FBI but I can ask them for you. You can do that yourself, you know. They rely upon you as a liaison to the Muslim community. This is what they want you to do."

Maha responded, "You and I both know if people are ever charged with a crime, they may have to produce her name if they know it."

"You are probably right but that is not for me to say."

"The Imam and I ask this. Will you speak with this woman, take what she tells you, and agree not to identify her in any way if that is all she knows. She can put Talat Mehmood with The Engineer but knows nothing else."

Patrick looked at Liz. She smiled.

"Why not? Been there, done that," said Patrick. "Besides home and work for me are close to the courthouse in the event I get called back by Bottom and his friends," said Patrick.

"Can you talk to her now?" asked Maha.

"Where?" asked Patrick.

"I can have her here in ten minutes. Would you mind speaking to her in your home?" asked Maha.

Patrick looked at Liz. "Can you do your thing with the camera?"

"I think so. Martin is on tonight. We can have him turn off the back camera before she comes in and again when she is leaving."

Maha looked somewhat perplexed.

"From time to time we have dinner guests whose appearance we do not wish recorded for all posterity. We arrange to shut off the camera covering the rear condo entrance and have the guests enter the building that way. As soon as the guests are ready to leave, the camera is briefly turned off again. We have always wanted our home to be a refuge and do not want our guests reviewed by just anyone who happens to get access to the disc."

Chapter 98

Liz did her thing with Martin in the guard booth. Fifteen minutes later there were two taps on the condo door. Liz answered and there was Maha Soufan with a young woman in Muslim headdress, including a full veil covering her face. She was of medium height and build. Her other clothes were Western style. She wore dungarees, a tweed suit jacket and a blue cloth shirt. Her dress was a distant cry from a black burka. Liz invited them in. Patrick's first impression was that she had beautiful eyes. It was amazing how the face veil directed your attention to the woman's eyes and how much you were able to tell about the person with a brief look. He knew she was a nice person.

"Please sit down," said Patrick. "For the purpose of this conversation I will call you Hagar, if that is permissible? That way Maha will not slip and use your name," said Patrick with a warm smile.

Hagar removed her veil from her face and smiled in return. She looked Patrick in the eye. "You were there this afternoon with the photograph."

"That is correct but now not relevant. Besides, I saw so many people today, I would not recognize any one of them. I am getting old and have a bad memory." Patrick smiled as he said this.

"I have told Hagar of your willingness to withhold her name or identification. This is agreeable to Hagar. Where do you want to start?"

"We understand you are talking about a person you saw with Talat Mehmood, is that correct?"

"Yes," said Hagar.

"Why don't you tell us what you saw and when you saw it. Start from the beginning. We can talk about Talat Mehmood after that." Patrick could tell she was nervous. He wanted her to speak at her own pace, telling her story in her own way, leaving her in charge of the presentation. He could ask questions later.

"I've worked nearby since winter one year ago. My hours are 4:00 pm to 12:00 pm. I work on a parking lot that abuts the harbor and the Harbor

Walk. Sometime after I started, I periodically noticed Talat Mehmood walking the Harbor Walk, usually in the company of one or more men but sometimes alone. I am in a booth. I see everyone in the area and they never see me, or if they do, they pay no attention to me. I have a lot of time to look around and observe people. I knew Talat Mehmood from a computer class at the mosque and before that from prayer service. I sometimes see his father at the mosque. I have never spoken with the father. I have not seen Mehmood at the mosque for almost two years."

They were all seated at the dining room table. Liz got up to get Hagar a glass of water and to make sure the tea water was ready.

"When it gets warmer, I often walk around outside the booth just so I don't have to sit all the time. One time Talat was walking alone. He looked over to the booth and saw me. I do not wear the veil when working, only the head covering. He could see it was me and I could tell he recognized me. I gave him a quick wave and he returned it and kept going. I thought it strange he would not speak to me, but some men are like that if the woman is not accompanied. Sometimes I see him sitting for long periods of time on a bench at the water's edge, at the rear of the parking lot. As the weather gets nicer many people enjoy this area and sit on the benches. I thought he must live in the area and uses this part of the Harbor Walk for his outdoor space."

"The tea kettle sounded and Liz got up to pour some tea. They waited for her to finish pouring and when the tea was on the table, Hagar resumed.

"The last week or two, I have seen Mehmood more frequently and each time he is in the company of the same man. He is the person in the photograph that was shown to me by whoever it was that came today. They were very nice but I was afraid to say anything to them. My father does not know I am working to support my husband's graduate studies."

"We understand that is the source of your concern and we will somehow work around that."

"Thank you," she said. "I have seen them sit on the bench in the park and look out over the water. I have seen Mehmood more then he realizes. I might be busy with a customer and will only see him from the side or the back, but I know it is him."

Hagar took a moment to sip her tea.

"What makes you think the person in the photograph is the same as the person you saw Mehmood with recently?" asked Patrick.

"About a week ago, they were seated on a Harbor Walk bench for a while before they got up and went to the back portion of the parking lot. I thought they were looking for a vehicle. Instead they turned and walked right down the middle of the lot directly past my booth and headed to Commercial Street. I felt compelled to at least say hello to Mehmood since he was so close to me. Instead, Mehmood looked directly at me as if to say don't recognize me. Then he looked away and they walked out of the lot to Commercial Street, turned right, and walked toward Franklin Wharf."

"So you got a good look at the man with Mehmood?" asked Patrick.

"Oh yes. He walked in front of me. I was wondering who he was that could force Mehmood not to say hello, especially when he was this close to me."

"Do you think Mehmood has ever told any of his friends about you?"

"No. Just the opposite. Should I tell you why?"

"Please," said Patrick.

"One particular night I saw him walking with a friend. When I get off at midnight, I walk up to Hanover Street in order to go to the T stop at Haymarket. At night there are mostly Middle Eastern men in the coffee shops. Sometimes I will get a coffee-to-go for the train ride. I saw Mehmood sitting at a table with the man he was walking with that same night. Also at the table were some other men I had seen walking with him before, but not that night. I looked at Mehmood and he looked away. He gave no indication to the men he knew me. These men never come close to the booth so they do not know me. No, I think he does not want these friends to know that he knows me."

Hagar had no idea where Mehmood lived, who his friends were or even where he went to school. She had no idea what he did for a living. He was just someone she knew from prayer and a computer class at the mosque. She has never known anything about his mother or siblings. Hagar was sure the Imam knew something of the family.

They spent more time getting physical descriptions of the different men she had seen walking with Mehmood. Over time she thought it was at least seven different men before the man in the photograph showed up.

When they had finished the interview and the tea, and as Hagar and Maha were about to leave, Hagar looked at Patrick and said: "You think I am in some sort of danger, don't you?"

Patrick looked surprised and then smiled. "You are observant. I was going to ask Maha to speak with you afterwards but I will ask you myself. Can you take a few days off from work?"

"Probably. My husband just finished exams and we were looking for a few days to ourselves. You don't want me at work?"

"There is a possibility these are bad people."

"Terrorists, you mean?"

Hagar is a smart person and she wants it straight, thought Patrick. "Yes," he responded. "It's possible."

"Why are you afraid I might be in danger? I don't know these men."

"Mehmood realizes you are there but will not let on to the others. Why? He is afraid that if they find out you know him and of his visits to that area, his friends may harm you. It is possible he may be ignoring you to help you. That is just a guess on my part. If you are not around for a few days it might be better for you."

"I understand," said Hagar.

Patrick said, "Please give Maha all your contact data and your plans so he can reach you at a moment's notice. We will pass your information onto the FBI. They will not be happy they cannot speak to you directly but hopefully we can work that out. I would like Maha to get the Imam's input as to how to address the concerns you have about your father. If we can relieve these concerns then you can talk with the FBI directly, which I think would be better. Is this okay with you Hagar?"

"Yes, and thank you all for your time, your kindness and your friendship in a cup of tea."

Patrick said to Maha, "When the FBI comes to see the Imam about Mehmood and his family and friends, will the Imam be cooperative?"

"He has already assured me he will be and told me to tell you that, also."

"That will be helpful. I am sure the FBI will be most thankful. I will have them contact you to set up a meeting with the Imam," said Patrick.

"That's fine. We are both available any time, including late tonight." said Maha.

"Thanks for all the help my friend," said Patrick.

Liz made sure the camera was turned off again. Hagar and Maha left.

"Your thoughts?" Patrick asked Liz.

"I agree the woman could be in danger. Mehmood may even be in danger, especially if he needs to keep the others from finding out he held out on them. They could do him in for a serious security breach."

"What is your idea for the next step?" asked Patrick.

"You do a brain dump with Baker. He will be glad to hear what you have to say but will be frustrated at not having direct contact with the source at the same time. I do think the Imam can help smooth things with the father so she can be in a position to talk to the FBI directly. There are possible sketches that can be done of the other men. She may even know more than she thinks. It will take more interview time to flesh that out."

"Quite so, my dear," responded Patrick as he sipped the last of his now cold tea.

"You did not mention the LNG tanker at all?" inquired Liz.

"It was intentional. I didn't want to put thoughts into her head. There are other ways of interviewing her without directly mentioning the tankers. Asking about specific dates, times, people around, what was the area activity, and sooner or later she will remember. We did not have the needed time tonight and it is not that important right now. We know something about where they are and what they may plan on doing," said Patrick.

"Call Baker and get this going. Time could be short. May I also suggest you put your toothbrush in your pocket just in case they don't agree with your need to protect Hagar on a temporary basis," said Liz, pretending a coy smile.

"The truth is, if they want to be jerks, they will probably guess who she is. Hopefully they will take the long view and appreciate that their years of efforts at building trust in the Boston Muslim community are paying off. If the Imam and Maha did not have trust in the FBI, this would not be happening. The help needed to solve these problems will have to come in part from the American Muslim community. This is a good start and hopefully no one will be pig-headed."

"Nice thoughts. Take your toothbrush, just in case," said Liz.

Chapter 99

At 10:00 pm, Patrick was sitting in Vince Baker's FBI office in Boston. Supervisor George Fisher and Agent Susan Crowley entered shortly after Patrick. If they were tired, thought Patrick, it did not show. They seemed to be glad of the possibility of some new information. Patrick explained his conversation with Soufan, their discussion about speaking with the woman, and finally the details of his conversation with Hagar. When he finished, Patrick waited for the possible criticism of having moved forward as he did. It did not come.

"We may have the young lady on video, along with Mehmood and The Engineer," explained Baker. "George, tell Patrick what you just learned."

"From the various videos we have gathered from the waterfront, we have three confirmed hits on The Engineer in the last four days. One was from the new Institute of Contemporary Art, another from Counting House Wharf, and a third from a camera in a condo building across from City Wharf. The last one is just before dusk and you can clearly see the men walk from the Harbor Walk at the water's edge, through the middle of the parking lot, past the parking attendant in her booth, and out onto Commercial Street where they turned north toward the Coast Guard yard. This is just what Hagar described. We have the whole crew in Charlestown working all the video we can find, to see how many people have been on the waterfront with The Engineer or Mehmood, in the hopes of identifying all the cell members. Hagar has just put a name on one, Talat Mehmood."

"Does the Imam mind us talking to him this late?" asked Baker.

"No," replied Patrick. "He realizes you may need to speak with him right away. Something else, I am unclear if the Imam was talking about Mehmood or someone else when he made reference to a father complaining about his son going on Hajj with people not from his mosque. As I thought about it afterwards, I realized our attention was on Hagar so, if you speak with him, would you clarify that point? He may have a second name of someone who went on the Hajj, which caused a father to complain. You want me to call Soufan now and tell them you are coming? I think he is with the Imam now."

"Yes, please," said Baker. "George, will you speak with the Imam and get the background ASAP? Susan can get with the JTTF AUSA and get some affidavits started. We need to get authority to monitor any form of communication Mehmood has with anyone and we need to do it now. From now on, anyone even speaking with Mehmood needs to be under an electronic blanket. We need to find the rest of the cell and their equipment. Whatever they are up to is not good."

"What about the LNG tanker?" asked Patrick.

Baker replied, "I'll call Wilkins. We have more facts. We should be able to get the Coast Guard to cooperate now. That LNG tanker should be coming up the East Coast. We need to hold it up but not have the delay publicized until we find Mehmood and put a physical and electronic coverage on him. Then it might work to our advantage. If they are thinking about this Thursday evening, when the next tanker is due to arrive, they will be in contact with each other to adjust their plans based on the ship's progress."

Patrick added, "There have been at least two instances over the last couple of years where an LNG tanker had engine failure at sea. One time the computers failed and shut down the boilers. The other time I don't know what caused the boiler failure, but in each case the Coast Guard had to go out with tugboats and mechanics to secure the tanker from drifting and get it back into operation. In both instances it took at least two days, as I recall. Why not use this type of excuse if and when the delay becomes public?"

"May I also suggest," added Patrick in the form of a caution, "that only the captain is made aware of the real reason for the delay. The ship's crew should actually believe they have a computer malfunction. I am worried the cell could have someone onboard keeping The Engineer posted as to the ship's progress. This person might be a martyr or perhaps has never been told the ship is the target."

"Agreed," said Baker. "I hadn't thought of that possibility."

Baker said to Crowley, "After I call Wilkins we will have a JTTF briefing. Get back to me with your new data so we can get it into affidavits and find Mehmood and his crew. We're not close to having a case against Mehmood so it's no use arresting him. However, if The Engineer is found, we have the John Doe warrant for him under the alias 'The Engineer' from New York. So he is fair game. We need to find that radioactive material. We will make it clear that no one is to act before discussing it with us unless it is a matter of life or death."

Fisher and his counterpart at the BPD met with the Imam and Soufan, who were still at the mosque. Fisher was up front and told the Imam they already had a video of Mehmood walking through a parking lot with the person they were seeking. He showed the Imam a photo copy of a frame and the Imam noted it was in fact Mehmood.

"I think we can work around Hagar for the moment" said Fisher. "We're just as glad if she is not around for a few days. If things go badly we don't want Mehmood or his friend thinking of Hagar as a potential witness."

Fisher then asked about the father who complained about the son going on Hajj with another mosque.

"I don't think it was Mehmood's father" said the Imam. "I could be confused but I really think it was the father of Jabbar Shaddi. Mehmood's father is a frequent visitor to the mosque, whereas Shaddi's is less frequent. I can ask the father if you like?"

"No, not just yet," responded Fisher. "It's a little too soon to ask questions openly. Do you know if Jabbar Shaddi and Talat Mehmood are friends?"

"No, I don't know," advised the Imam. "We keep very limited background information at the mosque on our members and their families.

You are welcome to what we do have. Everyone at the mosque has been told that if it comes to a terrorism investigation, we do not require a subpoena for any of our records. They are available to any law enforcement body. Tell us what you want and we will give it to you freely."

The Imam gave them copies of what little information he had for the Mehmood and Shaddi families.

On the way back, Fisher learned they had already identified Mehmood as living in an apartment in Allston. Subpoenas had been issued for phone, email, and banking records. They already obtained some general credit card data and were in the process of checking recent expenditures. Court orders had been obtained to attach tracking devices to any vehicle being used by Mehmood. They had some new equipment, which, besides being a GPS locator, recorded the exact streets traversed by the subject's vehicle. This data could be downloaded by the FBI electronically without physically going near the vehicle, so the surveillance teams would not to have to lock bumpers with the suspects and risk giving away their presence. Surveillance teams were in place, ready to jump on Mehmood once he was located.

Additionally, Baker set up fixed daylight surveillance points along the south and west sides of the harbor, from the Black Falcon Pier to the Charlestown Bridge. They needed to see everyone traversing this area and the fixed surveillance locations made this possible. The east side of the harbor had more open space and three high-vantage points had been set up to observe that area. Their hope that they would spot The Engineer was not to be.

Fisher called in the identifying data on Jabbar Shaddi. Within minutes they determined that his family lived in Dorchester but that Jabbar might be living in an East Boston apartment. His driving history also showed a recent speeding charge from East Boston. They would know as soon as they could check the actual court record.

Baker called Patrick just as he was going to bed. Baker told Patrick about the possibility of Jabbar Shaddi being of interest, based on what the Imam had said. Baker wanted to know if Hagar knew Jabbar Shaddi and if she had ever seen Shaddi with Mehmood. Patrick called Hagar. He explained there was no problem with the FBI needing her information directly. She did not know Shaddi's name and did not recall him or his family from the mosque. Hagar and her husband were leaving in the morning to visit relatives in Springfield. She would keep her cell on at all times in case they needed to reach her. She also gave them the address of where she was staying.

"What do you think?" asked Liz.

"They have picked up the scent again. It is now a question of time. If they can identify the cell members before they make their move, they have a better chance of getting them all at once. If things fall apart it could be hit or miss and some could get away, at least for awhile."

"What about the missiles and explosives?"

"That is a problem. If it's not all in one place, it is probably next to impossible to get the entire cell and the equipment at one time. If they get a sniff that people are right behind them, they could go underground and sit tight. It could be a long time before you pick up the trail again."

"What about the LNG tanker? Will they keep it out?"

"If the mayor allows me to write the script for his press conference, it will seem like a logical move," said Patrick with a slight smile.

"Will you be fermenting public demonstrations against the LNG tanker's presence, my dear?" asked Liz with a slight smile.

"At least," said Patrick.

Chapter 100

Baker was not going to get much sleep tonight. He didn't mind at all. They were starting to make some headway and the trail had been picked up. The most frustrating thing was to have no leads at all, no one to interview, no logical next step. Now they had plenty to do and what they had done in the last twenty-four hours was starting to pay off. The search of videos from all of the transportation centers in the city showed The Engineer had visited both North Station and South Station three days ago.

The Engineer was seen on the bus station video at South Station during the evening commute three days ago. After walking around the bus station terminal, he went to the adjacent train station where he examined the commuter rail and Amtrak rail ticket offices. He walked by the porters' bag storage area. Next, The Engineer sat at a table close to the door for track number eight, where he drank a cup of coffee. Toward the end of his visit he was met by a second man whom they think was Talat Mehmood. The man sat with The Engineer for a few minutes before they left together, walking out the front entrance.

One-half hour later, Mehmood, who they now could clearly make out on the video, and The Engineer appeared at North Station. There were no events at the Boston Garden and the commuter traffic had already departed. They mostly had the place to themselves. They walked together from the ticket office to the other end of the lobby. They looked at the escalator going up to the Garden from the station, but did not go up. They exited out the Zakim Bridge side of North Station, stood looking at the bridge, and then walked off toward the North End out of the range of any cameras.

Baker was meeting with Crowley, Fisher and the JTTF duty agent to discuss what else could be done right away.

"We have put a permanent fixed surveillance inside both North and South Stations. Their cameras are set in real time to identify either The Engineer or Mehmood if they return. Now the question is, what do we instruct the agents to do if either one of them returns?" asked Fisher.

"We have decided that already. The Engineer is to be arrested on sight. He is too dangerous to let out of our sight. We can arrest him on the Italian fugitive warrant." said Baker.

"What if Mehmood shows up without The Engineer," asked Crowley?

"I talked this over with Wilkins, the USA and the people at DOJ. We do not have enough probable cause yet against Mehmood to make an arrest. If he shows up we put him under surveillance and start building the case. If they show together, arrest The Engineer and attempt to interview Mehmood, then we stick to him like glue wherever he goes."

"The state police have loaded the photos of The Engineer and Mehmood into the Logan Airport security camera system. We have an agent with them 24/7 who will be given the same instructions," said Fisher.

"Have we made any progress with the video reviews from stores downtown that handle a large volume of cell phone sales? Any luck there?" asked Baker.

"None," said Crowley. "We also are delayed in getting the full credit reports for Mehmood. We had to get a subpoena and have it hand delivered before they would give us the information we asked for. We are hoping to trace his movements via credit card usage. From his bank records, we can possibly identify his cell phone carrier account number to get his call records. That way we don't have to waste time circulating all mobile carriers. His recent credit card charges may tell us a lot about where to look for him. We will also put a real time monitor on all of his credit cards so the moment one is used, we will know where it was used almost immediately."

The Engineer lay in his motel bed listening to the late night traffic on the Southeast Expressway. Forty-eight hours from now he would make history for Islam and himself. After reviewing all the plans, he truly believed they had a very good chance of success. He knew that some team members would be incinerated in the resulting LNG fire. But, if the element of surprise remained on their side, they would inflict serious damage on the City of Boston. More importantly, thought The Engineer, the combination of the LNG fire and the radioactive material being dispersed would take the fear of Islam to a whole new level for the American people.

The attack would send the Americans into a tailspin. No one would consider themself safe in any part of the country. These attacks would insure that impossible demands would be placed upon the US government. Citizens would insist on being fully protected from any form of terrorist attacks. This, of course, was not possible. Chaos would ensue. Trust in government would evaporate. Even moderate voices would fall by the wayside and the American respect for their rule of law would begin to crumble.

The demand to retaliate will be enormous, but against whom would America strike? The most logical person would be the former leader of al-Qaeda, whose demotion was not yet known in Western circles. The United States didn't even know where he was in hiding. Better they waste their energy searching for the former leader, thought the new current leader.

These attacks would enable al-Qaeda to reinvigorate their war against the infidels. al-Qaeda again would be a credible threat to any city in the United States. The Engineer knew from his discussions with al-Qaeda leadership that they had a long-term strategy to negatively impact and impair how the US government responded to their threats. They wanted the United States to over-respond. This in turn would negatively impact the exercise of daily freedoms by citizens. They did not think Homeland Security was nimble enough to realize their sometimes not well thought-out responses to security threats would create further fear and cause more tension between the government and its citizens.

al-Qaeda watched over the years as the US government slowly eroded the personal freedoms of its citizens in responding to al-Qaeda threats. It had been going on for so long now that citizens were almost like sheep being led from one pasture to another. If something needed to be done in the name of national security, or to purportedly preserve the public safety, it was expected that all citizens would simply and without question comply. Having your private parts examined by a total stranger in view of other passengers was just an example about how much indignity one could impose on a citizen in the name of "security." You can trust TSA when they say the electronic scanners hold no lifetime health hazards? You can trust the Homeland Security secretary who says, "the system worked," when in fact the President was forced to say the next day it had not?

How much had terrorism changed the lives of so many in just the last fifteen years? al-Qaeda believed there would come a time when the US government would press its citizens too far. In fact, they were counting on it. al-Qaeda planned to set the stage in such a way as to force the government to willfully bully its citizens into further personal, uncaring degradation, bordering almost on maliciousness. This was happening now. The Homeland Security secretary bluntly told the American flying public that if they did not like the new security procedures at airports, they could stop flying. This was the level of arrogance that al-Qaeda wanted to see government officials express to its citizens. They would just sit back and pick away at the scab to keep the sore bleeding and hopefully cause infection.

Small business in America was being forced to act as a base level screening apparatus for US immigration and, at the same time, pay for this effort out of their own pockets. Trains and buses were gaining customers. Amtrak advertised that if you traveled with them, you did not have to take your shoes off unless you wanted to make your feet more comfortable. Business travel was down substantially. Was it really due to the recession? What was the market telling the airlines with their stock prices?

The Engineer knew this was all part of al-Qaeda's long range planning. The Engineer knew that he was now going to be part of a historical event with long-term ramifications.

After the Dragon missiles were fired at the USS Constitution, The Engineer intended to leave the parking lot alone. Even if there were any survivors, he would not be meeting them in Lawrence. The Engineer believed he stood a better chance of escape if alone. Talat Mehmood would have served his purpose. The Engineer did not need a witness talking about him.

The Engineer also thought meeting with the team members prior to the attack was not necessary or in his best interests. He thought it was Mehmood who was demonstrating the need for emotional reinforcement. Everyone was in place. They had their equipment and instructions. This meeting was not necessary and could only represent a security risk. He would not have another New York result. His only necessary contact with a cell member would occur Thursday, when either he or Mehmood would deliver the canisters of radioactive material to each team.

Chapter 101

By the time Baker got to the office, after only a brief sleep and time to shower and shave, he had a call from Director Simms and Bob Wilkins. He could not believe what he was hearing.

"The Coast Guard said absent a specific threat to this or any other LNG tanker entering Boston Harbor, they will not halt or delay the ship," said Simms.

Baker exploded. "We have The Engineer and Mehmood all over the waterfront alone and together. They are clearly preparing for some activity in the area. What do they think that this means, with the information about the firepower we think they have? Are they crazy? What about the stock being shorted? What am I missing? Something here is not right."

"The Coast Guard will throw into your face that in New York all targets appeared to be commuter related. In Boston you now have The Engineer and Mehmood apparently conducting surveillance of North and South Stations. They will say this indicates more of a threat to those facilities than an LNG tanker," Simms pointed out with a neutral voice.

"So what happens when Mayor Corso holds a press conference bringing to the public's attention his lack of confidence in the judgment and abilities of the federal government to keep Boston safe from an LNG attack? He will say they are recklessly endangering the city? What is so important that these ships cannot be held up a few days until things are sorted out? That is entirely prudent under the circumstances we have now."

"Okay, Vince, now listen to me and I will tell you the rest of the story. I just came from my morning intelligence briefing with the President. I raised all these same issues. The President is concerned as he should be, but as of the moment, he is going to call the mayor and ask him not to discuss this publicly, as a matter of national security. The President is asking the mayor not to request a delay of this or any LNG tanker unless there is a more specific threat."

"Okay," said Baker, "I may be dumb, but I'm not stupid. What is the rest of this story?"

"This LNG tanker will be coming from Yemen."

Baker was dumbfounded.

After verifying their phone encryption, Director Simms continued. "Our country's most immediate, urgent and growing threat is al-Qaeda in the Arabian Peninsula (AQAP). al-Qaeda in recent months has taken over large geographical sections of Yemen. Yemen is a country with barely an existing government and with only an effective presence in two cities. There is no government rule elsewhere in the country. AQAP is being staffed and re-enforced by experienced al-Qaeda leaders who are leaving Afghanistan and Pakistan to escape the success of our drone missile attacks. The CIA, the military and the State Department have all been working with what exists as the Yemen government to get their 'permission' for the US to set up forward bases to conduct surveillance and combat operations. We need to attack al-Qaeda before it gets settled and while they are still in a mobile stage. This is being done under the auspices of training Yemen military in counterterrorism tactics. Yemen has agreed to accept US military 'training' so their troops can bring the battle to al-Qaeda, not us. So what we can or cannot do in Yemen is up in the air at this very moment."

"Isn't this what Pakistan did a few years back? That has worked really well. So far Pakistan intelligence and their military often serve al-Qaeda more than us," said Baker, with a clear edge in his voice.

Simms ignored Baker and continued. "Yemen is afraid of how they will be perceived in the Islamic world if they allow the US to directly and publicly operate against al-Qaeda on their sovereign territory. The clerics in Yemen are already threatening jihad against the existing Yemen government if they allow US troops on Yemen soil. Every day that negotiations drag out, they become more difficult. We have an opportunity in Yemen we did not have in Iraq or Afghanistan. Yemen is tomorrow's war we must fight today before al-Qaeda even gets started."

"How is this related to what I am doing?" asked Baker knowing, while he didn't know why, he was not going to like the answer.

"The government of Yemen is broke. They have no economy. They have almost no revenue. Their officials want the US to start carrying the country's financial load in order to enlist Yemen as an ally in the war on terror."

"So we pay them rent for space we lease for our military operations. What is the problem?" asked Baker.

"Vince, give the Director a chance to finish," asked Wilkins.

"Yemen wants to be treated as a full partner in many spheres of activity. Their first request is they want to sell LNG to a company that will load their ships in Yemen and immediately deliver LNG to the United States. They want to be paid COD. This has already been agreed to by us. Besides loading LNG in Trinidad, they will also load their ships in Yemen and deliver to Boston. These will be additional deliveries over and above what they already are delivering to Boston now."

Baker shook his head in disbelief. "How can they possibly consider this?"

Simms continued. "The CIA suspects some Yemen officials may have financial interests in the companies that stand to make the lion's share of the money once the shipments start. The Department of Energy and the Department of Commerce have been brought aboard to publicly support this plan. Homeland Security controls the Coast Guard so everyone is being asked to help fight the new terror war in Yemen now by making these LNG shipments work. It is the same company and personnel for the Boston LNG deliveries that the Coast Guard has been dealing with for years. They've never had a problem. If the Coast Guard were to delay an LNG shipment for any reason, especially the first one from Yemen, the CIA and military fear the Yemen government would perceive it as an affront and a delaying tactic. In retaliation they could immediately withdraw the limited support we have from them now against al-Qaeda."

"I find this almost unbelievable," said Baker. "When does the US learn to stop getting in bed with extortionists? Give into their demands and they will own you. What will they want next?"

"Everyone feels the same way," said Wilkins. "They are just asking for a little time right now. They will address these issues down the road, but not right now."

"I have yesterday's *Boston Globe* in front of me as I speak," said Baker. "It reports on the President's meeting with the intelligence community on Monday regarding the terrorist who tried to blow up the plane landing in Miami recently. The terrorist carried the explosive PETN in his underwear. According to the President, our entire intelligence community knew this could happen, had significant intelligence beforehand about the possible threat, and failed to 'connect the dots.' These many years after 9/11 and we hear the same thing. Failed to connect the dots? I am reading this just as a citizen, and, as a citizen, I believe that after billions of dollars have been spent, after huge increases in personnel and multiple reorganizations, it appears to the public that basically nothing of substance has changed in our national security effort since 9/11."

"Vince, why don't you just concentrate on doing your job? When you solve the problem with The Engineer then maybe someone will be interested in what you have to say," said Wilkins in a tone that was completely adversarial.

Baker ignored Wilkins and continued: "The Secretary of Homeland Security went on all the talk shows after the failed attempt to blow up the plane in Miami saying 'the system worked.' The President had to eat those words saying it did not. Now either the Secretary was intentionally lying, or someone in the administration put him up to do this to downplay the situation. Either way he has destroyed the little credibility the intelligence community has with the American public. Now you expect the people of Boston to believe that the intelligence community, the Secretary of Homeland Security, and the Coast Guard, which has never been under a direct attack by terrorists, should be entrusted to insure that a one mile circle around Boston Harbor will not be vaporized, and another one mile from that circle will not be put into flames?"

There was silence on the other end of the phone.

Baker continued finishing his thoughts: "The President wants to close Guantanamo immediately. It was his big campaign promise. Now he has two hundred terrorists left on that base that need to be moved ASAP. Ninety-eight of these terrorist prisoners are from Yemen. They were scheduled to be turned over to the Yemen government. That was confirmed this weekend by a presidential spokesperson. Now, on Monday, the President says that will not be the case. These prisoners will not be turned over to the Yemen government. It is pretty clear to any citizen following this in the media that the President has concluded he cannot trust the Yemen government to insure these terrorists will be kept confined, not allowed to 'escape,' nor given an outright release to return to the battle with al-Qaeda. All we would be doing is paying their way back to Yemen so they can join the battle against us sooner."

"What is your point?" asked Wilkins.

"We can't trust Yemen to even keep these terrorists locked up. Yet the people of Boston, and the nation, are supposed to believe that Yemen tankers, containing explosives five times more powerful than that dumped on Hiroshima, will not be a threat to the City of Boston. You are asking them to believe that Secretary of Homeland Security, American intelligence, and the Coast Guard can prevent any possible attack at this time that would destroy everything. I don't think that either of you believes this. Why try and sell it?"

"Vince, that is not entirely the situation," said Simms. "That tanker has not yet entered Boston Harbor. We just cannot fight this battle with what we presently have. Maybe the facts will change in the next few hours. Just keep working and we will continue the argument here as new facts come in. We know what you are saying. We have discussed all this down here," said Simms in a most professional tone.

"A little time is what I fear we do not have right now," said Baker. "Based on what you've told me, we will have to be much more aggressive in our investigative plan to find this cell. That requires us to take chances that would be unnecessary if we didn't have a sword hanging over our heads. If we take chances, we can expose what we know and still accomplish nothing."

"All of us are making tradeoffs trying to work as a team. You do what you have to under the circumstances you are dealt. None of us is operating under optimum conditions," said Simms.

Simms paused for a few moments, and then continued. "Vince, we make decisions every day that are not perfect because we do not have good, clear choices. What if the LNG is not a target? Even you have to admit that right now it is still a theory. You have to admit there is no direct evidence against the LNG. Your theory is sound, and probably correct, but there is another reality. The President needs to deal with Yemen today. You want him to tell the military they may have to put the brakes on the best opportunity they have against al-Qaeda for a theory. They have reality right now. They need to get the drone missile attacks started now but cannot because of the demands of the Yemen government. There are military teams and CIA agents secretly on the ground that need help at this very hour. These soldiers are in grave danger, facing death at this moment. That tanker will not arrive for two days," said Simms. "So we do have a few hours."

Baker was absorbing what Simms said. Baker respected Simms. He knew Simms to be an honorable man with strong convictions and not commonly subject to making decisions impacted by the political motivations of others. That is why Baker was willing to follow Simms in the past and why he would follow him now. You had to have some faith in someone.

"Vince," said Simms, "these are the President's orders for now. They are neither illegal nor immoral and have the full support of the Attorney General. We are sensitive to what you say. This is all being discussed at the highest levels right now. I repeat that tanker has not yet arrived. We have time. Let's use it. I know you are being forced into an expedited investigative schedule. Do the best you can. That is all any of us can so. By the way, Bottom threatened to go to the press if he was not put in charge of the JTTF investigation in Boston. They fired him last night with the additional understanding that if he says anything publicly he will be arrested. He is presently under a full physical surveillance, which is not discreet by any means. If they see him make a wrong move he'll be arrested."

"You have a couple of days before the LNG tanker is due to arrive," said Wilkins. "Work the case some more. You now have Mehmood who can possibly take you to the others. You have phone, bank and other records coming in to start determining his activities. In a couple of hours the whole scene can shift. Let's take it a few hours at a time. See what you can come up with. Maybe you can come up with something to break this open and identify the cell members so they can be neutralized."

"We have been going full speed since last night. I appreciate your listening to me" said Baker. "I am very concerned. Let me see what we can get going and I will get back to you." Baker hung up.

Sitting at his desk, Baker's body felt like he had been badly beaten in a bar brawl. His body hurt. He felt empty. He felt alone. He felt angry. At the same time he felt what Simms and Wilkins said made sense. They had time before the LNG tanker arrived. A few more facts could change the whole scenario.

"Maybe I am just tired and lack full perspective," murmured Baker to himself. "Perhaps there are situations that are so complicated there are no good answers, just one that would cause the least amount of damage."

Baker questioned whether he needed to have more respect for others who were trying as hard as he was to do the right thing to protect citizens. He did not need to be told that this discussion was not to go beyond him. He felt that he was entering a fight without all the necessary weapons at his disposal. He could not share this information with anyone right now. This would limit his ability to get input and ideas from his colleagues.

As he prepared for his next steps, Baker's thinking caused a slight smile to barely curl his lip. Baker realized that, between Corso and Patrick, that LNG tanker would never enter Boston Harbor as long as The Engineer and his cell were out there. Like Corso and Patrick, Baker knew how to stop it if he had to. Having recognized these possible scenarios, and turning over the implications in his own mind, his spirit was somewhat lightened and he was ready to move on.

Director Carter Simms put in a call to Patrick. "Can I ask a favor of you?"

"If I can help, I will. What is it?"

"Vince Baker is one of my best managers and investigators. I have complete confidence in him. However, after a few days in Boston, he is beginning to sound like you. I hear his voice but think I am talking to you. What is going on and how can I get Baker back?"

Patrick knew that Simms was only half serious. He could accept the humorous side of the comment but knew that Simms wanted something more from him. As always, Patrick said what he thought. "I like Vince. He is smart. He has integrity and tenacity. He is an improvement to your system. If he rubs off on your other leaders, the FBI will be a better organization. Don't try and get him back."

"Somehow I thought that is what you would say. I appreciate the help and just wanted to tell you that. Please continue to be a support to him. This case is getting very complicated. Enough now, you and I will talk when it is over."

Chapter 102

Baker called George Fisher and Susan Crowley into his office for an update before the scheduled JTTF meeting.

"Where do we stand with Mehmood at this moment?" asked Baker.

Fisher responded, "We had a court order signed early this morning authorizing roving electronic surveillance on Mehmood anywhere we find him. Because of the broad nature of the court order, we have to report back to the judge in three days for him to review his order and determine if we can continue. We also got a search warrant for his apartment in Allston. We have not found him or his car. He did not come home last night and we have no idea where he is right now. We went in to his apartment just before dawn and installed video cameras and microphones. We can only turn the equipment on once we know he is inside. We conducted a search and the results are not helpful. We found no computer and no evidence that he even owns one. There was no phone landline and no evidence of any cable service. He could be using a computer with Wi-Fi. There was nothing related to cell phones and we found nothing that would tell us anything about his recent activities. It looks as if he has been trained to keep a sterile environment with nothing around that would let you know who he is or what he does."

"What about his trash?" asked Baker.

"None," said Fisher. "That is what made us think he keeps a sanitary space where he sleeps. He must have someplace else. There was one thing that caught their eye."

"What was that?" asked Baker, with some expectation in his voice.

"There was a week-old community newspaper on a table next to the couch. It was folded open to an advertisement from a local Allston gas station listing the rental of small vans, trailers and trucks. This is a student and young-adult area so there is a lot of moving in and out. Behind the trash can on the floor was a small ball of papers that turned out to be receipts from the Sumner tunnel. He must have missed the trash can when he tossed them. It looks like he visits East Boston on a regular basis. The most recent receipt, though, was over a week old."

"So his apartment is abnormally clean, which tells us he probably is following some training regimen. At the same time, it means we have nothing to do until we find him."

"We are reluctant to put his car description and photo out on the police system because the press could pick that up. We are giving it to all the agents and JTTF people so they can look for him in their travels. If they see him they are to just call it in and stay with him until we can get full surveillance teams in place."

"Good plan," said Baker. "What do you have in mind about this advertisement that was seen?"

Crowley responded, "We want to send two Boston PD detectives on the JTTF into the gas station saying they want to see all records of active rentals as part of a hit and run accident investigation. This is common enough. Even if the gas station people know Mehmood, it should not raise any suspicions. Then we run every rental to the ground to see if he is involved."

"The state police are willing to put a cruiser on the toll booth at the Sumner Tunnel to see if they can spot him coming back from East Boston," added Fisher.

"Okay. Let's do all of that now. We need to move fast. I want every commercial and public database examined for any information about Mehmood. Follow up on the subpoena for his credit record. We need to find his bank and credit cards. Anything that can possibly locate him or get us on him must be done immediately."

"All of that is in progress and we should have the results before noon," said Crowley. She added, "Now that I think of it, why don't we get a list of all stolen, unrecovered vans within twenty miles of Boston for the last month? We can look for any of these vehicles as we get closer to the cell. They need transportation and all of it may not be rented."

Rose Phillips knocked on door to Baker's office. "Mark Patrick is on the phone and wants to know if you have a moment?"

Put him though. "Mark I am here with Fisher and Crowley. Do you want to go on speaker phone?"

"Sure," said Patrick.

"What's up?" asked Baker.

"I am thinking about what the Imam told Fisher last night. He offered the possibility that it could have been Shaddi's father who made the Hajj comment to him. We know al-Qaeda has been using the internet and social networking sites to generate interest in their cause with young Muslim American citizens. Wouldn't it be worth it to check with Shaddi's father to see if there is more there?"

"I am not sure we can expose ourselves just yet. Suppose word gets back to Mehmood via Shaddi that we are asking questions around the mosque. We have not found him yet, and if he hears something like that we might never find him."

"You don't have to ask the questions. Ask the Imam to chat the father up. If the father has concerns, he may have been trying to express them to the Imam who did not catch on at the time. At least ask the Imam if he knows the father well enough to do this. You can take it one step at a time."

"You think there could be more people involved at the mosque?"

"There is nothing to suggest that right now. I do think there are young men like Shaddi and Mehmood who could come under the sway of al-Qaeda through the internet, and this could well go unnoticed by family and friends. Perhaps they would only get a glimpse of something different. This could be what Shaddi's father was really noticing," said Patrick.

"Okay, Mark. We will talk this over. Thanks for calling."

After he hung up, Baker asked Crowley and Fisher, "What do you think?"

"If the Imam can do this as a natural follow up to a question he was previously asked by Shaddi's father, the approach should cause no alarm. It may be that it was him who made the comment," said Crowley.

"We should know who went on the Hajj with strangers that made a parent concerned enough to mention it to the Imam," said Baker.

Crowley replied, "Why don't I go back to the Imam and explain what we are thinking and find out if it is reasonable for him to follow up at this point in time with Shaddi's father. He can say yes or no. If the Imam believes it is logical to do so, we ask him to do it. We just take it one step at a time. I do think Patrick's right. Someone made that comment to the Imam and we need to follow it up."

"Okay. Ask the Imam if he can make a general inquiry to Shaddi's father. I think we need to do it now. We have not found Mehmood and we are running out of time and perhaps options. Let's get some background on Shaddi just in case."

Crowley and Fisher left the meeting with Baker. Fisher observed, "Something is different with him."

Crowley said, "Yea. I noticed the same thing. Maybe he is not getting enough sleep."

Chapter 103

Patrick was working at home when Maha Soufan called, just before lunch.

"Patrick, the Imam just met with Agent Crowley, who made certain requests of him and the mosque in general. The Imam would like you to meet with him to answer a few questions and perhaps give some practical advice. He does not have a sufficient comfort level and thought you might help."

"I would be more then glad to Maha. However, if the FBI wanted me present or involved they would have asked me. I don't want to appear to be butting into their business."

Maha replied, "I spoke directly with Agent Crowley after she met with the Imam. I told her the Imam wanted to speak with you and that you had given the mosque advice in the past. She told me that we were free to handle it as we saw best, and that included speaking with you."

"When?" asked Patrick.

"Now, if you can. It seems their needs are rather immediate."

"I will leave now and be there in twenty minutes."

When Patrick arrived at the mosque, Soufan and the Imam were standing in the interior public courtyard just inside the entrance. The space was so large that it was an excellent location in the mosque for a private conversation.

"In general, they want us to think about younger men who may have been affiliated with the mosque a few years back but not now. They are looking for young men who may have been recruited by the radical fundamentalists, perhaps through web social networking sites or chat rooms. Maha and I are going to meet with our senior colleagues after we speak to review our collective thinking and see if anyone or any family comes to mind. I have no problem with that, and we will do it right away."

Patrick said nothing.

The Imam continued. "They have asked me to contact the father of Jabbar Shaddi to follow up the conversation I had with him some time ago about his son going on the Hajj with strangers. They are wondering if I missed a signal that Shaddi really wanted to talk with me about his son."

"I spoke to them about this possibility earlier today. What, exactly, do they suggest you say when you contact Mr. Shaddi?" asked Patrick.

"They suggested I reference his previous comment about his son with strangers, noting that I never see Jabbar at prayer and ask him if everything is okay. If he is willing to speak about his son, they want to know what he is doing now and with whom. They want to know if he is acquainted with Talat Mehmood, the person that the young lady of ours spoke with you about."

"What is your question?" asked Patrick.

"I am not sure how to do it," said the Imam.

Patrick smiled. "You just described exactly how to do it. I would add that you should do this in person with Mr. Shaddi, rather than by phone. You want to make sure he is alone and able to communicate freely with you and also you want to be able to look into his eyes and judge his reaction as he responds."

"His business is in Dorchester, not far from here. I could drive over now."

"Would that be out of the ordinary?"

"Somewhat. But I have been to his business before. I would tell him I thought of him while in the area and decided to stop by and ask him about his son, as I rarely get a chance to speak with him after prayer."

"Sounds like a good way to do it to me," said Patrick.

The Imam paused for a moment, closed his eyes as if trying to see a conversation in his mind, and then continued. "As I think about it now, the father was concerned his son did not return from this most important event in the life of any Muslim, the Hajj, with the air of spirituality, personal fulfillment, and thanksgiving to Allah for the forgiveness of sins, which is bestowed by Allah upon those who make the Hajj in the true Muslim spirit."

This recollection by the Imam did not require any comment, and none was offered.

"Do you want me to call you when he gets back?" Maha asked Patrick.

"You and the Imam need to speak with Agent Crowley as soon as you can. If I can help you, then you call me. Okay?"

"Would you meet with us after I get back and after we confer to discuss any other persons we may wish to bring to their attention?" asked the Imam.

"I will help you any way I can. You must realize it is the FBI conducting the investigation, not me."

"We do. But we also recognize that this mosque has something of a history with you. We trust you, and tend to understand a little better after we speak with you," said Maha.

"Maha, you can call me on my cell anytime and I will be right over," replied Patrick.

At the same time Patrick was leaving the mosque, George Fisher was giving Vince Baker an update on both Mehmood and Shaddi.

"We ran Mehmood's photo through all the video we collected around the waterfront after we finished with The Engineer. We got some hits. We have picked him up on recent days at Central Wharf, King's Wharf by the MBTA Ferry Boats, North Wharf, behind the skating rink by the Charlestown Bridge, and across the Harbor Walk in Charlestown at Charlestown Plaza. The last time at North Wharf we think he is with The Engineer, but we can't be sure. At Charlestown Plaza we know he is with The Engineer."

"The skating rink and the Charlestown Plaza are within sight of North Station?"

"Yes," replied Fisher.

"So what we really know is that since The Engineer has been in Boston, he has been hanging around with Mehmood all along the downtown Boston side of the Harbor. What else?"

"We ran The Engineer's photo through all of the MBTA transit security camera systems. He is using the T and using it a lot. He has a Charlie Card which he updates with cash. We have him coming into Park Square on the Red Line and getting on the Green Line to Government Center and then the Blue Line to Aquarium. Using the same route he has taken the Blue Line to Maverick Station and again to the Airport Station. At the airport he is seen getting on the terminal bus system, but we can't put him at a specific terminal. We are having all of the sightings put into chart form for the analysts, and a copy will come to you in an hour."

"What about Mehmood and the MBTA" asked Baker?

"We are running him now, but it will take a while."

"No word on Mehmood's location?" asked Baker.

"No, not yet, but we do have some interesting news about Shaddi."

Baker nodded.

"Crowley has spoken with the Imam and he is willing to make the inquiry. He is also meeting with his senior advisers to review their member lists to see if they can think of anyone who could have been recruited by the fundamentalists. They also wanted to know if they could speak with Patrick, and she told them yes."

Baker nodded.

"We have the background on Shaddi. We have confirmed his address in East Boston, and have a surveillance team on him now. I realize he may not be involved but we had the manpower available and they might as well be on the street doing something. He graduated two years ago with a bachelor's degree in computer science. We think he mainly works out of his home for a computer repair service where he can log into the client's computer from home and repair software problems. We also think he writes software part time and goes to a repair shop once in a while to do physical repairs on computers. We got his photo from a college publication. He does not come up in any terrorist databases and appears to be a complete unknown. They are running his photograph though our waterfront videos now and will do the MBTA transit security videos as soon as they can. If he knows Mehmood or The Engineer, maybe we can put them together that way."

"As we get background on each of the potential suspects, I want it sent to the Psychological Profile Unit at Quantico. If we get to the interview stage, it would be nice to have their input on what approaches might work and which ones to avoid based on personality types and traits."

"They have all we know about The Engineer from here and New York. I will add Mehmood now and continue with Shaddi until told otherwise."

Baker's phone rang. Rose Phillips said a surveillance squad leader was on the radio and wanted to be patched through to Fisher right away. Baker told her to put the call through and he handed the phone to Fisher saying, "The radio room needs you."

Fisher took the phone, listened for a minute, and then said, "Call me on the encrypted phone please" and hung up. "That is the squad leader on the Shaddi team. They have seen something unusual and wanted to report it right away. He is calling in on a secure line now."

The phone rang and Fisher responded. "Hold on. I am going to put you on speaker with Baker. I am in his office."

Agent Jack Burke, the team leader on Shaddi, was in East Boston and. "We followed him to a coffee shop on Meridian Street where he met another man about his age who also appears to be of Middle Eastern descent. We sent in an Arab-speaking agent of the right age. The place was crowded enough so he could take a table and observe. He reports that Shaddi was in an extreme state of agitation bordering on hysteria. He was speaking in a low voice but at a very rapid pace, with lots of emotion, and never gave the other person a chance to talk. When he slowed down the other person seemed to enter a state of agitation. They lowered their heads to the table, kept looking around but did not stop talking and kept up a rapid exchange. The agent could not hear any of the conversation. The place was too noisy and they were too quiet. Then Shaddi just seemed to jump up and leave. As he walked by the agent, the agent thought he saw tears in Shaddi's eyes. Shaddi went back to his apartment. They followed the other man in his car back to an apartment about five blocks from the coffee shop. They are running his ID and data now, but I wanted to call this in."

"Thanks," said Fisher. "Keep us posted as to their movements."

"It will be interesting to see who Mr. Shaddi knows and what is bothering him," said Baker.

Chapter 104

The Engineer decided that Talat Mehmood should stay with him at the motel. They brought the van Mehmood had rented and parked it in the rear of the motel, where it could be seen from both their rooms. Under a false floor in the van were the two Dragon anti-tank missiles and their small arms. The van ignition was temporarily disabled to prevent it from being stolen. Mehmood had stored the bombs for South Station and North Station at a location unknown to The Engineer. All they needed was for The Engineer to provide two canisters of radioactive material to be attached to each bomb. Team one had their bomb ready for the airport. They would do the final connections. They needed one canister of the radioactive material, which The Engineer needed to get to them. Their bomb was already constructed and in the back of the van parked at a small garage in East Boston. Team three had a stolen van that they would use to transport their missiles and the five hundred pounds of Semtex to the Boston Marine Fire Station. The Semtex would be loaded onto the fireboat by teams three and four. The Engineer did not know where they had stored their van. However, The Engineer needed to deliver to team three the five canisters of radioactive material that was to be placed with the Semtex on the fireboat.

None of the cell members had been told the last component to their bombs would be a canister of radioactive material. These men were trained, but as of yet, untested warriors. Many had family and friends that could be negatively impacted by their actions. The Engineer did not want them thinking about that. The Engineer or Mehmood would not deliver the radioactive material to the teams until later tomorrow. Even then they would not tell the cell members what was in the canisters.

The Engineer designed ignition systems for the bombs that could be activated one of three ways. There was a manual control for immediate ignition in the event of a threat of immediate apprehension. The manual control also had a timer function where the detonation time could be preset. There was a coded radio signal activation control that would work up to a mile away. Lastly, he had included a device to detonate the bomb when activated by a cell phone call.

The Engineer had preset the timers for each bomb to explode when he calculated the approximate time the LNG tanker should arrive at the point of attack. Once placed, and if not manually detonated, these bombs would go off one way or another. Once activated, it would be nearly impossible for any bomb technician to master his wiring system in time to deactivate any of these bombs. He preferred that all the bombs go off at about the same time, and not until the attack on the LNG had already started. However, no matter what, they would all go off tomorrow night either together or separately.

The fireboat detonation system was designed to activate upon impact with the LNG tanker. If for any reason their boat could not get to the tanker, the bomb could be manually detonated by their boat driver. What team four was not told was that The Engineer also wired this bomb so he could detonate it from his vantage point in Charlestown by cell phone or radio. There was no question those five hundred pounds of Semtex, surrounded by radioactive material, would be ignited tomorrow night.

The Engineer was watching the news on TV when Mehmood knocked on his motel room door. He was excited.

Mehmood said, "We have to talk."

"Let's go outside," said The Engineer. They did.

Mehmood said, "I had a call from Shaddi's partner. He is concerned that Shaddi is very scared and may be changing his mind about being a martyr." Mehmood went on to explain what he had been told about the conversation inside the coffee shop. This was the same conversation the FBI could see but not hear.

"He questions if it is really Allah's will that so many innocent people must die. He does not want to let Allah down. He knows what he has promised to do. He also wants the respect that this act will give him in all of Islam. At times he was incoherent and nonsensical."

The Engineer responded with some degree of anger. "We need him to drive that boat. We need the damage that boat will do. You call him and tell him that he is just nervous, as is any true warrior before a battle. He should take one of the pills I gave him. I told him this might happen. Tell him to watch his own martyr video so he can recall why this is the will of Allah. Lastly, tell him that if he should falter from his sacred and sworn duties in any manner, I will not tolerate his failure. I will kill both of his parents and neither will be an easy death. Then I will do the same to him. Allah does not forgive traitors. Make the call now!" The Engineer turned and walked away.

Mehmood took out his cell phone and called Shaddi. His words, as dictated by The Engineer, actually seemed to sober Shaddi up. Shaddi seemed to regain control of his emotions, expressed resolution for his duties, and was again fully committed. Mehmood reported this back to The Engineer, who was satisfied.

Baker was now awash in information coming in about Mehmood and Shaddi. Shaddi's passport data showed his travel to Saudi Arabia at the same time as Mehmood. They were gone for the same extended period of several months. Like the others, it was more than needed for the Hajj. It was the same travel pattern evidenced by the New York terrorists traveling through the Bayonne mosque. They also found that Mehmood had rented a van about a week ago from the gas station near where he lived. They had the van description, markings, and license plate information. They also obtained a van key from the gas station, which they duplicated before returning it. The people in the gas station did not seem to know Mehmood personally. He was just a walk-in rental. He had a valid driver's license and an approved credit card in his name. Information was also being rapidly developed on a possible third cell member who was seen meeting with Shaddi at the coffee shop. His travel pattern matched that of Mehmood and Shaddi.

Fisher walked into Baker's office and said, "Crowley is on the phone and wants to speak to us both. She is with the Imam."

Baker put her on speaker phone and Crowley reported to them both.

"The Imam stopped into Shaddi's father's store in Dorchester. The father was glad to see him. It seems that Jabbar is friends with Talat Mehmood and it was Mehmood who got Jabbar to go on the Hajj with him. Jabbar knew Mehmood from earlier days at the mosque and Jabbar taught Mehmood how to use a personal computer. When the father questioned his son about his renewed relationship with Mehmood, and some of the ideas expressed by his son concerning jihad, Jabbar stopped talking to his father about anything having to do with Islam. He stopped coming to the mosque for prayer, saying it was not what Allah wanted him to do. His son became less spiritual after the Hajj, which the father thought was almost impossible for any devout Muslim. He thinks that Mehmood poisoned his son's mind and he is worried about his son who now seems so distant from him. The father broke down and cried. The Imam had to say nothing to engender conversation. The father really wanted to talk and wants help, as he fears his son is in trouble."

"What do you want to do now?" asked Baker.

"The Imam has offered to meet with both the father and the son at the mosque if his son will agree to come. The father said he would ask Jabbar and let the Imam know this afternoon. That is what the Imam thought seemed logical and natural to do when he stood in front of a distraught parent. Now the Imam wants to know if this is the right thing to do. What should he say? He is not acting now just as a religious adviser. He knows that. Yet it is still one of his important duties as the Imam."

"Let me check a few things and I will call you right back."

Baker hung up, then put in a call to the chief of the FBI Psychological Profile Unit headquartered at the FBI Academy in Quantico, Virginia. This unit had been reviewing all the data from both New York and Boston. After an additional update, Baker asked for their observations to see if they matched his thinking. They did.

Baker explained his thoughts. "I am sensing that this young man has agreed to do something and now is having conflicted and second thoughts. What the agents saw on surveillance tells me he was meeting with another cell member and came away distraught. Something is not right. I am thinking of asking the Imam to meet with the father and son, if the son is willing, and see if the son asks for help with his problem. We don't have a lot of time and I need an opening to expedite the investigation."

There was additional discussion, more questions from unit staff members, and finally agreement to a plan that could reasonably work. The consensus was that Jabbar Shaddi was presently under extreme stress and, if he accepted the father's invitation to meet with the Imam, there was a reasonable chance he was looking for help. If he attended the meeting and was recalcitrant and unwilling to speak, they would plant a micro-tracking device and microphone in his coat and start an intense, physical and electronic surveillance so they would know his every move and, hopefully, be led to The Engineer.

The other possibility was that Jabbar Shaddi may start making admissions and confess to the Imam. At that point the Imam would have to make some effort to advise Shaddi that the Imam was not the proper person for this conversation. The Imam would have to recommend and fully support that Shaddi immediately meet with the FBI. In fact, they would have an interview team in place at the mosque and ready to start an initial debriefing. They believed Shaddi and his father would feel less threatened at the mosque and the Imam could remain in the building and available if they wished to speak with him.

They discussed the composition of the interview team that could offer the best chance of success. It was agreed that one member of the team would be Shaddi's age and an Arabic speaker, and the other would be an older male. Using a female agent at this point was ruled out as it could act as an unneeded stressor to Shaddi at a critical point. These two agents would be the only ones speaking with Jabbar. They would transmit the interview contemporaneously from the mosque to other agents and Baker at the JTTF Office. The investigation could be directed from that point utilizing all available resources. If this plan worked, they would have a tiger by the tail and they would need everyone they had.

If Jabbar Shaddi maintained to the Imam that nothing was wrong, and he was just there out of respect for his father, then the chase would be on.

Baker called Wilkins and Simms. They both liked the plan and thought it was the best they could do under the circumstances.

Baker put in the call to Crowley who was with the Imam and Soufan at the mosque. Baker methodically explained to all present his conversation with the Psychological Profile Unit and his follow-up call with Director Simms and Wilkins. Baker told the Imam that he realized this was a decision that could have far reaching effects, and that Baker wanted the Imam to be fully informed as to what the FBI thought, what they planned to do, and what, specifically, they would ask the Imam to do. Then he asked for the Imam's help and consent.

"I thank you for your frankness and your willingness to explain to me what you did. You did not have to and I appreciate your confidence in me and our mosque. I recognize the potential downsides to my decision, either way. I have already discussed the potential adverse repercussions to this mosque with Mark Patrick. I see only one path. There is only one Allah. There is one Islam. No one can be allowed to pervert Islam to say that murder of innocents is allowed for any reason. I will not stand by and silently allow evil to prosper by my inaction or fear. I will do as you request and will pray that Allah blesses us all and that we remain true to him no matter how trying the circumstances." Then Imam added, "Mr. Shaddi called me. Jabbar has agreed to meet with me. They will be here in forty-five minutes."

The interview team was dispatched immediately along with a team of technical agents who would set up the equipment for the interview in the event Shaddi agreed to it. They would also tend to the technical needs of Shaddi's coat. Crowley was to remain at the mosque to coordinate these efforts but would not meet with Shaddi. Baker noted Crowley understood the problem without asking for an explanation. Not everyone had the ability to put their egos aside under such circumstances. Baker would not forget.

The JTTF coordinators were given a status briefing and everyone immediately started inventorying available manpower assets. Those with additional resources not on duty started calling them in. If it did not work out with Shaddi, they would need the help staying with him and with whomever he met. The Hostage Rescue Team was in route from Quantico and all agencies were lining up their SWAT teams and putting them on immediate standby. Technical agents were reviewing all equipment needs to make sure they had on hand whatever equipment was required. The LNG tanker was still scheduled to arrive in about thirty hours. They were running out of time.

Chapter 105

Shaddi entered the Imam's office accompanied by his father.

Jabbar looked to be in his mid-twenties, had dark, curly hair and a slim but wiry build. The Imam noticed his eyes above all. They were tired and he had been crying. He was outwardly nervous but appeared to have an inner resolve.

Jabbar had a firm handshake and looked at the Imam directly when they greeted each other. The trio sat down in the Imam's office, comfortable but by no means luxurious.

The Imam's place of business had more a look of home than an office. Comfortable but well-worn cloth chairs, a few lamps shaded with brightly colored glass, and a wall of pictures that introduced the Imam's family, friends, and fellow Muslims. The Imam offered a cup of tea to his guests as he checked his chrome electric pot already filled with water and plugged it into a wall outlet. Next he took out three white china tea cups of slightly different tints and shapes, along with a brown ceramic tea pot, and a box of tea bags bearing Arabic script.

The Imam's tea preparation was part custom, part ceremony, and additionally provided a few moments for Jabbar Shaddi to adjust to the room and the presence of the Imam. As the Imam waited on Jabbar and his father serving the tea, Jabbar felt he did not deserve this respect.

"I spoke with your father earlier this afternoon," the Imam began with a soft voice. "He is concerned. I asked if I could help. I see distress in your eyes. How can I help you, Jabbar?"

Jabbar did not respond. He looked down at the floor. Jabbar's father looked at him, then at the Imam, and then shrugged in disbelief. The Imam did not speak, he waited.

After a long silence, with eyes still downcast, Jabbar said, "I want you to see that my father and mother are protected and that no harm comes to them."

His father jumped excitedly from his chair. "Keep your mother and me from harm? Jabbar, what have you done?"

"Father, there is nothing you can do, the Imam can do, or that Allah can do to help me now."

"Jabbar," said the Imam with a kind look, "I would be most interested to hear what Allah is powerless to address. As Muslims, don't we pray to the all-powerful and all-understanding Allah?" His voice was still soft and calm. "You don't believe this anymore?"

"I don't know. I don't know what to believe."

"Your father says that you have completed the Hajj. Tell me about your journey. How did it feel to be in Medina, Mecca, to walk in the footsteps of the Prophet?"

The Imam got up, poured water from the kettle into the teapot, added the tea bags, and sat down with an expectant look on his lined but kindly face.

Jabbar seemed to relax for a moment. "It was the closest I have ever felt to Allah. I looked forward to my prayers every day."

"What happened to change that?" asked the Imam.

Jabbar did not answer. He looked at his feet.

"How did you go? Who went with you?" pressed the Imam.

At first Jabbar did not respond, but then began to speak excitedly: "You remember Talat Mehmood? I met him through a computer class at the mosque. He knew little about computers, and had a hard time in the class. I gave him some lessons. We became friends. He and I studied Islam together on the computer. He seemed to know a lot of websites that addressed questions young men have about Islam in today's world. Eventually he asked me to go on the Hajj with him and some of his friends from Boston. After, he said we could travel a little and see the Arabian Peninsula while we were there."

"Did you see the Arabian Peninsula while you were there?"

"Somewhat," responded Jabbar, regressing back to his near silence.

"I see," said the Imam. "These websites that you studied with Mehmood, did they talk about jihad?" The Imam knew that militant Muslim groups were using computers and the internet to recruit young Muslim men to jihad. He thought Jabbar fit the profile of being ripe for radicalization.

"Not at first. But later we looked at discussion groups on the computer where jihad was discussed. Talat also knew some special websites where we could learn more about today's injustices to Muslims and we were able to participate actively in these discussions."

"And what did you learn?"

"That the Muslim faith is not being respected." Jabbar's voice grew stronger. He was no longer whispering. "The infidel still has crusades. They just have taken a different form. Islam in the US has sold out to the comfortable secular life. The United States backs anything Israel does just to keep the Palestinian Muslims oppressed."

The Imam nodded. "Did you discuss these ideas with your father?"

"A little, but he did not want to hear it. He did not want a discussion with me about the real state of Islam in the US."

Jabbar's father had retaken his seat in the well-worn cloth chair. He sat there silently with rounded shoulders, looking down with a desperate look on his face.

"So you had these discussions with Mehmood and your new mutual friends on the computer?" asked the Imam. His voice continued to be calm and reassuring.

"Yes."

"What did you see in the Arabian Peninsula when you were there?"

"Basically what the Hajj included."

"So what did you do with your time after the Hajj ended?"

"We visited Afghanistan to see firsthand what the American troops were doing to the Taliban," Jabbar blurted out.

"You never told me you went to Afghanistan," said Jabbar's father quietly.

Jabbar said nothing. The Imam merely smiled at the father. He turned to Jabbar.

"And what did you see in Afghanistan? What cities or towns did you visit?"

Jabbar said nothing and continued to look down. He would not meet the Imam's eyes. The Imam knew the cause of his distress. He just wanted to make sure his parents were not murdered.

"Did you commit yourself to jihad during the Hajj or after?"

Without really thinking Jabbar responded, "After."

The Imam reached over, took a brown clay sugar bowl with a silver spoon and placed it on his desk in front of Mr. Shaddi and his son. He then poured three cups of tea from the pot and placed a cup in front of each of his guests. Jabbar fidgeted in his seat. His father sat there in shock but said nothing. The Imam was better at having conversation with his son. The ceremony of pouring tea seemed to bring peace and normalcy to Jabbar.

After he sipped his own tea, the Imam asked, "Does Talat Mehmood have anything to do with this potential danger to your parents, which causes you so much pain at this moment?"

"Yes," said Jabbar without looking up. Then he said, "It is not really him, though."

"I am wondering what kind of friends and fellow Muslims would threaten to do harm to your parents? Why?" The Imam said this as he slowly put his tea cup back on his desk.

Jabbar's father saw how calm the Imam was and wondered how he did it. The father was hearing things that no Muslim father wanted to hear from his son, yet the Imam was not angry or disturbed.

"Was Mehmood relaying the message for someone else?"

Jabbar nodded affirmatively.

"Did you tell them you did not want to be a terrorist? Is that what caused them to threaten the lives of your parents?"

"I cannot say anymore. It will only cause harm to my parents."

Jabbar's father was now visibly upset and unable to sit still. He was making strange guttural sounds. The Imam asked him to wait outside so he could speak alone with Jabbar. The father seemed more than willing to leave the room. He did not want to hear anymore.

When they were alone, the Imam continued in the same soft voice. "After the Hajj, you went to Afghanistan with Mehmood and others to train, right? You were recruited by people you talked with on the computer, people that Talat Mehmood put you in contact with?" asked the Imam with a new sense of authority in his voice.

Jabbar nodded yes but still would not look directly at the Imam.

"You agreed to participate in a terrorist act. You changed your mind. But now your new friends say it is too late for change, right? Now they threaten your parents if you do not follow through?"

Jabbar nodded yes.

"Jabbar look at me. Look into my eyes. Do you now think that these are the actions of someone who seeks to do the will of Allah? Does your reading of the Quran allow you to think that these people, whom you thought were friends and fellow Muslims, should threaten your parents?" said the Imam in words tinged with anger.

Jabbar now looked trapped. "I now realize that I was wrong, they are wrong, but it is too late. Nothing can be done now."

"You came today just to ask me to see that your parents are not harmed. How do you expect me to do that?" challenged the Imam.

"I don't know. You are an Imam, a prayer leader. I thought you would know."

"Suppose I do know the best chance to stop this. How do I know you would be willing to stand up and do what is necessary."

"What do you mean?" asked Jabbar.

"These people are going to do something evil very soon, and here in the Boston area?"

"Yes."

"The only way for you to protect your parents is to allow me to introduce you to the authorities with whom you need to cooperate. These people need to be arrested, taken into custody where they cannot carry out cowardly murder. Only when that happens will the threat to your parents end. If you don't do this now, they will have control of you forever, and through you, your parents."

"They won't control me because I will be dead. I agreed in Afghanistan to be a martyr."

The Imam was stunned. He hadn't considered this possibility. After he thought it through for a few moments, he realized it made little immediate difference. Jabbar would cooperate now or he would not.

Taking a sip of tea, and going back to his kind, soft voice, the Imam said: "It does not have to happen. You can live, your parents can live. But you must renounce your oaths to terrorism and to being a martyr. They are false oaths before Allah and not worthy of respect. You have been manipulated. It never was an honest discussion about Islam. That is what

401

they wanted you to think. It was always about convincing you to help them with their evil dream. Why isn't Talat Mehmood a martyr? Why does he get to threaten?"

Jabbar at that point bent forward in his chair and started sobbing uncontrollably. The Imam said and did nothing. He thought expiation was what Jabbar needed at this moment.

A minute or so later, the Imam reached over and placed Jabbar's tea cup directly in front of him. "Drink this and you will feel better."

Jabbar straightened up, sipped the tea, and regained control. The Imam still said nothing.

"What do you want me to do?" Jabbar finally asked.

"Do you trust me?" asked the Imam.

"Yes."

"I will introduce you to two FBI agents who will interview you about what is going on and who is involved. I do not need to be part of this conversation. There are things that are not meant for my ears. You must tell them the absolute truth to each question asked without fear of what might happen but, with my assurance to you, that this is the best thing for you to do. Allah forgives those who sin – only when they renounce their sin."

Jabbar nodded.

"I need to know you are doing this of your own free will because you realize this is the only way for you to remain true to Allah and to Islam."

Jabbar sat straight up, looked the Imam in the eye and said, "I am willing. I know it is the only solution for me and my parents. I don't want to be a martyr. I don't want to be a terrorist. I don't want the blood of innocents on my hands."

The Imam got up, walked out the door, down the hallway and into another room. He returned momentarily with two men. The Imam introduced them as FBI agents to Jabbar. Each agent showed Jabbar his credentials. Jabbar looked at each one and nodded.

Jabbar said to the Imam, "You knew what my problem was all along?"

The Imam nodded. "I had a pretty good idea. You are not the first, my son."

"I have spoken with Jabbar," said the Imam. "He is willing to cooperate with the FBI at my suggestion. He was recruited to be a terrorist and a martyr for jihad and was to participate in an act of terrorism to take place here in Boston in the near future. He regrets this action and tried to refuse to go forward. They have threatened to murder him and both of his parents if he fails to go through with the plan. Talat Mehmood is the person who started the recruitment, arranged for his going on the Hajj, and then to terrorist training in Afghanistan. He has told me that he will answer all your questions truthfully. Have I accurately stated everything Jabbar?"

"Yes," said Jabbar in a firm voice.

The younger, Arabic-looking agent asked Jabbar if he would read and sign a waiver stating he agreed to be interviewed of his own volition. He was asked to allow agents to record the interview, and transmit it contemporaneously to others who needed to respond immediately to what Jabbar might say. Jabbar agreed and signed the document, which was then witnessed by the Imam.

"Jabbar, I am leaving you now. However, I will be just down the hallway and will be available to speak with you or pray with you anytime you want. Do you understand that?"

"Yes. Thank you. Will you tell my father what else I told you and what I am doing now?"

"Yes," said the Imam.

The Imam left.

Chapter 106

Within one hour, Jabbar had provided the names and addresses of his eight fellow cell members. He identified Talat Mehmood, the ninth person, as the cell leader. They were all presently under the direction of a person called "The Engineer." Jabbar had briefly met The Engineer in training camp, not knowing he would later be giving the orders to Jabbar's cell. Jabbar identified the LNG tanker as the main target, the USS Constitution, and the three other sites where bombs would be placed before the attack on the LNG tanker began. He described the weapons that were to be used in all of the attacks. He knew about both the Javelins and the Dragons. Shaddi did not mention anything about radioactive materials. He seemed not to know about this element of the attacks. He did not know where The Engineer was staying but thought that Talat was with The Engineer because of the call this afternoon. To his knowledge there would be no meeting of the four cell teams prior to the attack. The Engineer had to visit teams one and three to complete some portion of their bombs. Shaddi did not know why.

The agents were working as fast as they could to get the basics. They would go back later for details. Right now they had to come up with a plan to halt the attacks, do it safely, and make sure no one escaped. They had to worry about how much more might be planned that even Jabbar did not know about.

After getting the basics, Jabbar was asked to immediately take a polygraph. He agreed. The agents brought in another agent carrying his computerized polygraph machine. The agent had ten relevant questions on which to test Jabbar, based on what Jabbar had told the agents within the last hour. Jabbar passed the polygraph on all ten questions. He was telling the truth.

State Department records confirmed the travel of Talat, and the eight others named by Jabbar, to Saudi Arabia for the period of the Hajj and for some months thereafter. There was no record of any travel outside of Saudi Arabia, and certainly none to Afghanistan. It was suspected that their contacts in Saudi Arabia provided them with Saudi passports under phony names that allowed them to travel to Afghanistan and wherever else they may have gone. When they got back to Saudi Arabia, they went back to using their US passports.

Surveillance teams were immediately dispatched to find the other team members. Jabbar's surveillance team was still standing by outside the mosque and would resume coverage of him once he left the mosque. Now this surveillance team was almost a personal protection detail to make sure nothing happened to Jabbar. He would be wired the whole time and they would monitor his every move and word.

Another surveillance team was still in place monitoring the person Jabbar had met in the East Boston coffee shop. They guessed right. He was another cell member.

Vince Baker was sitting in his office alone. Baker had three leading priorities. The first was nothing should be done that would increase risk of harm to the public. The second was that evidence of the use of weapons of mass destruction would be systematically collected and preserved to insure the successful prosecution of all. This was a case of terrorism but it was still a criminal case against US citizens and one foreign terrorist. They would be indicted and tried in a federal district court like any other criminal. The third priority was locating the radioactive material. They needed to get The Engineer into custody before something could go wrong.

Baker, Crowley and Supervisor Fisher were working out the details of execution of the plan with other agents and JTTF personnel. The surveillance teams were doing well in locating terrorist cell members and establishing fixed and roving surveillances on each one. Affidavits were being hammered out by the lawyers for probable cause to obtain electronic surveillance on all the parties wherever found. This would take some time. There was still a lot of background to collect. They had time, but not a lot.

Baker thought the only way to find The Engineer was to follow terrorist cells one and three until The Engineer met them to deliver what Baker was assuming was the radioactive material. They would have to arrest The Engineer the first time he was seen. He was too dangerous to let roam around while evidence was being gathered.

The Engineer and his teams had to believe the LNG tanker was coming in tomorrow night. Patrick previously suggested to Baker that The Engineer could have a mole on board the ship to tell him if it slowed down, changed position, or deviated in any way from its scheduled course. Baker now knew he would not let that tanker come into the harbor under any circumstances. It might get close to keep up appearances, but no more than that. If one team got loose and fired their missiles, all could be for naught. There could still be vast destruction and death if investigators made a mistake or good fortune abandoned them. The LNG tanker could not be used as bait, but it still had to seem that it was in play.

The FBI needed to stick to its knitting. Nothing fancy was needed. This was basic investigative work to include having good, clear communications where everyone understood their role and the case objectives. No cowboys need apply. Discipline was a necessity not only among the street agents but even more importantly among those who sought to direct the investigation starting with him. This is why Baker needed a few minutes alone to think things through. He took those minutes. Afterwards, Baker felt more organized and ready to move forward.

Baker placed his call to Wilkins and Simms.

"We have reviewed the material from the feed at Shaddi's interview and have already started feeding that material to the various intelligence agencies to see what the new data may turn up," said Wilkins. "This has really changed the equation. There is no question we will now have the LNG tanker halted where it is."

"We have been thinking more about that," said Baker. "Patrick was concerned that the terrorists may have their own person aboard the ship. If there is anything out of the ordinary or any delay, The Engineer may know that in short order."

"In the past, al-Qaeda has smuggled members into the country using LNG tankers. Having a source on board is not a far stretch. Most modern ships today have email for their crew. They will soon get close enough to shore to use a regular cell phone, much less a satellite phone," said Wilkins.

"Vince, what are you thinking?" asked Simms.

"Let the LNG tanker keep on trucking. It is not due here until late tomorrow evening. I would let it get within sight of Logan Airport and then have the Coast Guard stop it while jamming all signals coming from the ship. I would then isolate the crew, take away any form of personal communication, and start interviewing them. If we stop the tanker with this plan, it will not be a risk to public safety."

There was agreement on this point among the three of them. As far as Simms was concerned, only the President could tell him differently based on what they now knew. If the President was somehow persuaded to another point of view, he could find a new FBI Director.

The three of them understood that no matter what, if anything went wrong, it would be their collective fault. So be it. At this point such thoughts could not matter. They would make their moves and live with it. They thought themselves to be very lucky so far. If they made it through without anyone dying or anything blowing up, they would believe themselves more fortunate then skilled. The enemy could make many mistakes and just go back to the drawing board and try again. For them, even a near perfect batting average was not good enough. This was a tough business.

Simms, Wilkins and Baker were now all on the same page. They had enough available agents owing to the additional resources sent in a few days earlier. The Hostage Rescue Team was deployed in Boston and other SWAT Teams from the East Coast would be there within hours. They would be assigned to work with the other agency SWAT Teams on the JTTF.

"The clear expectation is that The Engineer needs to make a delivery to teams one and three. If he has radioactive material, he will probably have it with him to place with each bomb. So we stay with each cell member, but like glue with those on teams one and three. If they meet with The Engineer, we have to arrest The Engineer and any team members present."

"What about the other cell members," asked Wilkins?

"I don't think any of the teams will move until the LNG tanker is near the harbor entrance. All the teams need time to get in place before the ship gets to the point of attack which, according to Shaddi, is probably less than 250 yards south of the Coast Guard base. They want the tanker to drift after the missiles are fired so the hulk will settle over the tunnels to East Boston. If we halt the LNG at sea just short of Logan Airport, we should be able to take each terrorist cell team with the SWAT Teams we have available."

"What if our surveillance loses a cell?" asked Simms.

"We are using a lot of GPS transmitters. We will stick one on every individual if we get a chance. We have an idea of where each cell team plans to be when the attack starts so we hopefully know where to find them. But, you are right. It could happen. If we lose one team, we can have a very real problem. They cannot be allowed to detonate any bombs. We can prevent the direct attack on the LNG."

"What about Shaddi? Will they miss him?" asked Simms.

"Yes," said Baker. "If we don't return Shaddi to meet with his cell team partner, it could blow the whole plan. They need to believe that Shaddi is back on track and fully with the program. I'll bet his partner has to contact The Engineer to report on how Shaddi reacted to Talat's 'pep talk.' Shaddi could just as well come apart on us and tell his partner what he has done this afternoon. There are no guarantees."

"Are you wiring Shaddi?" asked Simms.

"Yes. We are putting one microphone and one GPS locater device on him that he will know about. We have sewn another of each, of the micro variety, into his jacket while he was being interviewed. If he thinks of losing the first two and turning on us, he will not know about the other two. If he makes one false move, he will be immediately taken into custody. In any event, he will be arrested with his partner and hopefully can continue to report during his incarceration if anything should go wrong."

"What about their takeover of the Marine Fire Station?" asked Simms.

"The Boston PD SWAT Units are in control of that area. If anyone makes it that far, which we presently doubt, they will be arrested on sight. The fireboat is being disabled as we speak. But, we desperately need to find the five hundred pounds of Semtex that Shaddi was to drive out to the tanker. Team three has that in a van someplace. We need to take team three when they meet with The Engineer. We have a list of all stolen and unrecovered vans from Boston and the surrounding area. The BFD personnel at Marine Unit are being pulled from the Marine Fire Station tomorrow night to 'staff other needs.' They are not being told why. We are not sure we know of everyone who might be giving the terrorists information about the Marine Unit from the inside."

They all knew that tomorrow's plan depended on how well they did the rest of the afternoon and night. They agreed to talk again at 1:00 am.

Baker felt relieved after the call. He knew they were working as a team and each was helping the other. He felt he had a lot of support from Simms and Wilkins. The rest would take care of itself.

Chapter 107

Maha Soufan and Patrick were standing at Court and Tremont Streets in downtown Boston.

"The Imam thanks you for your help," said Soufan. "He wants you to know that he has assisted the FBI as a citizen and the Shaddi family as an Imam. He finds his role in both compatible to his conscience and to Islam. Jabbar Shaddi has followed the advice of the Imam and is working with the FBI. As soon as the FBI resolves its present concerns, much of this may become public. The Imam would like us to continue to work with the FBI and the mosque to insure that what has occurred becomes a building block for the future, and not some instrument of divisiveness in the present."

"You know how we both feel," said Patrick. "You don't even have to ask."

"The Imam would also like your assistance to insure the mosque is made aware of any potential threats resulting from its ongoing cooperation."

Patrick nodded. Words weren't required.

They understood any further discussion at this point would serve no purpose. They would wait for the FBI to resolve the current threat.

Vince Baker was on the phone with Bob Wilkins and the Section Chief for Public Affairs at FBIHQ. The section chief explained he had just received a call from a senior National Public Radio reporter who regularly covered the FBI. The reporter wanted to know if the FBI had a link to the recent arrests in New York to a terrorist cell working in Boston. The section chief provided the standard response that the New York investigation was ongoing and the FBI did not respond or comment about an ongoing investigation.

The section chief continued, "Privately, I was told by this reporter that someone in a position to know within government was saying there was an active terrorist investigation in Boston as a continuation of the New York arrests. I don't think they are pursuing it at the moment, but I wanted you to know it is on the radar screen again."

While Baker was on the call, Rose Phillips passed him a note saying Claudia Bell was on the phone asking for Baker. She would only talk to Baker and not to the media agent.

"Put the call through, please" said Baker. He asked the other two to wait a minute and put them on hold.

"Mr. Baker, I have been told that the FBI has an active terrorist investigation here in Boston that is related to the arrests in New York. Will you confirm or deny that?"

"Ms. Bell, I don't understand why you felt compelled to demand to speak to me personally rather than your normal contact with the media agent?"

"I have some rather detailed information, which I may print in tomorrow's edition. I'm just looking for confirmation. I know the media agent does not have that authority," said Bell.

Baker replied, "I will tell you what the media agent would say. There is no comment on the New York investigation, noting that whatever information is presently available has already been furnished to the media."

"Can we go off the record?" asked Bell.

"You can consider it on the record or off the record. My answer is the same. Now if you will excuse me I do have another call waiting."

"Okay, I understand." said Bell. "Just a word of warning: Be prepared for more calls of this nature because there is a very angry person out there with a pocket full of dimes telling this story to anyone who will listen. If it is true, it is only a matter of time before someone runs with it."

The call ended.

Baker was back on with Wilkins and the section chief. He told them what Bell had to say.

"It has to be Bottom," said Wilkins. "At this point he is so out of control, almost unbalanced. The media is afraid to go with him without confirmation. To do anything now against Bottom would only confirm his information. Let's just go with what we are doing and we'll deal with him later. There is really no other practical choice."

The section chief suggested Baker immediately alert Patrick, who also knew this reporter. You could bet she would call Patrick and run the same questions by him. She had covered the case of Patrick's subpoena with Bottom. She would put it together that Patrick's case must have been about the New York arrests and the reported terror cell in Boston. It was also a question of how much Bottom may have told the reporter. Baker and Wilkins agreed.

Baker checked the status of all the physical surveillances they had going on cell members. Each cell member had been located. Some of their vehicles had GPS locators attached. None had microphones because the affidavits for electronic surveillance were not completed and couldn't yet be presented to the court. They could not move any faster. They hoped to have the authority soon. They had less than twenty-four hours before the LNG tanker was due in the harbor. All of the subjects appeared to be in a present state of inaction. "Patience and discipline," Baker said to himself.

Before Baker took the time to call Patrick, Claudia Bell put in her call to Patrick in an effort to get him to confirm the terrorist investigation in Boston. Patrick was not biting. He immediately figured it could only be Bottom, totally off on his personal lark regardless of possible arrest. When he learned from Bell of her call to Baker, Patrick could not understand why he had not been warned by Baker. After it was clear to Bell that Patrick had nothing to say, Bell made some personal comments to Patrick.

"I just wanted to educate you a little," said Bell. "Lots of times reporters hear things and do not go with them. You tend to see only your side of the story. I could go with this story. I have plenty, but I know it would be wrong. I know other reporters have been contacted by this person and they are not jumping on the story just to be first. Even if you confirmed, I would not go with the story but would use that information to trade for an exclusive when it was safer. I don't know how to tell you this Mark, but you don't have a lock on ethics or a conscience. We in the media have limits on what we are willing to do to be first. We will continue this conversation at a better time."

Chapter 108

The Engineer exited his motel room, went down one floor, and opened a closet door that contained some ladders, window washing equipment, and a cleaning cart. The Engineer had jammed the lock so the door could close, but the lock would not engage. In the back right corner behind the window cleaning equipment was a thirty-inch red fire extinguisher. The day work crew had gone home so The Engineer was not worried about being seen in the closet. He closed the closet door, turned on the overhead bulb, and proceeded to unscrew the top of the extinguisher. Once done he removed one gray metal canister about two inches high and just less than the internal circumference of the extinguisher. He screwed the top back on, left the closet, and walked to Talat Mehmood's room one floor below and knocked.

When Talat opened the door, The Engineer stepped inside, closed the door, and handed Talat the canister. "Take this to team one right now. Report back to me as soon as you return. We need to have no further contact with them until after the attack."

Talat reached for his jacket and walked out the door with The Engineer. Talat took the canister in his left hand, put his jacket over his arm, and walked to the parking lot and left in his car.

When Talat arrived at the apartment in East Boston used by team one, he parked on the street, looked around, saw nothing and went up the steps and rang the bell to the apartment. Before he was out of his car, the surveillance team knew who it was, had mobile units move into the area, and had a SWAT team placed nearby if needed. Baker was in his office listening to the events unfold over the radio.

Talat was buzzed in the front door. Everyone was now swearing. They had no court order and no electronic surveillance in the apartment. The terrorists were meeting and no one would know what they were saying. The fixed observation post radioed that a gray canister was in Mehmood's left hand.

About five minutes later, Mehmood and the two members of team one exited the front door, stood on the sidewalk for a moment, and turned left and walked up East Bennington Street. They walked two blocks, took a left, and went behind a three-decker house that had a five-space garage located at ground level in the rear of the house. There was a small sign on the front of the house saying "garage space for rent." The three entered a small door on the left side of the garage. Two minutes later, all three exited the same garage door and started walking back toward the apartment. It was immediately noted that Mehmood did not have the gray metal container in his hand. When they reached the area where Mehmood parked his vehicle, they approached another parked car nearby. One team member held up his electronic key and opened the trunk of the second vehicle. All three were looking into the trunk and paid no attention to the old lady walking by, rolling her barely functioning shopping cart. It would not move fast and neither could she. The lady did observe two duffle bags in the trunk, one of which had a zipper opened by a team member. Inside was a gray metal case. All of this was reported by the lady over the radio as she continued her journey slowly down the street. The bag was zipped back and the trunk closed. Mehmood exchanged a kiss with each of the men. They turned and went inside the apartment while Mehmood got into his car.

Baker's orders were quick and clear. Follow Mehmood. If either member or both members of team one exits the apartment and goes to either the parked vehicle or the garage, they were to be arrested. They could not to be allowed to enter, start or move either vehicle. Otherwise they were to remain as they were.

Mehmood drove his car to the end of the block, made two right turns and came out to the entrance to the Sumner Tunnel back into Boston. He drove by the state police cruiser parked nearby the toll booth. The trooper immediately saw Mehmood's vehicle and radioed in the sighting. The trooper was told a surveillance team was right behind Mehmood and they were trying to get aerial surveillance assistance on the other side of the tunnel. The trooper was to remain on station at the tunnel.

The tunnel prevented any member of the surveillance team from getting ahead of or flanking Mehmood. They could not do that until they got to the other side. It took Mehmood only five minutes to go from the apartment to the Boston side of the tunnel. There was no traffic at the end of the tunnel. He could exit to Government Center and go in two directions to the North End or the Surface Artery. He could also exit to go to Storrow Drive. The first three surveillance cars each took one of the options. They could not find Mehmood's vehicle. Three minutes later airplane surveillance arrived on the scene but had no luck in spotting the car in downtown traffic. With no chance to put a GPS device on the vehicle, they had no electronic tracking. Baker even jumped up from his chair to look out his office window trying to spot Mehmood. Mehmood may have just passed through Government Center. They didn't know where he was now.

Losing Mehmood was a bitter pill to swallow. Baker realized this and directed everyone back into their prior positions to be ready for the next event. There were a lot of people looking for Mehmood's car but none was in the flow of traffic on the Southeast Expressway as Mehmood returned to the motel.

Mehmood knocked on The Engineer's door. "It is done. I delivered it and I put it in the van next to the bomb. They will do the final hookup of the detonation system to the Semtex before they go out tomorrow. The missiles are in the trunk of the car parked on the street. The car has a kill switch so it can't be started except by them."

The Engineer nodded, said he would see Mehmood in the morning, and closed the door.

Chapter 109

The motel offered a light breakfast, which The Engineer took advantage of every morning. It gave him a chance to look over who was in the motel. In the lobby, where the breakfast was served, was a computer connected to the internet. Customers used it to print out airline tickets or to check email accounts.

The Engineer sat down at the computer and logged on to one of his several email accounts. He had no messages. It was time. He sent an email to the assistant cook aboard the LNG tanker. Most modern ships had at least email access via satellite for their crew to keep in contact with families and friends. This cook was ben Afad's direct contribution to the plan. Afad knew only recently about the shipment of LNG from Yemen to Boston. He moved quickly when he found out. The assistant cook aboard the LNG tanker was bribed by "drug dealers" to report on anything out of the ordinary on this voyage. He was led to believe that someone aboard ship was smuggling a large amount of drugs. He was to report anything strange or unusual immediately to the "drug boss" via email. The Engineer wanted to hear again from the assistant cook that nothing was amiss on the voyage. After he sent the email, he went back to his room to watch the news. One hour later he returned, checked his email account, and found a response. The assistant cook had nothing to report. The ship was on schedule and expected to dock at the terminal in Everett on schedule this evening. The Engineer knew his plan was going to work.

The Engineer went to his room, picked up a cloth bag, and returned to the closet one floor below. He unscrewed the fire extinguisher and removed five canisters and placed them in the cloth bag. He carried the bag to Mehmood's room where he knocked on the door. When it opened he went inside.

"I want you to immediately deliver these five canisters to team three. You have one pre- arranged contact delivery set up with them?"

"Yes. The Government Center MBTA Station one hour after they receive my call."

"Good. Call them and do it now. Report back to me immediately when you have completed this delivery." Mehmood nodded and The Engineer left.

The surveillance group assigned to monitor team three was sitting on an apartment in Chelsea not far from the produce market. It was a tough area in which to conduct surveillance without being noticed. There was a lot of truck traffic, little pedestrian traffic, and very few parked cars. They observed one of the team members come out of the apartment, get in a vehicle, and drive to the Maverick Square MBTA Station in East Boston. There he got on the Blue Line, which he took to State Street. He exited and walked less than a block and entered the Government Center MBTA Station. He went down the escalator and stood near the Green Line platform.

The team three member under surveillance looked at his watch a few times and then walked over to the coffee stand in the middle of the platform. He bought a paper, got a coffee and doughnut, spoke to no one, picked up a cloth bag and returned to where he was standing. At that point the surveillance team realized he had picked up a cloth bag from the floor in front of the coffee stand, but they did not see who put it on the floor. There were four people waiting on customers at the stand, which was very busy. Mehmood had his coffee and was back on the Green Line going to Park Square and the Red Line before the surveillance team even noticed the cloth bag.

The team three member, now with the cloth bag, took the escalator back to the street and walked back to the State Street MBTA where he took the Blue Line back to Maverick Square and his car. He drove back to the apartment and pulled up in front. A few seconds later his fellow team member came out and got in the car. They were followed one-half mile away where they pulled up to a garage in a busy industrial area. They took off a huge padlock and rolled up a metal overhead door. The surveillance agents could see a beige colored van parked inside. The front license plate was visible as the van was backed into the garage. The van was stolen two weeks ago. The team members went inside carrying the cloth bag, and rolled the garage door down after turning on an interior light. About ten minutes later, the garage door was rolled up again. The two exited the garage with nothing in their hands, rolled the door down, applied the padlock, and then drove to a nearby diner. They spent close to two hours eating and talking. No one could get close enough to pick up their conversation. When they finished they went back to the apartment in Chelsea.

Vince Baker was monitoring this surveillance. He felt he knew what was in the bag and where the five hundred pounds of Semtex they intended to put into the fireboat was stored. He also thought the Javelin missiles might be in the van or in the trunk of the car. In any event, these men could not get close to this potential bomb again. Baker ordered that if either one of the men, or preferably both, went to the immediate vicinity of the garage again they were to be arrested before they entered the garage. Agents should assume they had a way to remotely detonate any bomb present and the terrorist should be immediately immobilized.

Chapter 110

The surveillance on team two was problematic. One member was living in a South End apartment that was difficult to cover. There was no street parking available. It was in a congested neighborhood. It was difficult to cover with foot and vehicular traffic and remain unnoticed. The second member had an apartment about four blocks away but there was no sign he had been there in over twenty-four hours. They had no vehicle identified for GPS coverage so they had to be ready for anything.

About noontime, they saw the second member of the team walking up the street. He was carrying two clear plastic bags that appeared to be loaded with white Chinese food containers. If he had a car they had no idea where it was. According to Shaddi, this team had a van and was going to fire their two Javelin missiles from the parking lot just south of City Wharf. They were in the apartment now.

Baker wanted them and their missiles. The order was to try and follow them to the missiles. If there's a problem, don't lose them. Arrest them if you have too. If they head toward a van, arrest them before they are able to get the van in motion. There could be more than missiles in the van. Immobilize them as quickly as possible.

Jabbar Shaddi had been good to his word. After meeting with his fellow team member the night before and reviewing the entire plan with him, Shaddi left and went back to his apartment. He was to remain there until just before 7:30 pm when his teammate would pick him up and they would head to Merchants Wharf for the meeting with team three.

Shaddi was able to direct the evening conversation to get his fellow member to describe how he was a lifelong Muslim from parents that were deeply fundamentalist. He participated in conversations on the internet, at the request of Talat Mehmood in order to convert other people his age to the fundamentalist point of view. When he went on the Hajj, he knew when it was completed he was volunteering for terrorist training in Afghanistan. This cell member had discussed with his parents ahead of time whether he should consider being a martyr. They were not convinced at first, but when later told how al-Qaeda would support them financially because of the loss of their son, and how famous their family would be in Islam because of their son's great sacrifice, his mother gave him the required blessing to be a martyr.

Shaddi got his teammate to describe his interaction and planning with Talat Mehmood and the reputation that The Engineer enjoyed in the Islamic world of terrorism. They discussed what the other teams' assignments were and how they were being carried out. The team member seemed to know more than Jabbar did about the attack. He suggested that something even more historic was taking place, but would not or could not elaborate. In short, Jabbar had his partner confess to everything and that confession was being monitored and recorded by agents. They also got the impression that most teams would be in motion by 7:30 pm.

Baker still did not have a clue as to the location of Mehmood nor of The Engineer. Twice Mehmood had been lucky, or they had been unlucky. They were unable to follow him. They had not yet put out a police broadcast for Mehmood's vehicle but they were getting close to doing so. He would just have to take his chances with the word getting to the media.

Wilkins was on the phone and needed to speak with Baker immediately.

"A government agency has informed us that there has been some email traffic to and from the LNG tanker that may be of interest. While almost innocuous on its face, it appears that the assistant cook, with no known terrorist background, has exchanged emails with an email account that has been traced. We are ignoring the subscriber data for now as it looks phony. The message itself was a statement that the voyage was normal and nothing unusual has occurred. The message of origin and the assistant cook's response has been traced to an IP address of a motel just south of downtown Boston. This agency has located several other messages of a similar nature between the assistant cook and this IP address over the last couple of days."

"I take it we should not be using this information in an affidavit."

Wilkins smiled just a little. "That is correct. I'm also glad Patrick thought about the possibility of The Engineer having a mole aboard. The plan at present is still to have the ship stopped by the Coast Guard when it gets within sight of the airport. We will proceed as we discussed earlier. We will be monitoring your every move up there so we can adjust according to whatever you have to do."

"I appreciate that," said Baker. "I think the teams will make their move to get into firing positions around 7:30 pm, just before the tanker comes within sight of the airport."

"You think the stolen van in the Chelsea garage has the five hundred pounds of Semtex?"

"Yea," said a weary but not worn Baker.

"Do you think the gray canisters are the radioactive material?"

"Yes. I do. The description matches what was inside the fire extinguishers in New York. I will soon know for sure. We have the NEST doing drive-bys with their equipment at the garages in East Boston and Chelsea. In any event, we will not let anyone near those vehicles now."

When the call was over, Baker called the JTTF with the motel information and asked them to check it out discreetly as a possible location for The Engineer and Mehmood. No one asked where the address came from and he did not explain.

Chapter 111

Mehmood told The Engineer he was leaving to go pick up the bombs for South Station and North Station. He had to drive to a storage facility in Allston to pick them up. Did The Engineer want to come?

"No. I want to stay and monitor the news. I also need to check all the trigger numbers in my cell phone. When you come back give me a call and I will bring the last four canisters down to the truck. We can put them and the two bombs into the van."

This time luck was not on Mehmood's side. The first surveillance team was just arriving at the motel when they saw Mehmood pulling out of the motel, passing under the Southeast Expressway, and then taking a ramp onto the expressway heading north back to Boston. Within a minute he was fully flanked and a second surveillance team was nearby as backup. A third surveillance team was on its way to set up a fixed surveillance on the motel and immediate area.

Mehmood drove to a modern one-story storage facility within a half mile of his apartment. You needed a key code to get into the lot. Mehmood punched in his code and drove to a stall. He unlocked and opened the overhead rollup door. Mehmood removed one opaque plastic box about four-feet long and eighteen inches high. It had a solid blue top. He placed the container in the trunk of his car. He removed a duplicate container from the storage area and placed that on the back seat of his car and covered it with a piece of green plastic. He rolled the overhead door down, locked it, and drove out. His route was a direct return to the motel. When Mehmood arrived at the motel, he drove to the rear. The agents now knew that the van Mehmood had rented in Allston was parked there. They suspected The Engineer was also in the motel but they had not yet seen him. They did not have to wait any longer.

As Mehmood parked next to the van, The Engineer exited the rear door of the motel carrying a tan cloth bag. He walked over to the van, which Mehmood had unlocked. Mehmood took the plastic storage container from the trunk of his car and placed it in the rear of the van. The agents did not see anything else in the van. Mehmood took the second plastic container from the back seat and also placed it in the rear of the truck. Whatever was in the containers was not light. The Engineer could be seen placing two gray metal canisters into each plastic container. He then removed two sets of wires and laid them on the floor of the van.

The agents close enough to view this scene had no doubt they were looking at the two bombs The Engineer and Mehmood were to place in South and North Stations. As this information was being relayed to Baker,

Mehmood and The Engineer went back inside the motel. There wasn't enough time to execute an arrest that would prevent Mehmood or The Engineer any opportunity to detonate a bomb on the spot. By now other agents had checked into rooms at the motel and observed Mehmood and The Engineer going to their respective floors. They would wait until they could be sure they had the element of surprise on their side and could insure immediate control of their physical movements.

As this information was being reported to Baker, he also learned that the NEST people had found the garage in East Boston used by team one and the garage in Chelsea used by team three to be hot. Both registered for alpha and gamma particles just like in New York. Baker requested a check of the van at the parking lot at the motel. They were headed there now.

The surveillance team leader radioed: "Okay. They are in their rooms. We have people inside and outside. It looks like the bombs are not yet rigged for detonation, but we cannot be sure. We can start to evacuate the motel if necessary but we must be careful. It is a dense area with the Southeast Expressway right behind the motel. If The Engineer catches on to anything strange at the motel, he may be prepared to light up the whole area."

Baker radioed his own instructions. "If they come down together, arrest them both and immobilize them. If either one comes down alone, or it looks like he is leaving the motel, arrest that one party and get him out of the motel quickly and quietly. Under no circumstances do you let anyone near Mehmood's car or the truck."

The Hostage Rescue Team had arrived on site to execute these arrests. They were being assisted by a Massachusetts State Police SWAT Team.

As he finished with these instructions, Baker thought The Engineer's dream was going to come to an abrupt end very shortly. Hopefully no one would get killed.

About forty-five minutes later the NEST sweep of the area was completed. Mehmood's rental van was hot and so was the motel itself. Again both alpha and gamma readings were present. Whatever was present at this entire scene was not well protected from dispensing radiation.

Baker toyed with the idea of sneaking the stolen van out of the garage in East Boston. He was advised that if the bomb were there, it could be armed to go off via a motion detector if disturbed in any way. It could be booby trapped. Baker had to consider public safety equally with the need to apprehend. Given the area, and possible neighborhood watchers for team one, they had no ability to safely go near the garage until they could secure the team one members.

The same applied to the van in the Chelsea garage of team three. Luckily it was a more remote area, but the thought of five hundred pounds of Semtex going off was not good. Baker was advised that, like East Boston, this bomb could be booby trapped. Agents and the military ordinance disposal people did not feel an entry to either garage could be done safely in a clandestine manner. He agreed. They would have to wait.

Chapter 112

At 7:30 pm, one member of team one came out of the apartment, stepped onto the street, and took a good look in all directions. The second team one member joined him on the sidewalk a moment later. They talked briefly. Quite quickly, it seemed, one team member headed for the parked vehicle while the other started walking up the street. Two preset stun grenades went off. There were gigantic flashes accompanied by loud booms at the same time. One of the team members would say later they thought the bomb had gone off by accident. What did happen was after the stun grenades went off, agents and a SWAT Team appeared from nowhere. Both members of team one were hit with a stun gun, immobilized, had their fingers, hands and feet restrained while they were being searched and stripped where they lay. Boston police were on scene for crowd control. They also evacuated the area of the apartment, the parked vehicle, and the houses where the van was parked in the garage. Military ordinance disposal experts were now in the garage with agents. They soon discovered the detonation device had not yet been connected to the Semtex. The NEST members took control of safely handling the canister that was found. It was really hot!

Another military team was present when the trunk of the vehicle parked on the street was opened. They found two Javelin missiles inside the duffle bags. They were removed to safety. The naked prisoners by now had Velcro-joined jump suits thrown over their bodies. Hoods were placed over their heads, and they were whisked away for processing and confinement.

Within ten minutes Baker had the word that team one was secured, and that all dangerous material was recovered and being secured.

A few moments later, team three exited their apartment, got in their car and started driving toward the Chelsea garage where they had been earlier. As they were preparing to stop for a red light, the driver and passenger realized they were being taken from their vehicle and put onto the street while their vehicle was still slowly moving toward the stop light. Massachusetts State Police and FBI SWAT Teams had just performed a rolling vehicle stop and extraction to perfection. A trooper controlled their car and pulled it to the side of the street. The prisoners were immobilized and searched at the same time, with many hands all working in unison. Soon they were naked, then quickly covered with jump suits, hoods placed on their heads, and whisked away to join their fellow cell members.

The garage was entered. In it was the van. Inside the van were five hundred pounds of neatly stacked boxes of Semtex bricks ready to be loaded into the Boston Fire Department boat. Next to the Semtex was a cloth bag containing five canisters, which had to be immediately secured by NEST personnel. These canisters were quickly determined to be leaking radiation and not safe to be around. There was also a detonation system, in another bag, that had not yet been hooked to the bomb. The military separated the components. The NEST people took the five canisters. In front of the Semtex and closer to the driver and passenger seats were two duffle bags, each containing a Javelin missile in its case. The small arms and Javelins were unloaded after the canisters, followed by the detonation system. Finally the Semtex was split into a number of smaller batches and taken away by the military ordinance disposal teams.

Baker was elated to hear the news about team three. The five hundred pounds of Semtex and five canisters were a potential city disaster – almost beyond belief. Baker and Fisher wanted to celebrate but there was a lot more going on.

Chapter 113

Just after 7:30 pm, team two exited the apartment in the South End. They walked two blocks and entered a vehicle parked on the street. The surveillance team did not know anything about this car. They were following the arrest activity of the other teams and were expecting this group to make their move. Team two was followed as they drove from the South End through Boston traffic to a garage at Government Center in downtown Boston. They drove their vehicle to the fourth floor where they parked alongside a van. They got out of the car with nothing in their hands, entered the van, started it, and drove to the exit ramp. The agents could not get enough manpower to the fourth floor in time to safely make the arrests.

The van descended down the circular ramp from the fourth floor until they reached street level. When the van approached the ticket booth on the first floor, the occupants were pleasantly distracted by a young woman in a short skirt entering the ticket booth. She gave them a big smile. While they were smiling back, van doors opened, they were pulled out, thrown to the ground, and they felt hands all over their bodies. They could not move. It happened so fast they did not realize they were being arrested. Soon each was naked and cold. Standing over them were people in Boston police uniforms. Also standing over them was the young woman in the short skirt. She was now pointing a pistol at them and she was definitely not smiling. No one bothered to introduce the terrorists to Detective Gloria Sanchez of the BPD. Only now did they each realize they had been caught. Lying in the back of the van were two duffle bags. Each contained a Javelin missile. There was another bag with a Boston Police outer coat and cap, both with badges. Team two was no longer a threat to anyone.

Jabbar Shaddi was picked up by his fellow team four member at exactly 7:30 pm. Jabbar was still transmitting and the agents were still listening. His partner was in a less expansive mood than he was the night before. Jabbar asked him if he was scared. He said a little. Jabbar asked his partner if he wanted to change his mind and drop out of the plan. His partner looked at Jabbar with a scowl and said "no." That is too bad, thought Jabbar. You just made a big mistake.

Jabbar asked him if he had talked to anyone and he said no. They were not to talk until they met at Merchants Wharf with team three. Shaddi's partner drove them to North Wharf where they had the valet park the car in the garage. They walked next door to the shelter for the water taxi, where they were to wait for team three. When team three arrived, they would take over the Marine Unit next door at Merchants Wharf and start unloading the Semtex from team three's van.

After a few minutes, a young couple joined them in the waiting area. They were almost making out in front of them. Shaddi's partner thought this public display of affection was disgusting. Shaddi's partner turned away and was looking anxiously toward Commercial Street when he felt a cold piece of metal on the side of his head. The young woman said something about the FBI and then slammed him to the ground. He saw it was a gun. The man put something on his hands. Shaddi was also on the floor and the next thing he knew the whole waiting area was flooded with people and his clothes were being roughly taken off until he was naked. Then a jump suit device was put across his body and he was put in the back seat of a vehicle. He saw Shaddi being put into the car in front of him. He finally realized what had happened. He and Shaddi had been arrested.

At 7:40 pm, The Engineer got up from the lobby TV. He knew the other teams would be moving by 7:30 pm and so far there was nothing to indicate any problem. He would be glad to get through the evening. He felt like he was coming down with the flu, but, at the same time, he was excited. Within hours Muslim fundamentalists all over the world would be singing his praises and calling his name out to all as a true hero of Islam.

The Engineer previously decided that he would leave Boston alone after tonight's project was completed. Mehmood had been a good servant but, after the attack, The Engineer wanted to be on his own. Two Arab looking males would be suspects based on looks alone. He could travel faster and safer alone. It was not in his best interests to leave a witness behind. Within hours he would be in Canada. Mehmood had deluded himself that any of his team members would survive. They would not. In minutes the LNG fire would be over but the shore fires would just be getting started. The teams would be incinerated. He and Mehmood would be safe from the fire, but Mehmood might not be able to handle their deaths. Mehmood would not leave the back of their van.

Mehmood entered the lobby from the elevator and greeted The Engineer with a smile. Mehmood was cleaned up and wearing fresh clothes. Today, thought Mehmood, he would be famous in the world of Islam.

The Engineer's thoughts shifted to his need to connect the detonation device to the bombs in the van. He was going to do it right in the motel parking lot. It was as good a place as any, and it was simple enough to do.

As The Engineer walked out the rear door of the motel to the parking lot, he thought he heard something on the TV about arrests, but it was too late. He and Mehmood were swarmed from out of nowhere. He knew what was happening. He did not bother to resist. Something had gone terribly wrong. He could hear Mehmood yelling and struggling. How could this be? He had planned everything so well?"

Epilogue

The Engineer refused to identify himself. He would not even speak beyond what was otherwise necessary to communicate basic daily needs. They gave him complete medical attention to address his complaints of a cold and the flu. The Engineer initially refused to believe the doctors when they informed him that he was not suffering from the flu. The Engineer was told he was suffering from radiation poisoning. His case was sufficiently advanced to be his death sentence. He did not have long to live.

The Engineer continued his disbelief of the diagnosis until the doctors walked him through each test result. Agents described the radiation trail he left behind, starting with the cargo handler's locker at work, his car, the apartment in Palermo, and below The Engineer's bunk aboard ship. In the end, The Engineer knew they were telling him the truth. Mustaf ben Afad, probably at the direction of Said Ali al-Wahishi, destined him to be an unknowing martyr. Afad told The Engineer the canisters were safe for him to handle. They had no leakage. Now he was going to die, not for his beloved jihad, but only to insure there was no witness against Afad and Wahishi. No wonder they readily agreed to his request for operational secrecy. No one except the Engineer could describe their respective roles. Now he intended to do just that before he died.

The Engineer continued to refuse to identify himself but now it was out of shame, not operational necessity. He failed in his mission. He had been manipulated by the cause he believed in. He always knew al-Qaeda sometimes sacrificed an individual for the greater cause. He believed this time it was a case of two cowards corruptly acting to protect themselves at his expense. Now he wanted to tell what he knew of the new al-Qaeda leader, Said Ali al-Wahishi. He wanted to tell how Mustaf ben Afad was the person most responsible for helping him mount this attack. The Engineer now believed neither was worthy to be a member of al-Qaeda much less a leader.

With The Engineer's information, the FBI and British MI-5 did substantiate Vespa's information about al-Qaeda attempting to short the stock of the company owning the Boston bound LNG tanker. From this point they were able to follow the money trail both backward and forward and, with the help of allies, seized a substantial portion of al-Qaeda assets under Afad's control.

At first authorities were of two minds about arresting Afad. He didn't know The Engineer had talked. They could snuggle up next to him and learn more about the emerging al-Qaeda leadership and their remaining finances. Alternatively, they could immediately arrest Afad, preventing any chance of his escape. They wanted to give Afad a chance to confirm Wahishi was a full participant in the plan to use dirty bombs against the United States.

The decision finally favored was the arrest of Afad. When MI-5 and Scotland Yard went to Afad's London office, Afad escaped through an access tunnel into an adjacent building previously constructed for just that purpose. Afad made his way to the airport where he had a private jet available. They missed him, and now the chase was on. The word immediately went out to the international intelligence community. Afad was wanted. Really wanted. If you assisted him in any way, it would be at your great peril. There would be retribution. This was all said very nicely, diplomatically, but friend and foe alike understood. This was counter terrorism gone personal.

Pakistani Intelligence honored a CIA request to cover all airports in their country, as it was one of the most logical places for Afad to seek immediate sanctuary. They were right.

A Pakistani Intelligence officer spotted Afad exiting a private jet at Peshawar Airport. Waiting for Afad was a gray Nissan Pathfinder with a couple of well-armed toughs inside. Before the Nissan's engine was even started, the officer was on the phone with the CIA control room reporting his observations. The CIA, in turn, was able to immediately access a US military satellite that was making a routine pass over the Peshawar area. This satellite located the Nissan Pathfinder east of the airport traveling through local neighborhoods heading north. The Nissan next turned onto the N-5 Highway and headed west toward the mountains.

This military satellite would soon exit the Peshawar area and would be unable to continue the surveillance. Thanks to a forward thinking young CIA agent, who noted this problem at the outset, a CIA drone was earlier re-directed from its routine patrol assignment and tasked to pick up the surveillance on the Nissan. The drone located the Nissan on the N-5 West in a specific area called Shaqi Fort, on the Grand Trunk Road. After twenty minutes the drone cameras observed the Nissan being joined by two pickup trucks containing more armed men. One pickup traveled in front of the Nissan, and one behind. The caravan was still headed into the mountains.

The CIA and US military searched for coalition forces in the area to intercept and capture Afad and his entourage. However, there were none in the area of sufficient strength to take on this well-armed caravan. If Afad made it into the narrow mountain passes, even the drone might lose him. The drone might not see a brief stop with a passenger transferring to another vehicle.

The decision was made. Afad was not going to escape again. The drone on surveillance was a CIA MQ-9 Reaper armed with four Hellfire missiles. After the attack order came through the chain of command, the MQ-9 pilot, seated comfortably at his computer located at the drone control base in Afghanistan, flew the drone into an attack position over the Nissan entourage. After confirming he had the targets locked in, he again confirmed the fire order. It was confirmed. The pilot next fired three of his four Hellfire missiles at the Nissan and the two pickups. These three fast moving vehicles traveling this desolate area of the N-5 quickly became three distinct masses of fiery, non-recognizable metal grinding quickly to a halt.

The pilot dropped the drone to a lower altitude and slowly circled the smoldering mass of metal to inspect the wreckage. There was no need to fire the fourth missile. There was nothing left to fire at. Afad would never again mount another attack against the United States.

The Engineer and Shaddi both furnished the FBI details regarding the al-Qaeda training camp used to train the American jihadists. This camp was previously unknown to US intelligence. It did not take long to confirm their information as spot on. Those running the camp got no advance warning from al-Qaeda that their cover was blown. Their first warning came from the US Navy Tomahawk missiles fired with the intention of fully obliterating the camp, everything in it or around it, and literally creating a new agricultural valley where the camp previously stood. They were out to make a statement. They did.

After the training camp was obliterated and Mustaf ben Afad was wiped out by the drone attack, Said Ali al-Wahishi concluded The Engineer survived, was in custody, and had talked. Wahishi already generated leaks to Western intelligence that The Engineer was a tool of the former leader and the use of dirty bombs their aberration. He also thought The Engineer's plan to use the LNG tanker as the bomb remained practically sound. He would build the source of ignition inside the tanker's structure before it loaded in Yemen. The bomb would be complete the day the loaded tanker sailed for Boston. It could be ignited electronically by one person upon arrival. He would have put this plan into operation already, had it not been for attention drawn to Yemen LNG by an uncoordinated al-Qaeda affiliate group that blew up the Yemen LNG pipeline. He would wait for this minor attack to be forgotten before he began anew.

In an exercise of wishful thinking, Wahishi concluded that without Afad to corroborate what The Engineer knew, the United States would never be certain al-Wahishi knew of the planned dirty bomb attacks. The United States examined all the evidence and was convinced of Wahishi's role. Wahishi's face would not appear on any deck of cards. While the word assassination was never used, neither was the word arrest. There was going to be out and out personal retribution. The chase was on.

Patrick continued his friendship with the Boston Mosque. While the extent of their enormous contributions, which helped prevent the terrorist attack on the LNG tanker, were never fully made public, they were well known within law enforcement and Islamic communities. The event served as an example of what could be achieved in a space devoid of prejudice, where hearts and minds were in the right place.

It was a perfectly clear and warm evening in Boston. Patrick and Liz sat on their Franklin Wharf deck watching sailboats trying to catch the last of the harbor's evening breeze during an informal race. The departing sun cast a soft glow over the buildings in East Boston and on the waterfront. They could hear the train departing from North Station. They could see the airplanes landing at Logan Airport after passing over the Marine Terminal in South Boston. Once in a while they could feel a slight vibration from the vehicles using the Callahan and Sumner tunnels, located directly beneath them. All of the city's transportation systems were alive and well. It was a beautiful evening on the harbor. The vibrancy of Boston was on full display. Patrick turned his head when he noted the faint sound of helicopter engines in the distance.

Remaining quiet, martini in hand, Patrick nodded for Liz to look south in the harbor toward the federal courthouse. Rounding the bend in the harbor was the little changed flotilla of Coast Guard and police boats surrounding an incoming and heavily laden LNG tanker. There were a few more police boats in the flotilla, a few newer looking craft, and a few more police cruisers with blue lights blinking along the shoreline. It was all more of the same "threat mitigation procedures" that still would not stop a sophisticated, land-based terrorist attack, especially when the attackers were willing to give up their own lives. Patrick just shook his head.

Liz could see Patrick's face start to flush. Liz said, "Why is it that our congressional delegation, business and civic leaders, federal and state governmental agencies, have banded together in Fall River and have successfully opposed an LNG terminal in that city? Yet, here in Boston, it is business as usual. All these factions remain silent, or at best ineffective. I don't get it."

Patrick smiled. "Didn't you study physics?" he asked.

Liz looked perplexed.

Patrick continued, "An object at rest tends to remain at rest. An object in motion tends to remain in motion. I believe that's Newton's second law."

Liz then had to laugh and said, "As I sit here with Sir Isaac Newton, perhaps you would care to explain. Please don't bother dropping an apple from the balcony. I get that part."

"Years ago, before terrorism rose to the threat it is today, the voting populace and the entire government from the President on down favored LNG tankers offloading in Boston Harbor. All in the region wanted the promised, steady supply of cheap energy. When the terrorist threat level increased and questions of safety were later raised, it was already a done deal. LNG in Boston Harbor now needed to be defended as a sound political and economic policy with terrorist risks described as 'mitigated' through the application of 'increased security.' That is the status quo. That which is at rest tends to remain at rest. It takes too much energy and effort to undo what is at rest – unless there is a unified call to arms by many citizens. It is why blue laws remain on the books long after their enforcement has long ceased."

426

Liz was starting to follow Patrick's abused logic.

"Intellectually, I cannot refute your rather thin and spurious argument. I just refuse to accept it as an excuse," said Liz with a smile.

"So do I," admitted Patrick.

Liz followed up, "You believe the Boston LNG tanker is now even higher on every terrorist target list."

"In 1993, al-Qaeda just missed destroying one World Trade Center building when they parked their explosives laden truck too close to a garage wall, which deflected the blast impact. On 9/11, they returned to the same target, adjusted the form of attack utilizing fuel-laden, hijacked airplanes manned by martyrs, and succeeded. They were making a point. They don't give up. We need to listen," Patrick observed.

"Well, let's look on the positive side and review what your personal efforts have accomplished," said Liz with a devilish smile. .

Liz continued, "You've changed a lot. Bottom's posse and his friends at DOJ will look to get even or at least take away your pension. Some at FBIHQ think you should have coughed up Vespa at the start, made nice with Kirby and Bottom, and not generated any criticism or embarrassment that could fall upon the FBI. al-Qaeda now knows who you are and where to find you. To them you are an infidel who got in their way. Now, before your very eyes, you are witness to the substantial improvements in LNG tanker security! I am sure the discussions you want to take place, regarding informant guidelines and the need for a balance of intelligence gathering that will include human assets, will soon be scheduled. I am sure your invitation will be in the mail soon."

Patrick knew what Liz was doing. He loved her for it. Patrick leaned over the table and surprised Liz with a kiss. "I was able to do what I thought was right. I had you with me the whole time. I have faith the public will eventually demand more from their political leaders. I can't ask for more."

"To quote a priest named Father Gallitizin, 'we are all useful, but never necessary.'"

That admonition earned Liz a smile from Patrick.

Patrick spoke with Vespa several times by phone. He provided her the details of the arrests, seizure of weapons and explosives, and generally what The Engineer had to say. He explained to Vespa about ben Afad, his role with Wahishi, and how he came to meet his end. Patrick described the government's seizure of al-Qaeda assets in many countries. Patrick believed Vespa deserved this degree of detail and honesty. No one swore him to secrecy. He felt it only right that Vespa know. After all, she and her associates now bore potential personal risk from al-Qaeda for their help in preventing the planned attacks.

"I want to say thank you for what you and your associates did. There is no one else to tell you but me."

Liz later asked Patrick, "Do you know who Vespa is?"

"Not her name," Patrick said with a smile. "It wouldn't be difficult for me to find out. I know where to look."

Liz understood.

Patrick hoped the FBI would not forget about the possible third al-Qaeda US supply cell.

He wondered if he would ever speak with Vespa again.

About the Author

James Ring is a retired FBI Supervisory Special Agent who investigated the American La Cosa Nostra and the Sicilian Mafia in New England. Ring received the Department of Justice's highest award as the architect of the first and only electronic interception of the La Cosa Nostra/Mafia induction ceremony of new members, including the Omerta oath.

Ring has testified in federal court as an expert witness on La Cosa Nostra and has served as a media commentator on organized crime. He participated in a series by National Public Radio analyzing the current Department of Justice Informant Guidelines. Ring served on the Department of Defense advisory board mandated by Congress to review their civilian and military investigative capabilities. This review included the growing military preference of favoring electronic intelligence over human intelligence.

After retiring from the FBI, Ring founded a business information and investigative service within a prestigious Boston law firm where he remains today.

Ring resides in Boston and South Dartmouth, Massachusetts, with his wife, Merita A. Hopkins.

Made in the USA
Charleston, SC
25 October 2013